Hollow's End

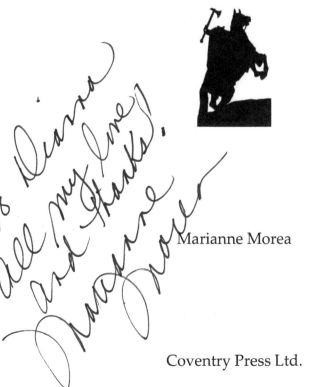

Marianne Morea

Coventry Press Ltd.

Coventry Press Ltd.
Somers, New York
http://www.coventrypressltd.com

ISBN-10: 0-9884396-3-8
ISBN-13: 978-0-9884396-3-4
First Edition: Coventry Press Ltd. 2013

Editor: Tina Winograd
Cover Design: The Killion Group, LLC.

Printed in the USA

For
Danielle, Anthony, and Sarah

Prologue

"He's coming! He's coming!" one of his soldiers cried, running past the crude tents. The devil himself on his heels. The sound of the black horse, its hooves tearing into the loamy earth echoed through the forest — the ominous herald announcing the rider's approach like the Angel of Death.

Both man and beast found nothing but agony waiting at the end of the man's sword. Slaughter and brutality his hallmark. He wielded them well.

His men fled, stomachs roiling with fear. The knowledge they had assisted his butchery, complying in mute terror, afraid to raise their eyes to his lest they be next. He swore he'd ride them to hell and back, their scalps hanging from his saddle, dripping bloody as tokens for the gods of war if they defied him. They would never be free...

Chapter 1

The alarm clock buzzed, its repetitive blare piercing what was left of my sleep. I opened my eyes half way and peered at the red digital numbers staring back at me through dim light. With a groan, I slammed my hand on the clock's hard plastic top, hoping to hit the snooze button and not the volume. Closing my eyes, I rolled over tucking one hand under my pillow and the other under my chin. But it was too late. My conscience was wide awake and already sparring with itself. *Get up! You're going to be late again. No, I won't, just five more minutes...*

"Rowen! It's six-thirty!" my mother's voice shot from the hall.

Five minutes. Just five more minutes.

"Rowen!"

"I heard you the first time!" I yelled at my closed bedroom door. Why did morning have to come so early and be so loud? I groaned again. If I didn't get out of bed soon, she'd come upstairs looking for me, and that was the last thing I wanted.

Yawning, I reached over my head and stretched, arching my back to let the blood flow into my resting muscles like a reveille call. *Up and at 'em, troops!*

My mother was up early, even by her standards. I wasn't surprised, though. It was that time of year again. The time when our little shop, *The Silver Cauldron*, became the town headquarters for spells and charmed candles and, of course, witches brew. The season when the quaint river town of Sleepy Hollow transformed into a mecca for all things creepy.

Marianne Morea

With my crazy mother organizing everything from the kids ragamuffin parade to the annual costume ball, there was never a spare minute to think or breathe. On top of everything else, she took over as coordinator for this year's Blaze—over 4,000 hand carved jack-o-lanterns lining the historic three hundred-year-old Van Cortlandt estate. It was no wonder I didn't want to get up. I was exhausted just being her daughter. My mother, Laura Corbett, was Sleepy Hollow's *unofficial* official town witch, and in a place where everyone knows everyone, that's saying a lot.

"It's just Halloween," I mumbled flipping my covers back, but in our house it was never *just Halloween*, nor was it ever just about trick-or-treating. It was the Witch's New Year and one of the biggest sabbats on the wheel of the year. Not that I believed in that sort of junk. That was my family's thing, not mine, even though my mother and grandmother had been trying to make it mine since the day I was born.

I swung my legs over the side of the bed and sat for a moment. I'd heard it a thousand times, "We're different, Rowen, embrace it. People would kill to be able to do what we can." Like people needed more reasons to think I was half a freak. And as to wanting to be like me, *uh...* I didn't think so. ~~witch or not?~~

"Rowen, hurry up! I need to talk to you before you leave," Mom's voice called again.

My room looked like a tornado hit. Clothes and shoes everywhere, and the books and math sheets I reviewed last night were still in a haphazard pile across my desk. Two empty Coke cans topped a pile of candy wrappers, and a large, half eaten bag of potato chips lay crumpled on the floor next to my backpack.

Oh God, I didn't.

At the incriminating sight, my hand shifted to my stomach, and a familiar self-loathing settled onto my shoulders. I slumped a bit, cringing inwardly at what the scale would read this morning.

With a sigh I pushed myself to stand and slid my gaze to the clothes I somehow remembered to set out. My lateness was reaching epic proportions, yet school was only halfway through the first semester. Most of the student body had learned to get out of the way when I came barreling in for homeroom.

Mom seemed to think my tardy nature would improve once I earned

my driver's license, but of course, that didn't happen. I was seventeen and already driving for the past year. We lived around the corner from the high school, and senior privilege or not, I didn't relish the idea of taking my mother's minivan.

Grabbing my outfit from the back of my desk chair, I walked into the bathroom and snapped on the light. I had no problem envisioning my mother, coffee cup in hand, impatiently waiting for me to come downstairs while she planned her latest concoction for the store.

When my mother says she needs to talk it usually means extra work for me, and considering how busy it's been I'm surprised it took her this long to ask. Not that I mind helping out at the shop with all its curiosities, but I can't seem to stomach the people who come in just to gawk. Of course, the townspeople wouldn't dare insult my mother that way, but the tourists loved to look at the whole lot, including us.

I took inventory of my face in the mirror, running fingers over the puffy skin beneath my eyes, trying to ignore the glare from the bathroom's overhead lights. Telltale dark smudges from my late date with calculus were evident beneath my lower lids, making my hazel eyes look a little muddy. "Now, that's attractive," I grumbled reaching for my makeup remover. Giving each eye a quick swipe, I checked my reflection for any marked improvement. No such luck.

Most of the time, I liked the way I looked. From the dark curls and high cheekbones I inherited from my dad, to winning the genetic lottery for great skin courtesy of mother's side of the family. Most of my friends hated that I never got zits or blemishes, but Mother Nature evened the playing field, seeing to it I gained weight if I so much as looked at junk food.

I muttered an expletive thinking about the bag of chips I'd massacred and pushed the bathroom scale under the vanity with my foot. One of these days I'd learn not to let the number glaring up at me from between my feet dictate the kind of day I would have, but today was not that day.

The Corbett's tended to be on the fleshy side, or at least that's what it looked like in all the family pictures. I wouldn't know firsthand, though, my dad having died when I was little, and his parents before I was born. Then again, having a mother who leaned more toward the vegetarian line helped a lot in that department.

Gathering my hair, I twisted it into a loose bun at the top of my head. There was a peculiar tension building in my stomach, and I didn't think it was the potato chips. I was out of sorts, restless for some reason, and a dull ache throbbed behind my eyes. I grabbed my toothbrush and turned on the tap, breaking one of the cardinal rules of my house by letting the water run while I brushed my teeth.

A calculus test was scheduled later this morning, but I was never one for being neurotic over grades. So why was I so edgy? I rinsed my mouth and stuck the toothbrush in its holder. The blunt pounding behind my eyes escalated and I winced, tilting my head down against the pain. That was when I saw it, or thought I saw it.

I stood motionless with my hand frozen in place as I stared at the water in the sink. The slow drain had allowed the flow to gather in the basin and ribbons of red curled and spread like blood streaming into the water. It didn't look like rust or red clay or anything else. It looked like blood, swirling and coating the white porcelain with streaks and tiny clots. Worse yet, it smelled like blood, with a sharp, metallic tang that lingered in my nose and throat. I gagged, squeezing my eyes shut.

A wave of dizziness hit and I gripped the edge of the vanity, sucking in short shallow breaths trying to work up enough air to yell for my mother. I swallowed against the sour bile taste in my mouth and counted to ten, and when I opened my eyes, only clear water flowed in the sink.

My hand shot forward turning off the tap, and I pumped the lever handle behind the faucet a bunch of times. I held my breath 'til the last of the water ran down the drain. *Did I say half a freak? How about a full-fledged weirdo, complete with psychotic visions?* Backing up, I grabbed hold of the towel rack and sank to the floor, the cold tile adding to my already goose-pimpled flesh.

Minutes passed and though my heart rate slowed, my mind raced. Was this some leftover nightmare skewed from Chiller TV? Part of me wanted to yell for my mother, but the other part knew she'd make a huge deal about it, and I didn't have time for a protection spell or whatever else she'd think to do.

The clock was ticking, and I needed to get myself together and out the door. Afraid to tempt fate and run the water in the sink again, I wet a washcloth under the bathtub tap. "No more sleep deprived delusions for me, thank you."

The problem was this didn't feel like a byproduct of too little sleep. Something happened, I sensed it. Gran told me the night of my birthday that my aura was bleeding. *Happy birthday, darling, and by the way... Gee, thanks. Love you too, Gran.*

That night my mother made light of it, telling me everyone's aura bled from time to time, it's part of coming into your own—yet I hadn't missed the look she shot my grandmother. And what the hell did that mean? Was I coming into my own as a strong, independent woman, or did some weird, cosmic witchiness hit me square in the face courtesy of my messed up gene pool? Right now, I didn't want to know. I wanted to go to school and take my exams like any other normal teenager.

After slapping on deodorant and body mist, I dressed, not bothering with make-up. I unfastened my claw clip and finger combed my hair before throwing it back into a messy bun, then grabbed my homework and shoved it into my bag. I allowed one last look in the mirror, hesitating about the no make-up, but no amount of cover-up would camouflage my fear-induced, chalk-white cheeks. Instead, I plastered a smile onto my face and headed downstairs, praying my mother's instincts would be too preoccupied to notice.

The blissful aroma of fresh brewed coffee filtered from the kitchen, making my mouth water before I walked through the doorway. Even more sublime, the scent of homemade pumpkin bread floated alongside the smell of fresh ground walnuts. "Hey," I mumbled, scraping one of the chairs back from the table. "Smells good. You had time to bake this morning?"

"I know how much you like pumpkin bread, so why not," my mother answered, putting a warm slice in front of me. "I thought it'd be nice for us to have a treat together, especially since I've been so busy lately and haven't been around much."

She thought right, and I took my first easy breath of the morning. "*Mmmmmm*, incredible," I said with my mouth full.

Reaching for her mug on the counter, she patted my shoulder and I cringed. The moment she touched me she'd know something was up. On cue she jerked her head around, eyes already probing.

I exhaled. "Cut it out, Mom, come on. I'm tired, that's all." I shrugged

her off purposefully, but she wasn't buying it. "I've got a huge math test today, and calc's been kicking my butt since the beginning of the year, so can we not do the Wicked Witch of Westchester County thing this morning?"

Taking a deep breath, my mother looked at me the way she looks at her rune stones when trying to divine a hidden meaning. "Okay, Rowen, if you say so. But whatever it was you saw…"

"I know, Mom, relax. Like I said, I'm just tired. Didn't you have something you needed to talk about? It must be important or why else would you need to bribe me," I said, waving my pumpkin bread her way before plopping another piece into my mouth.

My mother flashed me a half smile, knowing I'd used one of her trademark moves usually reserved for arguments with Gran. "You're right, but I think I could do better than pumpkin bread if I wanted to bribe you. Truth is, with New Year's a little less than two weeks away, the store is going to get crazy the closer it gets, and with everything I've got going I could really use your help."

"It's October, Mother. New Year's isn't for two months."

"You know what I mean, smart ass, *Samhain* is next week. And in case you've forgotten, Halloween is a fire sabbat that requires a ritual cleansing to protect the town and honor the wandering dead."

"Yeah, but jack-o-lanterns? Seriously?"

"Pumpkins are the easiest way to get everyone to participate without them really knowing. Unfortunately, they aren't going to carve themselves, and we're short of volunteers."

"I know," I said taking another bite of my pumpkin bread. "Don't worry, I'll do my part until every last jack-o-lantern is carved and placed." I wondered what the prissy town supervisor's wife would say if she knew my mother had orchestrated a pagan ritual involving the entire town right under her pious nose.

As if reading my mind, Mom smirked. "I knew I could count on you, Rowen, but do me a favor. Don't be such a teenager this week. The veil between the living and the dead is at its thinnest. I want you to pay attention, okay?"

I nodded, and she gave me a smile, but for the first time in my life my mother's smile didn't reach her eyes.

I walked to the corner and turned onto Main Street. Every lamp post was decked with the image of the Headless Horseman plastered on a flag billowing in the morning breeze. Indian summer was late this year, and a steady stream of warm days brought in business from all over. I waved to the owner of Main Street Bake Shoppe dressed in her red and white stripped apron with the motto, 'Let 'em eat cake!' emblazoned on the front. Local shops with all their quaint color were out in full force in anticipation of the seasonal rush.

The bells from St. Theresa's let me know it was almost 7:30 a.m., so I picked up my pace, my black, high heeled, peep-toe ankle boots clicking along the sidewalk like a metronome pacing my stride. The wind molded my long, slate blue tie-dyed skirt to my thighs, and I shivered, rubbing my arms through the sheer blouse beneath my denim vest. The morning air was cool, but the sky was clear and it looked like another beautiful day.

"It's about time!" Talia snorted between sips of her customary caramel latte. "It's only Tuesday, and your lateness has now passed epic and moved straight into legendary. As punishment for nearly ditching us, we've relegated you to the ranks of the latte-less this morning."

I grunted. "Some friends."

"You may keep your other friends waiting, but not us, Ro. Especially not this morning," Talia complained, shoving her pin-straight blond hair from her shoulder.

"Put a lid on it, Talia. Can't you see something's up?" Chloe snapped as the three of us stood on the corner across from school.

Talia smirked, swirling what was left of her whipped cream with a straw. "Well, it just so happens, something is up, or at least it will be Friday night." She giggled.

Chloe raised a suspicious eyebrow. "And what's *that* supposed to mean?"

High color stained Talia's cheeks as she moved closer. "I told Mike I'd go with him to Gory Brook Road."

"And?" I asked.

Talia gaped at me. "Douglas Park? Behind the cemetery? You know what I'm talking about," she said, tilting her head suggestively.

When my eyebrows shot up, Chloe burst out laughing. "Jeez, Rowen,

I think you need caffeine more than anyone this morning!" She looked from me to Talia and smirked. "So, you and Mike have a date with the backseat mambo, huh. Who'da thunk it? Talia Meyer, joining the ranks of the cemetery girls."

Talia's lips thinned in an annoyed frown. "Shut up, Chloe. At least I have a boyfriend. If you spent more time promoting your lady lumps instead of your right hook, you might actually interest someone. And *you...*," Talia turned her attention toward me, "that hippie-goth look you've got is cool and all, but most times it's more scary than sexy. Your mom may be the mayor of witch central, but you don't need to be her walking billboard."

Chloe's sharp breath said it all. Color rose in her cheeks making her usually creamy complexion blotched against her freckles. "Seriously, Talia? I'm so sick of listening to your mouth, lately. Have fun losing your *v-card*, but if Mike ditches you because you change your mind or worse, because he finally gets what he wants, don't bother calling. Rowen and I will be too busy to give a crap."

She stormed off, her bobbed auburn hair blowing in the breeze, leaving me and Talia staring after her in awkward silence.

"Rowen...," Talia whined, her tone demanding in a wheedling sort of way.

"Don't." I put my hand up, stopping her cold. "I know you don't mean it when you go off like that, but *Christ*, Talia, buy a filter! You're high maintenance and we know it, but this ego thing of yours is getting old. If it wasn't for the fact we've been friends since Pre-K, we would be so done."

I readjusted the strap to my messenger bag, annoyance pulling at the corners of my mouth. "You're not stupid, so do yourself a favor and dial it down or you'll be the one who's more than latte-less from now on." I turned on my heel and headed up the street, leaving her alone on the sidewalk.

Hippie-goth? Seriously? I dressed the way I liked, not because I was the quintessential poster child for the avant-garde. I straightened my shoulders, and even without the benefit of my trademark black eyeliner, I walked into school like I owned the place, ignoring the snide commentary from the cheerleaders sitting on the stone wall next to the main stairs.

They were all the same. *Plastics*, right out of the movie *Mean Girls*, and just as brainwashed to follow one girl, in this instance her name was Jenny Beamer. Her two-facedness was enough to make you sick. And she loved that her last name was the nickname for the archetypal suburban luxury car. Believe me, she never missed the opportunity to use the analogy, and considering the number of 'rides' she was rumored to have given boys, she wasn't that far off.

Jenny was hooked up with Tyler Cavanaugh, quarterback and first class jerk. A classic stereotype, but real enough to make you want to gag. He was gorgeous, of course, with sandy hair and eyes so blue they looked like candy. He ruled the school, or so he thought, spending as much time in the gym as he did in class. I tripped on my skirt once on the stairs, and I still remember the feel of his washboard stomach as he steadied me.

I was embarrassed, but thanked him anyway, and he seemed to revel in his role as hero, so much that he asked me out. My guess was he never expected me to say yes, but we went out anyway and actually had a good time. In fact, for a little while I even thought I misjudged him. Wrong. Tyler took me home after the movie, and to say it got ugly from there was an understatement. He was all hands and wouldn't let me out of his car. Self-defense 101 came in handy, although I'm glad I didn't hurt him too much, well...physically, anyway.

That was last spring, yet I still catch him looking at me like I was a prize he deserved to win, and didn't. As for Jenny, she was a classic backbiter, mean as a snake with the looks and money to back it up. Golden blond and pert, she and Tyler looked as though carved from ivory.

At my locker, I dropped my bag on the floor and grabbed the books I needed for the morning. Tyler's locker was three down from mine, and I surreptitiously glanced over, hoping he'd already left with his fan club. Again, no such luck.

A predatory grin spread across his too handsome face when he saw me. "Hey, Ro, what's up?" One eyebrow flicked upward in a flirty, yet snide question mark. "Going *au natural* today?"

Leave it to him to notice my fresh faced look, but even my uncharacteristically plain appearance didn't stop his eyes from giving my curves the once over, lingering too long where they shouldn't.

"Drop dead, Tyler—and don't call me Ro."

I should have known better than to acknowledge him. True to form, he took my rebuff as encouragement and positioned himself as close to me as possible without being obvious.

"Oooh, sorry, Mz. Corbett! What's the matter, the itchy witch got a bug up her butt?"

"I told you not to call me that, either."

"What?"

He knew what I meant. No one else called me itchy witch but him. He'd been doing it since we were little kids, teasing me about my favorite children's book called, *When Itchy Witchy Sneezes*.

Tyler's grin broadened to a leer and he reached out, skimming his knuckles across my upper arm. "That bug must be up there real good, but I know a way we can get rid of it. Whaddaya say, Rowen? I hear you Goth-chicks are into—*alternatives*." He paused for effect, stressing the word.

His innuendo and the way he over enunciated my name made his good looks suddenly ugly. I jerked myself sideways, dropping some of my books. "Keep your hands to yourself, Tyler. I don't think you want me to break a couple more of your fingers, not with it being football season and all. Besides, what excuse would you give your friends this time?"

His smile faded to a thin, harsh line. If looks could kill, I'd be dead on the white and red linoleum tiles in front of my locker. But who cares? I had lost all respect for him the night he wouldn't take no for an answer.

Tyler's eyes narrowed. He didn't say a word, but a nasty smirk formed on his lips before he walked back to his friends. When they all turned to look at me and laughed, I knew he said something gross to save face. He and his entire crew were pathetic. Then I noticed Hunter Morrissey looking directly at me. He hadn't laughed with the rest of them; in fact, he mouthed the words, "I'm sorry," before turning and heading off to class.

I blinked, watching him walk down the hall, wondering what the hell he was doing with such a bunch of losers. But who was I to judge? Tyler's appeal was an equal opportunity drain on the *IQ*.

As for Hunter, I didn't know him, really—not anymore. We were

friends at ten years old, before he moved to California. I was homeschooled at the time, but our mothers had been best friends, so we saw a lot of each other. We eventually lost touch, and then out of the blue, he moved back into town two months ago with just his mom.

He played on the football team, but he was also in a few of my honors classes. Go figure, a smart jock. Hunter was as good looking as Tyler, but in a much less Calvin Klein model sort of way. He was tall and dark with a laid-back California style and an easy smile that made you smile back. Tyler, on the other hand, was a *Kellan Lutz* wannabe, and it annoyed me how he was always posing, like life was some kind of ongoing photo shoot for underwear and perfect abs.

Hunter and I hadn't spoken since his mom and he stopped by the shop before term began. Since then, we exchanged a few polite words in the hallway and some ambiguous nods and quick glances in class, but that's all. Chloe and Talia loved to tease me whenever they caught him looking my way. And though it flattered my ego, Hunter Morrissey was Tyler's friend, and that was a huge *no-no* in my book.

I walked into A.P. English, and Hunter's eyes found mine the minute I came through the door. A half smile teased the corner of his mouth, but there was nothing snide about it. His expression was warm and even a little embarrassed, like I'd caught him in an unguarded moment. His gaze followed me as I slid into my seat three rows over, and we stared for the longest time. Self-conscious, I looked away, not wanting to feel more foolish, despite Chloe's *I told you so* grin from two seats away.

Mr. Conover finished scribbling on the smart board and turned, clapping his hands once. "Okay, people, we've been talking about American history and the role it played in inspiring certain works of literature. Considering the season, it naturally begs the discussion of Sleepy Hollow's favorite son, Washington Irving. Who can tell me the inspiration for his famous legend? Anyone?" He eased himself onto the edge of his desk and bounced his laser pointer up and down in his hand, waiting for an answer.

I raised my hand since no one else volunteered. Typical. Until the topic got heated, nobody opened their mouths.

"Yes, Rowen?"

"Some people say Irving got his inspiration for the Legend of Sleepy

Hollow from an old German folk tale he'd heard during his travels. He used real people from the area as the basis for crafting his characters, and a Revolutionary War setting for dramatic effect."

"Right. We all know the story; in fact it's a safe bet everyone in America knows the story. However, that's not what I was driving at. I want to talk about urban legends. We know Irving fictionalized his characters, but what about the lesser known tidbits? What about the accounts that remain untold except here in Sleepy Hollow? We know there's more to the legend than what's read on Halloween night."

A dull roar escalated in the room, with people talking back and forth among themselves. I shifted in my seat waiting for someone to say something rude about my family and its witchy inclinations, and of course, Jenny Beamer turned around eager to comply. A spiteful comment twisted on her lips, but Hunter's voice cut her off.

"Come on, Mr. Conover, seriously? You're telling us there's more to the story than some old folktale? It's been analyzed and decoded for over a century and every detail known is written and catalogued. Like Rowen said, some of the characters were based on real people. I'll be the first to admit the Van Tassells from the Legend are based on my mother's family tree. But the rest? Gimme a break."

The atmosphere tensed, and Mr. Conover's frown did nothing to help. "For the most part, you are correct, Hunter. Everyone concedes the story is pure fancy. No one actually believes the old town bridge is a supernatural checkpoint for evil spirits, or that Ichabod Crane was whisked to the underworld body and soul. That's not what I'm saying. There are local histories you're probably unaware of, intrigues and bits of scandal touched upon in the story that were very real at the time, and to which Irving was privy.

"The tidbits he embellished are the basis for the urban legends surrounding Sleepy Hollow to this day. Stories not well known outside our little village." He eyed Hunter specifically. "Your mother knows what I'm talking about. Perhaps you should ask her before you dismiss outright what you don't understand. There's what has been written, and then there's what has been passed down."

All eyes riveted to Hunter. His jaw tightened and the little muscle in his cheek clenched as he stared at the English teacher. Unfortunately, he'd

picked the wrong topic to argue against Mr. Conover.

"I don't need to talk to anyone, Mr. Conover. I may have spent the past seven years in California, but my heritage makes me more a part of this town's history than most. My mother told me the folklore surrounding your scandals, like the one about the Bronze Lady. How in the cemetery at night there's the sound of a woman crying bitterly, but it's not a woman, it's the bronze statue outside one of the old tombs. Legend claims if you climb into her lap and touch her cold, wet tears and say a prayer, she'll grant you her favor. On the other hand, if you mock her and slap her face, she'll haunt you to death. How tombstones are smeared with blood on All Hollows Eve with eyewitness accounts hidden in church documents.

"And according to those documents and my family's oral history, there's an unmarked grave at the center of the Old Dutch Cemetery, where the ground is black as pitch and nothing grows, and, of course, how could I leave out the Horseman's curse, promising to ride again when time and circumstance meet under a full moon. I know them all, Mr. Conover. I just don't believe them."

Mr. Conover slid his eyes toward me, his expression a little self-satisfied, like I was an ace in the hole. "And considering your family background, what do you think about all this, Rowen?"

Everyone's gaze followed, including Hunter's and my mouth went dry. "Me? What does my family have to do with this? We're not related to any families Washington Irving used in his story." Heat crawled up my neck and I felt my face flush. "God, I *hate* this time of year!"

Pressing my lips together, I gripped the side of my desk, trying to ignore Jenny's sniggering. Blurting was usually Talia's deal, not mine, so much so that I shocked myself along with everyone in the room. Even Mr. Conover had a hard time keeping a straight face at my unexpected outburst.

"Relax, Rowen, I'm not putting you on the spot," Mr. Conover assured. "I'm just curious about your opinion. These urban legends owe their longevity to a strong belief in the supernatural. Even the first few pages of Irving's story tell of this land as threaded with magic."

He reached behind his back for his glasses and a dog-eared copy of the Legend of Sleepy Hollow. He opened the book and cleared his throat.

Marianne Morea

'Certain it is, the place still continues under the sway of some witching power, that holds a spell over the minds of the good people, causing them to walk in continual reverie. They are given to all kinds of marvelous beliefs; are subject to trances and visions...'

Mr. Conover snapped the book closed, dropping his head to peer at me over the top rim of his glasses. "Everyone knows your mother and grandmother have been purveyors of the supernatural in this town for decades. As heir to their illustrious calling, what do you think?"

The bell rang and I breathed a sigh of relief. Gathering my books, I kept my head down, thanking God for small miracles.

"I'll be out tomorrow, people, so we'll continue this discussion the day after. Use that time to think about your answers. Concentrate on probability versus possibility." Mr. Conover shouted as we filed out.

"He really put you in the hot seat. Has he always been like that?" Hunter asked, coming up behind me in the hall.

Running a hand through my bangs, I fluffed my hair, but it was more residual tension than nervous flirting. "Nah, he's just a townie who's very into our history. Trust me, he's harmless."

Hunter snorted. "He didn't sound harmless when he put me on the spot. I saw the 'F' I'll get forming in his mind."

I laughed, flashing him a bright smile at how real he sounded. For the first time since he moved back, I recognized the same Hunter I remembered, regardless of his choice of friends. He wasn't at all a poser. It dawned how nice he was, that he hadn't lost his kindheartedness with everything he'd been through—plus, Hunter was as smart as he was handsome.

The fact he was tall and built hadn't escaped my noticed, not to mention the way his t-shirt clung to the six-pack hidden beneath the soft cotton. He wore his brown hair short and somewhat spiked, but not in a pretentious, 'I use a pound of gel every morning,' kind of way. I found myself mesmerized by his deep coffee colored eyes and how they glistened with warmth when he smiled. *Simpatico*. That's the word Señora Clark would use in Spanish class to describe Hunter. My own eyes were glued to his face, and at some point I realized I was staring.

His lips twitched, one side of his mouth curling up at my all too obvious ogling. "You okay?"

Sifting through clever things I could say, I couldn't form words and ended up babbling. "Yeah…I mean, no…I mean, I'm good. Just a little scattered after being put on the spot like that, but I'm fine, really."

He smiled, a full on gorgeous grin. "Good, because it looked to me like I'd lost you there for a sec."

Too nervous to chance opening my mouth again, I gave him a little poke with my elbow. Moments ticked, lapsing into an awkward silence and I fidgeted with my books. Shuffling my feet, I shifted my weight onto my heels, and like something out of America's most embarrassing moments, my heel caught a raised seam in the linoleum. I was going down hard. I groaned inwardly knowing it wasn't going to be pretty.

Hunter's hand shot out, grabbing my elbow. I managed to mumble a thank you, bracing myself for the inevitable laughter—but he didn't laugh or move away. Instead he held my forearm, running his thumb back and forth across my skin.

"It's a wonder you don't kill yourself in those things," he said, glancing at my shoes. Then eyeing me with a ghost of a smirk, he leaned forward. "But they're definitely killing *me* with how hot they look."

If I could've swallowed my tongue I would have. Thank God someone he knew walked by taking his direct attention. I must've been every shade of red on the color wheel, but when he turned back I had composed myself enough to whisper, "Death by stilettos, it's the only way to go."

Flashing me a wry smile, he winked. "Quick on the uptake, Rowen. I like that about you."

I almost choked. God, he was cute, and there was plenty I liked about him, too. "So… where are you headed, now? I've got calculus, then gym."

He laughed out loud. "Gym? I hope you brought sneakers, or it's going to be very interesting watching you play volleyball in those things, sexy as they are."

"I guess that means you've got gym the same time." No sooner than the words left my mouth, I cringed. *Duh?* Of course we were in the same gym class, and had been for the past month and a half. *Oh god, babble much?*

Overlooking my obvious brain burp, he nodded. "Yup, along with Tyler and Ben. I know they're not your favorite people, but they're

harmless, like Mr. Conover. Trust me, their bark is worse than their bite. Besides, the next time they get out of line you've got me to step in and block."

I smiled at his football analogy, but the truth was I'd ignored Tyler and his crew for so long that I never gave Hunter more than the covert glance I'd give any good-looking guy. As much as I liked him, he was still friends with the rest of those jerks, so the jury was still out. I thought about telling him about Tyler and what happened last spring, but it would open a can of worms I wasn't prepared to deal with. Besides, I could handle Tyler myself.

I shrugged, playing it cool. "They're your friends... but in the meantime, I've got this huge calculus test I'm about to fail, so I'd better run. See you later?" I asked, the flirty lilt in my voice sounding silly in my ears.

He smiled. "Definitely." His soft brown eyes crinkled at the corners a bit before glancing at the clock above the stairwell. "I'd love to walk you to class, but I've got to book it upstairs to physics or risk a lecture from Mr. Schaefer." With a wink and one of those gorgeous smiles, he disappeared through the double doors.

I sighed quietly and turned on my heel, a secret smile on my face. Hunter liked me, I was sure of it. What made matters worse was I liked him, too. It should be easy. Boy meets girl, boy likes girl. Girl likes boy back. Simple. Just then I felt a set of eyes on me. Tyler was leaning on the door to Mr. Garret's history class, his gaze tracking me. *Did I say simple? Not.*

The clock didn't budge, or at least that's how it seemed every time I looked up from my paper. The second hand moved. I watched it round the twelve, over and over, but the minute hand dragged.

I couldn't concentrate, and Mr. Shannon knew it. He peered at me from his desk, tapping the papers in front of him with his index finger when he caught my eye. Forehead in hand, I tucked a few loose strands behind my ear and tried to focus. Failure wasn't an option. At the very least, I wanted something to show for my late night study efforts, plus the giant bag of chips I demolished, but my thoughts wouldn't cooperate.

I was preoccupied with seeing Hunter again, and the idea of me

looking forward to gym class was so alien a thought, I actually laughed out loud, earning myself a few more desk-taps from Mr. Shannon. *Concentrate, Rowen… Calculus first. Cute guy later.*

I took a deep breath, calming my mind and marshaling my thoughts. The extra study paid off, and I swear my analytically-challenged brain sat up and yelled, *"Ah ha!"* The bell rang as I scribbled my last few answers, and I slammed my pencil down in my own version of, "yeah, baby!" Mr. Shannon shot me another half-mooned glare, but I didn't care. Excess adrenaline raced through my blood like I'd finished a marathon, but my stomach jumped for a different reason.

*He's popular…come on, Rowen, guys like him don't bother with girls like you unless they want something…*I ignored the little warning voice in the back of my head, and waited while Mr. Shannon took his time collecting the tests. I sat, cross-legged with the slim edge of my heel clicking against the hard linoleum floor. He made everyone late, and I raced out of the room and smack into Hunter's chest. The look on my face must have been rocked-back shock, because the *whoomph* that came out of my mouth was nothing short of embarrassing.

I bounced off of him, balancing on one heel like a drunken tightrope walker. "Take it easy killer, where's the fire?" he said, his arms taking hold of mine, stopping me from falling over myself, yet again.

My eyes wouldn't focus and I lost my breath. Blood was everywhere, on my hands, on the ground, and Hunter's face and chest. We weren't in the hallway anymore. In fact, we weren't anywhere I recognized. The school's polished white and red floor was now a grassy knoll, scorched black and slick with blood.

Hunter wore a blousy, linen shirt and britches—torn and bloody, a long gash crossed his torso from shoulder to belly. Crimson rivulets dripped from his forehead. I choked, vomit rising in my throat at the sight of his gleaming white skull showing where his hairline should have been. He'd been partially scalped and his throat cut.

Desperate to tell me something, the phantom Hunter tried to speak, but only gurgled. A long hiss escaped from the slice at his throat and he crumpled to the ground.

When I came to, someone was screaming in the hazy background. Didn't take long to realize it was me. Gulping down breaths, the terror

lingered along with the taste of vomit. It had to be a vision, but it was as real as the cold floor beneath me.

My eyesight cleared and I grabbed Hunter's arm, digging my fingers into his bicep. He took hold of my shoulders and shook me. He called my name, but his voice was thick and slow in my ears.

I crumpled into sobs, slumping against his chest, half lying on the floor, half in his arms. Sweat trickled between my breasts, and I couldn't catch my breath.

A small crowd formed around us outside the calculus lab, and Mr. Shannon shouted to get the nurse. Hunter helped me off the floor, but even with his protective arm around my shoulders, I felt everyone staring. I was the undisputed, *Queen du Freak*, and this nailed the title above my head for the rest of my life.

Talia rushed over despite this morning's fight. "Oh my God, Rowen!" she said, helping Hunter get me to my feet. "What the hell happened?"

Mr. Shannon waved her off. "Dial it down, people. This doesn't qualify as high drama. She fainted, that's all. I'm sure Mrs. Webber will take good care of her. Mr. Morrissey..." he said, turning his attention to Hunter. "Take Ms. Corbett to the nurse. The rest of you get back to class, show's over!" Mr. Shannon's voice echoed down the hall as he cleared the area.

"I'm sor...sorry," I mumbled into Hunter's shoulder as he half-carried, half-dragged me down the hall.

"*Shhh.* We're almost there," he murmured, tucking me further under his arm.

"Mrs. Webber?" Hunter called, using his shoulder to push open the door to the nurse's office.

"Oh my goodness, what happened?" Flipping her stethoscope onto her neck, Mrs. Webber jumped up from her desk chair to help sit me on the green cot next to the bathroom. Pursing her lips, she felt my forehead. "You're as white as a sheet. Is Mrs. McCafferty doing dissections again?"

A sweet lady with fondness for pink scrubs, Mrs. Webber had been the school nurse for almost twenty years. She was round, with little square reading glasses that sat neatly at the end of her nose, but she was no nonsense.

"No, more like a tough calculus test and a collision in the hallway,"

Hunter said with a wink, trying to make me smile.

"Ah, and with whom did we collide?" Mrs. Webber asked with a hint of a smile herself.

"Him," I croaked. "But, I'm not really sure what happened after that." I lied trying not to sound as frightened as I was.

With two fingers on my wrist and her eyes on her wristwatch, she didn't miss a beat telling Hunter to get me a cup of water from the cooler. "Hmmm. Your pulse *is* fast," she added frowning a bit. "How much coffee did you have before school this morning?"

"None." I managed to answer.

Hunter handed Mrs. Webber the paper cup and she gave it to me. "Take small sips. Your skin is clammy, are you nauseated? You have no fever, but your cheeks are flushed. Have you been sick at all recently, Rowen?"

I almost said, "Not unless you count the two psychotic episodes I had this morning," but didn't. Mrs. Webber meant well, but she wasn't who I needed right now. I needed my mother. "No, ma'am," I answered shaking my head, quietly.

"Getting the wind knocked out of you like that can certainly leave you a little disoriented, and it's no wonder you're crashing around like a bull in a china shop, just look at those shoes! You kids really need to slow down or more of you are going to end up in here."

Putting her stethoscope back in her pocket, she fixed me with one of her looks. "I want you to lie back, and we'll see how you feel after you've rested for a while."

Mrs. Webber went back to her paperwork and Hunter sat next to me on the cot. I couldn't stop looking at him. He was all right, not a mark on him. Even so, I reached up to run my fingers over his face, pushing my hands through his hair to satisfy myself his scalp was still attached to his head. "You're okay…you're really okay," I mumbled.

Stunned, he just looked at me. "Yeah, I'm okay. I've got guys way bigger than you crashing into me on the field every day. But what about you? Jeez, Rowen, what the hell was that? You ran out of class like a bat out of hell, crash head on into my chest, and the next thing I know you're catatonic on the floor, staring at me in terror. I kept calling you, but it's like you couldn't hear me, and then you started screaming."

My mouth was open, but no words came. How could I explain what happened when I didn't understand myself? "Hunter, I...I need to go home," I stuttered, my eyes searching his.

Taking my hand he winked, flashing me a calculated smile. "I'll see what I can do."

Mrs. Webber looked up from her desk. "Considering all the chitchat going on over there, I can only assume you're feeling better, Rowen."

Getting up, she checked my color and my pulse again, her mouth set in a thin line as she made notes on her clipboard. "You're heart rate is still a little too high for my liking. I can't keep you in school, sweetie, the last thing we need is you face down in your lunch tray. Just stay put and I'll call your mother to come get you."

"Wait...," Hunter piped up. "*Uh*...I'm more or less done for the day, so if it's okay with you I can take Rowen home."

The nurse raised an eyebrow, her no-nonsense gaze falling on him. "Well, which is it Mr. Morrissey, more done or less done?"

"That's a matter of opinion." He shrugged flashing a persuasive smile, but when her eyebrow shot even higher, he cleared his throat, wiping the grin off his face. "I've got lunch in about fifteen minutes and then study hall. My last afternoon class is calculus at 1:20."

Pursing her lips, she pointed a finger in my direction. "I'm still going to call your mother. I trust you'll go straight home, so no shenanigans. Got it?" Her eyes looked from me to Hunter and back again.

I nodded.

Chuckling, she walked back to her desk and took two passes and a pen from her top drawer. Scribbling on one, she handed it to me. "Yours is for the remainder of the day. If you don't start feeling better by tonight, have your mother take you to the doctor."

Switching her gaze to Hunter, she smirked, writing out the other pass. "However charming and noble you are, Mr. Morrissey, yours is only for study hall, so I suggest you get Rowen's books and then see her home. Now get going before I change my mind," she said, winking at me as she sat at her desk.

Hunter didn't waste any time, and before I knew it, we were pushing our way through the heavy double doors and into the sunshine. The weather was just as I expected, and the sun felt incredible on my face and

skin. I closed my eyes imagining away the odd chill that had seeped into my bones.

"It's beautiful out. Too bad we can't blow off the rest of the day together," Hunter remarked, giving me a sideways glance as he led us through the senior parking lot to the sidewalk. "We could head down to Kingsland Point like we used to when we were kids."

The idea of blowing off classes and hanging with Hunter all day made my heart skip a beat, but I had no brain cells left at this point to give it more than a cursory thought. Everything that happened was too real for me to ignore, and the residual panic churning my stomach was a jagged explanation point driving that fact home. Reaching over I took Hunter's hand and squeezed it. "Rain check?" I said, my voice cracking a bit.

"Sure, rain check." he winked, squeezing my hand back as if telling me no sweat. "Come on, I'll drive you home."

Drive? He pressed the crosswalk button on the pole near the curb, and we waited for the light to change. Neither one of us said a word, but he continued to hold my hand—probably just making sure I didn't take off down the street, screaming like a lunatic. Not that I blamed him. At this point I wasn't sure either.

The light changed, and he steered me toward the municipal lot behind the coffee shop on the corner. Keys in hand, he clicked the black fob at the end of his key ring, and a quick, high pitched chirp turned me toward a line of cars to our right. At the end of the row sat a brand new, cobalt blue Mustang, its lights flashing in time with the chirp.

It figured. The car had California style, plates and all, and was almost as striking as he was. I glanced up at him sideways. "You know, you could've just walked me home. I only live around the corner, remember?" I said, crooking my finger in the direction of my house.

He smiled that full on gorgeous grin, the one that was quickly becoming my favorite thing about him. "Yeah, but then I'd have to walk back, instead of hanging out with you a little longer." Walking around the front of the car, he unlocked the passenger side door and held it open for me.

Freaked out or not, complicated or not, did I mention how much I wanted to kiss him?

Chapter 2

My mother hadn't yet arrived when Hunter pulled in front of my house, but I knew she was on her way. We lived in a Tudor style duplex with a private residence on one side and our store on the other. When my mother opened the Silver Cauldron, we lived in the apartment upstairs, but as her business grew, she expanded, buying the attached house and renovating the layout so the shop and the house were linked and easy to manage.

I unlocked the front door, the scents of lavender and burnt sage filling my nose as I stepped inside. Mom had been burning incense, and most likely had smudged the house with white sage to cleanse it of whatever was making me so edgy. After what happened at school, I had a sneaking suspicion she needed to put in for a bigger supply.

"Come on in," I said over my shoulder as I kicked off my boots. "But take your shoes off."

Still carrying my messenger bag, Hunter put it down and took a deep breath, holding it for a moment. I frowned, knowing the residual scent of burnt sage can sometimes smell like pot. "It's not what you think," I said trying to sound relaxed, but I'd been through enough today, and even a hint of disapproval on Hunter's face was going to push me over the edge.

He smiled like he knew exactly what I meant. "Sage. My mom used to burn it, fanning the smoke through the house every time my dad had one of his business associates over. She said it got rid of bad vibes and the

stench of phony friends. California is full of pretentious jerks, just like New York." He chuckled.

I couldn't help but burst out laughing, and some of the tension lodged between my shoulder blades loosened. "And here I was afraid you'd think my family was up to its hippie worst. You wouldn't believe the reaction we get from people who aren't familiar with the practice of burning sage. Now my mom just smudges the place after people leave. It's less complicated."

Standing in his white socks with his hands in his pockets, Hunter looked uncomfortable. Guilt edged its way past my own preoccupation, and I felt awful. He'd been totally kind and totally cool, while everyone else was whispering about how freaky I was. "I know you said you'd wait with me, but I don't want you to get into trouble on my account. My mother will be here any minute." And if I knew my mom, she was airborne the minute she hung up with Mrs. Webber.

Taking his hands out of his pockets, he crossed his arms in front of his chest. "You think I'm going to leave you on your own after the episode you had?"

Chewing on my lower lip, I went into the living room and stood near the couch with my back to him. I knew it was too good to be true. He'd only held my hand because he felt sorry for me. Setting my jaw, I turned and looked him square in the face. "I'm fine, Hunter. I just need to talk to my mother, so you can stop treating me like I belong in a psych ward."

"Psych ward? You're really clueless, aren't you? Can't you see I don't care what everyone else thinks? I know you're not a freak, Rowen, but your collapse this morning scared the crap out me. Something happened, something most people can't or won't understand. I know we really haven't gotten to know each other again, but you've got to trust me, I'll understand."

I threw my hands in the air in frustration. "You're kidding, right? I know I scared you. Hell, I scared myself, but how do you expect me to believe you'll understand, when I don't understand myself?"

"You saw something, didn't you?" he said taking a step toward me, his voice apprehensive.

His eyes looked through me, and my mouth went dry. "What makes you think that?"

He opened his mouth but hesitated, as if he was taking a calculated risk with what he was about to say. "My mother was the same way. Not so much anymore, but it used to happen a lot when I was younger. Scary thing was, her visions almost always came true. Just tell me one thing, did you see me die?" he asked his face serious.

My tongue felt like sandpaper stuck to the roof of my mouth. I swallowed, trying to work up enough spit to form words. I kept shaking my head trying to wrap my mind around it all. "It was you, but not you..." was all I managed. My voice trailed off, and on cue, my mother's car pulled in. She came in like a firestorm, and I knew there was no way I could finish telling him, even if I had found my voice. We stared at each other, those few words hanging in the air between us.

"Rowen! Are you okay, honey? I knew something was up this morning, but as usual you didn't want to talk about it..."

I don't know what my mother expected to find, but she stopped short like someone threw cold water in her face. "Hunter? What's going on? The school called and..."

I cut her off, needing to clear the tension between me and Hunter and at the same time, circumvent my mother's bat senses. When it came to sniffing out facts, Laura Corbett could give the FBI a run for its money. "Hunter brought me home and waited with me 'til you got here, but now that you're home he's got to get back to class."

He stepped forward and put out his hand. "It's nice to see you again, Mrs. Corbett," he said offering her a quick smile.

Scrutinizing his face, my mother's eyes seemed to weigh every nuance of his expression and I groaned inwardly. *Please, not the Star Chamber inquisition, not now....*

"Of course. How are you, sweetie?" she said, taking his hand in both of hers and the air around us suddenly felt thick. "I'm sorry, I don't mean to stare. I still can't get over how much you've grown. You'll have to forgive me, but I'm having a hard time getting past the image I have in my head of you and Rowen as little kids."

He shrugged, sliding his eyes sideways toward me. He was embarrassed, and there was nothing I could do to help. My mother's antennae were up and targeted on us.

A huge grin spread across my mother's beautiful face. "Your mom

mentioned you were moving into the old Van Wart place. Are you all settled in?"

A shadow passed over Hunter's face, but it was gone as fast as it came. "It's just me and Mom, now. Dad's still in California, I think. But yeah, we're all settled."

I watched my mother's eyes soften and her face grow a little pained for him and for his mother. "I'm sorry about your dad, Hunter. Your mom mentioned the separation when I saw her last, but I didn't want to press. Oceans of time and all."

Hunter looked down at his socks. "Separation is just a polite way of saying divorce, I guess." He picked up his head and flashed my mother half a smile. "But it is what it is."

I wanted to crawl under the floorboards. "Hunter, don't you need to get back to school?" I said, surreptitiously motioning to the door with my head. No way was I taking the chance of my mother embarrassing him any further, or God-forbid, embarrassing me in front of him.

She looked at him, her gaze bright. "Well, California's loss is Sleepy Hollow's gain, and I'm sure Rowen is certainly happy you've come home."

Oh man, don't go there, please...

I couldn't believe it, Hunter actually blushed. "Yeah, me too, but Rowen's right. I really should get back to class."

I eyed them both, not really knowing what to say. Hunter picked up his shoes and headed for the front door, but rather than stand there in awkward silence, or worse yet, have my mother start my inevitable interrogation in front of him, I followed him to the door. The two of us were silent as he slipped on his sneakers, but he shot me a look that told me our conversation was far from over.

My mom followed behind, but walked to the credenza to put down her keys. "It was nice to see you again, Hunter, and thank you for everything. Please tell your mother to give me a call. I'd love to see her, again." Turning on her heel, she made it clear the time for small talk was over, and I needed to get down to the business of telling her what happened.

I walked him onto the front porch, but before I could open my mouth to say anything, he handed me his cell phone. "Put in your number. I

have football practice late, but I'll call you at some point tonight."

A little unsure, I punched my number into his phone and handed him mine to do the same. I didn't know what to say as I watched him add his number to my contact list, but I also didn't want to leave things hanging. "Hunter, whatever I saw, there's got to be a reasonable explanation. I'll figure it out, I promise."

He shrugged, handing me back my phone. "I know you will." His voice was guarded and he glanced past me through the screen door to my mother as she puttered around the kitchen. Looking back, he dropped his gaze to mine. "We'd both better get going."

With a nod he started down the stairs and then stopped, glancing back. "I trust you, Rowen." His expression was an odd mix of unease and hope.

I nodded once, not really sure how to respond. I mean, what could I say? Thanks for trusting I'm not some kind of nutcase? That I'm confident I can figure this out when in reality I'm scared witless and haven't a clue? I watched him pull away and let go of the breath I didn't realize I'd been holding.

"He's cute," my mother said fixing herself a cup of tea at the kitchen counter. She didn't look up from steeping her crescent-moon shaped infuser, but a faint smile played on her lips.

I stood in the doorway a little perplexed, surprised she hadn't jumped on what happened at school the minute Hunter left. My mother was calm about things, except when it came to me and my safety, and considering our background, she was also pretty good with weird. This situation hit home on both counts, and though she hadn't found me comatose or sitting in the corner rocking back and forth, I expected more of a reaction.

"I guess," I shot back, a little irritated. Walking to the table, I flopped into one of the chairs and toyed with the end of a linen placement, her steady calm unnerving me a bit.

She fiddled with the tea kettle, placing it on the back burner before putting her cup on the table. The sound of her chair scraping against the tile as she sat down adding to my tension. "So...,"she asked, spooning sugar into her cup and eyeing me circumspectly.

Tears pricked the corners of my eyes and I almost lost it. I had been

holding it together since I left school grounds, not wanting to fall to pieces in front of Hunter any more than I already had. I was angry and scared, and my body flushed with heat at the thought of no longer being in control of my own thoughts or actions. Both my mother and my grandmother always said to let things happen, to let whatever was sent roll over me like a wave. Well, this was no wave. This was a tsunami.

"I've been having visions. They're bloody and they're violent and they're terrifying the crap out of me. It's happened twice—once this morning in the bathroom and then again at school. *Bam*! Blindsided out of nowhere and the next thing I know, I'm sucked into some kind of supernatural time warp."

"What you were doing when they occurred?" she asked stirring her tea, her delicate fingers on the edge of her teaspoon, moving it round and round the way she stirred one of her brews.

I exhaled sharply, throwing my hands up. "That's just it, I wasn't doing anything. I was just going about my normal routine, like any other day!"

Laying the spoon on her napkin, she picked up her teacup and blew over the rim. "Don't get yourself worked up, Rowen, or you'll trigger another one. It's a sure bet this is somehow related to who you were with at the time."

"Then it has to do with me, I guess, because the first one hit while I was brushing my teeth in the bathroom this morning, and the other when I accidentally crashed into Hunter at school."

"You crashed into Hunter?" she said her lips twitching in yet another half-smile.

"*Jesus*, Mom, can we focus here, please? Yes, I crashed into him in the hallway, and it triggered some sort of *Dr. Who*, out of body, space and time-travel thing! I saw him, or at least someone who looked like him. He had been tortured, bleeding everywhere, and he couldn't speak though he tried to tell me something. Mom. It was horrible!"

"When."

"I just told you, it happened in school this morning."

"No, Rowen, you said it triggered some kind of time warp. Forward or back is what I'm asking."

"Back. The Hunter in my vision was dressed like somebody from the

Revolutionary War."

My mother didn't say anything, just sipped her tea, her eyes narrowing as she stared ahead at nothing. Except those looks were never *at nothing*.

"Mom? Hello? You still with me, or are you having your own out of body experience?"

Putting her cup down, she shook her head. "What you had wasn't an out of body experience, Rowen. *You* didn't leave your body and go anywhere; your *mind* took you back in time. I'm pretty sure what you experienced was a temporal wave. A ripple effect of something that happened long ago, now felt in the present. Think of it as someone throwing a rock into a cosmic lake 200 years ago, and the ripples are just now reaching the shore. My question is why?"

"I don't really care why. I just want you to make it stop."

"It goes hand in hand, sweetheart. If we can figure out what your vision was trying to tell you, then the message in the cosmic bottle will have been delivered, loud and clear."

"Great, so I'm a clearinghouse for paranormal junk mail?"

"Don't get cute, but in a nutshell, yes. Visions are nothing more than scraps of information, supernatural snippets warning us of things to happen, or things that have already happened that may have some meaning for future events. It's up to us to divine which. And just so you know, the snippets are hardly ever junk."

With my palms on the table I stood in a rant, the chair clattering to the floor in the process. "So what does that mean? I saw Hunter die and it was awful! The scary thing is, he guessed it, said his mother used to have visions all the time."

I was just short of a full blown nervous breakdown, but my mother was still irritatingly calm. "Sit down, Rowen. You're not helping the situation getting carried away by panic. However vicious the event, you have to remember it happened in the past. It wasn't Hunter. This vision was meant to warn him, or perhaps help him with something now. Like you were told on your birthday last month, things are changing for you.

"You're coming into your own, and your bleeding aura may be connected to this in some way. This is not something to be taken lightly. In this instance, you may find yourself to be more than just a messenger.

Have Hunter ask his mother if she knows of any ancestors that died in the revolution, also if she's ever had visions similar to yours. Back in the day, the Van Tassells were a very prominent family in Sleepy Hollow, and my guess is they kept impeccable records."

I woke early, weak morning light crisscrossing my room like a laser grid warning me to stay in bed. My head weighed ten pounds, at least that's how it felt. My mouth was dry and I tried to swallow, but didn't have enough spit to down the cotton balls lodged at the back of my throat. With one arm across my eyes, it didn't take long for me to drop back into the edgy, preoccupied mindset from the night before.

I rolled onto my side away from the windows to try and coax sleep, but the towel I used to wrap my wet hair slid onto my shoulder. I didn't remember lying down with it still on my head. Had I passed out? Pulling it off, I dumped it on the floor and flopped onto my back. A thousand little vibrations tingled along my scalp as I ran my fingers through my still damp hair.

It was then I remembered the tea my mother had brought to me before I went to bed. The empty cup sat on my nightstand. I reached out wrapping my fingers around the porcelain handle and lifted it to my nose. It was my mother's proprietary blend of nighttime tea mixed with the unmistakable, underlying scent of alcohol, and I groaned.

A few left over tea leaves adhered themselves to the porcelain, while others swirled in the remaining brown liquid. I wrinkled my nose. Perhaps I should ask my mother to read them for any bad omens. Snorting at the idea, a dull ache shot through my forehead like a cosmic wrist slap. Corbett's worked serious magic, not cheap carnival tricks.

A soft knock came outside my bedroom door and I croaked, "Come in," already knowing it was my mother.

"Oh my," she said taking one look at me.

Putting the cup back on its saucer, I groaned again, lying back on my pillow. I was officially revoking the title of 'mother' until my head stopped pounding. "You do know it's considered bad parenting to drug your children, Laura. What the hell did you give me last night?"

With a limp hand, I gestured to my hair, the towel on the floor and the fact I was still in my terry robe with nothing underneath. "All

evidence points to my passing out, don't you think?"

Bending to pick up the towel from the floor, she hung it over my desk chair. "Don't be so dramatic, Rowen. Mothers have been rubbing whiskey on their baby's gums for centuries, it soothes them, and what I did was no different. I only gave you a drop, and the tea is no different from what I always give you when you can't sleep. I just added an extra ingredient to make sure you didn't dream."

"Was it supposed to cement my tongue to the roof of my mouth?"

"From the sound of your griping, your tongue is working just fine. But since I knew you'd be out of sorts this morning, I've brought something to perk you up and clear away the cobwebs." Handing me another teacup, I eyed it and her warily.

"What is it?"

"If you paid more attention to the recipes and spell books in the kitchen, you'd know what it is. Just drink it, it'll help."

I took a tentative sip and smiled. *Peppermint and green tea.*

With a knowing look she smiled back, tapping the side of her temple. "Mama knows best." Then putting both hands out she gestured for me to get up. "Come on, I'll keep you company while you get dressed."

I gulped down the rest of my pick-me-up, burping in the process, making us both laugh. I knew she had a million and one things to do, but keeping me company was her way of lessening my fear of zoning out. I loved her for it. Grabbing my clothes I went into the bathroom, but kept the door ajar so we could talk.

"Did this ever happen to you when you were my age?" I asked while washing my face and brushing my teeth.

"No, honey, I wasn't lucky enough."

Lucky? Through the crack in the doorway, I saw her as she went about straightening my room.

"I know right now you don't think of it as lucky," she added like she could read my mind. Tucking in the corners of my duvet she continued, "However, this shows how psychic you really are, and it's a blessing whether you realize it or not. Just think of what you'll be able do with your talent once you learn to harness it."

I laughed, throwing my hair over my head, trying to gel my curls into submission. "Wanna trade?"

"Ha. Don't thumb your nose at the fates; you never know what might piss them off."

Dressed in black jeans, black high tops and a gray lace camisole, I finished applying my mascara and eyeliner. It was like putting on my armor. I was back and ready for whatever the cosmos threw at me. Grabbing a dark steampunk style jacket, I shrugged into it and turned toward my mother sitting on the end of my bed. "Whaddaya think?"

"Perfect, except for one thing." In her hand was a tiny black bag attached to a black silken cord. "Slip this over your neck."

Rolling my eyes, I moaned. "Forget it. I'm not wearing a mojo bag. No way."

Dangling it from her fingers, she fixed me with a look that would rival Mrs. Webber's. "Rowen." The lilt she added to the end of my name told me she wasn't taking no for an answer.

With a halfhearted sigh, I took the bag from her and opened the drawstring. "What's in it? Nothing that smells, I hope." I shook the contents out into my palm, a bloodstone, a sprig of rosemary, a piece of rose quartz and comfrey—tiny stones and herbs all for protection, courage and calm. Fingering the pink stone, I gave my mother curious look. Rose quartz wasn't just for peace; it was also a love stone.

My mother shrugged. "Hey, you're going to be talking to Hunter at some point today, so why not kill two birds with one 'love' stone?"

I opened my mouth to retort, but then snapped it shut. *Crap! Hunter.* He was supposed to have called last night. My eyes flew to my cell phone and I grabbed it off the nightstand. I scrolled through my messages and missed calls. Yup, he called just as he said he would, and I missed it because my own mother drugged me into a stupor.

"Everything okay?"

Distracted, I looked up at her. "What? Yeah, just a missed call, that's all." Pressing the end button on my touch screen, I stuck it back in its clip and hooked it to my hip.

"Rowen, it's better you talk to him in person anyway," she said reading the disappointment in my face. "But make sure you wear the bag, or at least put it in your pocket. It'll stop you from having visions while you're at school—and speaking of school, can you ask Chloe and maybe one or two of your other friends if they can help out at the Blaze site this

weekend? We need help to be ready in time for the exhibition on Halloween night. So far we've been okay maintaining our regular tour display, but this warm weather has been kicking our butts, to use your phrase, and we could really use a few extra hands. Ask Hunter to come, too. I've warded the place myself, so you should be vision free, but if any get through at least I'll be there to help."

It almost sounded like she hoped something would happen, just so she could see firsthand what I'm seeing. For a moment I was put off, but then I realized if she went through it with me, maybe we could figure out things.

Nodding absently, I hunted for my earrings. "Okay, I'll see who's around. Do you still need me to cover the shop today?"

Pushing up from the bed, she stood behind me at my dresser with her hands on my shoulders, both our reflections looking back at us from my mirror as I fastened my silver hoops. "If you're not up to it, sweetheart, I can get someone to cover, although it's short notice at this point."

I covered her hand with mine. "Don't worry, I got it."

"You're sure? It'll only be 'til 4:00, and then Gran can take over."

I nodded, and a feeling of comfort stole over me, like together we could do anything.

Chapter 3

I hadn't seen Hunter all day. He was a no show in English, despite the fact Mr. Conover was out, and I hadn't seen him in the hallway. Distracted to say the least, I forced myself to focus in class. No one seemed to know where he was, not even his friends. I texted him before school about missing his call, but he hadn't texted back. Was this his standard, or was he just pissed I didn't phone him back last night?

My adrenaline level soared off the charts worrying that while I was in an herbal induced coma, something terrible happened. I checked messages like an addict looking for the next fix, but my only unread text was from Chloe, telling me she was sick and couldn't hang out later. The fact she ended her text with a string of winks, wanting to know details about me and Hunter, told me the whole school was talking about us.

Talia must have texted her, along with everyone else looking for the 411. As far as helping with the Blaze this weekend, she was too busy. No surprise, there. So far nobody was willing to volunteer, but then again who else was crazy enough to work free manual labor on the weekend but me?

I ran up the stairs practically carrying my entire locker with me, and pushed my way into the girl's changing room to get ready for gym. Dropping my books, my pack, and my purse on the wooden bench in front of the lockers, I exhaled, peeling my jacket off my shoulders. Class hadn't even started, and I was already a sweaty mess. Why the school put

the locker rooms upstairs from the gym was beyond me.

I bent over to untie my high tops, forgetting the mojo bag tucked into the shelf bra of my camisole. It fell forward, swinging in front of me like pendulum.

"Nice necklace, Rowen, what's in it, eye of newt or maybe this time it's a dried cat's tongue." Jenny Beamer laughed, the high pitched tinkle making everyone cringe, even her friends. For someone so pretty, her voice was like a heat seeking missile aimed at finding the most vulnerable spot in your ear and making it bleed.

I shot her my most deadpan look, eyeing her straight on. "Very funny, but I'd be worried about my own tongue if I were you. People might be tempted to cut it out to shut you up."

The girl visibly flinched, and I bit the inside of my cheek to keep from laughing.

"You're such a freak, Rowen!" she said, stomping her designer shoe clad feet like a petulant toddler.

I shrugged. "Yeah, but every guy in school knows *exactly* what you are. It's classic. Mommy and Daddy don't give you enough attention, so you look for it in the backseat of any car you can crawl into."

Clenching her fists, splotches of red broke out across Jenny's face and neck. "Go to hell!"

"Very original, Jen. Anything new to add, or can we move on?" My question must have thrown her, because all she did was blink. Jenny Beamer wasn't the sharpest tool in the shed. "Didn't think so," I added, shaking my head.

In a fit of temper she yelled for Tyler as she stormed out of the locker room, her bubble-headed clique a line of ducks quacking behind her.

Chuckling, I finished changing in peace, tucking my mother's mojo bag into my sports bra, just in case.

I walked onto the lacquered gym floor, ducking at the last second as a dodge ball flew past my head. "Watch where you're walking, Row-en," Tyler guffawed, over-emphasizing my name again as Jenny tucked herself under his arm, a nasty smile stretching across her pink glossed mouth.

Disgusted, I ignored them and knelt to retie my high tops. I waved to my friends sitting on the bleachers, thinking I would join them in the

Hollow's End

hope of going unnoticed when it came time for choosing up sides. Gym class was a joke, more like a free period with indiscriminate sports thrown in for the hell of it.

A pair of black Nike cross trainers attached to an unbelievable set of calves stopped right in front of me. "What's the matter, you forget to charge your phone, or did you just decide it was more fun to blow me off."

I lifted my eyes, taking in every inch of the Greek god standing in front of me. The unbelievable calves gave way to powerful thighs, a flat stomach, broad shoulders and the face that had haunted my thoughts since I woke up. *Hunter*.

I got to my feet and he flashed me that wonderful grin, but I was too annoyed with myself to care. "Feeling better now that you made me feel like crap? I texted you what happened, or did *you* forget to charge *your* phone?"

Taken aback, his eyebrows rose slightly. "No need to take my head off. I was just kidding."

When I didn't say anything, his eyes narrowed and he studied me closer. I exhaled, dropping my gaze to my hands fidgeting with the bottom hem of my tee shirt. No doubt he thought I had another episode, but no way was I letting him know Jenny and her wannabes got under my skin.

"Stop looking at me like that. I'm fine," I mumbled, looking up but not really making eye contact.

He took a step forward and grabbed my forearm. "Come on, Rowen, I'm not stupid. Something happened."

Jerking my arm away, I snapped at him. "Not that it's any of your business, but if you need to know I had a run in with Jenny in the locker room. It's no big deal, I've been dealing with her kind my whole life, but of course, you wouldn't understand."

"Jenny? Why? And why are you so sure I wouldn't understand?"

His expression was a mixed bag, but I didn't expect Hunter to get it. Guys just don't, but from the look on his face he wasn't going to take no for an answer.

I blew out a breath, waving my hand futilely. "You're a part of Tyler's crew, as he likes to call it. You hang with them." I said, making bunny ear

quotation marks in the air. "How could you possibly understand what it feels like to be lumped with the U.P.s?"

"U.P.s?"

I stared at him. Was he fishing for me to explain? "You're kidding, right? Unpopular verses popular? It's not exactly a new trend, Hunter."

He stood contemplative for a moment, his expression the way he used to look when we were kids and he was planning something he knew I'd hate. "Come with me," he said. It was more directive than request, and he took my arm again, steering me toward the other side of the gym.

I stopped short, jerking my arm away for the second time. "Forget it, Hunter. There's no way I'm going over there with you."

I flicked my gaze toward the basketball court where, surprise, surprise, Tyler was watching us. He held up the basketball waving for Hunter to join him, and threw in a rude gesture for my benefit.

A disgusted noise escaped my lips and Hunter chuckled. "Lighten up, Rowen. You might surprise yourself and actually have a good time with us."

I shot him a dirty look, and much to my chagrin, he laughed harder. In one fluid motion he stepped in front of me, a soft, half smile playing on his lips. "I'll be the first to admit Tyler does boneheaded things, but he doesn't mean anything by it. It's just Tyler being Tyler. You've gotta know he only does it because he gets a rise out of you every time." Hunter took another step closer, his knuckles skimming the side of my forearm. "Once you get to know him, you'll understand what I mean."

I crossed my arms in front of my chest. "I know him a lot better than you think." I gave him a pointed look, hoping he was astute enough to read between the lines. One day I'd pluck up the nerve to tell him how much of a creep his friend was, but today wasn't that day.

"Why don't you hang out with us before you make up your mind to lump all of us together, to use your word? If you still think my friends are a bunch of jerks, I promise to lay off."

I didn't answer; I looked at his handsome face and the cajoling smile he wore.

"A bunch of us are sticking around after we set up for the candlelight tour at the Old Dutch Church. The tour is Halloween night and from what I hear, it's a popular stop before people head over to the Blaze."

Hollow's End

"I know about the tour, Hunter. I'm not the one who just moved back, remember?"

"Ha, ha," he shot back, teasingly annoyed. "Coach is making the team help set up as part of our community service requirement. It's Saturday night, and the party is afterward—in the cemetery."

He leaned closer almost whispering the last part like it was supposed to scare or shock me. I'd heard about these clandestine cemetery parties, but had never attended one. It sounded creepy, but I didn't care. Right now, it was all I could do to not sigh. The feel of Hunter's fingers on my bare skin sent shivers across my lower belly. I wanted him to wrap his arms around my waist and pull me against his hard, flat stomach.

"Come with me, it'll be fun," he said, tilting his head, his smile making the butterflies in my stomach loop di loop.

I squeezed my arms even tighter across my chest. "Maybe...but I'm still not going with you to the basketball court."

Grinning, he ran his hand across my skin once more before letting it drop to his side. "Okay, you win, but we still have an important conversation to finish. How about we drive to Kingsland Point after school? You owe me a rain check, remember?"

How could I forget? Chewing on my bottom lip, I hedged. "Okay... but don't you have football practice?"

"Coach has some meeting or something, so practice doesn't start until later." He cocked his head to the side. "Why? Not sure you want to hang out with me, after all?" he asked teasingly.

Heat rushed to my cheeks at the way he looked at me. "No, it's fine," I hesitated again. *Why did I have to promise my mother I'd work this afternoon?* "It's just it'll have to wait until four, if that's okay. I promised my mother I'd help at the shop until then."

He smiled. "It's a date, then."

I nodded. *If only.* "Okay. See you, later."

The rest of the day dragged as I plowed through the list of dull tasks my mother left for me to do in the shop. I opened FedEx boxes with last minute stock, organizing the new items on the shelves and marking the packing slips for my mother to check against the invoices. Finishing up early, I tried not to watch the clock as time moved closer to four p.m.

The doorbells chimed and I looked up from behind the register where I sat doing homework. Hunter stood in the doorway, the gold and red hues from the late afternoon sun making him look even more Greek god-like.

"Hey," I said flipping my notebook closed.

He walked to the counter with both hands in his jacket pockets. "Are we still on for Kingsland Point?" he asked, gesturing toward my AP History textbook.

I nodded. "Yeah. We weren't busy, so I used the time to catch up on homework." I sat awkwardly with my pen in hand before realizing he was waiting for me to pack up. Mentally chastising myself, I shoved my books into my messenger bag and tucked it behind the chair next to the register. "I'll be a sec," I said, and slipped behind the curtain separating the shop from my mother's office and our back storage room.

When I came back out, Hunter was waiting by the door.

"Ready?" he asked.

I nodded again, sticking one hand in my jacket pocket so as not to fidget too much. "Let's go."

Hunter held the door open, and just then my grandmother's voice called from the backroom and I cringed inwardly.

"I'm leaving, Gran, didn't you hear me tell you?" I answered, hoping she wouldn't come out front and do what she always does where I'm concerned. Gran was formidable, and her unblinking scrutiny creeped out most of my friends.

When she simply yelled, "Okay, honey, I'll see you later..." I practically pushed Hunter out the door so as not to tempt fate. Had I told her I was leaving with someone, especially a boy, Gran would have been out front like a shot. She must be as preoccupied as my mother these days for her not to have sensed it.

With one quick click, Hunter unlocked the car doors and I slid into the passenger seat while he went around to the other side to get in.

"Want to stop and eat?" he asked, putting the key in the ignition. "We could pick up a couple of sandwiches, if you want, and eat by the water."

"No, I'm good. Maybe a soda and some chips..." I stopped, remembering I'd already filled my quota for junk food this week. "Nah, forget it. I'm fine."

Hunter laughed and started the car. "I figured you say as much, so I came prepared."

At first I didn't know what he meant, but then he gestured toward the back and the large brown paper bag filled with junk food sitting on the seat behind him.

I slid my gaze back to his, and watched a playful smirk toy with the corner of his mouth. "It's just us going to the Point, right?" I asked.

He looked at me strangely, but nodded just the same. "Yeah, just you and me...why?"

I shrugged, flicking my gaze toward the monstrous sack. "Oh, I don't know, maybe because you brought enough food to feed the entire football team?"

His playful smirk spread into a gorgeous full-on smile. "Well, that proves one thing..." he murmured, pausing to look over his shoulder before pulling an illegal U-turn to head up Main Street. "You definitely need to hang out with me more often. That bag wouldn't feed our quarterback, let alone the whole team. I grabbed a bunch of things, not sure what you like."

I didn't reply, but I couldn't help but feel gratified at the obvious thought he'd put into our 'conversation' time.

We stopped at the traffic light at the corner across from the high school and then turned left onto Broadway. Technically, it was U.S. Route 9, and the main thoroughfare linking all the river towns along the eastern side of the Hudson. High sloping hills surrounded the village, and many of the houses along the stretch of road were historic landmarks with breathtaking views. I glanced west as we drove, looking down at the white caps and dark water. "Maybe this isn't such a great idea, after all," I mumbled.

Hunter glanced at me. "Why? What's wrong?"

I pulled my eyes away from the river, heat flushing to my face at being caught muttering to myself.

"Nothing. It's going to be dark in about forty-five minutes, so maybe going to the Point isn't such a good idea. Kingsland closes at dusk, remember?"

Hunter considered what I said, then reached over and took my hand. "We can talk anyplace, Rowen. Where do you want to go?"

His hand was warm, and for the first time since I agreed to meet him, I relaxed. The butterflies in my stomach were still there, but they weren't winging around at the speed of light.

"You know what? Leave the bag of goodies. Let's head over to JJ's. It's far enough away that we won't run into anyone we know from school. Plus, it won't be crowded now, and we can find a corner in the back."

Of course, what I really meant was we could find a corner where no one would overhear how crazy I was.

Hunter gave me another smile and let go of my hand to click on the turning signal. "Now, that sounds like a plan."

Jean Jacques, or JJ's as we all called it, was two towns from Sleepy Hollow and a safe bet for privacy. The fact they served amazing pastries and great coffee was a complete bonus.

Most of the day had been clear and fine, but as expected for this time of year, the temperature had dropped as the afternoon waned. Anticipating as much, I traded in my gray lace camisole for a long sleeved, dove gray silk blouse I happened to borrow from my mother's closet. I loved the way the ruffled front looked against the steampunk style buttons of my jacket.

Hunter was quiet. Music from his iPod streamed from speakers on both sides of the front dash, and he had turned the heat on low, probably for my benefit.

I shivered, and a sneeze wrinkled my nose.

"There's a package of tissues in the center glove box," he said, gesturing to console between the seats.

I slid open the top and found the travel size tissue pack, but that's not what caught my eye.

Directly beneath the tissue pack was a photograph, and even in the dim light I recognized the fence from my backyard peeking at me from the corner. Tissues forgotten, I slipped the picture out and looked at it. It was a picture of Hunter's parents taken the day before their family moved to California. Hunter and I were in the background, sitting on a picnic blanket eating watermelon. I stared at the photograph, remembering like it was yesterday.

"My mother found that when we were packing to come back to New

York. She was making piles of what to keep and what to throw away. I rescued that from the garbage pile."

I glanced at him, not sure what to say. I knew his mom and dad were divorcing, but I didn't know why and I certainly wasn't going to ask if he didn't feel like sharing. Based on what he said, I could only guess how hard it must be to be caught in the middle. My father died when I was little. I didn't remember him much, just images like shadows, but I did remember feeling cheated that he was taken from me—but to have someone leave by choice? I couldn't even imagine.

Weirdness settled between us, and I tucked the photo back beneath the tissues. "I'm sorry," I mumbled.

He shrugged, but didn't say a word.

I felt awful, like I opened a wound or eavesdropped on his pain. I kept stealing glances at him from the corner of my eye, and finally I just blurted, "Okay, I'm nosy, but I recognized my backyard in the corner of the photograph! I'm not trying to pry or anything..."

He rolled his eyes, and his doubtful smirk made me want to crawl under the seat.

"You can exhale, Rowen. Seriously. It's fine. He's still my father, regardless of what's going on between him and my mom. I kept the picture because it reminds me that things weren't always bad—and you and I are in it, too."

We pulled into a space down the block from the café. Hunter kept his hands in his pockets as we walked up the sidewalk, and I closed my eyes for a moment, hoping my nosiness hadn't ruined things.

The doorbells jangled and again, Hunter held the door for me as I walked in. The place was more crowded than I expected, but we found a small table in the back by one of the large portrait windows facing the street. I sat and took off my coat.

"So, what's good here?" he asked, tossing his coat over the back of his chair.

"Everything," I replied, rubbing my hands together. "Although, their chocolate croissants win hands down for me, every time."

"*Mmmmm*, that sounds great. Coffee?"

"You got it."

Hunter went to order, and I did a quick inventory of my hair and

makeup. I never carry a purse, and I'd left my messenger bag with everything in it at the shop. Thank God the napkin holder was polished stainless steel, and not a cheapo chrome one that made your reflection look like something out of a funhouse.

My curls were still good, not a frizz in sight, but my eyeliner had smudged onto my lower lids. Not quite raccoon eyes, but enough that I needed a careful swipe with the corner of a napkin.

As expected, the place was empty of anyone I knew. I smoothed the ruffles on the front of my shirt, making sure my mother's mojo bag was where it should be, just in case. The last thing I wanted was another creepy vision earning me a reputation in this town as well.

Hunter returned with two coffees and the most delicious looking croissants I'd seen. He put them on the table and the scents of raspberry, butter, and chocolate made my mouth water.

"This place is amazing," he said peeling back the travel tab on his coffee.

I sipped my coffee, letting the sweet warmth roll on my tongue. "Perfect," I answered softly, wiping foam from my upper lip. "Don't they have French pastry shops in California?"

He chewed a flaky mouthful, obviously enjoying himself. "Yeah, but not like this."

I laughed, "Poor baby, made to eat all that health food in the land of fruit and nuts."

"Hey!"

I chuckled. "You walked right into that, sorry."

Hunter picked a crunchy bit of chocolate off the edge of his croissant and plopped it into his mouth. "Yeah, well, California doesn't own the monopoly on crazy. I've seen some real nut cases right here..." he stopped short.

I stiffened, my hand frozen with my coffee half way to my lips.

"I'm such an idiot..." he muttered, closing his eyes in embarrassment. When he opened them again, he reached across the table for my hand. "I didn't mean you, Rowen. I wouldn't be here if I did," he added softly, his expression as embarrassed as it was sorry.

I shrugged, casually pulling my hand away from his and crossing my arms on the table. "It's okay. It doesn't really matter one way or the

other."

He blew out a breath and watched the cars on the street. "I can't figure you out," he murmured half to himself, but when he turned back, his eyes were dark and intense. "It does matter, to me anyway. You take my head off in gym for nothing, and now you shrug like you're Miss Casual and couldn't care less. Is that what you do? Either blow up or blow off?"

I pulled my arms in closer to my chest. "Why do you care?"

We sat silently for a moment, my question lingering in the air between us along with the scent of chocolate. Finally he shook his head slowly. "To be honest, I don't know why. You've said it yourself. We don't have much in common; except for the fact we were friends first." He paused and considering me intently. "I like you, Rowen. A lot... apart from that nasty temper of yours."

I gave him a closed mouth smile that was half smirk, but inside it was an ear to ear grin.

I glanced down at my crossed arms, realizing my fingers had unconsciously twisted the inside edge of both sleeves. I forced myself to take a breath and met his waiting gaze. "I like you, too, Hunter, and you're right. We were friends first."

He opened his mouth as if to say something, but closed it, taking a sip of coffee, instead.

"What?" I asked, immediately concerned things had shifted from possibility back to awkward in a matter of seconds.

He picked at the top of his travel lid, his eyes flicking to mine. "It's nothing, just a thought."

"What?" My voice was low, but insistent.

"I was thinking. Maybe it's because of our connection that you had that weird vision about me dying."

I didn't want to talk about my visions, but I knew we had to. It was time for me to let go of my fantasy that there was anything more to this than a fact finding mission. I sucked in a deep breath through my nose and exhaled quietly, my fingers gripping the string of my mother's mojo bag through my blouse.

"I don't know, Hunter...maybe. But, why now? Why not when we were kids? We hardly know each other anymore, and until recently, we

haven't hung out. My mother thinks my visions are some cosmic message from the past. Something aimed specifically at you or me, or both of us."

His brows furrowed and he pushed his coffee cup aside. "A message? What kind of message?"

I threw one of my hands up, frustration pouring through me again. "You think I know? I'm as freaked out as I've ever been. Like I already told you, it was you in my vision, but not you. It was you, but from the past. My mother wants you to ask your mom if she knows of any of your ancestors who died in the revolution, and if she's ever had a vision similar to mine."

"Why," he asked, shaking his head.

"I don't know. I'm just the messenger, in every sense of the word." My shoulders slumped, but my tone was just shy of antagonistic and Hunter raised an eyebrow in surprise.

"Don't look at me that way, you'd be testy too if horrible visions about people who look like people you care about hit you out of nowhere." I knew I was babbling, but I didn't care.

Hunter covered my hand with his again. "I'll find out what I can, but you've got to calm down. Maybe if you relaxed you wouldn't be as vulnerable to whatever is using you as a message board."

"Ha."

He shrugged. "It's actually kind of cool that you're psychic. I'd love to be able to see what you see."

I swallowed, remembering the helpless disorientation, the dizziness and the nausea. I shook my head. "No, you wouldn't. Trust me."

He squeezed my hand, chuckling at how serious I must have seemed. "If you say so. Look, let's make a deal. You promise to tell me if anything else hits you from out of the blue and you'll let me help if possible, and I promise to find out as much as I can on my end."

He let go of my hand and raised his coffee cup, holding it in front of him.

I lifted my chin and looked at his honest expression. He meant what he was saying. "Okay," I answered lifting my cup to his.

"One more thing," he said, pulling his cup back before I touched it with mine. "You have to promise me we can have a real date. One where 'conversation' is optional."

I laughed out loud. "Just tell me when."

He took the coffee cup from my hand and put it on the table next to his. "This calls for more than a pinky-promise." He leaned across the table and took my hands in his, pulling me forward, kissing me lightly on the mouth.

"That should hold us," he said, sitting back down.

I swallowed against the nervous energy blooming in my lower belly. "Hold us for what?"

He smiled and leaned back in his chair. "For whatever comes next."

Chapter 4

Getting up and out of the house this morning was worse than usual. You'd think after spending time with Hunter yesterday I'd be rushing through the door to see him. From the minute I opened my eyes I've had a stupid smile on my face, that is until I realized the time and bolted for the door.

My breath caught in my throat each time his words ran through my head. *For whatever comes next...*

After leaving JJs, we sat in his car and talked, even though Hunter risked running laps 'til he threw up if he was late for practice. My stomach jumped thinking about how good he smelled and how he held our goodbye kiss long enough for me to grasp what he meant by whatever came next.

I went through my morning classes in a daze, chewing on my lip until the bell finally rang for English and I darted for the hall.

"Hey, Rowen, where's the fire?" Tyler asked, grabbing my arm as I rounded the corner. "If you're looking for Morrissey, lover boy's inside." He gestured toward the open door to the math lab.

As if on cue, Hunter stepped through the doorway books in hand, pausing long enough to give Tyler a hard look. "Dude, don't be such a tool," he replied in kind, only to earn wiseass kissy noises in response.

I shot Tyler a disgusted look, but that's all. This time I wasn't about to give him the satisfaction of getting a rise out of me, and focused my

attention on Hunter.

"Conover's back. Are you ready for round two in us versus the English teacher?" I asked, completely ignoring Tyler.

"I am if you are," he answered disregarding his friend's sarcastic snort, instead taking my messenger bag from me and slipping it onto his own shoulder. He shot Tyler a warning look before steering me away from the door.

"Whipped!" Tyler called after us with a laugh as we headed down the hall toward English.

"Why does he have to be such a jerk when it comes to me?" I muttered, half to myself, half to Hunter.

Hunter turned at that point to look at me, a slight frown creasing his forehead. His expression was the perfect blend of uncertainty and annoyance, as if he'd been wondering the same thing. "Don't let him bother you, Rowen. He's not worth letting it rent space in your head."

Maybe Hunter didn't need me to enlighten him about Tyler. The jerk was doing a good job of showing his true colors all by himself.

Mr. Conover's classroom sat at the far end of the hall, and suddenly I had the sensation of the corridor narrowing and stretching. I hated being the focus of attention, and Conover put me at the forefront every chance he got. Guessing my hesitation, Hunter shifted my messenger bag to his other shoulder and slid his arm around mine. "Solidarity, baby. Like the song says, let's give'em something to talk about," he smiled, leaning over to kiss my temple.

I felt people staring, as if the sight of me with Hunter threw the balance of life off kilter, but for that tiny display of affection alone, I would gladly stand center ring in full spot light.

Chloe's mouth dropped open the minute Hunter and I walked into class together, and more than a few sets of eyes followed as he walked me to my desk and handed me my bag. Less than a second later, my phone buzzed with a text from Chloe.

"WTF?"

"No comment."

"Rowen!"

"No."

I heard her hand slap the desk. Chloe hated when I was evasive, and

the only thing saving me from a barrage of texts was Mr. Conover looking at us from his laptop. My phone buzzed once more.

"Lunch. And you better not ditch..."

I looked up to find her eyeing me, her lips molded into a shrewd side smirk. She knew I didn't stand a snowball's chance in hell of avoiding her, so I nodded, letting my shoulders slump for effect. She was my best friend, how could I say no?

On the other hand, luck was on my side because Jenny's desk was unexpectedly empty, and I exhaled whatever was left of my apprehension. I was overreacting and I knew it, but contrary to popular belief, I wasn't as confident as I appeared. Most days my bravado was as much to convince myself as everyone else that I was beyond letting people get to me.

Chloe could grill me for details and speculate about us all the way to prom, but right now my friendship with Hunter was at a provocative crossroads, and that was enough for me. Playing the odds were never my style, and with all else I had going I needed to keep things in perspective.

I squared my shoulders and sat up straight, catching Hunter's grin of approval. How he 'got' me so well and so quickly was a mystery, but one that left me with a secret smile on my face and butterflies in my stomach. I winked at him and then dragged my notebook onto my desk, opening it to the notes we started the day before yesterday.

Mr. Conover closed his laptop and stood, pushing in his desk chair with a loud squeak. "Okay, people. You've had two days to think about what we discussed in class, and I hope you did because I've had plenty of time to think myself, and I've decided this is the perfect topic for a research project."

The groans that erupted were more than gratuitous. No one liked research projects, let alone with a major creep factor.

"That's enough, everyone, come on..." he continued despite the complaints. "It's not as bad as you think. I've decided to let you pair up, and you can choose your own research partner. Each pair is responsible for delving into the truths behind our local urban legends. Pick whichever one interests you the most. What counts is what you find out and how you tie it back to the legend. Halloween is a week from this Saturday, so that gives you eight days. Be ready to present your findings

on Friday, the thirtieth."

I raised my hand in the middle of the unhappy hum.

"Yes, Rowen?"

I hesitated, not wanting to start Mr. Conover on another historic tear or worse. "Um, I guess I'm not sure what you're asking us to research. You said *our urban legends...*" I paused again, glancing quickly at Hunter before continuing. "Correct me if I'm wrong, Mr. Conover, but doesn't that suggest there would be no official record or formal accounting anywhere for us to examine? Where do you propose we start looking? Can you give us hint?"

The room fell quiet, and everyone watched as Mr. Conover took off his glasses and tapped them in his palm. "That's a valid question, Rowen, and my suggestion is you conduct this like any other investigation compromised by circumstantial evidence. You talk to people. Canvas the townies. Take a walk to the Historical Society and see what they have in terms of diaries and eyewitness accounts. Plus don't forget there's a treasure trove of artifacts in the basement. Libby Scarborough is the person you'll need to speak with.

"Most of you know her as the executive director of the Historical Society, but you might not know she's also an archeologist. You'll need to make an appointment with her I'm sure, as she's very busy, especially this time of year. Also, the seniors at Cedar Manor Nursing Home are an exceptionally good resource. Their memories are long, and they would love the chance to recount their take on the stories and what they learned from those who came before them."

He paused, putting his glasses back onto his long nose. "I'll tell you what, as an extra bonus, consider this project twofold. If you visit the nursing home, I'll give you credit toward the service hours you need to graduate come June."

Regardless of how magnanimous Mr. Conover seemed to think his offer was, nobody was happy about the assignment, but thankfully he moved to droning on about the qualities of literary analysis, whatever that meant.

The bell rang, finally, and Hunter waited for me by the door as I collected my books.

"I told you he was already forming my 'F' in his head," he said,

gesturing toward his temple with his free hand as he took my bag.

Lockers slammed on either side of us as the first lunch period began. I was supposed to drop off my books at my locker and meet Chloe in the cafeteria, and I knew Hunter had to get to history.

"That's ridiculous. He'd have to give me the same 'F' and I have no intention of bombing this assignment regardless of how lame it is." I stopped in front of my locker and took my bag from Hunter, letting it slide to the shiny, white and red tiled floor.

He shook his head, watching me do my combination. "Why would he do that? You're a townie." He made quotation marks in the air, his tone less than appreciative.

"Because…"I said, shoving my entire bag into my locker. "…research partners always get the same grade." I shut the rectangular metal door, pressing on it with my shoulder while turning the dial on my combination lock.

A slow half smile crooked at the corner of his mouth and he leaned down, running his fingers along the line of my cheek. "Partners, huh?"

I nodded. "Partners. Unless there's someone else you'd rather hook up with?"

He shook his head. "Nah, you're all I can handle right now." With one swift move, he slid his fingers behind my head and leaned in, kissing me in front of God and everyone in the hall.

The late bell rang once, giving its one minute warning. Hunter broke our kiss and stepped back. "Okay, partner. I'll see you later."

My vocal chords disconnected from the rest of my throat, so I nodded, watching as he sprinted down the hall.

I closed my eyes and shouted a silent squeal! Chloe was not going to believe this.

I was late for lunch, of course, and Chloe practically yanked me off the cafeteria line, tray and all, barely giving me time to pay for my food.

"Well?" Her whisper was more irritated than curious.

"Chloe, can I at least get to the table and put my tray down before you start interrogating me? I haven't eaten a thing since last night and I'm starved."

She rolled her eyes. "How can you think of your stomach? I'm

surprised you can even eat."

"Seriously, Chlo? Take a pill. Your OCD need to know everything is going to give you hives. I may get butterflies when Hunter's around, but otherwise my appetite is totally fine." I slid my tray onto the table and pulled the chair out, making as much noise as possible on purpose.

She scowled, watching me slide into my chair, probably as much from the noise as from my offhand attitude. "Fine. Eat your lunch. I guess you're not interested in what everyone is saying, then, huh?"

I stopped with a single french fry halfway to my mouth. "What are you talking about? The only people stupid enough to say anything are Jenny and Tyler, and Hunter already put Tyler in his place once today. Jenny, on the other hand, is M.I.A, thank God."

No sooner did the words leave my mouth than I heard her high pitched, baby doll voice behind me.

"Well, look who's decided to run with the big dogs. That was some kiss in the hallway, Rowen. And to think, Tyler told everyone you were a cold fish."

She slipped around to the front of the table, purposely leaning her elbows on the cream-colored Formica, her low-scooped neckline putting her less than an inch away from a wardrobe malfunction.

I took a sip from my Snapple, eyeing her with matching disdain. "Missed you in class, Jen." My gaze flicked over her outfit and the purplish hickey marks dotting the swell of her small breasts. "Cute top, by the way, but you might want to rethink it, unless you like walking around like a clotting victim."

Jenny sniffed. "What would you know about it? At least I know how to keep my guy satisfied, and that's more than you'll ever be able to say. I give it until Halloween before Hunter comes looking for me."

I raised an eyebrow. "Wow. I wonder what Tyler would say about that. He's not exactly the sharing type."

She frowned. "Me, as in my crew, you freak. Any of my girls would be glad to tap that," she said, snapping her fingers. "I think I'll put Constance up to it—yeah, she'll make Hunter very happy. That girl could suck nails out of a board."

I stood, pushing my chair out more abruptly than before, making Jenny take a step back. "You need to keep your eyes on what's yours,

Jen." I glanced past her shoulder to where Constance leaned provocatively across Tyler's table talking to Ben, but clearly giving Tyler an eyeful. "'Cause from here, it looks like it wouldn't take much to persuade Constance to show Tyler how skilled she is."

Jenny's head jerked around to follow my line of sight, and when she turned back, the smirk plastered across her lips lacked its previous bravado. "You wish," she huffed, before making a beeline back to where she came from.

"Soooo," Chloe started. "I guess you know what everyone is saying, now, hmmm?"

I nodded, with a slight frown. Inhaling through my nose, I exhaled the same way, letting my shoulders drop. "Look, Chlo, I appreciate the heads up, but it doesn't matter. No one is going to collect on any bets, because right now Hunter and I are a non-entity."

Chloe snorted. "Oh come on, Ro. You can't be that dense. If you two are such a non-entity then why does Jenny have her panties in a twist? Sure, she likes to stick it to you, but she wouldn't waste good lip-gloss on this if she didn't feel threatened or exposed in some way. She may be hooked up with Tyler, but everyone knows Hunter has never given her the time of day, making him guilty of the unforgiveable sin of not finding her irresistible. Did you know she's gone so far as to suggest he bats for the pink team? Now you come along and suddenly Hunter's all about P.D.A. Sort of throws her justifications in the toilet."

I wadded my napkin and dropped it onto my tray. "Hunter is not all about public displays of affection, thank you. He's just got my back, that's all…" I stopped fidgeting and glanced at Chloe and the other girls at our table before looking down at my tray. "Forget it."

"Has your back for what?" Chloe asked, keeping her voice low.

My first inclination may have been to tell her everything, but after this latest scene with Jenny, I didn't need any more gossip and the cafeteria had more ears than a corn field.

"Oh, no you don't. I knew there was a reason behind your being so evasive," she said, throwing one of my own french fries at me. "What's going on, Rowen?"

I leaned onto the table and crooked my finger. Chloe's eyes darted left then right before she leaned forward to meet me half way.

"So? Spill it."

I shook my head. "Nothing."

"What?" She looked at me perplexed.

I shrugged, knowing I was about to piss her off. "There's nothing going on. That's the big secret, Chloe."

She slumped back into her chair, shooting me the dirtiest look. "Yeah right. Tell me another one, Rowen. You don't normally censure yourself, at least not with me."

I sighed, sinking into my chair, as well. "Chlo, please understand. I can't tell you anything because there's nothing to tell, or at least nothing I know how to explain." I leaned forward and lowered my voice. "Let's just say my inherited maternal gene pool is messing with my life and Hunter happened to be there to pick up the pieces."

Chloe threw her hands up. "And what does that mean, exactly?"

"That's just it! I. Don't. Know. If I did, don't you think I'd tell you?" Irritation edged its way into my voice. "Even my mother isn't certain what's happening with me or why, but one thing is sure, I don't want to talk about it—not here, anyway."

My skin prickled as heat spread from my neck to my cheeks. Tiny shards jabbed at the back of my eyes, and I leaned on my elbows, my fingers massaging my temples. Nausea gripped my stomach as the air around me started to swim, the same way it does over the asphalt in summer. *No, no, not again!*

My peripheral vision narrowed, but not enough for me to miss the faint image of ropes tying my wrists together and blood trickling from the base of my palms from where the rough hemp dug into the tender flesh. I closed my eyes, jamming my fingertips deeper into the sides of my forehead trying to will away forming images.

Desperate not to let myself be taken over, I dropped one hand to the mojo bag still around my neck and squeezed. This morning, my mother added yellow agrimony flowers to the mix, as well as a sprinkle of angelica to help bolster the warding. The bag warmed in my hand and the outline of the bloodstone and rose quartz pressed into my palm, as I waited for the wave to pass.

"Rowen! Are you sick? What's going on?"

I waved my free hand at Chloe, ignoring the alarm in her voice. After

a moment, the air stilled and I sucked in a breath, finally opening my eyes. *Damn, my mother was good.*

Chloe stared at me, her eyes wide with concern. "Are you okay?"

I nodded, exhaling slowly.

"You sure, 'cause it looked like you were hit with the migraine of the century."

Taking a swig from my Snapple, I laughed, but there was no humor in it, despite my dribbling some of the amber tea down my chin.

"Now, that's attractive," Chloe added in a droll attempt to make me laugh.

I breathed out a half-hearted chuckle. "Tell me about it." I wiped my hand across my chin, but Chloe still eyed me like she expected me to spew pea soup or something. I threw my crumpled napkin at her. "I'm fine, Chlo...really. It's probably the french fries."

She shook her head. "I don't think so, Rowen." She lowered her voice, her tone softening along with her expression. "I'm worried about you. I've known you forever, and this is not your average, everyday Corbett weirdness. Listen, I'm around later if you want to talk."

My eyes met hers. Was I that obvious?

"Hey, I've got a ton of homework, and on top of everything, I've got this research project to do for Mr. Conover, and you know how I love those. Forgive me for being a little stressed."

Chloe smirked, swirling one of my fries in ketchup. "Sure, I know all about your research, and who you're researching with..." She trailed off, plopping the fry in her mouth.

I pressed my lips together, giving her a closed mouth smile. She was like a dog with a bone. "Since gossip has obviously replaced football as the game of choice around here, maybe we should change the school banner to read, The Bigmouths, instead of The Horseman."

Chloe sniffed, her nose wrinkling along with her freckles. "You do realize Talia filled me in on the kiss heard 'round the school?"

My mouth fell open, and she confirmed my disbelief with a nod. "Yup. She was standing with Jenny next to Señora Clark's desk when Hunter kissed you in the hallway outside Spanish. She texted me immediately. Oh, man did she have a field day with Jenny! You would be so proud."

"Proud?" I shot back cutting her off. It was hard enough having to deal with Tyler and his extended entourage, but my own friends, too? "So all this…" I said, flinging my hand out in Jenny's general direction, "…was Talia's doing? She's the one stirring the crap?"

Chloe nodded again, stuffing the last of the fries into her mouth.

Irritated, I shoved my tray towards the center of the table. "So much for putting friendship first," I muttered, letting my voice trail into an annoyed exhale.

Taking a sip from her Diet Coke, Chloe eyed me again, before screwing the cap back on her bottle, slowly. "See, this is what I'm talking about. We all know I'm the type to fly off the handle, especially where Talia is concerned. But you, you're the level headed one. Talia's always been over the top, but her antics never bothered you before. Whether you want to see it or not, she had your back with Jenny, earlier. Also, she told me how you went off on her after I left you guys at the corner the other day. Whatever is up with you, you'd better get a handle on it soon. I said it before, and I'll say it again…I'm worried for you, Ro. We all are."

I didn't answer, just glanced down at my hands, not a trace of blood visible. *Me too, Chloe… me too.*

I headed toward my locker, my eyes glued to my feet. I hadn't even asked Chloe if she would help at the Blaze on Saturday. I needed to get my head straight, and all I wanted to do was dump my books and head home. Unfortunately, I had gym, yet again, and couldn't afford another cut. At least I'd see Hunter.

The girl's locker room was empty by the time I got there. I slipped on my sneakers, not bothering with changing into my shorts and t-shirt. I'd take the demerit. I didn't care.

I rushed down the stairs and snuck in through the gym's double doors. Loitering in the corner, I tried to make myself as inconspicuous as possible. From the way things looked we were starting a new unit. Treadmills, weight machines and free weights had been set up on hard foam mats along the polished floor, with yoga balls large enough to sit on placed in between stations. Oh goodie.

"Ready to feel the burn?" Hunter asked as he slid next to me.

Throwing my hair into a ponytail, I shook my head. "Not really. And

Marianne Morea

what's up with all these gym classes? What happened to twice a week?"

"It's part of the school board's new initiative on health, or so I've heard."

I snorted, smoothing the sides of my hair back. "I guess I must have missed the memo."

He laughed. "Oh, come on, circuit training can be fun. I'll even spot you on the free weights. You can work in with me and Ben."

Obviously Hunter was confusing me with someone else. "Me? Pump iron? Not in your life. I'm more the sit and watch type."

"Ha. Speaking of sitting and watching, why don't you come and hang out at the field this afternoon? You can watch me practice, and then we can grab something to eat, maybe plan our attack on the town's urban legends."

Lucky for me the whistle blew for class to begin, and when I turned to where Mr. Faulkner stood, he had his finger crooked at me.

Wonderful. With my luck today, I'd end up with detention simply because I wasn't a pump before you primp kind of girl.

Faulkner had been the school's gym teacher for as long as anyone could remember. Rumor had it he was some sort of All-American during in his college years, which explained his penchant for boring the class to tears with stories from his glory days.

Of course, I had to walk past half the class to get where Mr. Faulkner waited, his legs shoulder width apart and his hands hooked onto his hips.

"Is there a reason you're not joining us today, Ms. Corbett?" His slightly thinning comb-over drooped onto his forehead as he waited for me to answer.

"I'm not feeling so well, Mr. Faulkner."

The man fiddled with the red nylon cord attached to his whistle, repeatedly twisting and untwisting it around his fingers while he studied my face. "Do you need to use the girl's restroom, or is it something else?"

His voice was steady and professional, but his face sprouted the same color pink as the breast cancer awareness ribbon pinned to his polo shirt. It was obvious this was his attempt at being politically correct in case it was women's issues at the root of my non-participation. It was all I could do not to cringe.

A loud crash yanked everyone's attention toward the bench press

57

station. His eyes flicked between me and the meathead from the wrestling team who was jumping around holding his foot. "We'll revisit this later, Ms. Corbett. Have a seat on the bleachers. You can do the baseline circuit next class."

I headed back to Hunter, with Mr. Faulkner yelling behind me for everyone to be more careful.

Hunter stood with his arms folded, trying not to laugh. "That was a calculated, text book bail," he tsked, shaking his head.

I pushed at his shoulder. "Yeah, right. And members of the football team never get out of homework or have extensions granted simply because they have an important game."

He grinned. "Hey, I don't make the double standards, but you've got to admit, you girls have it easy, sometimes. Especially you pretty ones. Faulkner would never have bought that line, otherwise. Unless, of course, you hit him with some of that Corbett family hoodoo." He unfolded his arms to wiggle his fingers at me.

"Hunter!"

His grin spread wider, making his eyes glow with mischief. "You know you could share the luck, and whip up a little magic for the team this Saturday."

I shot him a look. "Not funny." I scuffed my sneaker against the hardwood. "Why? What's happening Saturday?"

"The big game against Ossining? Jeez, Rowen, it's not like there aren't posters all over the school."

I raised my chin, making a face. "I don't do football, Hunter. You know that."

He slid his arm around my shoulders. "I know. But you can't blame a guy for trying."

I looked at him. This time he wasn't teasing, just hopeful, and I was immediately sorry for bordering on being a brat. "You sure you want to waste your time on me? I don't know much about the game."

"Well, it's about time you learned. Come to my game." When I hesitated, he gave my shoulder a squeeze. "Come on, Rowen, it'll be fun. Let's make it a real date, you can wear my away jersey and I'll take you out for pizza afterward, whaddaya say?"

I couldn't say no, even though sitting on cold aluminum bleachers

watching a bunch of Neanderthals kill each other was not my idea of fun, but Hunter wanted me there and I wanted Hunter. No contest.

"Okay," I nodded. "But I get to pick the pizza toppings."

"Deal. You'll get to see me in action, and I get to look up into the stands and see you cheering me on. Win-win."

"You have a warped sense of fun, don't you?"

His smile, full and sexy, spread in a way that matched the mischief in his eyes. "Makes for keeping things interesting," he whispered with his face a little too close to mine for gym class and I shivered inside, wanting nothing more than to curl my fingers through his hair and pull his mouth to mine.

"What are you doing later? I've got practice until 5:30, but I can drop by afterward if you want to hang out. We can plan our attack for Conover's research project."

Playing it cool, I shrugged, intentionally ignoring the nervous dive-bombs in my stomach. "Okay. In the meantime I can ask my gran what she remembers. Except for Libby, she knows more about this town and its history than anyone."

He looked at me curiously, and then glanced down at his feet, almost as if he was suddenly nervous, too. "You know, the day before a big game we always have a walk through practice followed by a team dinner."

"And?"

"Would you like to go with me?" Hunter cleared his throat, giving me a sheepish grin.

"To your team dinner?"

"No, to wash the dishes afterwards. Of course, to the dinner. It's usually just the varsity team, but sometimes the JV team and the cheerleaders come too…"

I held up my hand, stepping out from under his arm. "Uh, you can stop right there. I'll pass."

He raised an eyebrow, and I couldn't tell if he was surprised or offended at how quickly I answered him. "Come on, Rowen. You said you would hang out with us, and this is the perfect opportunity to give my friends a chance."

I shook my head. Of course, I wanted to spend as much time with

Hunter as I could, but there was no way this lamb was going to be led to the slaughter. I'd rather have my teeth drilled than give Tyler Cavanaugh and Jenny Beamer two hours of unrestrained jibe throwing.

"How late does the dinner go? Maybe I could meet up with you afterward?"

There was no question he was disappointed, but to his credit, he didn't push. "It goes until about eight p.m. I guess we can meet up then."

I smiled. "Good. Maybe we can grab some ice cream at Main Street Sweets." He nodded, giving me a closed lipped smile, but it was clear he was not happy with my continued reluctance. I reached out, resting my hand on his arm. "I'll hang out with your friends, Hunter, I promise. I'll be the first to admit I'm the one dragging my feet, but the last thing I need is to be caught in a sea of pumped up testosterone egging on more visions. I'd never live it down if I fainted again."

His gaze softened, and he tweaked my nose. "I understand. Ice cream it is then, but I'm holding you to coming to the game Saturday. I won't take no for an answer, Rowen. I mean it....bring Chloe and anyone else you want, but I want to look up and know you're there in the stands."

I pursed my lips, considering him for a moment "I'll make you a deal," I offered, hooking my hands on either side of my waist. "I'll come to the game and I'll even cheer for the Horsemen if you promise to come with me to the Van Cortlandt Estate afterward."

He eyed me, tilting his head suspiciously. "Pumpkins, right? So this is all just a ploy for manual labor."

I chuckled. "No, not really. But if that's what it takes to get you to help me, then whatever."

Hunter leaned over and kissed my cheek. "All you need to do is ask," he whispered low, his deep voice suggestive and intoxicating. With a smirk, he walked off to meet Ben waiting for him to start their workout. *God he was gorgeous.*

Ben usually shadowed Tyler, but both Tyler and Jen were conspicuously missing—again. Between English this morning and now cutting gym, the girl was flirting with suspension, but Jen's parents were the M.I.A. type, so it didn't matter.

Someone had cracked open the side door, letting cool air drift in from the back parking lot. Despite the jeans and black sweater I threw on this

morning, I crossed my arms, rubbing them to stave off the chill.

The wooden bleachers had been pulled out from the wall, allowing for the bottom three rows to extend onto the gym floor. I settled myself on the third tier where I had a bird's eye view of Hunter working out. From the corner of my eye, I spotted Talia picking her way across the far end toward me, her black bike shorts and lacrosse pinny highlighting her lithe figure and long legs.

"Hey," she said a little out of breath as she plopped down next to me.

Talia looked wind-swept and flushed with loose strands fanning around her face where they escaped from her high ponytail.

"What happened to you? You're a mess." I chuckled, knowing how she was about her appearance.

Talia huffed, her hands smoothing down the flyaway strands. "Faulkner didn't like all my chatter, so he made me run laps around the field." She made a face. "I should have told him I had cramps. He'd have turned ten shades of red and had me sit here with you."

"Ha. So your mouth is the reason I'm sitting here freezing."

She grinned. "Yeah, but it was worth it. I caught Jenny and Tyler outside in the parking lot."

"So?"

Her grin grew even wider. "So, let's just say paybacks are sweet." She leaned back, curling her hands around the edge of the flat wooden bench, her expression smug.

"And?"

"And nothing. I sort of let it slip to the school Resource Officer they were about to spark up, if you know what I mean."

I looked at her almost speechless. "You caught them smoking weed?"

She lifted one shoulder and let it drop. "Technically, no. They were hanging out by the upper parking lot headed toward the Aqueduct trails, and everyone knows that's where the local loadies go to get high." With a wink and a nod, she gestured toward the two of them being led through the gym by school security. Tyler's head was down, but Jen's eyes burned as she stared at the two of us sitting on the bleachers.

"Great, Tal...thanks. Now she thinks I had a hand in it, too." I inhaled through my nose, pressing my lips together.

Sitting up straight, Talia snorted, folding her arms in front of her

chest. "Since when do you care what she thinks? For years that girl has waltzed around this school like she owns it, talking trash and ruining people's lives just for sport. Jen deserves what she's getting and more."

I peered at Talia like I didn't know her. Whatever Jenny had said or done in the past, she didn't deserve to face suspension or worse for something she didn't do.

"I can't believe you did this, Tal. Do you have any idea of the consequences they might face, now? And what about you? If the school finds out you purposely lied?" I exhaled sharply, my stomach tight thinking about the implications.

Talia gestured offhandedly. "You're making too much of this. They'll get sent home and maybe have to pee in a cup. Big deal," she added with a snort.

My mouth fell open and I blinked, not believing the callous tone in her voice. "Listen to me, neither one of them is high on my list of favorite people, but this is wrong. You can't go around accusing people of things they didn't do. Even if they were going to spark up, it's none of your business. If they do and they get caught, it's their funeral. Lord knows we've done some questionable things, too, or did you forget Mike's Labor Day pool party?"

Talia's face hardened. "How could I forget? And you want to know what I remember most? How about Jenny slipping into the cabana shower with Mike later that same night."

She glanced at me, and her usually perky smile seemed almost sinister. "You're not the only one who can make things happen, Rowen, and what goes around comes around." Her eyes trailed to where Mike stood with his friends, and she frowned before looking back at me. "You'd be smart to remember that. You want to dance with the devil, prepare to pay."

My kneejerk reaction was to shift away from her, but I forced myself to sit and meet here gaze head on. "That sounds like a threat, Talia. What are you going to do, start a rumor about me, too?"

She didn't answer, just put her hands on her knees and pushed herself to stand. With a sniff she adjusted the hem of her bike shorts and then stepped down to the next row of bleachers. She paused, turning to glance up at me. "Friends don't do things like that to each other, Rowen.

And we're friends, right?"

At this point, I didn't know what to make of either her or this whole situation. Talia was being all weird and cryptic, so I just nodded.

She smiled, but again it was off. "Good. Then we have nothing to worry about, do we?" She winked, and then jumped over the bottom row, landing on the balls of her feet like a cat. She headed toward Hunter and Ben working through their circuit, her eyes skimming over her shoulder in my direction as she passed them.

Floored, I didn't know how to react. What the hell did she mean by dance with the devil? Could Talia be behind the visions and everything else happening with me, lately? She always said she wished she could be like me. I shook my head, rejecting the thought.

Nah. No way. Even if Talia got the idea to play with spell craft, she wasn't of the blood, as Gran would say. How much damage could she do, really? I shook my head again at the ridiculous thought. Talia was just being vindictive.

Not that I blamed her. Chloe and I were the only girls in three school districts Mike hadn't hit on, probably because he was afraid I'd hex his private parts, and he'd get nothing but a right hook from Chloe. Nevertheless, he was as guilty as Jenny in the whole Labor Day fiasco, and everyone knew it, even Talia, only now it was clear her view was skewed. *Yeah, like Fatal Attraction skewed.*

Hunter caught my eye when he saw Jenny and Tyler doing the walk of shame, but I couldn't respond, not with Talia being all threatening and creepy. He must have seen Jenny glare my way, but when he looked at me again, all I could do was shrug, shaking my head. Hopefully, I would get the chance to talk to him before this all hit the fan. If Jenny thought I was involved, then that meant Tyler did, too. Not good. Not for me, not for them, and not for Hunter.

Chapter 5

The rest of the day remained uneventful. No uninvited visions and no fallout from the incident in the gym. Chloe practically pulled my arm off when she yanked me into the girl's bathroom to question me about Talia's not so little prank.

"You've got to be kidding. Why would Talia put herself in the position to be proved a liar?" Chloe's mouth hung open, disbelief clearly written across her creased forehead.

All I could do was shrug, unwilling to let Talia's antics suck me in any further. "Beats me, but I don't believe what she said, anyway. Tyler's a jerk most of the time, but he's a jock first. Football is his life. Plus, Mike told me college scouts have been sniffing around. According to him, scouts keep an eye on teams from a distance, but won't talk to any of the players until March, or so. Spring is a long way off, Chlo, and Tyler's not stupid enough to risk his chance at a scholarship for a quick toke. I have no idea what's going through Talia's head, but I am not about to call her on it, again. I made my feelings clear in the gym."

If Talia didn't get how fundamentally wrong she was, then nothing either Chloe or I said was going to change her mind. At this point, I'd had enough drama to last me the rest of the school year and wasn't about to add to it.

Chloe left me by my locker, promising to drop by the shop later to

talk. She didn't say it, but I knew she was going to try and guilt me into doing her version of a friendtervention, but I wasn't having it. My reluctance to confront Talia made me sound like the world's worst friend, but the girl knew right from wrong, and I had my own problems to figure out. For once I welcomed the mundane chores waiting for me at the Silver Cauldron. I even looked forward to calling Gran about the town legends like I promised. After all, Hunter was coming over.

I smiled to myself, feeling my cheeks warm at the thought of him and me alone in my room with no one else around. It would give us a real chance to talk. *Talk, yes…and whatever came next.*

No one had seen Tyler since he was escorted out through the gym, though the halls were buzzing with speculation. Nevertheless, the 411 on what was happening to him was still a big zero.

I slung my messenger bag over my shoulder and made a beeline for music. The music wing was located on the far side on the building, across from the school's two gyms. Introduction to musical theory was my last class of the day, and the only core requirement I had yet to fulfill for graduation.

It wasn't a far walk, and the sun had warmed the glass lined corridor connecting the wings. I peeled off the black sweater I had layered over a vintage graphic t-shirt and bolted up the sloped passageway. Noise further up told me something was going on outside the McCleery Gym, and though I couldn't see that far ahead, I heard the reason for the commotion. Sucking in a breath, I sprinted the rest of the way, my stomach knotted as a huge crash echoed down the connecting hallway.

"She set me up!" Tyler yelled, shoving Hunter into the vending machine against the wall, his books and backpack on the floor in a heap.

Arms out, Hunter's head snapped, his shoulders smacking into the blue Plexiglas front. The vending machine rocked back, knocking a few soda cans loose, dropping them into the beverage dispenser.

I stayed back, watching the whole thing from the side entrance. No way was I getting between them, plus Hunter didn't need me distracting him.

Pushing himself up, Hunter wiped his hand across his mouth. "Leave it to a coward to hit me when I'm not looking. Maybe I should return the favor on the field."

Tyler's face hardened and he lunged, his fist swinging wide for Hunter's head. With one step, Hunter grabbed Tyler's arm and shoved him toward the curved lobby outside the gym, the boy's own momentum sending him flying. Tyler crashed to the ground, and rolled to his side holding his arm.

Hunter stood over him, fists clenched. "I told you once and I'll say it again, Rowen had nothing to do with what happened. She was with me the whole time. I don't give a damn what your bubble headed girlfriend says."

Tyler sat up, giving his head a quick shake to clear it. "Jenny doesn't lie, at least not to me, she doesn't."

"Are you really that oblivious? Jenny lies for the hell of it, especially to you. Or are you blind as well as stupid?" Hunter shot back, shoving his hand through his hair.

Tyler got to his feet and took a step closer to Hunter, watching him. "And what's that supposed to mean?"

Hunter considered him for a moment then shook his head. "Look, I don't give a crap about you and your hook ups. You want to be played by some backseat slash in a mini-skirt, that's your choice. But I'm warning you. Back off Rowen. She had nothing to with it."

Tyler snorted. "Whatever, man. I know who narced on me. The blond your girlfriend hangs out with blew the whistle, but nothing's going to convince me Rowen didn't know about it."

With a guttural exhale, Hunter shook his head. "She knew about it all right. *After the fact*. The same way I knew about it along with the rest of the school."

Tyler pushed past Hunter, shoving his shoulder back in the process. "Whatever, man..." He paused, bending down to pick up Hunter's backpack. "Coach can't bench me since it's hearsay, and unless my parents agree to have me drug tested, the school can't do anything about it, either," he added with a smirk. "Innocent until proven guilty."

Hunter threw his arm up, his expression a picture of amazed frustration. "Then why do you have such a hard-on about this? About Rowen? She said you were a jerk, but I've been telling her to give you a chance. Don't make me a liar by being a complete tool. She didn't have anything to do with this, and you know it. Did you ever think maybe

your girlfriend is the reason Talia did what she did?"

Tyler tossed Hunter's pack at him. "Man, stop tap dancing and say whatever it is you have to say."

Hunter slung his pack over his shoulder, shaking his head. "Nah. It's not me you need to ask. It's Mike. Ask him about his pool party and his late night cabana surprise."

Jaw tight, Tyler didn't say a word, just stared Hunter down before stalking away. The crowd that gathered dispersed as quickly as they came, and Hunter bent to pick up the rest of his books. He straightened, glancing toward the glass corridor where I stood next to the wall.

"You can come out now," he said with a smirk.

Walking with my head down, I kept my eyes on the ground not wanting to make eye contact with anyone. This whole situation struck me as ridiculous. Tyler and Jenny had any number of people lined up to get even with them, but they automatically honed in on me. What had I done to deserve their undivided attention?

"Is there a reason why you won't look at me?"

My face must have said it all because Hunter burst out laughing. "That bad, huh?"

"What?" I said jerking my eyes to his.

"Me."

Confused, I scrambled trying to figure out what he meant. I was not letting him take the heat for any of this.

Shaking my head, my eyes searched his. "No. It's me. I won't let you get sucked in any more to whatever black hole is following me. Now you're getting into fights. Maybe it's best if we didn't hang out." I nearly choked on the words, but I couldn't risk Hunter getting hurt, or worse, become an outcast like me. Talia was so getting a face full from me after school for causing all this.

Hunter eyed me carefully. "You're serious, aren't you?"

I nodded.

He kept his eyes on mine, but shook his head, his face as grim as mine. "That's not happening, Rowen. Tyler was just being the jerk we all know him to be. I can handle myself, so don't worry."

My throat tightened and for the first time since my father died, I wanted to crawl into someone's arms and cry. Preferably Hunter's.

As if he read my thoughts, he dropped his pack and gathered me to him. Tears threatened, but thankfully they didn't come. I hitched a breath and slid my arms around his waist, resting my head on his chest. I relaxed into his embrace, my mother's mojo bag crushed between us.

A sense of déjà vu passed over me, and I closed my eyes. Hunter had held me before, but this was different. The feeling was older, settled, like I belonged right where I was at this very moment. I opened my eyes and my vision swam. I was still in Hunter's arms but we were in a paddock next to a split rail fence. The scent of animals and fresh hay filled my nose, and in the background I heard the sound of a waterwheel.

I lifted my head and turned to see a white, two-story cottage with a black door and black shuttered windows. A young boy in a tricorn hat played in the front garden with a little girl. She had brown curls tied with bright blue ribbon. They turned toward me and smiled, waving. I lifted my hand to wave back, but the vision faded, and I was once again with Hunter in front of the McCleery gym.

At least this time the vision wasn't of something horrible. In fact, I smiled to myself, my spirits lighter than they had been all day.

Hunter glanced down at me. "What's that smile for?"

I shook my head. "Nothing. I'd better get to music before I'm so late it's considered a cut." I went up on my tip toes and kissed his cheek, then stepped back, out of his arms. "Will I see you later?"

He winked, picking up his backpack. "You bet."

I walked into the shop and both my mother and Britt Morrissey looked up from the register.

"Hey, Mrs. Morrissey. Hey, Mom," I said as the door closed behind me.

"Hi, sweetie. How was school?" my mother asked.

I dropped my messenger bag onto the front counter and let my breath out in one quick huff.

"Uh oh," Britt chuckled. "I hope Hunter isn't the reason for your trouble."

With a sheepish smile I shook my head. "Nah, just girl drama."

She laughed. "I guess some things never change." She gathered her bag and leaned over to give my mother a hug. "I'd better get going then,

so you two can talk. How about lunch on Friday?"

My mom nodded. "Absolutely, just say when and where."

"Good. I'll call you later."

Britt patted my arm as she passed. "Girl fights never last, honey. So don't stress too much. It'll ruin your gorgeous complexion." With a quick wave she left, and as the door closed behind her I exhaled again.

"That bad?" my mother asked, handing me a cup of green tea she poured from the electric kettle on the work shelf behind the counter.

I shrugged, taking the mug and blowing across the top of the pale yellow-green liquid. "Not the whole day. Talia went all sniper in gym class, targeting Jenny Beamer and Tyler Cavanaugh."

My mother regarded me, confused. "What do you mean she went all sniper?"

I exhaled sharply, again. "Talia was outside running laps for talking over Mr. Faulkner in gym class." I paused to watch my mother's reaction. Mr. Faulkner was not one of her favorite people, and her grimaced smirk made it clear what she thought of him.

"And?"

"And, when Talia saw Jenny and Tyler headed toward the Aqueduct…"

"Uh oh," my mother replied, cringing a little. The Aqueduct was notorious.

"Yup. But the kicker is Tal never saw Jen nor Ty *do* anything. She just told the Resource Officer she did. Then on top of it, she comes and tells me all about it. She was practically crowing."

"What did you say?"

Swirling the top rim of the cup with my index finger, I shrugged again. "I called her out, and she made veiled threats, but that's about it. Talia blames Jenny for Mike scamming on her over the summer, but you and I know that's bull. Unfortunately, now Tyler thinks I had something to do with it. Probably because that's what Jenny told him."

"You?"

I half snorted, half chuckled, but there was no humor in it. "Yeah. Stupid, right. Hunter set him straight, though."

"Really." My mother sat back on her stool, a smirk tickling the corner of her mouth as she took a sip from her own cup.

"Mom! Cut it out. Hunter's supposed to come over tonight so we can work on a research project we have for English, but if you're going to be all weird, I'll text him and tell him not to come."

My mother put her cup on the counter and got up, palms out neutral. "Relax. I'm not even going to be around tonight. Believe it or not, your grandmother and I are going to a planning meeting at the Warner Library, and then out for coffee with a few people."

"Gran's not going to be around?"

My mother considered me, no doubt surprised I wasn't palpably relieved Gran wasn't going to drop by with Hunter here.

"No, she's not. Why?" she asked, her head titled suspiciously.

I shook my head. "No reason. It's just Hunter and I have this research project on the town's urban legends, and Gran was our first stop."

"Oh, well then, she's coming for dinner around six before we leave for the meeting. You can interview her then and fill Hunter in later."

I mentally calculated the time Hunter would take to get here from practice, silently praying coach would keep the team later than usual. I knew he'd want to grab a shower before coming. I crossed my fingers hoping we'd end up with a simple hello/goodbye scenario with Gran. I could handle my grandmother, but there wasn't any way I was forcing that gimlet-eyed stare of hers on Hunter. It was unnerving when she gave *me* her once over, and I've known her my whole life.

My mother chuckled. "Look at you, gnawing on your bottom lip like you were going to face the inquisitor general. I'll keep Gran away from Hunter, if that's what's worrying you. Relax. Go on upstairs to the kitchen and start your homework. It's always better if you're prepared when you approach Gran, so write down whatever it is you want to ask."

Embarrassed, I knew I was as red as a beet, but it didn't matter. My mother knew me better than anyone, and she was right. Gran scared the crud out of me. *And everyone else in town.*

I pushed myself up, hopping onto the counter just enough to plant a kiss on my mother's cheek. "You're the best!" I slid off, taking my bag with me.

I headed toward the back storeroom and the secret door that led from the shop into our basement.

"And don't you forget it!" my mother called after me with a snort.

Maybe tonight would be a good night after all.

I stopped in the kitchen and rummaged the counter and bread box for a snack, finding fresh zucchini bread wrapped in plastic wrap next to the bagels. It came from the Bake Shoppe, but I didn't care. Once the Witch's New Year had come and gone, Mom and I would bake and freeze enough winter breads to last all season.

My phone buzzed with a text from Chloe saying she'd call me later, but was too swamped with homework to stop by as promised. It was just as well. I wasn't in the mood to play Dr. Phil with Talia and her love life.

Taking a bottle of ginger ale from the fridge, I put my messenger bag on the kitchen table and washed my hands. I flinched before putting my hands in the running water, afraid I might see blood pouring from the faucet, but my mother had warded the house into a protective bubble, so it was all good.

Homemade whole wheat pasta lay drying on the counter and the last of the Indian summer plum tomatoes were piled beside a container of pine nuts. I knew I'd find a similar container in the fridge filled with fresh feta cheese. Dinner. Yum.

Thinking about my mother's pasta made my mouth water, so I dried my hands and grabbed a couple of napkins, cutting myself a nice slice of the bread before sitting down to my lessons. I sat in silence while I worked, arranging my books in order of homework importance, leaving a blank yellow legal pad on the bottom for the questions I would ask Gran. Each night I had a couple of hours worth of homework, yet procrastination was something I was raising to an art form. Tonight was different, though. I wanted Hunter to myself with no unnecessary distractions.

I made a mental list of what needed to be done. I finished eating and cleared my crumbs, placing my empty soda bottle in the recycling bin next to the trashcan. Messy was an understatement when it came to my room and bathroom, and I was not letting Hunter anywhere near my bedroom unless I cleaned it up. Leaving my books on the table, I pulled out a garbage bag, paper towels and an all-purpose cleaner from under the sink and trudged up the stairs.

Half the mess went straight into the trash bag, the other half, mostly

clothes, where tossed into the hamper hidden in my closet. I made my bed and gave the bathroom a quick wipe down, deciding to top it off by running the vacuum. The scented candle on my nightstand, the final touch.

Standing in the middle of the room, I gave everything a swift once over. Scenarios of where we would sit and what we would say to each other drifted through my mind—from the beanbag chairs in the corner, to the little couch near my TV. My eyes drifted to the bed. I pictured Hunter propped up against my headboard, pillows wedged behind his back as we watched a movie, the soft rise and fall of his lean, muscular chest under my head and our legs intertwined.

My breath quickened at the natural intimacy of the image and suddenly I wanted to call Hunter and tell him not to come.

Don't be a coward. Grimacing, I closed my eyes. *Hunter is not Tyler. You have nothing to worry about.*

Downstairs, I heard the backdoor open and close, and I glanced at the clock on the night table. Five p.m. Gran was early.

I swallowed my nonsense, giving myself a quick glance in the mirror. "You want this. Remember?" With a swift breath, I gathered empty plates and cups on my desk and headed out of the room.

"Rowen?" My grandmother called from the bottom of the stairs.

"Coming, Gran."

She watched as I carried the dirty dishes down the steps, a mixed look of surprise and suspicion on her face as she eyed my contraband.

"Eating upstairs again? You know your mother will go ballistic if she sees you with all that," she said, gesturing with her hand.

"I know. That's why I'm cleaning up while she's in the shop," I replied, ignoring her harrumph of disproval. Not quite making eye contact with her, I loaded the dishes and cups into the dishwasher.

"What's all this?" she asked, eyeing the table and my pile of books.

"Homework. I'll move it into the dining room if it's in your way."

She shook her head. "That won't be necessary. Your mother called and said you needed my help with something, some sort of research or whatnot."

I nodded, closing the dishwasher door. "Yes. Mr. Conover has assigned the class a research project, asking each of us to find out as

Marianne Morea

much as we can about the town's urban legends."

My grandmother's hand flew up in a flippant gesture, a disgusted grunt echoing from somewhere in the back of her throat. "That hysterical fool just can't let things lie. He assigns this idiotic project in one form or another every year hoping that one of his students will uncover some clue to what actually happened."

Actually happened? I had no idea what Gran meant. I eyed her, watching as she put the kettle on, puttering in the cabinet for her favorite caramel tea. She continued to shake her head, as if mentally taking Mr. Conover to task.

"I suppose you want me to recount all the stories I've collected over the years, hmmm?" she asked over her shoulder.

Behind her back I frowned, not sure I wanted her to tell me anything, but there was no going back. She had come over early to help. "I guess," I replied with a small sigh. "Mr. Conover has been a little hard on me this semester, so I need to make the most of this to get him off my back."

Gran turned, her mouth set into a thin line. "Leave it to Gerry Conover to take his limitations out on an Ekert."

I made a face. "An Ekert? I don't get it." Ekert was my mother's maiden name.

"Your mother. Your teacher," she said with an offhand wave. "Gerry Conover had a thing for your mom back in the day, but she was already dating your father. Let's just say he didn't take kindly to Laura's polite rebuff. Whether you realize it or not, he's partly responsible for the whispering that has followed this family for the last twenty years."

Dumfounded, I stared at my grandmother. "I still don't understand. Mom always told me to be proud of our family's uniqueness." I made bunny ears with my fingers at the word. "I know for a fact some people in town wish they had the same claim to fame."

Gran shrugged, carrying her mug of tea to the table and sitting across from where I stood. "That's very true, but envy takes many forms and not all of them good. Sit down, honey, and let me tell you one of the stories that will help with this research of yours. It will illustrate how bad jealousy can be, and how rumors turn into legends."

I moved slowly, pulling the chair out. If this was about my mother, I wasn't prepared to hear that she suffered any more than I already knew.

Mom had a tough time after Dad died, and people were cruel, especially whenever fear and superstition combined. Our family history was steeped in it. Only through hard work, and years of community service and volunteering for everything under the sun, did my mother turn things around from distrust to admiration and respect. She made things easier for me, although there were still a few puritanical hold-outs in town that let me know I was hell bound every chance they got. Ironically, Tyler Cavanaugh's family was one of them. Maybe that's why he acted the way he did around me.

Elbows on the table, Gran laced her fingers together, eyeing me over the top of her rings. Two ornate stones worn on each index finger, she was never without them, so much so they had become her trademark. One was a large moonstone. Opaque milky white with a hint of blue set in what was tantamount to a silver claw. The other was a large emerald, oval, and so faceted its green depths glittered in even the dimmest light.

"You know the story behind the Bronze Lady?" she asked, leaning her chin forward.

"Of course," I answered matter-of-factly. "Everyone in town knows about the weeping statue. But it's a farce. The metal reacts with the air and it seems like she's crying."

Gran's eyebrow shot up, and her lips half hidden behind her fingers pulled down. Never a good sign. "Really. And you believe that?"

I didn't know what to say. I had seen enough magic in my life, particularly over the last couple of weeks, to never discount metaphysics altogether, but to think an inanimate object could affect people's lives directly? "I guess…" I replied, immediately adding, "I don't know," to the end of my statement when her eyebrow shot up further into her hairline.

"Hmmph. Well, at least that's an honest answer." She pursed her lips.

Gran was quiet, sipping her tea. The clock above the stove ticked loudly, accenting the uncomfortable silence. Why couldn't Gran be like other grandmothers? Always happy to see you and full of hugs and praise?

"Sorry, Gran. I didn't mean anything by that. I don't know what to believe anymore."

She smiled. "That's fair enough. The facts behind the statue of the

Bronze lady are easy, it's the legend that's hard. She was commissioned by the widow of Civil War General, Samuel Thomas. It was a very impressive piece for its day. It's real name is *Recuillement* or Grief, and was intended as a memorial figure to be placed outside the general's tomb. The story goes that the artist was pleased with the sculpture, but when the widow saw the finished product in his Paris studio, she was disappointed in the expression, that it wasn't cheerful enough. The artist told the general's wife to come back in one week, where he showed her a new head with a happy expression, then politely smashed it on the floor."

I listened as I started dinner, chopping tomatoes with fresh basil and boiling water for the pasta.

"Wow, looks like people lose heads all over Sleepy Hollow Cemetery," I added with snort, earning one of Gran's withering looks.

She cleared her throat. "Pay attention, Rowen. You asked for my help on our urban legends, and this is one that most people don't know. "

I cringed, making sure to straighten my face before looking at her over my shoulder. "Sorry, Gran."

She waved me off. "Anyway, the story that follows is that a chambermaid from the Thomas household in Manhattan found her way back to the cemetery after the funeral, and for days wouldn't leave. By all accounts, the poor lady cried over how she loved the general and never got the chance to tell him. The gatekeeper would find her drunk, often to the point of being passed out at the foot of the general's mausoleum. He would then cart the girl back to his lodging to sober up, not being the kind of man to call the police on a grieving woman. My own grandmother told me the story when I was a little girl. After all, it was 1903 when the scandal hit, and she remembered the event like it was yesterday.

"Mrs. Thomas, of course, scoffed at her maid's claims and used her considerable wealth and influence to have the girl banned from the cemetery and the story hushed up, but the poor chambermaid always came back—that is until the morning the gatekeeper found her missing from her cot in his house. He found her dead on the marble steps of the tomb, wrists slit."

"So, the statue's tears belonged to the girl that killed herself?"

Gran nodded. "Shortly after that, rumors of the weeping statue began

to surface, though what is intriguing about the story is what was left out of the police report. The girl's blood had run from the marble base of the tomb in a direct line, pooling in a perfect circle around the statue, saturating the ground. My grandmother said townspeople claimed the excessive amount of blood at the site baffled the coroner's office, but as there was no other body found, police let the case go.

"Such strong emotion, especially with such a violent act attached, invariably leaves a mark on this world. That statue embodies the poor woman's grief and unrequited love. People who have visited the grave and scoffed at her story, always, and I mean always, find themselves paying for their callousness. But those who show compassion for her pain reap her favor. Good luck and all that."

I drained the pasta, adding a little fresh olive oil and garlic along with the pine nuts and feta before tossing it together with the tomatoes in a serving dish.

"Gran, I get how rumor and sensational headlines can pave the way for an urban legend, but finding out about the lesser known stories was only part of the assignment. Mr. Conover wants us to try and tie it back to Irving's legend. In his mind, it's the only legend that matters."

She considered my words as I set out three dishes, putting forks and napkins down at each plate and then calling down to my mother dinner was ready.

"You can tie at least part of this next legend to Washington Irving's story, but I warn you, you're not going to like it."

I stopped short, serving spoon in hand with a large helping of pasta half way to Gran's dish. "Why?"

"Did you ever hear the story of a Revolutionary War captain by the name of Emmerick?"

I shook my head, and slowly finished spooning dinner onto her plate.

"Emmerick was a Hessian soldier who earned a command of his own during the war."

"A Hessian? Are you saying what I think your saying?"

Gran chuckled. "No. Andreas Emmerick was not the Headless Horseman. But that's another story. In fact, he was executed by a firing squad much later. During the Revolutionary War his men were an unruly group, with no respect for people or property. He and his Tory

counterpart, Joshua Barnes, were notorious. They ruled the area under the protection of Governor Tryon. He gave the infamous order to, 'Burn Tarrytown.' That order drove these men to burn most of the patriot houses in the area, many times with no regard for the people still inside."

I put the spoon on the table and slid into my chair. "They burned people alive?" The shock in my voice must have echoed the stunned look on my face, because my grandmother reached out to pat my hand.

"Yes, honey. Many cruel things were done in the name of King George, but also in the name of freedom. Neither side was guiltless. However, that's not what I was getting at. You see, besides being cruel, both Emmerick and Barnes were greedy. They craved material things almost as much as they craved power, and knowing this, some of the local families bartered with them to save themselves and their homes, even if that meant bartering their own flesh."

Confused, I looked at her.

"Fathers sacrificed their own daughters, handing them over to be used and discarded in exchange for their houses and lands being spared."

I swallowed hard, my appetite gone just thinking about what that meant for girls doubtless younger than me.

"Emmerick had a special fondness for local girls, particularly ones with Dutch last names. He preyed upon those families, in all likelihood because it was from their church pulpit that his actions were most severely judged."

"And nobody did anything about it?" I asked, aghast.

Gran shook her head. "War makes for very strange bedfellows. Of course, none of the families wanted reminders of their sordid dealings, so their daughters were sent away to give birth to their ill-gotten children. Afterward, these same daughters were married off to the first men who asked, often for a price."

"Sounds more like sold off," I mumbled.

With a shrug, Gran took a bite of her pasta. "That about sums it up. It was all very hush-hush, and church fathers made sure to keep it that way, especially when it came to Emmerick's doings. Even so, every birth, death, and marriage was recorded, even the ones they tried to sweep under the carpet."

"I can't believe the townspeople allowed this to go on, I mean really,

Gran? And the girls went along with it?"

She pointed her fork in my direction, bouncing it up and down slightly. "You're looking at this from a twenty-first century mindset. These girls didn't stand a chance. Townsfolk spoke of Emmerick as less than kind when he took these girls. They were delivered to him gift wrapped, and in most cases he viewed them as bought and paid for, and treated them as such."

Her eyes met mine. "Here's where you can link the oral history with the legend. Claims have been made that Emmerick and the stories surrounding him may have been the basis for the character of Brom Bones."

I wrinkled my nose. "I don't think so, Gran. Brom Bones in the story was mischievous and a prankster, but he wasn't cruel. "

Her eyebrows hiked up and her eyes widened. "Very good, Rowen. Yes, the character was mischievous, with frat boy charm, but, according to accounts, so was Emmerick. He was cruel, but he was also charming and strong. He had arrogance and swagger and a quick wit. How else would a Hessian make it all the way to Lieutenant Colonel?"

"But you said he was a captain."

She nodded. "He was, at the time of the burnings. But Emmerick managed to charm his way into a higher rank. He had a favorite among the girls he took advantage of in town. She was his counterpart, in that she reveled in taunting the other girls, priding herself with the idea that she was different, that she had been chosen. When she became pregnant, she carried her burgeoning belly as a sign of honor. But when Emmerick left the area, he refused to take her with him, and once he was gone, she was shunned."

"I don't understand. Her family let her flaunt her illicit affair with him?"

Gran shrugged again. "When it benefited them, yes. But as soon as it was clear she was cast aside, they planned a public flogging. She ran to the deacon of the church, claiming that Emmerick had bewitched her, begging to be re-baptized."

The food in my dish was ice cold at this point, and I pushed it aside, pouring myself a glass of apple cider. "What became of her? I mean, would they have really whipped a pregnant girl?"

Holding out her glass to me, I filled it with cider, too. "Of course they would. But it's ironic really. She ended up seducing the deacon and married him, becoming a pillar of the reformed church. Stories say the deacon adopted her son, and they were transformed into a model family of piety and goodness."

"Hmmph. Sounds like some of the families we have around here," I replied grabbing my notebook next to my half empty plate and scribbling down some of what Gran said.

"They are," she added quietly. "One and the same."

I glanced up from my notes as my mother came upstairs. She seemed exhausted, and sat at the table with and audible sigh of relief. She picked in the serving dish, plopping a finger full of pasta into her mouth. "What are you two so intent about?"

"Pious assholes, both past and present." I answered.

She glanced between Gran and me and then back to Gran.

"I was enlightening Rowen about the families whose histories tie to Captain Emmerick."

My mother's face was a picture of distaste, and Gran nodded patting my mother's hand. "A nasty bunch, the lot of them. Even today, they are the same families happy to help Gerry Conover spread his venom against your mother and our Wiccan ways."

My head was spinning. Many town families were tied to the church at that time. Did that mean one or more of them were linked to the heartache caused by that Hessian creep?

"Gran, is this just hearsay or are there records I could examine? If there are diaries or conversations that noted Emmerick's messed up attitude as some of the inspiration for Brom Bones, then I'll not only make Mr. Conover's day, I might even get an 'A' in English for once."

She looked at my mother and then at me. "Like I said, there are birth and death records, genealogies and such at the Historical Society and in the vaults of the reformed church. But this is something you would have to dig for. There was much that was done quietly, since at that time neighbor turned on neighbor when it came to Tory versus Patriot. It was all linked to politics and money, just like today, but then again when it came to events that happened on the wrong side of the sheets, secrets were not uncommon."

I suddenly couldn't wait for Hunter to get here. We had a major lead and a definite direction to search in. "What if I turn up more than just hearsay? What if I find skeletons rattling that will hurt people? People we know."

My mother pushed up from the table. "That was delicious, Rowen. Thanks for putting dinner together. I've been rushing around all day..." she stopped, glancing down at her watch. "...and it looks like it'll be that way all evening, too," she added with a frown. "Mom, we've got to run. We were supposed to be at the library fifteen minutes ago."

They deliberately left my question hanging. Maybe there was more chance of me finding juicy town tidbits than either wanted to admit. I glanced at the clock above the stove and issued a silent thank you they weren't the only ones running behind. Hunter would eventually meet Gran. Just not tonight.

Chapter 6

I wasted no time cleaning up after my mother and Gran left, and sure enough, no sooner did I close the last cabinet and hang the damp dish towel on the sink, then there was a knock on the backdoor.

I smiled, smoothing my curls and checking my teeth for rogue bits of food in the mirrored plaque on the side wall. "Coming," I said loudly, and walked to open the door.

Hunter looked amazing in light wash jeans and a soft, deep blue fleece that highlighted his broad shoulders. His hair was still damp, and as he stepped into the kitchen to give me a hug, I inhaled, taking in his clean scent.

"How was practice? Did you have time to eat?" I asked, giving him a quick squeeze back, reluctant to give up my close proximity for etiquette's sake.

He nodded taking a look around the kitchen. "I grabbed something from the vending machine at school..." He stopped and sniffed the air. "It certainly wasn't as good as whatever you ate. It smells incredible in here."

I smiled. "Just pasta with fresh tomato, basil and a little feta cheese. Want some?"

Hunter didn't answer, just pulled out a chair and sat, moving one of the linen placemats in front of him.

Chuckling, I opened the fridge and took out the serving platter, the base of which was still warm. "I'm guessing that's a yes." I said closing the refrigerator with my hip.

Hunter ate three helpings while I told him what Gran had said. He didn't comment, really, but paused once, fork in hand when I told him about Emmerick and his barter system.

"Man, that is just messed up. And it's creepy to think some of his descendants might be walking around town now."

I busied myself with a paper napkin, twisting pieces into thin sprigs. "Maybe. Maybe not. Gran said the families usually sent the girls away."

"Hmmph. Yeah, all but that one. I wonder whose family tree it is."

Scooping my napkin pieces into my hand, I got up to throw them in the garbage. "I don't know. And I'm not sure I want to find out."

Hunter wiped his mouth, and then carried his dish to the sink. "Come on, Rowen. It's not like it matters. What's one got to do with the other? My family has been around here for over 250 years. Do I have anything in common with my ancestors?"

He burst out laughing at the face I gave him, lifting his hands, palms out in surrender. "Okay. I take that back. But metaphysical weirdness notwithstanding, do I?"

I chewed on my lip, shrugging slowly. "I suppose not."

"Exactly," he said, stepping on the chrome pedal at the base of the trash, tossing his napkin into the open bin. "The only person likely to be upset by what we find is Mr. Conover, because he'll have no choice but to give us an 'A'. Maybe it will floor him enough to get him off our backs for the rest of the year."

Hmmm. "If you say so."

Hunter took his foot off the pedal and released the lid on the trash can with soft thunk. I crossed toward the table, eyeing him over my shoulder as he stood with his arms folded in front of his chest.

"What?"

He flashed one of his killer smiles. "Nothing…" he paused. "It's just I didn't expect to get here and have it be mission accomplished. Since you did all the legwork, and we have our research objective, I can call Mrs. Scarborough tomorrow and set up an appointment with her at the Historical Society."

Nodding, I smirked. "And?"

"And nothing."

"Ha. You're getting off easy."

He laughed, giving me a closed lip smile. "You think so, but wait 'til we're digging through piles of papers and genealogies. Then you'll see me in action. I have a photographic memory," he said tapping the side of his head.

"Oh, really?"

He nodded, walking up to me by the table. "Yup. I'll prove it. I've only been here once in the last seven years or so, right?"

I bobbed my head.

"So how do I know your bedroom is the second door on the left upstairs?"

I burst out laughing, pushing him back a step. "Okay, Edward Cullen. Are you sneaking in like a stalker and watching me sleep, too?"

Hunter's grin went from ear to ear, and his cheeks actually pinked at the analogy. "No. But that vampire story had it right. I would give anything to watch you drool syrup onto your pillow."

"Eeeww! Hunter!"

"Ha. Now you're blushing. Come on, Cinderella. Show me your room before your mother gets back and turns you into a pumpkin and me into a frog." He gestured toward the hallway with his head.

Laughing, I took his hand in mine and headed for the door, leading him toward the stairs. At the base, I hesitated with one foot on the first step. I looked back at him, my face suddenly hot. My palms were clammy, and I wished I could disengage my hand from his for just a second to wipe it on my jeans. I opened my mouth to say something, but on second thought, closed it.

He tugged on my hand. And I knew it wasn't to urge me forward, but to stop me from stressing. "If you're uncomfortable with us going upstairs, Rowen, we can hang out in here," he said gesturing toward the living room. "I just want to spend some time with you—that's all. I don't care where."

Hunter didn't wait for me to reply. He took the lead, pulling me behind him as he turned left into my living room. "You got any decent music down here?"

I didn't know what to say. Was I now a dork because I didn't know how to properly accomplish a seduction scene? I should have been cool and sexy leading him upstairs, but instead I probably seemed to him like I was heading toward death row. God, I'm such a loser.

As if he could read the emotion on my face, he pulled me to him. Stroking my hair, he traced the line of my cheek, running his finger over my bottom lip. "Rowen, stop mentally questioning everything we do or don't do, everything we say or don't say. Like I said, I want to spend time with you. The rest will come. Whatever comes next? Remember? And what's next is me getting to know you and you getting to know me. So, it's all good."

He leaned down to kiss me, and we sank to the couch together, my foot catching the leg of the coffee table making it screech against the hardwood.

"Now, that's classy," he said with a laugh at the fart-like noise.

"Hunter!"

He kissed me again, then handed me his iPod. "Plug this in and hit playlist number five. I made it for us, just for the occasion."

Regarding him curiously, I took the device. My mother had a Bose iPod dock on the fireplace mantel, so I set it up as instructed and hit play.

One Direction's *Little Things* played immediately, and I glanced at Hunter. I didn't know one girl who didn't tear up at this song. Even Jenny wasn't immune. The fact that Hunter chose it as the first song I'd hear on his playlist said a lot, and I knew it wasn't a clever manipulation. Again, I didn't know how, but Hunter just 'got' me.

I slid onto the couch next to him. "Good choice."

He nodded. "Whoever wrote this song is a genius."

I smacked his arm playfully, and he caught my wrist, bringing my hand to his mouth. "I meant that in a good way. I can't imagine not thinking of you every time I hear it."

I felt myself blush.

"And considering it's every other song played on the radio these days, I've been thinking about you a lot!"

I smirked. "Ha. Ha."

"Just kidding," he said dipping his head to kiss me again.

I sighed against his lips, not caring the audible exhale left no question

about what he did to me. I put my palms against the flat planes of his stomach, feeling the hard lines of his chest beneath my fingers. My hand inched across his belly in a shy attempt at a caress, and I heard his breath hitch. Smiling against his mouth, I kissed him back...deeper; happy I wasn't the only one affected.

"Dance with me," he whispered, feathering kisses along my jaw and up toward my ear.

"What?" I craned my head back to look at him.

"Dance. You know, when two people get up and move in time to music together?"

My mouth quirked up in a half embarrassed smile. "You're risking your toes with that request, Mr. Morrissey. I'm pretty sure I have two left feet."

He chuckled, pecking the tip of my nose before standing. "I have two right feet. We're a perfectly matched set."

Hunter held out his hand, and biting the corner of my lip, I slid my fingers into his waiting palm. "You have a big game in less than forty-eight hours. Are you sure you want to risk it?"

He pulled me into his arms, his hands gliding around my waist. "I'm willing if you are."

The next song began. Another perfect pick, and as the music to Taylor Swift's *Fifteen* swelled, all I heard was my own heart beating in my ears. Like the song said, Hunter was the boy from the football team, but I wasn't fifteen and he wasn't my first kiss. Even so, no one had ever made me feel like this.

"Relax, Rowen. There's no one else on the planet right now, just you and me." Hunter turned, spinning with me in his arms like something out of Dancing With The Stars. I closed my eyes hoping I didn't trip or step on his feet. His scent, clean and undeniably masculine filled my nose, and I pressed my cheek to his chest just to breath in more. My arms were around his neck, and Hunter slowed our pace 'til we swayed back and forth in each other's arms in time with the music.

"Do you still want to see upstairs?" I asked, despite the shy tone behind my question.

He leaned his chin on the top of my head, and his chest shook with a low chuckle. "Now that's a question. What do you think?"

Without missing a beat he slipped his hand behind my neck and urged me to look at him. "Of course, I want to *see upstairs*, as you so politely put it." A soft smile played on his lips, and he dipped me, his breath fanning my throat as he kissed my neck all the way to my mouth. "But I think for tonight I'm good right where I am — for now, at least," he whispered.

I fought my own embarrassment as he brought me back to standing, hoping I wasn't fifty shades of red while trying to act all fifty shades of grey.

"How about some popcorn?" he asked changing the subject, doubtless because I looked like I wanted to swallow my own tongue.

I blinked, trying to regroup. "Sure. Why not?" I said. "Gimme a sec, and I'll put some in the micro."

Straightening my shirt, I headed to the kitchen. For some reason I couldn't find the popcorn, and I opened and closed cabinets all over the pantry trying not to seem like a total loser in my own kitchen. Finally, I found a stray box wedged between barley bags and dried lentils.

"Everything okay?" Hunter asked, making me jump. He was standing outside the pantry closet and had probably heard me arguing with myself. My cheeks burned at being caught unaware, and I nodded like a mute, ripping the plastic wrapper off one of the popcorn bags with my teeth.

"Rowen..."

"Do you want melted butter? This brand is a plain, air popped, but I could melt some butter to pour on top."

"Rowen," he began again, but this time he grabbed my arm so I'd have to look at him. "Why are you so tense? Did I do something?"

I swallowed, shaking my head. "No, why?"

He let go of my arm and frowned, shrugging one shoulder. "Oh, I don't know. Maybe because the vibe I'm getting from you makes me think you want me to leave but don't know how to tell me."

I opened my mouth, but closed it quickly, biting back on the panicked "Nooooo!" cocked and ready for fire off tip of my tongue. "I don't want you leave, Hunter. That's the last thing I want." Clearing my throat a little, I added. "So...what do *you* want?"

He looked at me like a bell had gone off in his head, and his confused

frown softened. "Rowen, do you think I don't want to go upstairs with you? Is that why you're all jumpy and weird with me now?"

I shut the microwave door, but the sound bordered more on slam. "I am not all jumpy and I'm certainly not weird, not with you or anyone."

His frown was back, but this time it was annoyed rather than confused. "I didn't mean it that way and you know it. I just meant you're blowing hot and cold again."

I groaned, and not in a pretty way, giving him my back so I wouldn't have to see the disappointment in his face.

"What did I say?" Hunter put his hand on my arm, but didn't force me to turn. "You know, I really have to thank Jenny for the head job she's done on all you girls, because obviously you think going to your bedroom is the only way to prove how much I like you, how much I want to be with you."

I whirled around, my mouth open. "That's not what I think…" I paused. "Oh hell, I don't know what I think. I've never been in a situation where I *wanted* to go upstairs with anyone."

"Well, that sounds promising."

Now it was my turn to frown. "What does that mean?"

He smiled sheepishly. "It means you're not the only one confused by how fast this is moving."

At this point the microwave dinged, and both of us turned to look at it. Hunter opened the door and took out the steaming bag, gingerly passing it back and forth between his hands so as not to burn his fingers. "Come on, grab a bowl and let's talk."

Relieved, I opened the bottom cabinet for a large clear glass bowl and told Hunter to grab two Coke cans from the back of the pantry where I kept my contraband soda hidden from my mother.

He opened the popcorn bag, pouring the contents into the bowl. Without asking, I took out a stick of Irish butter and put it into a small bowl, setting the microwave to melt it to a liquid gold.

"*Mmmmm.* You read my mind," he said, taking the melted butter from me and pouring it over the fluffy white kernels. "You'd better grab some more napkins, this is going to get messy!" Grabbing a handful of popcorn, he stuffed half into his mouth before putting the rest on a paper towel.

"Easy, killer," I said with a chuckle. "Don't you ever get full?"

Chewing, he winked. "Not during football season," he replied behind his hand.

With so much still hanging in the air between us, I changed direction. "So tell me about California. Were you more beach or Disney? Wine country or mountains?"

He shrugged, swallowing a gulp from his Coke. "Beach. And to tell the truth, except for the palm trees, the temperate climate and the Pacific Ocean, it wasn't too different from living here."

"Oh come on, no surfing every day after school, no selling maps to movie stars homes instead of a paper route for extra cash?"

"Paper route? What am I twelve?" He chuckled. "In all my years of living in L.A., no one I knew ever bought one of those maps they sell on the roadside listing the homes of famous actors. When you grow up in L.A., celebrity spotting isn't something you do. None of my friends would be caught dead trolling the gold stars on Hollywood's Walk of Fame, or putting their hands and feet in the cement imprints outside the old Grauman's Chinese Theater."

"Too touristy for you, huh?"

He tilted his head, wearing a smirk. "When's the last time you went to the Statue of Liberty or the Empire State Building?"

Grinning, I threw a piece of popcorn at him. "Point taken."

Hunter played with the aluminum tab at the top of his soda can. "My life in California was normal. I had friends, I went to school, I played little league, I went to the beach. I learned how to drive in Laguna Beach along the Pacific Coast Highway, how many kids can say that? Mom and Dad rented a house for the summer there, the year I got my permit. Most of the time it was just me and Mom, with Dad commuting an hour into the city every day. Once I got good enough behind the wheel, my mom would let me drive through town to the Pacific Coast Highway. There we would cruise with the windows down. There's nothing like the smell of the ocean."

I rested my chin on my hands listening to him talk. He was sitting in the kitchen with me, but his eyes were thousands of miles away, remembering.

"Sounds wonderful."

He inhaled through his nose, his chest rising quickly before he exhaled. "It was."

As the words left his mouth he looked so unhappy, and I didn't know what to say. "If you don't want to talk about California anymore, I get it." I said, knowing full well how lame I sounded.

"It's okay, Rowen. That summer was kind of the beginning of the end for my family as I knew it. My dad started staying in the city more and more, leaving us at the beach, alone. My mother would make excuses, but I was old enough to figure out what was happening, and by the time mid-August rolled around and Mom and I headed back to L.A. for school, things had really changed.

"My dad was working all the time, obsessed. He's a good lawyer, but he put himself on some kind of fast track to make senior partner. As if there were some unwritten deadline he needed to complete by age forty. When he did come home, he'd eat dinner and then lock himself in his downstairs office to work until all hours. The only time he wanted to socialize at home, it usually revolved around some creepy client he brought to the house for us to entertain."

I nodded, watching the repulsed expression on his face. "You mentioned something about that the other day."

He shot me a wry grin. "Yeah. My mom and her smudge stick. It's funny, you know. Even though Laguna Beach is definitely a monied town, my mom's artistic nature and witchy inclinations never seemed out of place. Just the opposite, in fact. People seemed drawn to her. But at home in L.A., the people my dad dealt with looked down on her...on me."

Mouth open, I blinked. "Why? I don't get it, you guys are great."

He looked at me, again. "Yeah, you do. Truthfully, you're the one who labeled it for me, only then I didn't realize it had a name."

Puzzled, my brows knotted as I tried think, but he answered my silent questioning with a skeptical tilt of his head. "Your *U.P.s*. Remember?"

"Yeah, but that's just high school."

"Rowen, for somebody so smart, you say some dumbass things, sometimes."

"Hey!" I launched another kernel at him.

"Whatever label it carries, you know as well as I, that kind of

prejudice is everywhere. In this case, it was in the creeps my dad brought home for cocktails. They looked at us like we were backwards— especially my mother. The wives couldn't get past the way she dressed, and that she didn't believe in Botox or have a plastic surgeon on speed dial. That she actually shopped at Target and Kohls, instead of Rodeo Drive."

"Ha. I thought nobody shopped on Rodeo Drive," I joked, getting up to grab two more Cokes from the backend of the pantry.

Now it was his turn to throw a piece of popcorn at me. "I'm just making a point."

I closed the pantry door and turned. Hunter was looking down at his hands, and that preoccupied air was back. I wanted to ask him what he was thinking, but I didn't want to embarrass him, and I certainly didn't want to embarrass myself. I handing him a soda and sat. "Is it true that everything in L.A. is set up so any place in the city is only twenty minutes away from the freeway?"

"No. Who told you that?"

I shrugged opening my soda and taking a sip. "I don't remember where I heard it. Probably some dumb movie or something. Did you travel a lot when you were there? Go skiing in Lake Tahoe or head down to Baha, Mexico?"

He grinned stuffing a few more kernels into his mouth. "You sound like the Travel Channel."

I smirked, flipping my hand up in a mock gesture of defeat. "Yep. You caught me. I'm an undercover travel detective luring you here for your biased take on living in LaLa land."

Hunter glanced at the table again, fidgeting with the edge of the placemat. "I liked my life, Rowen. We were happy, or at least I thought we were. That is 'til my dad messed things up with his mid-life crisis. If I had to choose between being here in New York alone with my mom and having my family back the way it was, I would still be in California." He sighed. "But we don't always get what we want, do we? I mean, if you could have your dad back, wouldn't you?"

His eyes met mine and I saw they were wet. Hunter glanced away, blinking to clear his unshed tears, and it was in that moment I realized he hadn't shared this with anyone else, probably not even his mom.

Reaching out, I took his hand, half expecting him to do the guy thing and blow off his unguarded emotional moment. But he didn't. He let me take his hand and met my gaze, steady and dry eyed.

"What happened, Hunter? It sounds like you and your mom were pretty settled in California, even without your dad. What made you want to come back to New York?"

He shrugged. "I didn't." He slid his hand away from mine and opened his soda, the telltale hiss punctuating his words. "My dad met someone else. An actress named Carly. She's twenty-six. Coming to New York was for my mother. I told her I wanted to move, but the truth is I did it for her. Just don't tell anybody, okay? If it got back to my mother it would hurt her feelings, and she's been hurt enough."

I nodded, murmuring I wouldn't say a word, but an awkward quiet fell between us, and not knowing what else to say I got up to straighten the kitchen. I put Hunter's dinner dishes in the dishwasher, and rinsed the sink, wiping down the counter before hanging the dishtowel on the edge of the stainless steel once again. Hunter leaned back in his chair, tipping it off its front legs. He stretched, and a huge yawn left his mouth.

With a muffled thud, he set the chair back onto four legs and pushed back from the table. "I guess I'd better be getting home. It's after ten."

I glanced up at the ceramic clock hanging above the stove It was 10:05 p.m. Was he really tired, or had talking about his family depressed him? "You don't have to go yet. My mother won't be back for another hour or so."

"I know, but I think all this talk has brought this party down." He paused, fixing me with a straight look. "You know, it's not like I came back to New York dragging my heels. The idea of leaving my friends and spending my senior year in a strange high school didn't exactly thrill me, but I wanted a clean break for my mother."

I knew he had more to say, but his eyes dropped to his hands on the table. Flattening them, he pushed himself up from his chair and came around to where I stood by the sink. His face had softened, and he put his finger under my chin, pulling my gaze up to meet his. "All things considered, it's been a very interesting transition."

My cheeks burned. "Interesting, hmmm?"

He nodded. "Yep. And I'm very encouraged." He pulled me close,

molding my body to his.

I laughed, pushing his shoulder back. "Encouraged, huh? Well, we'll just have to see about that."

Exasperated, he let me go, but there was a smile in his eyes. "Rowen Corbett, you are many things, but never once did I think you were a tease! Guess I was wrong."

I put my hands on my hips, and lifted my chin. "I suppose I should take that as a compliment."

A huge grin spread across his face to match the glint in his eyes, and he stepped forward, cupping my face. "Absolutely," he whispered into a gentle kiss.

Hunter let go of my chin and with a wink, gathered the last of the mess from the table.

"Just put everything in the sink, I'll get to it later."

Depositing the popcorn bowl and empty soda cans in the basin, he wiped his hands on his jeans. "So, are we still on for ice cream tomorrow night?"

I nodded, crossing my arms against the chill drifting in from worn weather stripping on the back door. "You bet. I'll meet you at Main Street Sweets around eight, okay?"

"Sounds like a plan." He watched me for a moment, a slight frown creasing his forehead.

"What?" I asked, worried he remembered a prior commitment, or had second thoughts about being seen out with me locally.

"You do realize that Jenny, Ty, and Ben will probably be there — possibly a few others from my team, too. I can't very well tell them not to come."

I hesitated, but then nodded. "I know. I expected as much. It's all good, Hunter. I told you I'd hang out with your friends, and I meant it." I tilted my head, teasingly. "Just be prepared to run interference for me if I need it, okay."

He laughed, giving my nose a tweak. "You got it." Pulling the door open, he stepped halfway onto the back porch, but stopped, turning to look at me again. "You know you're the best part of moving back here, right?"

My stomach flip-flopped and a strange tingling spread along my belly

making my knees weak. I wanted to pull him back inside and never let him go, but all I did was nod. "Me, too," I added lamely.

He walked down the stairs to the driveway, and I watched as he backed into the street.

If I messed this up I was going to hate myself forever.

School was uneventful, and I was grateful it was finally Friday. Hunter and I had one week left before we handed in our joint research project, and then it was Halloween and the Fire Sabbat event planned for the Blaze. However, what I looked forward to the most was our candlelight tour at the Old Dutch Church and then sneaking back later with everyone for the clandestine cemetery party.

I still didn't know how the football team planned to carry this off, especially knowing the cops would be out in full force Halloween night. I didn't care, though. I could use a little excitement in my life.

The store had been busy for hours, but as it got closer to dinner time, I took advantage of the much needed lull to do something for fun. I grabbed three pumpkin-shaped candles and climbed into the store's front window. Arranging them around the cast iron cauldron at the center, I situated a large painted witch holding a crooked broom behind it. The scene looked as though the witch was stirring a brew, and for giggles, I stuck a battery operated fog machine inside the black iron pot, and turned it on.

Smoke billowed from the mouth of the cauldron, filling the window. Choking and waving my hands around, I scrambled to turn the fog machine off. *Well, so much for artistry.* I slumped back on the large window frame, thanking God it was just water vapor, and much to my embarrassment, I spotted Chloe across the street.

The door jingled.

"Hey," Chloe chirped from the doorway.

"Come on in, you can stand guard and make sure I don't kill myself with my own bright ideas, "I added wryly.

She giggled. "I saw. Maybe if you put the fog machine on low or empty out some of the soap mix it would work better."

I rolled my eyes. "Maybe. But if that doesn't work, that witch's brew is being served cold."

Chloe put down her bag and peeled off her jean jacket. "Here, give me the fog machine and I'll dump out half the soap in the bathroom sink."

I dropped my chin, giving Chloe a lopsided smile. "Thanks. And when you get back you can help me string these up with fishing wire so it looks like the witch is making them float around to eerie music." I said, pointing to the toy instruments lying by my feet. "My mom's got some ghostly music she wants to play in combination with the animatronic witch."

Wearing an excited smile, Chloe bounced toward the backroom. Man, that girl needed to get out more than I did.

Behind the register, I rummaged through my mother's tool box for a roll of clear fishing line and plastic hooks. I stuck five hooks in my mouth and grabbed the staple gun, as Chloe came back with the fog machine.

"All done," she said with a bright smile. "Wanna try it again?"

It was only water vapor, so what did we have to lose? I let Chloe place it in the bottom of the cauldron and then turn the switch to low. *Viola! Whaddaya know?* A tiny tendril of smoke-like steam rose from the center of the black pot.

Chloe clapped her hands once. "See, I'm not as much of a lost cause as you thought, Miss Artsy Fartsy pants!"

Half cringing, half laughing, I threw a plastic hook at her. "Artsy Fartsy pants? What are we, ten?"

She blew a razzberry my way. "Well, even without my expert suggestions, the window looks amazing."

"Thanks. We try."

"Ha. Try my butt cheeks. You guys have set the bar around here for window decorations. Have you seen what the ice cream shop is doing to keep up? In their window they've got vampire figurines scooping red velvet ice cream out of coffin shaped tubs!"

I guffawed. "No! That's great. I'll check it out tonight when I head over to meet Hunter and his crew after the team dinner. Wanna come with?"

She shook her head handing me one of the plastic brass-colored trumpets. "Nah. I don't want to be a third wheel."

I stopped what I was doing and looked at her. "Chloe, there's going to

be a crowd of people there. You won't be a third wheel. Plus Jenny is going to be there with Tyler. I could really use a friendly face, I mean, other than Hunter's."

She considered for a minute, before handing me the faux flute. "Maybe. I'll see what's going on later. If I can, I'll meet you there. What time?"

"Eight o'clock," I garbled through the thumb tacks in my teeth. I finished fastening the last of the wire and grabbed the clear hooks from the package lying on the floor. "I promise I won't hold you to it. Believe me, the idea of hanging out with the football crowd is as alien to me as it is to you, but Hunter asked, and I can't say no. It was my compromise after turning him down to be his date for the team dinner."

Chloe held out a plastic drum, which she pulled back when I reached for it. "You turned him *down*? Rowen! What is the matter with you? You don't turn down someone like Hunter Morrissey."

I laughed and yanked the drum from her hand. "It's all good, Chlo. We talked about it and Hunter understands. It's why I suggested going for ice cream afterward."

She hmmphed, her skepticism underlined by the sarcastic set of her jaw. "You suggested? Did that suggestion include the team and their entourage as well?"

I hesitated, my hand hooking the last instrument to the wire and adjusting its positioning. "No," I answered quietly. "But you know how nosy they all are. Hunter warned me last night that they would probably show, and to be honest, I expected as much."

Chloe inhaled with a loud sniff. "Okay, boss. I'll try to make it tonight, if only to watch the fireworks."

At the teasing remark, I threw another plastic hook at her. "You better watch it or I'll have my mother turn you into a permanent window display."

"Now, now, Rowen. Threats are Talia's deal, not yours."

"Ha. Tell me about it. You talk to her today?"

Chloe shook her head. "Nope. But her big date with Mike is tonight, so I didn't expect to. I'm sure the last thing she wants is me or you raining on her parade. I hope to God she doesn't do anything stupid."

I shrugged, climbing out of the window and closing the partition. "It's

her choice, and we can't do anything to change that. Come on, let's see what this looks like outside."

Chloe and I stood by the curb facing the store window. "Not bad," I said with a smile.

Chloe squinted at me. "I told you."

A horn beeped and we both turned. Talia was leaning out the passenger window of Mike's car. "Hey! Looks great, Rowen. See you tonight!"

Her voice trailed off as Mike sped off, his souped-up engine roaring noise pollution up and down Main Street. Typical.

Chloe looked at me. "Guess I will be tagging along tonight after all."

I laughed. "Good. Bring some popcorn. I think it's going to be quite a show."

Chapter 7

Main Street Sweets was crammed with customers despite the chilly evening. Indian summer may have claimed the daytime of late, but the night definitely belonged to Jack Frost. The wind off the river wasn't cooperating, and I shivered in my black leggings and cranberry colored hi-lo shirt dress, making me regret the decision to walk to the ice cream shop. I shivered again, pulling open the polished wood and glass door, praying for a drama free night.

Hunter was already inside, and I plastered a smile on my face for his benefit. I wasn't going to be the one to ruin this, adding to my plea that Jenny and Tyler were in an accommodating mood.

I walked in to the smell of homemade waffle cones and sweet cream. Bright and cheerful, with little round café tables and checkered tablecloths, the place hummed with low chatter, with the majority of the buzz coming from a few tables in the back. No surprise there, considering that's where Hunter sat with the rest of his gang.

He looked up, and the minute his gaze met mine, every other sight and sound fell away. His smile flashed full and gorgeous, and he walked over to where I stood like a paralytic inside the doorway.

"You made it," he said giving my cheek a quick peck. "I was starting to think you bailed."

I didn't have a chance to answer. Tyler had gotten up as well, and

followed on Hunter's heels.

"Well, look who decided to go slumming."

Hunter shot him a nasty look, but I managed to catch his eye, giving my head a quick shake. Hunter let the slight go, and I exhaled. I wasn't going to ruin this, but neither was I going to let Tyler Cavanaugh do it for me.

"You're right, Ty. I am slumming tonight. I decided to hang out with a bunch of smelly, ball-hugging Neanderthals—but then again, I didn't have much else going, so why not see how the other half lives?"

Tyler blinked, a momentary lapse in bravado leaving his mouth hanging open. Either my sarcasm went right over his head or he was floored I responded in such a civil manner.

When he opened his mouth and closed it again, I looked at Hunter and we both laughed. "Now, that's a first," Hunter said between chuckles.

One hurdle down.

Hunter introduced me around, which I thought silly since I knew everyone there by name, if not by previous introduction. Jenny sat to Tyler's right between him and Benny. She was conspicuously quiet, and only nodded her acknowledged hello, not a sarcastic quip in sight. Was she holding out for the right moment to zing one at me, or had she decided to call a truce? I studied her from the corner of my eye while Hunter left to get me a waffle cone with two scoops of pure pistachio.

Jenny wasn't her usual self. At least three different conversations were going on at the various tables where we all sat, and she was usually at the center of each one. Maybe being escorted out of the gym by the school Resource Officer on Thursday scared her. Tyler on the other hand was up to his old tricks. He plopped down in Hunter's chair while he was at the counter, and pulled himself so close to me that our arms touched.

"Your nice and toasty, Rowen, and you smell good. What's that scent? Love Potion #9?"

I smiled sweetly refusing to let him bait me. At the love potion joke, Ben laughed, but Jenny didn't even crack a smile.

Hunter glanced over, both annoyed at Tyler and concerned for me. I blew him a kiss. Like he had said once before—*Solidarity, baby.*

"Benny, you idiot!" Jenny shrilled, sounding like herself for the first

time since I got there. "Do you think you could eat like a human instead of a pig in a trough? Look at my sweater!"

Benny had reached across the table to snag Tyler's Coke, slopping raspberry chocolate truffle ice cream across the front of Jenny's white silk sweater. She pushed her stool back from the table with a huff. Jenny wasn't my favorite person, but I felt bad for her as she headed toward the ladies room. I never carry a purse, but tonight I was making an effort and borrowed one from my mom. I knew there was probably a Tide stain stick somewhere in the inside zipper pocket. My mother kept one in every bag she owned.

"Excuse me," I murmured, sliding out from my seat and crossing behind Benny to the open floor.

I opened the door to the ladies room trying not to be obvious. The sound of soft crying greeted me beside the hum of the overhead heater. Unsure, I hesitated, turning in a halfhearted retreat back to the table when the crying stopped. Muffled sniffles followed the sound of toilet paper being pulled from the roll, and I waited another moment, not wanting to intrude any further into Jenny's trouble than I already had.

"You can come in, Rowen. I'm done," she called from behind the stall door.

I didn't know what to say. "I'm not trying to butt in, Jen. I found a stain stick in my bag and I thought it might help." When she didn't reply, I placed the pen-like stain remover on the white porcelain and opened the door to head back to the table. "I'll leave it here on the sink. You can keep it."

Feeling stupid, I walked back to the others with my head down. Why did I think she'd even bother to say thank you?

Loud snickering and Benny's snort of laughter shot across the room. "She looks good wrapped around you, Morrissey." Tyler's voice prompted and my head snapped up.

I had to blink twice at the sight of Constance draped across Hunter's lap. As if struck by a sudden loss of motor skills, I froze, dropping my bag and everything in it to the floor.

"Rowen!" Hunter called out, pushing his chair back in a rough screech, depositing Constance in an unflattering heap to the floor.

With calm I didn't know I possessed, I gathered up my bag and

walked the rest of the way to the table. Someone had placed my melting ice cream in a bowl with the cone pointed up. To me it looked like the dunce cap I deserved for agreeing to come here tonight.

Was Hunter at the center of this? No. Of that I was sure. Just as I was sure I didn't belong here. Not with his friends, and maybe not even with him. Who was I kidding? It's not like he asked me to be his girlfriend or anything. If Jenny wasn't feeling sorry for herself in the bathroom, I would have bet she was behind Connie's antics just to spite me—but one look at Ty and I knew he and 'the boys' were having a little fun— probably encouraged Constance while at the same time egging Hunter on, telling him it was just a joke. Except this time the joke was on me. *Not.*

Maybe Hunter wasn't as perfect as I had made myself believe. I mean, he stood up to Tyler when he blamed me for what happened with the resource officer, yet at the same time makes excuses for the boy. How much benefit of the doubt can you give before it makes you look like a first class chump? Hunter was too good to be true. But maybe being too good, was his biggest fault.

I slipped my bag over my arm and straightened my shoulders, ready to leave. "Don't anyone get up on my account."

"Rowen!" Hunter was up and out of his seat in a flash, his hand a staying force on my forearm. "It's not what you think?"

"Why do you care what I think? It's not like I'm your girlfriend or anything. You can have any bimbo you want give you a lap dance, but if this is what you meant by *whatever comes next,* then I pass."

His face looked like I had just slapped him.

Crap. My face grew hot, and I wanted to bite my tongue until I tasted blood. I didn't mean to, but I'd hurt his feelings, but then again he was the one with another girl sitting on his lap. To his immense credit, instead of blowing me off like most of his friends would, he kept his hand on my arm and his eyes locked on mine.

"Rowen, Constance's heel broke and she was falling. I caught her before she smashed her head on the edge of the table, and the two of us fell back onto my chair. She was catching her breath when you came out of the bathroom." Hunter slid his eyes to Tyler and the look he gave his friend would have withered anything with a pulse. "As to our resident A-hole and his verbal diarrhea, Tyler was just being the jerk he always is."

Behind Hunter, Constance nodded, holding her shoe in one hand and the broken heel in the other for me to see. "I know how it looks, Rowen, and I don't blame you for freaking, but Hunter's telling the truth."

Jenny came out of the room scrubbing the front of her sweater with a paper towel, my stain remover between her teeth. She stopped short, looking a bit like an elegant golden retriever with a stick in its mouth. Her eyes went from me and Hunter to Constance and then finally, to Tyler and Benny. She spit the stain pen into her hand, and wiped her mouth on her sleeve. "What'd I miss?"

With a sharp exhale, Hunter let go of my arm and put his hand up. "Nothing, Jenny. Just a misunderstanding between me and my girlfriend." He swiveled his gaze back to me, one eyebrow raised, daring me to argue the point again.

I cleared my voice, trying to sound cool instead of the jelly-legged mess I really was. "Well, it's not like you asked me or anything." I mumbled, knowing how lame I sounded.

Hunter's lips slid into a grin that slowly spread across his full mouth. "Asked, huh?" Slipping his hands over my shoulders and down my arms, he unlocked the vice grip I had across my chest and moved in even closer. He cupped the back of my head and glided his other arm around my waist, pulling me against him.

My breath caught in my throat as his mouth skimmed over mine. For a second I forgot where we were, and I wrapped my arms around his neck and kissed him back.

At the hoots and cat calls from the other tables, flames shot straight into my cheeks and I tensed. Hunter took a step back, snaking his arm around my shoulder. I wiped my mouth with the side of my hand, and pressed my face into his chest to hide my embarrassment.

Chuckling, he lifted my chin. "Well, Ms. Corbett how's that for asking?"

I was still trying to remember how to speak, when one of the managers asked if we could either sit down or take it outside.

We walked arm in arm to our table, and from the corner of my eye I caught Tyler's expression as he stared at Hunter with his arm around my shoulders. An odd chill crept up my spine, and as if sensing it, Hunter pressed a kiss along my temple, and that's all it took to chase the errant

shiver back where it belonged.

I let the weird feeling pass, focusing instead on my boyfriend's gorgeous and talented mouth. *Boyfriend.* It was all I could do not to squeal like a fan-girl at a One Direction concert. I was on cloud nine, and nothing was going to ruin this for me, not even the dirty look Jenny shot my way.

"Rowen, are you listening to me or do I need to kiss you again to get you to pay attention?"

"Only if you feel it's necessary," I said, smiling up at him.

"I scheduled an appointment for us at the Historical Society on Tuesday, right after school. Mrs. Scarborough's going to be there for only a little while, but she said we could stay after as long as the intern helping her with cataloging can let us out."

"Sounds good."

"Also, there are only a few afternoon tours scheduled over the next week or so at the Old Dutch Church. After that, they stop for the winter. I talked to the groundskeeper. He said we could poke around in the vaults below the chapel after services this Sunday if we were quiet and kept it short."

Tyler snorted. He had one arm slung over the back of Jenny's chair, and the other in his lap, his hand shoved into the top of his waistband. "Morrissey you are turning into a first class geek. First, honors classes and now you're hanging out in cemeteries. What gives?" He leaned forward taking his straw from his glass and sucked the remaining chocolate shake from inside. Sitting back with his legs splayed, he chewed on the straw's end waiting for Hunter to jump on the defensive.

It turned my stomach, and I couldn't believe I ever found him attractive. Tyler liked seeing how far he could push it. In fact, I'd heard stories about how he liked to force girls into dangerous situations and then take advantage of their fear, forcing them to do things they wouldn't normally do. I chalked it up to gossip, but now I wasn't so sure.

"If I remember correctly, dude, you like hanging out at cemeteries, too." Both eyebrows hiked up attached to a pointed look, and everyone knew Hunter was referring to the party set for next week.

"*Pffft.* That's different, man. Nothing like a boneyard on Halloween for a scare fest."

Hunter slapped his forehead and even Benny shot Tyler a look. To her

credit, Jenny gave Tyler a hard pinch for being obtuse and broadcasting our plans to the general public.

"Oww! What was that for?"

"For Christ sake, Tyler, put a cork in it! Do you want us busted for trespassing before we even get there Saturday night?"

Tyler made a face, but Jenny's words shut him up.

Pouting, she pushed from the table. "I'm bored. Let's get out of here." Turning on her heel to leave, she hesitated by my chair. I met her sideways glance, bracing for a snide comment, but instead she gave me a closed lipped smile. "Thanks," she mumbled, and then whined again for Tyler to hurry up.

They left, followed shortly after by Benny and the others.

Hunter spooned up the last of his Oreo bomb ice cream, licking it clean. "It never changes, does it?"

I shook my head. "Nope, but at least they're consistent."

I kept watching the door wondering what had kept Chloe, but as it was already ten p.m., I knew she wasn't coming. Talia and Mike were no shows, too.

"Listen, after the game tomorrow, I'll meet you by my car in the senior parking lot. We can grab that pizza I promised you, and then we can head to the Blaze to help your mom."

I turned my attention back to Hunter. "I think pizza might have to wait. I promised my mother we'd be there by five."

"You expect me to do manual labor on an empty stomach?"

"Never," I said with a laugh. "We can call ahead and pick it up on the way."

"Come on," he said handing me my purse. "Coach already gave us the *women weaken legs* speech from Rocky, so I'd better take you home. I've got to run rings around Tyler tomorrow and I don't need extra laps because coach thinks I'm doggin' it on the field."

I groaned.

"Oh no…You promised," he said with a sharp lilt that matched his *no excuses, you will be there* expression.

"One o'clock, sharp. Right?"

Hunter's lips parted into a ghost of a smirk. "Bring hot chocolate. Pom-poms optional."

Hollow's End

Saturday dawned bright and clear. The air was crisp, and according to the radio, a perfect day for football. I rolled over, fumbling on my nightstand to mute the *too perky for this early in the morning* voice that just ruined my day. The weather spell I dug out of my mother's arsenal wasn't giving me the nor'easter I'd hoped for. It was cosmically settled, then. I was going to a football game.

I padded into the kitchen, my shearling slippers making a scuff, scuff sound as I dragged my butt into a chair.

"Aren't you a bundle of sunshine this morning? Did we not sleep well last night?" my mother asked, her chipper tone grating on my nerves as much as the weather.

"Hmmph. A lot you care. You wouldn't help me with my climate charm last night, so now I get to be all Rah, Rah, Go Horseman!"

My mother looked at me, her tangible disappointment making me wince as much as her steady gaze. "You sound like a brat, so cut it out, Rowen. Did you ever think you might enjoy yourself?"

Coffee was perking on the stove, and the scent of fresh rolls lifted my spirits a little. "Why would you think that?"

She raised an eyebrow, pouring me a cup of coffee with a dollop of cinnamon sweet cream, her mouth curving into one of her troublemaking smiles. "Because, smarty pants, you've never been to a football game."

"So?"

"So, how can you know you won't like something, if you never try it?"

I exhaled. "Mother, this isn't like trying a new food. I've seen enough football in bits and pieces to make an educated guess."

She handed me the mug of coffee and then leaned on the table facing me. "That may be so, but watching snippets on TV won't give you the whole experience, plus you've never seen Hunter in his football uniform.

"…and again, so?"

She smirked. "You're really not thinking outside the box this morning, are you? I know you think Hunter and his teammates are a bunch of bullies knocking their heads together for a stupid ball—and there's validity to your argument—but there is also something to be said for watching the play of testosterone on the field. And let's not forget the

fringe benefit of how football pants and shoulder pads accentuate the male body—especially when that body is already very nicely put together.

"Eeeww, Mom!"

"Relax, Rowen," she replied, walking to the counter to top up her own mug. "I'm not going all cougar on Hunter. I was talking about your dad. He was a Horseman too, you know."

I swiveled in my seat to face her, and the expression on my face must have been laughable. Mom almost spewed her Italian roast.

Wiping her mouth on the back of her hand, she put her cup down and grabbed a napkin from the holder next to the coffeepot. "Don't look so shocked," she said, dabbing the side of her mouth "He was a fullback, and let me tell you he filled out that red and white uniform, very, very nicely." Waggling her eyebrows at me, she crumpled her napkin and tossed it into the trash.

"Mom!" I wanted to stick my fingers in my ears and sing the alphabet song. "Jeez, Mother, what's next, you telling me you were a cheerleader, like Jenny?'

Her playful smile faded, her demeanor taking on a slightly dispirited feel. "No. I was very much like you. Growing up with Gran wasn't easy, and I didn't have the same…" she paused, considering me. "…the same freedoms, I give you. I went to your father's games because they were the only normal things I had in my life."

She was quiet after that, and I didn't know what to say. My mother never elaborated, but from the comments Gran let fall around here, I knew she made my mother's life claustrophobic, especially when it came to the study of spell craft.

"Mom…"

She shook her head. "Problems long past, sweetheart, and time has mellowed my memory, if not your grandmother. Besides, I was lucky. I got to marry my football star and had a happily ever after. The cheerleader lost out. You remember that."

She grabbed her mug off the counter and walked over to where I sat, wordless. Reaching out, she brushed the hair from my eyes like she did when I was small, and then rested her hand on my cheek. "Go to the game and have fun," she murmured. "Hunter wants you there. That

should be enough." With no other word, her hand slid from my cheek to pat my arm, and she left, taking her coffee into her work room, leaving me to fend for myself for breakfast.

I puttered around the kitchen thinking about what she said. My mother never shared that part of her past unless there was something she wanted me to learn. When it came to my dad, my memories were faded at best. He was a carpenter, a man who loved to design and build things with his hands. I never would have linked him with the celebrated meatheads I see strutting through the halls at school.

Appetite gone, I stopped scrambling eggs and cheese, and pushed away the bowl with the soupy yellow mixture. God, my mother was good. Whether I wanted to admit it or not, I needed an attitude adjustment when it came to Hunter and his friends. I was guilty of lumping them together with Tyler and Jenny, when I didn't know them well enough to say anything more than hello or goodbye. Tyler was one person, and Hunter had been trying to get me to see that all along.

Suddenly the idea of seeing Hunter in his uniform and watching him run the field in those tight white pants had me squirming in my seat. I finished cooking breakfast and poured a cup of warm cider, not wanting a second cup of coffee, taking them both to my room to plan. If I was going to Hunter's game, I was going to do it up right.

I opened my drawer and took out a pair of skinny jeans and the one red and white Horseman sweatshirt I owned. The doorbell rang downstairs and I heard my mother walk across the foyer to answer it.

Unconcerned, I headed into the bathroom and hung my bathrobe on the hook behind the door, surprised when my mother's voice and soft knock happened at my bedroom door.

"Rowen?"

"I'm just getting into the shower, Mom. What is it?"

"A package came for you."

Puzzled, I threw on my robe, tying a clumsy knot at my waist before opening my bedroom door. In my mother's hand was a plastic grocery bag.

"What is it?" I asked, glancing at the lumpy sack dangling from my mother's fingers. "Who dropped it off?"

"Don't know," she said, letting one shoulder rise and fall, but the

teasing look on her face told me she positively did know. "Just untie it and see for yourself."

I took the bag from her and fumbled with the knot, finally resorting to ripping the plastic with my fingers. A large white football jersey with red trim fell into my hand.

I blinked at it and then looked at my mother, her knowing smile making my cheeks grow warm. It was Hunter's away jersey, just as he promised.

Red collegiate lettering on the front spelled out Sleepy Hollow, and when I turned it over it had Hunter's number on the back.

"Forty-Four. Good solid number, grounded and stable just like Hunter," my mom said. "Very telling, don't you think?"

The question was rhetorical, but that didn't stop her from tilting her head as if expecting me to answer.

"Take your shower," she added, gesturing toward my bathroom before turning to head back downstairs. "...and I would wear a tee-shirt underneath, if I were you. It tends to get breezy on the stands."

I closed my door, tossing the plastic bag in the trash bin beneath my desk. So I was taking pre-game fashion advice from my mother, of all people. Who would have thought?

With a shaky breath, I held the white polyester blend up to my body and looked in the full length mirror hanging on the back of my bathroom door. My bathrobe made the jersey's outline look bumpy and unflattering, but on its own with the right pair of pants or leggings, I could definitely make this work.

As I looked at my reflection it hit me. Wearing Hunter's jersey to the game made a statement. And as the thought crossed my mind, my old fear reached up and grabbed me by my throat. The same fear that said, "Keep to yourself; don't let anyone in because you might get hurt." I squashed the errant and hurtful thought and replaced it with how I knew Hunter would look when he saw me wearing his number.

The idea of making him happy and proud brought a smile to my face, and I swear, if I had the pom-poms he teased me about, I would have done an all-American cheer.

Chapter 8

Where have you been?" Chloe hissed at me as I climbed to sit next to her on the top row of the bleachers. "Jeez, Rowen, Hunter's been searching the stands for you for the last a half hour."

"Sorry, time just got away from me."

Everyone around us was sitting, so I took advantage and stepped onto the metal bench to look for Hunter. "Where is he, Chlo?"

She pointed to the row of red clad monsters lining the side of the field. They were in their home jerseys, and immediately, I saw what my mother was talking about. They looked like Titans in their tidy whites. Not a Neanderthal in sight.

I spotted Hunter's number at the center of the group, and he looked amazing. The tight white material contoured his strong, muscled thighs and his shoulder pads gave him an even broader god-like physique. He turned then, and my breath caught in my throat.

"He looks good, huh?" Chloe said with a giggle.

I didn't answer. I just stared, licking my lips.

"Well, don't stand there like an idiot, call him," she said holding a makeshift bullhorn curled from the game day program.

I took it from her, hesitating for a moment before holding it up to my mouth.

"Hunter!" I shouted, and he turned to face the stands, his hand

coming up to shield the sun from his eyes.

I waved, swinging my arms side to side above my head like a crazed fan. He grinned, waving back. Then pointing to me, he tugged the sleeve of his own jersey, shooting me thumbs up.

Just as I thought, he was clearly pleased I wore the jersey, and I turned, modeling his number on my back, blowing him a kiss. His grin spread to a full on gorgeous smile, and he nodded, blowing me a kiss right back. In that moment I wasn't on top of the bleachers. I was on top of the world.

The horn blew for the start of the game, and Chloe pulled me down next to her. "Don't distract him. Just cheer when I tell you to and you'll be fine," she said, handing me one end of her red fleece Horseman blanket to spread over our legs.

I sat mesmerized for the next hour and a half, getting up to stretch only when the Sleepy Hollow pep band took the field at half time.

"Do you want to grab something to eat? Now's the time to do it, because the game is close and you're not going to want to get up and walk past the Ossining kids, not wearing what your wearing. Hunter is tearing up the field and he and Tyler are sticking it to the Ossining QB every chance they get."

"Good. Whatever that means. As for Ossining, I don't care if they talk trash." I got up from my spot on the bleachers. "Come on, let's get a hot dog."

Chloe looked at me funny.

"What?"

"Who are you, and what have you done with my best friend?"

"What?" I said, again.

"Hot dogs? I know you do chips and soda from time to time, but never processed meat."

I laughed. "Okay, so maybe not a hot dog, but I've got to eat something or I'll scare people by the time this game is over with how ravenous I am."

Chloe put her hands on her knees and got up with a puffed exhale. "Let's go, but leave the blanket so no one takes or spot. Maybe they'll have tofu dogs and all will be right with the world again."

We stood in the refreshment line, and I caught Jenny looking at me

from the cotton candy stand. I lifted my chin, giving her a quick smile of acknowledgement, but didn't push it. She was wearing Tyler's away jersey, and I knew she was eyeing me in Hunter's.

I should have known. Just like with Tyler, any bit of encouragement was viewed as an invitation, and she came walking over, but I didn't care. It was as if Hunter's jersey was a kind of protective armor, giving me a true confidence I'd only faked in the past.

"Hi," Jenny said in her high pitched squeak.

"Jen," I nodded once. "Enjoying the game so far?"

Her eyes narrowed momentarily, as if trying to decipher any hidden sarcasm in my question, but after a moment she relaxed back into her normal perkiness, albeit a tone usually reserved for her friends.

"Yeah, it's a good game. Hunter's playing well, don't you think?"

I looked at Chloe who had turned away, her wide eyed, *what the hell is up with this* look, hidden behind the super-sized slushy she just paid for.

"I guess. It seems exciting, but I don't really understand most of what's happening. Chloe is filling me in as we go."

At the mention of her name, Chloe had the good manners to turn around and nod to Jen, but then shot me a sideways look as she handed me my soda, telling me in unspoken words to leave her out of whatever trouble Jen was stirring.

Ignoring Chloe altogether, Jenny flipped her long gold hair back over her shoulder. "Well, that's good. You need to know what's going on so you can understand what Hunter is gushing about later."

I nodded, but had no intention of sitting bright eyed and adoring as Hunter relived his glory moments. We didn't work that way. I was proud of him, and I would tell him so, but I wasn't about to turn into a fantasy football groupie.

"Where's your other friend, the blonde. What's her name?"

My gaze tightened. Now we were getting to the real reason she walked over. I tilted my head suspiciously. "Talia? I haven't seen her. Why?"

Jenny took a breath and flashed a small tight smile. "No reason. I thought the three of you were inseparable, that's all."

Chloe turned around at this point, her eyes daggers pointed right at Jen. "We're friends, Jen. Just like you and your crew. Then again, we're

not joined at the hip and we don't follow one person around while doing the 'we're not worthy' bow."

I shot Chloe a look.

Jen's eyes gave Chloe a once over, and in that moment Jen let her perky veneer slip to what was truly beneath all her sugar. "I heard she and Mike had quite a date last night."

Her snide tone drifted off for effect, and she raised both eyebrows setting the bait for either me or Chloe to react. Both Chloe and I stared her down, though, neither giving her an inch.

A melodramatic sigh escaped Jenny's lips, and she signaled for her crew to fall back in tow as her plan clearly wasn't eliciting the response she expected. "Well, there's no accounting for taste on Mike's part." She backpedalled but still turned her attention to me, a single flick of her eyes indicating Hunter's jersey. "When you want to play with the big girls, Rowen, you know where to find me."

Expletives exploded in a whispered rant from under Chloe's breath, and I burst out laughing. "So much for staying on neutral ground, Ms. Switzerland."

"Oh, pleeeese! The only reason she came over was to start trouble with Talia."

"I can't figure Jen out anymore. One minute she's queen shrew, and the next she's crying into her Coca-Cola." I told Chloe about the stain remover incident and she nearly choked on her blue raspberry slush.

I pounded her on the back, and she laughed even harder.

"Take it easy or that blue stuff is going to come out your nose."

She took a second to catch her breath before grabbing my hand and pulling me behind the kids jumping castle.

"Stop it, Chlo, what are you doing? You're going to spill that blue crap all over me."

She pulled me to a halt and then peered around the plastic bumper through the nylon mesh in the direction Jen had gone. "We should follow her."

"Who?"

She shot me a look.

When it dawned on me, I shook my head, waving my hands in a definitive 'no' motion in front of me. "No way, Chloe. Talia's

conspicuously M.I.A. because she's afraid to show her face now the entire school knows the stunt she pulled. No ma'am. I'm not stirring the pot on this brew. If you think I want to be any more of a social outcast than I already am, you're crazy."

Chloe's face hardened. "Social outcast? Correct me if I'm wrong, but didn't you just get the equivalent of an engraved invitation to hang with the queen?"

I frowned, my mouth half way between a sneer and a disappointed moue. "Yeah. Right. And it's not hard to guess the reasons behind her comradely display. First, because she wanted to stick it to you and Talia, and second because I'm wearing Hunter's jersey. She has to ask me now that I'm his girlfriend."

"What? Is there some messed up 2013 version of the Pink Lady Code I'm unaware of?"

I gave her a blank stare.

"The Pink Ladies? From the movie, *Grease*?"

People turned at the very unladylike noise that resonated from my mouth. "Gimme just a small break, Chlo, willya?"

The horn sounded for the beginning of the second half, and we walked back to the stands in silence.

The fact that Talia was a no show again, was beginning to make me worry. I fingered my cell phone in the pocket of my jeans, but decided not to call. She'd catch up with us at some point—if not tomorrow, then Monday morning for lattes, and I made a promise to myself not to be late.

We got back to our seats and no sooner had we weaved through the sea of knees and laps, then the entire stadium was on its feet. Hunter had intercepted a pass and was barreling down the field taking yard after yard on his way to the end zone and a much needed touchdown. I held my breath when he tumbled over the white painted line in the grass and the opposing team piled on him as if they wanted to grind him into the earth. Chloe grabbed my hand, and the entire stands exploded in cheers when he still held the ball. The Horseman gained a tremendous lead and still had possession of the ball...or at least that's what the guy next to us said.

All I knew was Hunter was okay after that pile up and I took an easy breath as the team set up for another play. They had only ten yards to go,

and the center snapped the ball to Tyler and in a fake out pass he rushed the ball, passing it back handed to Hunter who ran the last ten yards to score giving the Horseman a seven point lead.

"Did you see that? That was amazing! Say what you want about Tyler, but that boy can play football!" Chloe hooted and hollered, and when someone asked who scored the touchdown, she turned me around, showing everyone that my boyfriend was the one who just scored for the red and white.

"Here ya' go, 44-girl!" someone shouted, tossing me a multicolored beach ball. "Let's get a wave going!"

Someone else clapped, telling me to toss the ball to them, and before long it was batted back and forth through the crowd to the tune of "Let's go, Horseman!" Laughing at the cheers and cat calls for Hunter and Tyler, I ducked the beach ball volley, not wanting to ruin it with my lack of coordination, but on the last pass it was coming right at me so I reached for it, squeezing my eyes shut.

"Way to go, Ro!" Chloe cheered, when my hands actually locked onto the silly ball.

I opened my eyes, and vertigo hit hard and fast, dizziness taking me as my eyesight faltered and I fell back against the bleachers. Chloe screamed, and I heard her yelling for me, but it was at a distance, the same way Hunter's voice sounded when I passed out in the hallway outside calculus.

My fingers squeezed the plastic, but the feel of it was slick, wet, stringy. A stench reeked of moldy earth and rot. I gulped in air, and forced my fingers to let go of whatever I grasped. As it rolled from my hands, I felt the contours of cheekbones, a nose, and mouth. There was no doubt. I held a severed head.

I waited, counting to ten as I took short, shallow breaths. Chloe's voice and the voices of the people around me became clearer, more distinct, and when I could smell Chloe's blue raspberry slush that spilled on the bleacher when she dropped her cup to catch me, I knew it was safe to open my eyes.

Her gaze searched mine, and she helped me to sit straight.

I ran a hand over my forehead and tried to smile. "See, I told you I should have gotten a hot dog." I gave her a sheepish look, and she

smacked my shoulder before bursting out in laughter, half from annoyance and the other half from me scaring the crud out of her.

"Since when do you suffer from low blood sugar? I think you're just swoony over your jock boyfriend," she said with a smirk, and pulled a Snickers bar from her sweatshirt pocket.

"Where the hell did you get that?"

"I bought it when I got the slushy. Now, eat before you get pissy like in one of those commercials."

"I do not get grouchy or diva-like when hungry."

"Okay, Crabby Miss Pass-Out Pants. Whatever you say." She unwrapped half the candy bar and handed it to me.

I didn't want to argue the point. Let her think it was low blood sugar. There was no way I was explaining my cosmic near miss to her or anyone else. Despite myself, I was actually having a blast, and later I would have my sexy football player all to myself…well, for a little while anyway until we headed to the Blaze.

The game ended around four p.m., giving me just enough time to change my clothes and be back before Hunter got out of the locker room. We grabbed a quick pizza and headed up to the Van Cortlandt estate, pulling up to the gates a little after five p.m. My mother hated tardiness, and I prayed she wouldn't make a big deal about it. After all, we were here and the first tour wasn't for another two hours.

The gatekeeper waved Hunter's car through as soon he saw he was with me. My mother was probably hard at work organizing the grounds like a five star general. The decorations were incredible, with each themed section casting an eerie glow in the dark, as the place buzzed with last minute activity. Disney's Haunted Mansion had nothing on Van Cortlandt Manor during the Blaze. It was nature and art incarnate.

"This is great! It's just as spooky as the Horseman's Hollow," Hunter said pulling around to the visitor's parking lot. "Even better, because it's a beautiful, classy sort of creepy."

"Seriously? You can't compare that cheesy fright night event with the Blaze. Vampires, ghouls and psychos waiting to jump from dark corners and scare the crap out of everyone. I don't think so. What was it you said to Mr. Conover…gimme a break?"

Hunter grinned parking the car under a security light close to the path. "Some kind of witch you are, scared of things that go bump in the night."

"Yeah, right," I murmured back, a frown pulling at the corners of my mouth. "Take a walk around the inside of my head, and then come talk to me about being scared. Cheesy special effects and people running around in costumes are not going to haunt my nightmares."

His smiled faded and his forehead creased. "Sorry, Rowen. I didn't mean anything by it, I was just kidding around."

I shrugged. "I know."

Leaning over, he cupped his hand behind my head, pressing his lips to mine. My entire body sighed at the feel, and I went a little limp. His tongue darted around with mine and the sweet taste of his mouth made my lower belly jump.

"How long before your mother sends her own minions of darkness looking for us?" he whispered against my mouth between kisses.

I couldn't help but smile. "Now that's a scary thought."

Chuckling, he caressed the back of my neck, his fingers trailing along the scooped edge of my knit top. "No joke. But I'll chance it if you will," he said raising a curious eyebrow.

I kissed him this time, running my fingers through his dark hair and wrapping my arms around the back of his neck. Lost in the kiss, I barely noticed the pinpoint glow of a flashlight and the sound of someone tapping on the driver's side window.

"Hey! You two aren't supposed to be here!" A muffled voice yelled through the slightly fogged up glass. "Hey! You hear me in there? Don't make me have to call the cops."

Hunter and I flew apart like someone sprayed us with a garden hose. *Crap!* Clearing his voice, he rolled down the window. "Sorry, we were just getting out."

The security guard's eyes widened when he saw it was me in the passenger seat. "Rowen. Your mother just asked me if I'd seen you. You'd better get going or I'm not the one you'll have to worry about!"

Hunter glanced at me and got out of the car first. I did a quick check in the vanity mirror behind the visor and climbed out of the car as well. "Sorry, Joe," I said straightening my jacket self-consciously. "Is my mom

still out back by the ferry house?"

"Yeah, and she's got her hands full, too. The staff had to carve a whole bunch of new Jacks a.s.a.p. because of all the warm weather. They need to be pulled out or by tomorrow we'll be buried in rotten, hollowed out gruesome ghouls and fairies, with a mob of unhappy tourists on our heels."

Hunter coughed back a snort. "We're on it. Come on, Rowen."

"Here…take my extra flashlight," Joe said handing it to Hunter, fixing him with a hard look. "I wouldn't want you two to get lost or sidetracked. Follow the path past the main house and then head straight."

My cheeks burned at his insinuation, and I was glad it was dark or my embarrassment would have been triple. Hunter slid his arm around my shoulder and clicked on the flashlight. "Thanks, man," was all he said and steered us toward the path.

I gave Joe a lame wave and buried my face in Hunter's chest.

"There you are!" my mother said peeling a pair of gardening gloves from her hands as she came toward us. They were covered in dirt and bits of pumpkin, and made a wet splat when she tossed them on the stone bench to the side of the tented carving area. "What happened? I expected you an hour ago."

She gave of us each a hug, and I knew she didn't really need an answer because her face told me she already knew. "Getting to know each other, huh?" she said with too wide a smile.

"Mom!" I half groaned, half hissed. "You said five o'clock was fine."

"Oh stop it, I'm teasing." Hooking one arm in mine and the other in Hunter's, she led us where volunteers were working. "Everyone, you remember my daughter, Rowen…and this is Hunter."

The telltale nuance she employed while introducing Hunter left me mortified and I immediately shot him an apologetic look. Much to my chagrin, he wore an ear to ear grin.

"Ha. Just wait 'til you meet my grandmother then we'll see who has the last laugh," I sniffed.

He burst out laughing and even my mother fought back a smile. I bit back on the snarky remark I had waiting, instead resigning myself to my mother's good-natured teasing. I shot Hunter another look, consoling myself with the fact that paybacks are indeed sweet.

"Come on you two, there's a lot to do. Hunter, will you get the schematic for the north part of the path, the one that winds past the Infinity theme? It's inside on the table," she smiled waving him off.

Still laughing, he shrugged and headed toward the front stairs of the ferry house.

"So, how was your day? Did you enjoy the game? Besides your little make out session in the car, anything else I should know about?" she asked with a playful glint in her eyes.

"Mom!" I hissed again.

"I'm sorry sweetie, I can't help it. You two are just too cute together."

"Ugh, will you stop!"

"Okay, okay. But seriously, anything else happen today? Any visions?"

I sighed, shaking my head, but also making sure to avoid her eyes. Technically it wasn't a lie, as I didn't have a vision as much as a tactile episode. I didn't 'see' anything, just felt it.

"No, thank God. I guess the mojo bag worked or maybe it was just a freaky glitch and now it's over."

"We'll see, I guess," she replied and then turned with a smile as Hunter walked back and handed her the schematic. "Thanks. This is where the two of you will be headed with the mini pickup truck. You'll be working on replacing the pumpkins around the giant spider's web. Hunter, can you drive a standard shift?"

"Sure, why?"

"The mini is a four wheel drive standard, and Rowen can't drive a stick shift. I'll follow behind with one of the others. It's going to take four of us to unload and then replace the Jacks accordingly. If you go with Leslie, the two of you can bring the trucks around so we can load up. She's one of our set designers."

Hunter followed Leslie toward the Manor house, and I glanced at the flood of work surrounding us. I was amazed. The place was like a military tactical unit, only with pumpkins.

"So, has Hunter said anything about his family's history yet? Anyone we can link to these visions of yours?"

Before I could answer, Leslie pulled up next to the carving tent with Hunter right behind. Everyone pitched in and the pumpkins were

loaded, and I jumped into the cab with Hunter, while my mother went with Leslie. We followed them, the gravel crunching under the tires echoing louder in the darkness the farther away we got from the carving site.

The headlights gleamed, but the light refracting off the ground fog gave the atmosphere a creepy, almost sinister feel. Hunter and I hadn't said a word, and my fingers played with the cord holding the mojo bag around my neck almost of their own volition.

"You're too quiet. What's the matter?"

I shook my head, but kept my eyes trained on the road. "Nothing really. I was just thinking about how surreal this place looks."

"Seriously. But after the last week or so, it fits."

"I suppose," I muttered. But I wasn't thinking about that. I was all too aware of Hunter, and how his close proximity made my heart skip beats.

"What?"

I turned my head and took in the perfect curve of his profile. Was he getting lessons from my mother on how to see into my head? "What, yourself?"

He was silent for a moment then slid his eyes sideways, a concern evident in the way he looked at me. "Something's got you by the tail and it's not the visions you've been having. Is it me?"

In the dark, with the glow from the full moon, he was breathtaking. Part of me wanted to tell him how he unnerved me, the other part just wanted to tuck myself under his arm and let my fingers glide over the hard planes of his chest.

As if he'd read my mind, he swung his arm over and pulled me in close to his side. He drove with one hand draped over the steering wheel and the other draped over my shoulder until he saw Leslie's brake lights, and had to downshift to pull up behind her and park.

The spider's web was to our left and it was enormous. Like most of the themed exhibits, it was a massive undertaking, but it was easy to see why the staff was in a panic. There were hundreds of jack-o-lanterns placed on the grass and in the surrounding areas that needed to be removed.

The sun had done a number on many of the fresh pumpkins, and it was all the staff of twenty carvers could do to keep up. They had over 900

volunteers scooping, but it was solely the responsibility of the staff and a few extra helpers to carve and place all 4,000 pumpkins for the event. No wonder Mom needed help tonight.

We climbed out of the truck, and Hunter grabbed the two battery operated camp lanterns Leslie had put in the back of the flatbed along with the Jacks. Handing one to me, we joined my mother, already unloading the back of her truck.

"We'll have to unload here first, and then carry in the jack-o-lanterns one at a time. We'll swap them out as we go, and carry the ruined ones back to the trucks. You two get started toward the left, and Leslie and I will take the right," my mother said picking up a twenty-five pound Jack like it weighed nothing.

I resisted the urge to salute, instead picking up a jack-o-lantern myself and heading toward the left as instructed, with Hunter carrying two large pumpkins in his arms alongside me.

"Are you trying to give yourself a hernia, or you just showing off?" I teased picking my way through the creepy maze of round, unlit faces.

"Funny. But, hey, if it turns you on…" he shot back with a sexy shrug, letting his voice trail off.

My face flushed and I was thankful once again that it was dark. Putting down his arm load near mine, he lifted two ruined pumpkins and handed one my way, leaning in to brush his lips across mine in the process.

I held my breath, completely unused to the attention, but loving it all the same. An image of Hunter taking me by the hand and pulling me down next to him in the grass went through my mind, and I closed my eyes. Now that was the sort of vision I didn't mind barging through my head. My hand rested on my stomach and I exhaled trying to quell the butterflies that had taken up permanent residence since our first kiss.

Somehow I managed to keep my hands to myself, and we carried pumpkins for about an hour. We took a short break, and my mother handed us each a bottle of water. I surveyed the area, rolling my shoulders against a dull ache that had formed at the base of my neck. We were about half way done.

Hunter grabbed another run, and I blew him a kiss. I was actually enjoying myself despite the sweat and manual labor, and when Hunter

pulled off his jacket and t-shirt I almost died right there in the pumpkin patch. He wore a white muscle tank underneath, and it molded to his body like paint on skin. His jeans dipped a little low, and hugged his hips and firm butt and it was clear how well-proportioned he was...everywhere. *Oh my God!*

He turned toward me and flashed one of those gorgeous smiles and my stomach dropped. I couldn't believe he chose to be with me. He could have his pick of anyone in the school, and the knowledge gave me both warm-fuzzies and anxiety. I grabbed the closest pumpkin and walked toward him, my legs not quite working the way they should. I stumbled as always, and Hunter caught me yet again.

My eyesight went, and suddenly everything was a giant flame colored blur. My legs buckled, sending me to my knees in the grass. The pumpkin rolled from my hands; except it wasn't a jack-o-lantern's carved eyes gaping up at me, it was a human face. A severed head lay at the base of my lap. Its body, only God knew where. Without question it was the same head that materialized from the beach ball at Hunter's football game. Like something from a *Final Destination* horror movie, the vision was meant to happen, meant be seen and I refused to look. Now it wouldn't' let go until I witnessed every detail.

Gray lips peeled back in a perpetual death shriek from a maggot-infested mouth. Rotted teeth were jagged shards and its nose and eyes, nothing but decayed, empty orifices. Its long, stringy hair held the remnants of a blue bow at the base of the skull, tied to what seemed to be a revolutionary style ponytail. Obviously this horror had once been a young man.

I covered my eyes and screamed, my fingers clawing at my own skin. I knew Hunter's hands gripped my shoulders, and I heard my mother's voice along with his yelling my name. My mother's fingers pulled my own from my face, and she held my hands in hers pressing her forehead to mine. She whispered something in Latin and suddenly she was there with me in my head.

I saw with a duel sight, my mother's vision combining with mine like a split screen television: me screaming at a lifeless head on one side, my mother scrambling to pull me back from the edge on the other. Her face was determined but she wasn't strong enough, and I sensed her reach for

Hunter's hand and the three of us were linked, and he was in my mind as well.

They witnessed everything I saw, everything I felt. I heard my mother's voice call to me again and I jerked my head up. They were both there, tangible but not. Hunter reached out grabbing hold of my arms, and I flung myself into his chest and a great whooshing pulled at my mind, and I was back.

I fell forward, crashing into reality as I collapsed into my mother's arms. She rocked me back and forth like she did when I was a child, and Hunter picked up his jacket and wrapped it around my shoulders.

"Did you see?" I croaked as my mother smoothed my hair.

"Yes. Just be still, we'll get to the bottom of this, sweetheart. I promise," she cooed.

Lifting my head, I saw the way she looked at Hunter, and I could almost hear her mind working. The last few visions happened when I was with him.

"Mom, I know what you're thinking, but you're wrong." My eyes pleaded with her. I was not going to have her make Hunter the catalyst for this. "Can't we do some kind of spell reversal or attach a trace or something? What about a banishing spell?"

"*Shhh.* Let's get you home. We'll worry about that later," she said kissing my temple.

Hunter held out his hands to help me off my mother's lap. He wrapped his arms around my shoulders and I shrank into his chest. I couldn't get close enough and I started to shiver.

"She's going into shock, maybe we should take her to the hospital," he said to my mother, concern edging his voice.

She shook her head. "It's not shock. It's what happens sometimes after having a vision, especially if it's intense. Just get her home, Hunter, I know exactly what to do. I'll be right behind you, but I need to speak to Leslie, first." The poor woman was both frightened and confused, and now it was more than pumpkins that required triage.

Hunter helped me to the truck. I gritted my teeth against the spasms racking my body, trying not to cry. He lifted me onto the seat, swearing under his breath as he tucked his jacket even tighter around my body and buckled my seatbelt. Starting the engine he backed up onto the gravel

path and took off, the all terrain tires shooting the tiny rocks like mini projectiles. He wrapped his arm around my shoulders, the tension in his muscles obvious through my panicked and exhausted state.

"I'm okay...really," I rasped.

He stayed silent, instead tightening his grip on my shoulder. "Hunter, please..." I said craning my neck to see his face.

This time he looked down at me, and his expression was as dark as his eyes. It was clear the same thought had crossed his mind as to who was the cause of my horrific glimpses into the past. He still didn't say a word, but pressed a kiss to the top of my head.

"Not your fault," was all I managed through the tears that threatened and the new fear choking at my throat. This was going to cost me Hunter, and now my body shook from the thought alone.

Chapter 9

We sat in the kitchen waiting for my mother to arrive. It was like déjà vu from last week, only now I realized the visions weren't random like I originally thought and the situation wasn't stopping on its own. I needed high magic to prevent this from happening again, and high magic meant Gran.

The backdoor opened and closed, and I looked up from my tea expecting it to be my mother. Instead, my grandmother walked in holding a black embroidered carpetbag. The thing looked like something from another century. Growing up I remembered relatives joking about Gran and her infamous witch doctor bag, and all at once the image of my grandmother dressed as Madame Pomfrey from *Harry Potter* popped into my mind.

Gran's face pinched severe. All business, not a hint of the lady who sometimes brought me cookies and chicken soup. Walking in, she didn't say a word, just dropped the ominous black bag on the kitchen table. Without missing a beat she took my chin in her hand and turned my face from side to side watching my eyes, evaluating. I tried to swallow, but my mouth tasted like sand as I did my best to cooperate. Her mouth was a thin line when she finally let go of my face and directed her attention to Hunter.

"So you're the one causing all the metaphysical fallout around here, huh?" she asked, and I held my breath hoping Hunter wouldn't try and

answer. Gran was big on rhetorical questions, but not a fan of rebuttal.

Her tone had a bite to it, as if being Britt Van Tassell's son was reason enough to lay blame at Hunter's feet. "I knew your mother growing up. She was Laura's best friend." She pursed her lips looking at him the same way she looked at any dubious new arrival. "My guess is she never bothered to teach you anything about the craft? Well, I can't say Laura has done much with that either."

In one sentence her tone had changed from accessing and judgmental to disappointed, and I nearly choked on my chamomile. "Gran! Mom gave me the choice you never gave her; it's not her fault I never showed much interest. And what's going on with me has nothing to do with Hunter. It just so happens, the first episode occurred *before* I started hanging out with him."

Her eyes narrowed. I didn't need to be a rocket scientist to see how annoyed she was in general, but right now her irritation was clearly directed at me and my big mouth. "Oh, and I suppose you never set eyes on him before that morning in your bathroom, eh?"

I wasn't surprised Gran knew about the bloody water in the bathroom. She always just knew. Over the years she had earned the title of town historian, or depending on your point of view, town busybody — but she was always right, and now that uncanny intuition of hers ratcheted my anxiety to the point of cracking. I swear if she pulled an interrogation room spotlight out of that bag it wouldn't have shocked me in the least.

I chewed on my thumb listening to the sound of the clock ticking above the stove while I tried to think of something to say. The last thing I wanted was to embarrass either me or Hunter by admitting to weeks of flirting or that I was his girlfriend. My grandmother's scrutiny was unwavering, and just when I thought I couldn't bear anymore my mother walked in, shifting Gran's attention from me to her.

"Laura Elizabeth Eckert Corbett! Why under heaven's eyes would you allow this situation to intensify to this point? Rowen is far too young and far too inexperienced to deal with this sort of thing on her own." Gran's mouth was more of a slash, and for a split second my mother's expression was as intimidated as mine, giving me a small glimpse of what it must have been like for her growing up.

But the insecure shadow passed from my mother's face as quickly as it came, leaving the same strong, confident, loving woman I knew. Squaring her shoulders, she spared me a quick glance before meeting Gran's icy gaze.

"I'm handling this mother, and only called you because we need at least three women to do a combined spell, and right now it's important to keep this in the family. Rowen needs a scrying ritual so we can trace what's causing this and why. Now, you can either help or you can go home. I don't have to ask to know you've been giving her a hard time about Hunter—it's written all over her face. He's not the cause of this, but to be sure I've called Britt to meet us here as well. She's his mother and I'm sure you can't dispute the Van Tassell lineage when it comes to powerful practitioners."

I bit back a smile, because Gran's face puckered like she'd sucked lemons. She wasn't used to having her say negated. You don't get the mama cat angry, and in this case Laura was one ticked off tabby. Without a word, Gran picked up her bag and tucked it under her arm. She turned on her heel to head out the same way she came in, but hesitated by the door. This was *so* not good, and I braced myself for her verbal barrage.

Gran's face was indecipherable when she turned back and I cringed, expecting nothing less than cold condescension and steaming hot guilt. With her chin high looked straight at my mother and then at me. "You're right. We need to do what's best for Rowen."

My jaw hit the table. Never in a million years would I have expected my grandmother, the formidable Anne Dederick Eckert, to defer to someone else, let alone my mother.

Gran's gaze softened and she reached for my mother's hand. "I taught you well, Laura. Now if we could only do something about our girl and that snippy nose of hers in the air about such things."

Oh. My. God. There was no way they were turning this into some warped, witchy Hallmark moment. "Gran! Jeez! Let's not go there, okay? Don't we have enough to deal with without dragging everyone through the do's and don'ts of witchy parenting?" I was glad they managed to get past it and meet in the middle without catching me in the crossfire...but hell!

Hunter looked like he didn't know whether to laugh or run screaming

from the house. I reached over to rest my hand on his as he picked at the edges of the placemats. "They'll behave better once your mother gets here, I promise." It was all I could say and I secretly hoped I was right.

His eyes were full to the brim with questions I couldn't answer. It was going to be a long night, but at least we were all on the same page. Gran had a plan. I was sure of it, otherwise she wouldn't have let my mother off so easily—plus I was okay for now, and with all of them here I knew that permanently okay was just around the corner and I was safe.

There was nothing to do except wait for Britt. Scraping my chair back I stood, motioning for Hunter to do the same. "We're gonna head upstairs, just call us when Hunter's mom gets here."

With her elbows resting against the counter, my mother drummed her fingers on the dark green granite, considering me with discerning eyes. "Honey, I don't think that's such a great idea."

"What? No trust, Mother? With you *and* Gran in the house?"

Gran leaned on the counter as well, mimicking my mom's stance. Her height barely reached Mom's shoulders, but she drummed her fingers in time with my mother's in matriarchal solidarity. "You got that right," she answered for them both.

This whole messed up situation wasn't exactly a great way to start things with a new boyfriend. It was bad enough we had to be here at all, but I refused to waste what little alone time I could grab with Hunter to sit in a fishbowl. "What are you more afraid of, me going upstairs with Hunter or that I'll have another vision?"

My mother stopped her drumming and cracked a smile. Her eyes twinkled, and it was one of those moments when I knew she got it...got me. "It's a toss-up," she winked.

Rolling my eyes, I walked around the side of the table and took Hunter's hand. "Okay then..."

The immediate tension ebbed and Hunter's shoulders visibly relaxed, despite his beet red face. I suffered a twinge of guilt at having embarrassed him. But hey, he laughed at me earlier.

He didn't say a word as we headed into the hall, but his body language spoke volumes. He was relieved we were out from under the microscope, as well.

"Was that as surreal for you as it was for me?" I asked going up the

stairs ahead of him.

He exhaled, cracking a smile. "Worse. Your family's no joke, but I thought they at least *had* to like you."

I frowned. My family was difficult, but hey...they were still my family. "What do you mean?"

His eyes flicked to the deplorable school portraits hung along the stairwell, each marking the awkward stages of my childhood in the same sadistic manner most parents employ to embarrass their kids.

My mouth fell open, and I balked in defense. "And I suppose you looked like the perfect California surfer dude back in the sixth grade, huh?"

He laughed, putting his hand to his heart. "Ouch."

I stifled a giggle. "Sorry, Mr. Running Back. I didn't realize you were so touchy."

With a dexterity learned on the football field, his hand shot around my waist, pulling me the rest of the way upstairs. "Only around you," he breathed, his lips hovering just above mine.

His arms were solid strength around me, and through my flimsy leggings his thighs were bands of muscle, rock hard like his chest. My own legs were Jell-O, and the tension I'd felt earlier was replaced by a new variety, one that suffused my skin with heat and electricity, making my lower belly jump and tingle. If this was what he meant by touchy, then bring it on! Breathless, I licked my lips already anticipating the crush of his on mine, but instead he gave me a quick peck and let go of my waist.

The quick shift from overdrive into neutral left me completely unsettled, and it took a moment for my brain to unscramble itself.

"So, this is your room, huh?" he asked, his mouth a wicked half smile as he leaned against the wall to the right of my bedroom door.

I raked a nervous hand through my hair, still trying to recover. His crooked smile stretched across his full mouth as I pushed the door open, like he secretly enjoyed his ability to make me come unglued.

"Yup, this is it," I gestured with my arm, silently thanking God my room wasn't its usual disaster.

Contemplating my books and my collection of CDs and classic vinyl, he flipped through the stack of old albums piled on my desk. "Seriously

not what I expected," he murmured, picking up an original pressing of Bon Jovi's debut album from 1984.

"What's that supposed to mean?" I'd never reacted this way to anyone, *ever*...and watching him as he continued his inspection of my dad's old albums, it hit me how little I knew about him and how much I actually cared about what he thought.

He sized up my brass bed, the antique armoire and matching dresser and the roll top desk that had been in my family for generations, and putting down the albums, he leaned against the back of my chair. "Nothing. It's just not what I expected your room to look like."

I sat on my bed, tucking one leg under the other. "And what did you expect? Stuffed animals everywhere and pink and white walls covered with silly posters and cutouts from People Magazine?"

He chuckled. "Pretty much."

Even surrounded by my chaos, he was beautiful, if you could use such a word to describe a guy. The butterflies, which had gone catatonic since we left the Blaze site, started fluttering around my stomach. To distract myself, I got up and moved to the other side of the bed.

"Well, just so as not to disappoint you..." I reached behind my pillow and pulled out a tiny unicorn beanie baby, complete with a sparkly pink horn and gold braided harness.

He laughed out loud, propping another pillow against the headboard and climbing up next to me on the bed. "I knew it all along." he said taking the stuffed toy from my hand. "I'm glad, too."

"Glad?"

"That you like unicorns," he said idly stoking the white faux fur with his index finger. "They're unique, they're beautiful, and they're full of magic...just like you."

My butterflies went wild and I bit my lower lip to squelch the nervous feeling. I looked down and traced the floral pattern on my bedspread. "I don't know about beautiful and magical, but I've always liked the idea of unique," I said trying to sound normal.

Hunter put the unicorn on the bed and reached across the pillow to run his fingers across my cheek. "Trust me," he whispered tilting my head so he could look into my eyes. "Definitely, all three."

His hand dropped to the bed and he slid closer to me. We were hip to

hip and this time his kiss was no peck as his hand fisted the back of my hair and his mouth sought mine. My hands snaked around to his back, clutching his shirt and urged him to deepen our kiss.

His breath came sharp and fast and he skimmed my waist with his palm. Sliding his hand upward, it rested on my ribs just below my breast, his thumb stroking its full, rounded curve. My body tingled with the promise of his touch and I pressed myself closer to him. I wanted to feel him, him to feel me, and a soft moan escaped my throat.

His hand dropped to my back and his fingers traveled the length of my spine. Holding me against him, he guided my body down next to his, and with our legs intertwined the motion skimmed my waist pushing up the camisole beneath my blouse and over sensitive peaks, sending tiny, electric shocks shooting through my body. I moaned again, this time pulling him over so his weight straddled mine.

I couldn't get close enough. It was like I wanted him to crawl inside me, and me inside him, 'til neither of us knew where one stopped and the other started. My mind was fuzzy and thick, drunk on the feel and the smell of him. His mouth trailed across my collarbone, the rough feel of his chin grazing the scooped edge of my tee-shirt.

"Rowen?" My mother's voice sounded from outside my door. Her knock was a dowsing of ice water, sending the two of us shooting to either side of the bed. I couldn't find my voice. I couldn't answer my mother's knock, nor did I know what to say to Hunter. All I could do was stare at his back as he sat on the edge of the bed, his breathing rapid and ragged as my own.

"Rowen... I'm sorry." Hunter's voice was a rough whisper full of guilt and regret, and his apologetic tone left tears pricking at the corners of my eyes.

I wasn't letting him blame himself, not when I was the one who spurred him on. I scooted over wrapping my arms around his and pressed my cheek to his back. I half expected him to shrug me off, but he didn't, instead he relaxed back into my arms.

"Don't be sorry, Hunter, I'm not. It's not your fault. If anyone's hormones are to blame, they're mine. I'm the one who got carried away..."

Another knock followed the first, only louder. "Okay, Mom! We'll be

right down," I called back hoping my voice didn't sound as shaky as it felt.

I sat back on my heels and Hunter shifted, moving to one side so our knees touched. I looked at him, my eyes needing him to say something, anything, but my mother's voice outside the door brought us crashing back to the situation at hand. We had a job to do tonight and we needed clear heads and focus.

Hunter got up from the bed and held out his hand for me. There was so much I wanted to say, but since he still hadn't said a word, I didn't know where or how to begin. I scooted further toward the edge of the mattress and he pulled me to standing, wrapping his arms around my shoulders.

"You really need to stop chewing on your lower lip. It's going to look even more like we've been making out. There's nothing that needs to be said, nothing to be ashamed of and nothing to worry about. I'm not sorry we got carried away, and I'm not upset. I'm together with you, and that's all that matters. The rest will come. You're different, Rowen. You're not like any other girl I've ever been with and I want this to be special...for both of us."

I clung to him, a tumult of uncertainty and hope mixed with desire and fear. "I'm crazy about you," I murmured into his chest. Truth was, it was more like I was falling for him, and Hunter was smart enough to read between the lines.

A thousand thoughts clamored through my head the minute the words left my mouth. Hadn't he said he didn't want to rush things? We'd been together a few short weeks, what the hell was I thinking? I closed my eyes not wanting to see what was written on his face.

"Look at me, Rowen."

His fingers gently traced the curve of my cheek, sliding his index finger under my chin. He lifted my face, brushing my lips with his. "And here I thought I was the only one," he whispered against my mouth.

It didn't make any sense. How he could feel the same about me, especially with all the trouble I'd caused? I was an outcast with a metaphysical monkey on my back, and he was perfect.

"Open your eyes so I know you heard me."

The fates had sent Hunter into my life, and whatever their reason, I

wasn't going to question them. I opened my eyes, embracing their gift with open arms. This was the happiest I'd ever been, but it was tempered by the fact we had to go downstairs and face whatever my mother and grandmother had cooked up.

"They're waiting," Hunter reminded, gently disengaging my arms from behind his back. "Why don't I go down ahead? I'll tell them you're in the bathroom, that way you can wash your face or do whatever it is you girls do to freshen up."

He was just amazing. I went up on tip toes and pressed a kiss to his lips. "I don't know what I did to deserve you, but when we get downstairs I'm sending a big, fat thank you into the universe just in case. What about you? Are you sure you're okay?"

One eyebrow shot up and his eyes sparkled with laughter. "I'm a guy, Rowen, with a beautiful girlfriend who's got the potential to be a nymphomaniac. I'd say I'm more than just okay."

When I came downstairs all conversation came to a dead stop, and four sets of eyes turned to meet me in the doorway of the living room. The room was completely prepared. My mother had rolled up the area rug, revealing a perfect Wiccan circle etched into the hardwood beneath.

Salt had been poured into the grooves of the ring and in the lines carved by design at the center to form a pentacle. White beeswax candles inscribed with runes and ritual symbols burned at the head and foot and each corner. They represented the universe and the four directions, as well as the five wounds of Christ.

As a child, I'd seen this ritual done. It was a lesser banishing ritual, but done with a high magic invocation. Gran was going to perform a rite of the Celtic cross and call to the guardian watchtowers, beginning in the east and working clockwise to the north. Through the Sign of the Enterer and the Sign of Silence, the circle and everyone within would be protected. After that Gran would take the lead and scry for what was causing my trouble.

Hunter and I were placed at the center of the pentagram, while my mother, Gran, and Britt took positions of power along the inner circle. Tracing a pentacle entwined with a cross in the air to the east, Gran intoned the ancient words, her arms shooting forward to pierce the five

pointed star with an ancient ritual knife. A white light radiated from the end of the black handled athame as it struck center, and she pulled it along the circle's edge repeating the invocation for each direction.

Everything inside the circle vibrated with white and blue light as energy built. My body trembled and shook from the inside out. Blood thrust through my veins, pounding in my heart like liquid jackhammers. I caught a glimpse of myself in the mirror above the couch and gasped. My skin was alight and wisps of my hair stood on end as if charged with static electricity. Hunter's body glowed bluish. As Gran circled back around to the east the vibrations were unbearable.

My knees buckled. Hunter caught me, but his touch skewered my body. I screamed in pain. There was nothing he could do to help me. Clutching my middle, I sunk to the floor as Gran threw one arm out to the side and the other shot upward toward the ceiling. She gave the final call, invoking the arch angels, Rafael, Gabriel, Michael and Uriel to lend their strength and banish and reverse the evil piercing my mind. Suddenly everything stopped, and my pain disappeared. Hunter's relief was palpable and he stepped toward me, but my mother held up her hand. There would be time for comfort soon enough, but the task at hand was far from over.

Gran stepped back. Her face sober, eyes glinting with satisfaction from a job well done. Nothing was getting into this circle, and the power surrounding us was so pure it would surely furnish whatever answers we needed.

Britt walked forward and anointed Hunter with ritual oils. She traced a swirl in a counterclockwise motion along the seven chakra points of his body that marked the flow of energy in all creatures. She stepped back and my mother came forward to do the same for me.

The oils glowed, each in the correct alignment and color of the chakra spectrum. Gran opened her black, embroidered bag and took out an ornate, purple glass bottle. It was the length and width of her hand, with Celtic writing inscribed in silver around a beautiful Celtic cross. I knew what it was. Holy water from St. Brigid's well in Ireland. The patron of fire and healing, Brigid was the first pagan goddess to be named a saint, and her water was seen as a portal to the otherworld and a source for wisdom and healing.

We were ready. The circle had been purified and protected. Time to get the truth. Gran approached me first, motioning for me to kneel, not because she was so powerful a practitioner, but for the simple fact I was so much taller. She stood over me, and a nervous chuckle escaped my mouth. She cracked a smile and gave me a wink, but then quickly sobered.

In words that sounded like Latin, she poured the water over the crown of my head, my face and chest and down my belly. It trickled onto the floor and my instincts knew better than to move or disturb the little puddle. With her arms stretched high, Gran repeated the same with Hunter.

As I knelt on the hard floor, I itched to hold Hunter's hand, but knew it would compromise everything Gran had just done. We had each been cleansed, consecrated and energy whizzed through me like a current.

Tiny pools of cloudy water traced a path over the places our mothers' had marked like puddles on the street mixed with gasoline after a light rain.

Gran opened her bag again and took out a scrying stone, a crystal pendulum hanging from a silver chain. Standing in front of me, she held it over the water and invoked the spirit world, asking for the source of my chaotic visions.

The pendulum swayed, moving side to side in an ellipse, faster and faster, until a circular pattern formed. Water swirled. Residual oils separated from the liquid mixture, forming a perfect circle within the circle. Inside the ring, the now clear water reflected as a mirror.

Images crept to the surface. From my vantage point they were inverted, but I recognized the figure revealed in the water. Hunter. But this time it was obvious the image was his ancestor. He wore a smile, laughing mischievously with a beautiful dark haired beauty dressed in white lace. They danced in a courtyard, with ribbons streaming from poles decorated with flowers and vines.

The water whirlpooled and the image changed. Revolutionary Hunter appeared older. He stood behind his dark haired beauty with one hand on her shoulder while he gazed at the baby in her arms.

The scene shifted. Night time. British soldiers held the screaming woman by the arms. Her child was gone and revolutionary Hunter lay on

the ground, beaten.

She fought to free herself, gesturing toward their house in panicked pleas, but her cries were ignored. At their commander's signal, soldiers hurled blazing torches through the upstairs windows. Glass exploded into the garden as flames ate toward the sky.

The man in charge watched, a cruel smirk on his face at a job well done. The woman sobbed, her arms desperately reaching to the inferno as her husband was dragged away, wrists tied to the tail of one of the cattle the soldiers appropriated along with valuables from the house.

The images faded to a vision of a little girl. She was brown haired and fresh faced. When she looked up, I sucked in a breath. She had Hunter's eyes. A bright blue dress and a checkered ribbon in her hair ruffled in the breeze as she picked flowers in a springtime meadow. Laughing, she waved to us, then her face changed. She aged before my eyes, skin turned grey and sloughed off. Her eyes and nose rotted away until a decomposed skeleton remained.

The visions and the people were linked, but how? Why? After the stories Gran told me about the burnings, I wonder if the visions were related. And why was I chosen for torment? Britt Morrissey and my mother stood at Gran's side. Britt's face anguished as she watched the images unfold. It was clear she understood more than she wanted.

The figures disintegrated to black and the water was still and void once more. But Gran was far from done. She repeated the same invocation over the water pooled at Hunter's knees.

At his first image, air choked in my throat. My face stared back at me along with his. We stood in tandem. My arms reached toward the heavens. Above my head an eerie shaft of light penetrated the space between my hands. My crown chakra glowed, but not of clean, white light. Mottled with red it throbbed like a beating heart. My aura bled into the channel.

A new vision popped up. Hunter stood, arms crossed over his chest. Insubstantial wisps of black and red, gold and white circled his body. They were not of this world, yet they clung to him.

The image shifted. This time the two of us were intertwined. Our arms were around each other and the shaft of light above my head churned with the black and red wisps circling Hunter. White light

shimmered in the midst of the black, bloody mess, but winked in and out as if overpowered. The water turned dark and was void, reflecting nothing but the surrounding candlelight.

My mother helped me to my feet, and Britt did the same for Hunter. My body ached with exhaustion, and my legs wobbled. Everyone looked drawn and worried, but Gran' face creased, her mind already wrestling out the puzzle pieces.

With a sweep of her hand, Gran drew everyone's focus to the task at hand. "Once the watchtowers are released, we need to talk about what we saw. Everyone, hold hands to reverse the energy and open the circle."

I reached for Hunter, but his mother grabbed my wrist, stopping me. "No. You need to hold someone else's hand," she said.

Perplexed and a little hurt, I stared at her for several seconds before looking to my grandmother for an explanation.

"It's necessary, Rowen. Britt's not trying to be unkind. There are things happening that I can't explain right now. Cooperate and I'll answer your questions as best I can once we're done." I opened my mouth to argue, but Gran eyed me.

I pressed my lips together. Hunter shot me a sympathetic look, but was smart enough to keep opinions to himself.

The three women reversed the directions, each bidding thanks and farewell to the guardians. They swept the perimeter salt that marked the pentacle into the scrying water and wiped it clean with white cloth before burning it in the fireplace. My mother set the white beeswax candles aside and then she and Britt went into the kitchen for food and drinks.

Cakes and wine were a standard part of any post circle ceremony, but tonight the tradition felt more like a debriefing. Gran sat in the chair closest to the fireplace, gazing into the fire. Her expression was calm, but I knew she was preoccupied with what she saw.

Mom and Britt carried in trays with fruit and cheese, crisp sliced bread and spiced cider. They set the platters on the coffee table and sat.

I reached for the cider, but froze half way to the cups. Gran's gaze had shifted from the fire and set on me. My mother eased my arm down, and finished pouring me a cup. I took it from her, but couldn't lift it to take a sip, not with the dread spiraling in my stomach as Gran continued to study me.

"What?" My voice cracked with fear and anxiety. "Whatever it is you have to say, just spit it out. Staring at me like I've sprouted horns is creeping me out."

My mother handed a cup of cider to Hunter and Britt, and then poured one for Gran, as well. Gran held it without saying a word, sipping slowly.

"Gran, please!"

She took another sip and put her cup on the chair side table. Folding her hands in her lap, she exhaled. "Rowen, your visions have been getting progressively worse over the past couple of weeks, almost as if the closer it gets to Samhain, the more disturbing they become. Each of your visions involves people from Britt and Hunter's past. Long past. We don't know why, but of course, that wasn't the purpose of this circle. Tonight we simply wanted to know the source, to find out why they hit with such intensity whenever the two of you are together, and now we know.

"You, my darling child, are a conduit for the spirit world, and Hunter, for lack of a better word, is a magnet. He draws spirits without even knowing it, and you give them the channel they crave to make contact or wreak havoc or whatever be their intent. You, Rowen, are a natural medium."

Hunter and I exchanged looks, and it was obvious he was as confused as I was. "I don't get it. Are you saying that together, Hunter and I form some kind of turbo-charged exit ramp off the spirit world superhighway? If that's the case, put up a road block or some metaphysical version of a DWI checkpoint. I don't care why it's happening or how we handle it. I want it to stop."

Hunter's eyes flashed to mine and then to Gran's. "How can you say this is happening because Rowen and I are together? We hadn't really spoken when Rowen had her first vision."

Gran's eyes softened. "Hunter, it has to do with proximity. You moved to town and every day for the past two months the two of you have been together in school, in class. Think of it like plate tectonics, the two of you fit together like a perfectly matched puzzle that happens to cause metaphysical cataclysms."

Britt interjected before either of us could say another word. "They're

just kids, Anne. There has to be something we can do to block this, or at least channel the energies into a different medium. I mean, they have to go to school. There's no way we can prevent them from seeing each other."

I sat without moving, my eyes locked on Hunter. This was it. I knew in my heart exactly what my Gran was going to say, and I dreaded hearing the words.

"Yes, Britt, that's exactly what I'm saying. Laura knows it as well, don't you, honey? As difficult and it's going to be, the two of them need to stay away from each other for the time being, or at least until we can figure out what to do. Right now the only thing I can think to do is bind their powers, but I don't think either of you want that."

Britt and my mother exchanged glances, and in tandem both shook their heads.

I stood shaking my head as well, my nerve endings zinging with adrenaline. "Wait a minute! Why are you looking at Mom and Britt? Shouldn't the decision be up to me and Hunter? Don't we have a say on how to handle this?"

My mother pulled me back into my chair and I glanced at Hunter again. Everything came to a crashing halt, and I wasn't buying it. I'd waited too long to feel the way I did with Hunter to let something like this be a barrier. Not now, not before we even had the chance to really begin. "No, Mom! There has to be another way!"

She regarded me sadly. "Sweetie, at this point I won't allow your power to be bound. You're too young, and the backlash could be devastating. I won't risk it, and neither will Britt."

Hunter rose and walked behind my chair. "Mrs. Eckert, both Rowen and I understand the severity of this situation, and we're willing to do whatever it takes to help."

"Hunter!" I twisted around in my chair to look up at him. He stared at me like I was missing something obvious, and his gaze told me to shut the hell up and let him finish. He was resolute. I exhaled grudgingly, hoping he knew what he was doing and turned around.

"You said 'until you figure things out.' Between the three of you there has to be some idea of what to do, because the idea of Rowen and me staying apart until further notice is entirely impractical."

His mother sighed. "I won't risk Hunter's well being with the kind of binding spell this would need. It's serious magic and I for one consider it bad practice." She glanced at us. "The spell's essence is the removal of free will, and I think we should try every other possible solution before we consider overpowering the kids' natural abilities. Even *permanent* bindings are rarely permanent, and both Hunter and Rowen would be in a constant battle with the spell, even unconsciously. Trying to make someone go against their nature is one of the most difficult things to accomplish, and eventually we'd be back to square one. But Hunter's right about one thing, we need a plan of attack."

My mother offered, "What about a banishing spell together with a blocking ritual to reverse or alternate the channel? It'll leave their powers unbound, but they'll still be protected. Something like Rowen jokingly suggested, a metaphysical road block."

Gran pursed her lips. "It could work, but we wouldn't be able to start for a while. The new moon is two weeks out, and this requires the circle to be cast under Hecate's moon."

Britt chewed the tip of her finger. "Two weeks is a long time, Anne. It's impractical—and their teenagers…" she let her words and their meaning drift off with a gesture that said, "kids will be kids."

At Gran's look of impatience, Britt held up her hand, letting her know she wasn't finished. "All the same, I do have an idea how we can work around that rule."

All eyes turned to watch Gran's reaction, and her raised eyebrow was enough for Britt to continue.

"If we bind their powers to each of us, instead of binding them completely, then we could temper the flow, keep it to a trickle. We wouldn't be able to stop it, but then again, we wouldn't want to, not with the kind of metaphysical back up it would cause."

Now it was Gran's turn to consider. Her face took on an almost brooding appearance, but I knew it was just the way Gran seemed when someone said something worth thinking about.

She glanced from Britt to my mother and then back to Britt, and she actually smiled. I didn't know whether to be hopeful or very afraid.

Gran's expression changed from ominous to appreciative as she took in Britt, her gaze studying her as if truly seeing her for the first time.

"You're an asset to your line, Britt Van Tassell Morrissey. Your late grandmother Sofie would be proud. I think your idea might work, and it will buy us time, as well. And if the situation escalates, our combined power will give us the strength we need to banish whatever this is back to the hell in which it came. That is if it has the balls to show its face."

She fixed Hunter and me with one of her looks. "Do you think the two of you could manage to keep your hormones in check for the time being? Two weeks, that's all we'll need to see this put to rest the right way, but with Samhain a week from tonight, I want to stack the odds in our favor. At the pace these visions are growing, if we don't, who knows what could happen or come through."

I started to protest, but Hunter's fingers squeezed my shoulders, in effect telling me to be quiet yet again. "I think we can manage that, Mrs. Eckert. Two weeks is a small price for everyone's peace of mind."

"Hunter!" I craned my neck and shot him a dirty look. *Traitor.*

"Good. It's nice to see one of you is thinking straight," Gran said with a smile. "I think perhaps I may have been too hasty in my opinions. You may have inherited your great-grandmother Sofie's good sense as well, Hunter. Gives me hope for this one, yet," she joked, jerking her head my way.

"Gran!" I huffed.

A huge grin broke across her wrinkled face. "It's all set then. Your mothers can help me use this week to prepare. In the mean time, perhaps we could move this little powwow into the kitchen. I hate crumbs on the floor almost as much as I hate petulant grandchildren. We can brew the binding spell there and still invoke it before the moon sets."

Hunter gave my shoulders another quick squeeze. "You need to relax. It'll be okay, I promise."

Gran got up from her chair and stretched. "Absolutely. Certain spells require a true blood moon, and they only happen once every six years, so I'd count my blessings if I were you, Rowen."

Clutching the seat cushions with both hands, part of me wanted to kick my legs and yell and scream. But I didn't say a word, neither did I offer to help as Britt and my mom collected everything from the coffee table. They were right—all of them, but that didn't mean I liked it.

I knew what they were asking was for the best, but at this moment

they might as well have been the three witches from Shakespeare's King Lear—mysterious, solemn and full of dread as they wheeled a thunderstorm with their intervention. I sighed and released my vice grip on the chair. "Whatever you say, Gran."

Chapter 10

"Rowen! Breakfast!" My mother's voiced carried from the bottom of the stairs. It's not unusual for her to call me from there, but after last night I had a sneaking suspicion she was purposefully keeping her distance. I wasn't exactly what you'd call a happy camper.

I heaved a small sigh and got out of bed. Monday's were always tough, but today was going to be a very long day, and the idea of seeing Hunter and not do more than just talk left me flat as the banana chocolate chip pancakes I smelled coming from the kitchen. I knew I was being unreasonable, and I was aware of how much worse this situation could have been if Britt hadn't had her light bulb moment. But I couldn't help myself. Gran didn't want us to have any physical contact. Not even hand holding. And I didn't want to just talk to Hunter. I wanted to wrap my arms around him every chance I got.

The delicious scent told me my mother was going all out trying to cheer me up. Like dessert for breakfast was going to do the trick. Yeah, right, maybe if I was still five.

I guess I should be happy she let Hunter and me stay alone together in the living room after the circle was completed. One last concession before the physical ban took effect at midnight. I suppose she figured the room had been über-purified, and I was sure the *Three Stygians*, as I now referred to my mother, Gran and Britt, were confident nothing was getting through as they talked and strategized in the kitchen.

The Stygian Witches from Greek mythology were epic, scary women, capable of tremendous prophecy and power, and nobody messed with them. Both Hunter and I knew better than to mess with our own three, regardless of how much we hated their edict.

"Rowen…"

I gritted my teeth. Her tone was the same she used when I was little and trying to coax me into eating something I hated. Again, not five anymore…I mean, *really*.

I didn't answer, just grabbed my clothes and plodded into the bathroom. Turning on the tap I stared at the water, almost hoping the faucet would spout blood clots or body parts, anything to chase away this glum mood. To hope for horror as an antidote for feeling sorry for myself was ridiculous, even by my overly dramatic standards. Again, I knew I was being difficult…petulant, even, but I wanted to live my life. I never wanted any part of my so called heritage. I hadn't asked for this, and now this metaphysical nightmare was messing with me when my life was starting to get good.

But the water in the sink stayed clear, as if the universe thumbed its nose at me saying, *"don't call us, we'll call you."* I let out a disgusted sigh, and brushed my teeth before getting into the shower. I usually liked luxuriating in the hot water, but this morning I lathered, rinsed, and repeated in a perfunctory manner and got out almost as quickly as I got in.

All I wanted to do was leave the house. I ran a brush through my hair and pulled on a pair of black leggings and a black, off the shoulder tunic and headed directly for the front door, not bothering with breakfast. I didn't want to see the, "I know you hate me for this, but it's for your own good," look on my mother's face. The faster I got the day started, the faster it would end.

Chloe was waiting for me when I crossed the street by the firehouse. "Hey. What's up?" I asked trying to sound casual, but missing the mark by a long shot.

One glimpse at my approach with caution outfit and she whistled low and long. "I'm good, but from the looks of that get up, your sullen has gone scary this morning, and I don't mean just your clothes. What happened between yesterday and today?"

I rolled my eyes and exhaled. "You wouldn't believe me if I told you."

"Try me." Chloe's chin length, bobbed hair wafted around her like a halo in the morning breeze as she scrutinized my face.

"You saw your Gran last night, didn't you?" her voice clipped. She had no patience for my grandmother and her overbearing matriarchy, and she blew her auburn bangs off her forehead punctuating her annoyance. "You gotta stop letting her get under your skin. I mean, she practically ruined your birthday with her whole *Oooh, your aura is bleeding* garbage. What did she say this time?"

Chloe knew my family history and all, but the last thing I needed was someone else telling me what to do. I shook my head. "Just drop it, Chloe, I'll tell you about it later, but right now I don't want to talk about it."

She didn't comment, and though I knew she was itching to push the issue, I was glad she didn't. Hiking the strap of her purple messenger bag onto her shoulder, she turned and headed up the street with me. It was like any other morning, except I kept catching her watching me from the corner of her eye. At the light across the street from the school I had enough. "Will you stop looking at me like you're waiting for my head to explode? I'm fine, but I won't be if you don't quit already!"

She laughed. "Sorry, but you know how I get sometimes…okay, no more watching for weirdness, I promise. Hey, speaking of weirdness, you hear about the party Saturday night at the cemetery? I heard Tyler's been squawking about it all over school. Talk about dumb as a stump. Doesn't he realize the more he opens his mouth the more likely the cops will break it up before it even gets started?"

I had to give Chloe props for changing the subject so adeptly, especially since she knew cracking on Tyler's incessant stupidity was usually a sure fire way to bring a smile to my face. "Yeah, he did the same thing Friday night. In fact Jenny practically took his head off for being so dense. Guess the lesson didn't penetrate. Hunter and I were gonna go, but now I think I'm just gonna pass."

"What! You can't! Benny asked me to go with him and I only said yes because he told me you were going with Hunter."

"Yeah, well. That was yesterday."

My face must have shouted disappointment and self-loathing, because Chloe's eyes narrowed to protective slits. "Oh, no he didn't!

Hollow's End

Please tell me he didn't pull the same crap as Tyler last spring? *Ugh.* When are you going to learn to follow your head and not your hormones? Those guys are all the same, Rowen, or did you forget it was only by the grace of God and a well-aimed kick you got away the last time. Well, be thankful it didn't take Hunter long to show his true colors."

"Chloe! Stop, and lower your voice!" We were in front of the school at this point, and all ears were focused on us, especially Jenny's well trained toadies. "Hunter didn't do anything, in fact he's just as amazing as I originally thought, even more so. It's complicated and I can't go into it, but a party right now isn't such a good thing, that's all...and for the record I didn't kick Tyler, I broke his hand."

"Not a good thing? Why? The two of you just got together, and from the texts flying back and forth all day yesterday it seemed obvious the two of you hit hot and heavy from the get go."

I exhaled, squelching the urge to sulk.

Her eyes widened. "Ha! I knew it! Your Gran told you to stay away from him, didn't she?"

"Something like that," I answered simply. "But not for the reasons you think. Gran actually likes him, but right now things are way more complicated than you can imagine. It has nothing to do with me or Hunter or how we feel when we're together." I closed my eyes for a moment, remembering the taste of his mouth on mine and the feel of his arms around my waist. My breath caught in my throat. I opened my eyes meeting Chloe's questioning gaze. "Trust me, in two weeks things will definitely be back to hot and heavy."

Chloe followed me to my locker, and after seeing my reaction how could I expect she'd leave things alone, she was all pit-bull. "Why then?" she asked, not even trying to appreciate how difficult this was for me. "People are going notice, Rowen, and you know they're just gonna chalk it up to another popular jock getting over on yet another unpopular girl. They'll laugh, making you the butt of all their jokes, and I won't have any ammo to shut them up unless you tell me the real reasons why?"

I loved Chloe like a sister, but in this instance there was too much at stake for me to take a chance. She never quite got the concept that cooler heads prevail, and I was positive she'd blurt out exactly what was happening in a fit of defensive anger if she knew the truth...not that

anyone would believe her, but still. I shook my head. "Can't be helped."

Her lips were a thin line, and two red splotches formed on her cheeks before spreading down across her throat. I'd hurt her feelings, and she was pissed. "Look, Chloe, it's not that I *don't* want to tell you, truth is I *can't*. There's more involved than just my word, but I promise you'll be the first person I tell when I can talk about it. In the meantime, don't worry about what everyone else is saying behind my back. You've got to trust me. If the wannabees end up talking trash, ignore it...or better yet, tell them Hunter and I are secretly engaged. That'll definitely drive them batty wondering if it's true, and if he knocked me up."

She laughed so loud, she snorted, and for the first time this morning I felt like I could breath. "I gotta run," I said closing my locker. Shifting my books to one hip, I gave her a quick hug. "See you at lunch?"

"Absolutely," she said with a grin. "Maybe I'll grab a copy of *The Girlfriend's Guide to Pregnancy* and keep it on the table next to my lunch tray!"

Now it was my turn to laugh. "And you said I was scary this morning?" I blew her a kiss and headed down the hall. Chloe's first class was across from my locker. Glancing back, I chuckled again as she pushed the corners of her mouth up in a mock grin. Even pissed, she was still trying to make me laugh.

With a wave I turned the corner and headed for two hours of boring calculus. Today was a block day, and that meant double science and double math. Since Hunter and I were in different classes for those subjects it meant he'd be on the other side of the building for the better part of the day. Even with a reprieve from dealing with our temporary stasis, the idea of listening to Mr. Shannon spout calc functions had my mood plummeting from bad to worse.

After the longest two hours of my life, the bell rang, but I hung back, intentionally letting everyone shuffle out first. Grabbing my pack from under the desk, I looked up and spotted Jenny standing just inside the door.

"Benny told me Hunter's taking you to the party Saturday night." Walking toward the front row, she dropped her books on the first desk, the sound echoing in the empty room. "Makes sense, really. After all, dead things belong in the cemetery, and from what Tyler told me you've

got to be dead, 'cause no one could be *that* frigid."

Shoving my bag onto my shoulder, I pushed past her, knocking her books and purse to the floor in a loud clatter. "Tyler just loves fiction, doesn't he? On the other hand, what he tells everyone about you is not only fact, it's been footnoted by half the football team, and the margin notes on the walls of the boy's bathroom are read by every guy in the school."

Jenny flinched as I swung my bag to my opposite shoulder and walked out, swearing to myself I would never feel sorry for her again. For once, I'd left her speechless—well, at least today wasn't going to be a complete blow.

I made it to chemistry after the bell, but thankfully Mrs. McCafferty wasn't there yet, either. I slid into my seat and opened my book. It wasn't like her to be late, but ever since Mr. Bixler was let go because of an explosion using potassium chlorate, she was covering both biology as well as chem. The Bixler Blast made news across the county, blowing out the windows in the classroom and injuring six students. Taking over after a freak accident like that, I guess it was understandable why Mrs. McCafferty was a little edgy.

My phone buzzed with a text from Hunter.

"Hey."

"Hey urself."

"Feel like going to church?"

"Huh?"

"LOL! The gatekeeper at the Old Dutch said we could poke around after school."

"Nope."

"Scared?"

"Um, yeah. And u should b too."

'Come on. It's research. No one gets to see the vaults. Maybe we'll find something."

"Not worried about us finding something. I'm worried about some "thing" finding us."

"Chicken."

"Bock, bock."

"KK. I'll just go myself. I'll let you know if I find anything."

I chewed on my lip staring at the blue word bubble on my phone screen. *Go himself? Uh, no way.* I had two options. I could call in the

Stygian witches to put the kibosh on his plan, or I could go with him.

We were supposed to have paid a visit to the vaults yesterday, but of course, that didn't work courtesy of Saturday's vision fright fest and Wiccan mediation. Plus, Gran's circle had taken its toll on all of us, me and Hunter especially. We spent the day sacked out on the couch with Netflix, under the distant yet perceptive eyes of both our mothers.

Supposedly, Hunter and I would be fine and dandy as long as we kept our libidos in check. Problem was all I had to do was look at him, and all bets were off in that department.

Exhaling loudly, I hit reply.

"No. I'll go too. Just wait for me by your car."

"☺ Kk. C u later"

Mrs. McCafferty walked in, and I shut off my phone. Chemistry wasn't my strongest class, and I didn't need the distraction. Based on our plans for this afternoon, there was enough distraction lined up already.

Both Talia and Chloe sat at our usual table in the cafeteria by the time I arrived. Tray in hand, I slid in next to Chloe.

"Hey stranger, where have you been?" I asked, giving Talia a genuine smile. I had been worried about her no shows of late, and was actually glad to see her.

She shrugged, picking at the bits of lettuce sticking out from her chicken wrap. "I've been with Mike."

Chloe threw a french fry at her. "And?"

That was all it took, and Talia's lips stretched into a grin. She wiggled herself closer to the table and leaned in, motioning for us to do the same, her top teeth digging into her lip in anticipation.

"Friday after we saw you two outside the shop, Mike drove us to Croton Point. He had an afternoon picnic all planned, down to a flowers and basket full of goodies hidden in the trunk of his car."

Impressed, Chloe's face showed her surprise. Hunter as a romantic, yes…But Mike? Not a chance.

Talia beamed. "He spread the blanket on the grass beneath one of the trees overlooking the water. It was wonderful. We talked. I mean really talked."

"So, did the blanket make it into the backseat with you?"

"It wasn't like that, Chloe. And you two say I'm the one with the dirty mind, jeez. It was a romantic date. We stayed in the park until it got too cold and too dark to see the water anymore, but then he took us to Isabella's for dinner. The place is so romantic, and they make the best thin crust pizza just like the kind we had in Italy when I went with my family last summer. Mike and I sat across from each other at a tiny table for two all night. We were going to head up to meet you guys for dessert, but decided to have gelato there instead. We ended up closing the place."

"Wow. He dropped some serious coin on you, then."

Talia made a face, and even I shot Chloe a look at that. "That's not the point, Chlo. He spent *time* on me. *That's* what matters."

"What happened to the two of you heading over to Douglas Park? I thought that was the whole point of you two getting together Friday night? To take your relationship to the next level."

Looking down at her sandwich, Talia shrugged saying nothing.

"Tal… are you okay?" I asked.

She nodded, but glanced away and I looked at Chloe, gesturing with my eyes and my head for her to say something.

"Oh, I get it. You had second thoughts and this whole romantic scene was just Mike's way of trying to get you to change your mind."

"Chloe!" I glared at her. I wanted her to say something, but that was definitely not it.

Giving my best friend another withering look, I reached across the table for Talia's hand. "So, you said no. So what? You're allowed to change your mind, Tal. It's not like deciding on a pair of shoes or what to eat for dinner. This is a big step, and if you weren't ready, then Mike will just have to deal with it. And if he really cares about you, he will."

She turned back to look at us, her eyes wet. "You sound like my mother."

"You discussed Mike and horizontal WrestleMania with your mom?" Chloe blurted, entirely forgoing her filter.

"Chloe!" Talia and I both shouted in stereo.

For a minute no one said a word, and then all three of us burst out laughing. Talia laughed so hard she actually snorted, and the tears that threatened earlier spilled down her cheeks, but at least now they were cheerful. She wiped her eyes with her sleeve, and I bumped Chloe with

my elbow for being such a brat. Still the end result justified the means. Talia was laughing again, and that was all that mattered.

"Wait…I'm trying to picture it!" Chloe said, pushing my elbow away.

"Picture what? My mom spewing her coffee from the shock?"

"No, Mike's face when you dropped the bomb on him."

Talia stopped laughing, and the light in her eyes faded along with her smile. She glanced down at her uneaten lunch, her face miserable and uncertain.

"Mike is the first popular guy to pay any attention to me. We've been together since the fireworks on July 4th." She picked up a fry, and with a sigh let it drop back onto her plate. "It's my fault. Maybe if I didn't get cold feet every time he asked…" Her voice broke and she hesitated, exhaling before she continued. "…maybe he would have told Jenny to take a hike instead of inviting her into the shower."

I scooted my chair closer, wanting to make sure Talia heard me loud and clear. "Don't you dare blame yourself!" I replied at full volume, not caring who overheard what I had to say about Jenny's nefarious nocturnal skulking. "Only a self-deluded, insecure loser would crawl into the shower with another girl's boyfriend." I paused before plunging in with the rest of what had to be said. "And whether you're ready to admit it or not, the truth is Mike is just as guilty."

I waited for Talia to explode or dissolve into tears, but to her credit she did neither, she waited patiently for me to finish.

"Talia, you saying yes or no to anything Mike wants should have no bearing on what he did with Jenny. He should have stepped up. He's selfish, and no matter how much you like him, or how much he does for your social status, it's still Mike's way or the highway."

She considered me, and whereas ten minutes ago she was at a crossroads with tears threatening over the pressure Mike put on her, now she looked almost calm.

"You're right, Ro."

The bell rang, and Talia didn't say another word, just gave me a hug before grabbing her tray and heading toward the trash can and the door to the hall.

I eyed Chloe gathering her stuff. "What do you make of that?"

Hollow's End

She shook her head. "I don't know, but something you said clicked. I hope it was the right button."

Hunter leaned on the back end of his mustang, the sight of him relaxed against its cobalt blue with the bright sun reflecting on his brown hair made my heart skip a beat. I hurried to my locker, grabbing my jean jacket and anything else I needed before dashing to meet him in the parking lot.

"Ready?" he asked, his hand already reaching for my bag. Taking it by the strap, his arm jerked downward under its weight. "Christ, Rowen, what do you have in here? Your entire locker?"

"I've got a ton of homework and two exams tomorrow." I answered with a breathy exhale, aggravated by the amount of work I had and the little time I had to do it.

He opened the car door, placing my bag next to his on the backseat. "Do you still want to do this today? I mean, if a trip to the church is going to set you back, we can always reschedule."

"No, we can't. We're running out of time on this research project, too. Tomorrow we have our appointment with Libby at the Historical Society, and that leaves us two days to finish writing the whole report. I'll hit the books after dinner, and whatever I don't get done I can catch up on in study hall."

He shut the rear car door, and I walked around to the passenger side to get in, Hunter sliding in after me on the opposite side.

"Then let's go play in the cemetery," he teased, buckling his seat belt.

He pulled out of his space and headed down the hill to the traffic light at the school's entrance. Making a right on red, he merged into the northbound lane and headed up Route 9, bearing left at the fork in the road toward the church.

"Are you up for giving our oral presentation?" he asked, clicking on his right turn signal and guiding the car through the open cemetery gates.

"What are you talking about?"

"The oral synopsis of our findings. You do realize Mr. Conover expects each of us to get up and tell the class what we uncovered, if anything."

Mouth open, I shook my head. "*Ahhh*, no…"

150

Hunter nodded. "Sure, he mentioned it in class Friday."

"I must have zoned out or something, because I don't remember him saying that. Are you sure, or are you teasing me?" I sat staring at him, hoping he wasn't serious.

"Positive."

My mouth went dry at the thought of all those eyes watching me stumble over my own words. "Hunter, I don't think I can."

He parked along the side of the road that led to the graves and turned the ignition off. "Yes, you can," he said shifting in his seat to face me. "We'll do it together, and if you get nervous, look at me. Just tell it to me."

Giving him what I knew was a doubtful look, I shrugged. "If you say so."

"You'll be fine," he murmured, and then leaned over giving me a quick kiss. "Come on. I'm not sure how much time this guy is going to give us. I think the only reason he agreed to let us in afterhours is because I'm a Van Tassell and my family is related to half the people buried here."

"So?"

He eyed me, his head cocked to one side. "So, who do you think is buried in the vaults under the church?"

I swallowed hard. "Vaults? As in mausoleum-like grave thingies?"

He nodded. "Yeah, what did you think I meant?"

Incredulous, I just gaped. "I don't know. Bank vaults or record vaults. I didn't think you meant a crypt!'

He laughed, opening the car door. "Oh, come on. You had to have had an inkling or else you wouldn't have made that comment about *things* finding us. You're just getting cold feet."

Hunter got out of the car, and held out his hand for me to do the same. "Let's go." he said, steering me toward the path that led to the front of the church. "I'll hold your hand the whole time we're underground, I promise."

Underground?

I swallowed again. "Good. Because I'm not planning on letting go until we pull out of the parking lot and head home."

The door to the church was closed, but unlocked. Hunter knocked twice before we let ourselves in.

"Hello? Mr. Grayson?" he called.

"Up here, boy." A deep voice called above us.

Inside, the church was small, maybe the size of a large living room. A wide planked floor held approximately twenty pews facing a stark alter with a polished wood pulpit, both situated between two paned arched windows.

"So, the two of you are on a scavenger hunt, eh?" the voice called again.

We turned to see a heavy set man with a long white beard, wearing a Greek fisherman's cap, staring down at us from the choir loft.

Mr. Grayson came down the stairs, his movements careful and slow. "This place takes on a mystical quality come dusk," he said with a wheezy chuckle. "Such a small, unadorned place to inspire such imaginings, don'tcha think?" he continued, crossing toward us, neither of us sure what to say.

"You must be Laura's daughter," he said, eyeing me with a small sideways tilt of his head. "Fine lady, that one. Never understood why some folks insisted on giving her and your Gran such a hard time. Then again, these walls have seen and heard plenty of long nosed stares and wicked whisperings." He moved past us.

I looked at Hunter, and his shoulders inched up and dropped in a question mark.

"*Um*, thanks for letting us in, Mr. Grayson. I know it's not church etiquette to let people in after hours," Hunter said, his voice amplified in the quiet.

Mr. Grayson stopped, turning ever so slightly as he stepped into his chosen row. "Your family pew is there," he said to Hunter, pointing toward a bench on the left. "In fact, it was there your ancestor Eleanor sat when she caught the eye of a very young Washington Irving."

A teasing smile spread to the corners of his mouth, and he glanced up to where he was earlier. "Yes sir, it was from his perch way up in the loft that the young man first spied the Dutch beauty. Town legend has it, she was the inspiration behind his character, Katrina—but then again you know how gossip goes."

He sat, easing himself onto one of the narrow pews, motioning for us to do the same.

"Every one of the original families is related in some way or another. The Storms, the Van Tassells, the Philipses, the Van Lents, the Romers..." He looked at me. "Even the Ekerts."

At my raised eyebrow he smiled, giving me a nod. "Yep, all of them as intertwined as the stories that surround them. Master Irving's legend may be the most famous, but this land has more stories attached to it and its original families than you can shake a stick at."

I raised my hand, interrupting him before he could go on. "Excuse me, Mr. Grayson, but you said scavenger hunt..." I paused, letting my curiosity edge past the reservation in my voice. "Mr. Conover didn't ask us to look for anything but information and connections. Do people come here—kids, I mean—looking to take items from the church and its grounds?"

He shook his head and gave us another wheezy laugh. "No, child. This place is locked up tight and the security system rivals Fort Knox. No, by scavenger hunt, I was referring to the hunt for evidence as you just said. The difference this time is they didn't have me to help." He winked, laying his finger on the side of his nose in a creepy Santa Claus impression.

Hunter and I exchanged glances, and Mr. Grayson threw his head back and laughed, his shoulders shaking until he dissolved into a fit of coughing.

Taking out a handkerchief, he wiped his mouth before stuffing the folded white square back into his pocket. "Come on. Let me show you what I mean."

He led us out the main doors and around to the back of the church through the ancient grave stones. The graves seemed out of a horror movie, but the worst part was passing all the last names—names I knew as well as my own. I shivered, taking Hunter's hand and tightening my grip, not caring that physical contact was a no-no until Gran said otherwise.

We followed Mr. Grayson down a grass path to a fieldstone structure built into the hill beneath where the church and adjacent graveyard resided. The entrance was guarded by an iron gate, and the old man took an antique skeleton key from his breast pocket, holding it up for us to see.

"The Philipse family crypt is beneath the church, directly under the

center row of pews," he said, gesturing toward the church. "There used to be a trap door set into the floor near the back of the church that led directly into the tomb, but it was sealed off when some of the floorboards were removed due to dry rot."

He inserted the key in the weathered lock and turned it to the right. The tumblers engaged with a grinding whine, followed by a creepy screech as the man swung open the gate. "A few years later, another entrance was discovered. A secret one."

Mr. Grayson pulled a flashlight from his back pocket and led us toward another door, this one a stained, weather-beaten bronze. With as much ordeal, he opened it, leading us across a stone corridor, the temperature dropping several degrees the farther in we went.

"Who's buried out here?" I asked, wrinkling my nose at the smell of mold and decay.

Mr. Grayson didn't even glance up. "That's not your concern. What matters is where this outside tomb leads."

From the mysterious way the old man spoke, I half expected to find torches on the wall ensconced in iron that lit themselves as we passed, but as it was, all we had was a narrow beam of light coming from the man's flashlight.

Hunter fished in his back pocket, pulling out his cellphone. Next thing I knew the cold, wet stone walls were awash in light. He had managed to scroll for his iPhone flashlight.

Mr. Grayson looked over his shoulder, and smiled wide. "Now that's a resourceful young man. No wonder you're a Van Tassell."

With a nod the man held out his hand, his flashlight illuminating another door half hidden by moss and roots. Producing a second key from his pocket, he turned the lock, revealing a narrow stone passageway. We followed him up a tight incline until a rectangular room opened ahead. An ornate granite sepulcher was housed at its center flanked by two smaller ones on either side. Many of the smaller wood coffins set into the walls had rotted, collapsing one on top of the other and scattering bones to the stone floor.

I didn't have to look at my hands to know my knuckles were white, and from the look on Hunter's face he was as creeped out as I was.

"This crypt dates back to 1702 when church founder, Frederick

Philipse, died. He was interred with his first and second wives laid to rest on either side of him," he said, pointing to the three prominent graves. "But, I didn't bring you here to show you the resting place of a few old bones." He turned his head and directed his flashlight to the base of the stone wall at the head of the room.

Hunter let go of my hand and I protested, but he held up his palm and I shut up. He moved forward, shining his light on what turned out to be markings etched into the rock. He stopped, unsure about approaching further, but Mr. Grayson urged him on until Hunter was close enough to squat down and run his fingers across the writing.

"This isn't a formal inscription; it wasn't chiseled into the stone. This was carved into the rock with a knife or a blade."

"That's right, son. It was."

I looked from Hunter, whose face was now in shadow, back to Mr. Grayson. "If it's not an inscription for the Philipse's, then what is it? Who put it there? I mean who would desecrate a burial crypt with graffiti?"

The words left my mouth incredulous, but truth was I could think of at least a handful of people I knew personally who'd do it just for kicks.

I put my hand up, waving it gently to cancel my last question. "Don't answer that. I know there are enough creeps walking around to even be shocked."

Even in the dim light, Mr. Grayson's eyes seemed to soften. "I'm well aware of what people are capable of, love. You forget, I'm the gatekeeper here."

Hunter looked over his shoulder at us. "The writing is Dutch, isn't it?"

Mr. Grayson nodded. "Yes, it is. It reads, *Wraak en gerechtigheid alleen gevonden als bloed en waarheid voldoen aan.*"

At our matched set of blank looks, the man smirked. "Sorry. Just showing off a bit. It means, 'Revenge and justice are only found when blood and truth meet.'"

"What do you think it means?" I asked, not sure what this clandestine trip into the crypt was supposed to serve.

Hunter stood, wiping his palms one at a time on the front of his pants. "Mr. Grayson. How long has that writing been there?"

The old man considered the two of us, and in the eerie refracted glow

from the flashlight on the walls, he seemed almost ghost like.

"Over two-hundred years," he replied. "I can't tell you much more than that, but this crypt was used in secret by the patriots during the revolution to plan their strategies against the British—and in some cases, their revenge. You might want to keep that in mind while you're searching through Libby's records at the Historical Society. Very eye opening."

He gave us that same knowing look he did earlier, and then turned, gesturing for us to follow him out.

Hunter and I left the church, neither of us much for talking. Mr. Grayson may have thought he was pointing us in the right direction, but I was more confused than ever. Gran said many families were wronged by the loyalist members of the village, and I wondered if the writing on the crypt wall had anything to do with my visions, or some historic plan for revenge sought among the church brethren.

Marianne Morea

Chapter 11

I sat in study hall, watching the clock crawl while trying to concentrate on the chemistry lab I didn't get to the night before. Everything we learned from Mr. Grayson was still front and center in my mind. After Hunter and I left the Old Dutch Church, we headed to Horsefeathers Pub to grab something to eat, and spent the better part of the next two hours speculating on what we'd heard. Of course, that made Hunter late for practice and me late to the Silver Cauldron.

While I was in no jeopardy of being assigned laps for my tardiness, my guess was coach wouldn't be too hard on Hunter either, not after the wicked tight game he played on Saturday. But then again, there was no telling with jocks.

Of the two exams I had lined up today, AP History had gone well, thank God, considering I barely studied. I was too preoccupied after Hunter dropped me off at home to retain anything I read, yet my luck seemed to hold because Señora Clark was absent today, which meant no Spanish test.

The day had been drama free for the most part, even though Chloe had a mini nervous breakdown at lunch. She was nearly failing English, and this morning found out her research partner was out with mono for the next month, leaving her high and dry with only days left to complete the project on her own. She had been counting on a good grade to help boost her quarter average.

Mr. Conover gave her the choice to either triple up with Jenny and Constance, or go it alone. It was no surprise she decided to go solo, but what shocked me was how she managed to con Benny into helping her, even though he wasn't in AP English. Perhaps she was taking Talia's dating advice, after all. *God, I hoped not.*

The bell rang and I gathered my books, ready to face whatever formulas Mrs. McCafferty threw at me. I wasn't paying much attention, and didn't notice Jen standing beside her locker as I turned the corner. She slammed the rectangular door with a bang and turned to lean against the red steel.

"Saw Hunter's car parked at the Old Dutch yesterday. You two planning to tie the knot?" The lilt of her voice dripped candy, despite her too loud question broadcast to everyone within earshot.

Saying nothing, I let it pass, allowing my dirty look do the talking for me. As half expected, Jen pushed herself away from the lockers and fell into step with me, still fishing for a reaction.

"I don't get you, Rowen," she began. "You're rude, and you walk around like you're better than half the school, then out of the blue you come to my rescue in the bathroom like my BFF. What gives?"

I stopped short, and she jerked to a halt pivoting on her heeled sneakers to stay neck and neck with me.

Slack jawed, I just stared at her. "Do you actually hear what you say or do the words just fall onto your tongue like a gumball machine?"

Heat flushed to my cheeks as I stared her down, and it was all I could do not to yell. "You insult people, spewing verbal shrapnel for sport every chance you get, yet *I'm* rude? You've got to be kidding me. I refuse to put up with your nonsense, yet I still felt sorry for you the other night. Trust me, it'll never happen again."

Jen snorted. "*You* felt sorry for *me*? Yeah right. What happened was you finally realized being with Hunter meant *his* crew was now *your* crew. Face it, Rowen, you're one of us now, and membership does have its privileges. But don't sweat it, sweetie. I can only imagine how hard it is for you to shake the loser-tude that's been stuck to you for all these years. Must feel good, a girl like you with a guy like him? Goes to show miracles do happen."

Her bogus welcome to the club made my jaw hurt. "What is it you

want me to say, Jen? Thank you? Do you want me to apologize for the fact Hunter likes me and I like him?" I shook my head in a slow, deliberate gesture. "I think you know that's not going to happen."

Irritation pricked at me as we traded glares, but I ignored the sting, turning away before she could respond.

"Yeah, well. Enjoy the attention while it lasts." Her voice followed.

Now it was my turn to stop short. I wheeled around and stormed back to where she stood with her chin high and her eyes daring me to start something.

What did this chick want from me?

"You know, you and Tyler truly deserve each other," I said, watching her expression flick between sarcastic self-assurance and questioning doubt. "You're both selfish, with way too high an opinion of yourselves. It's pathetic. You're throwing tantrums because you didn't get what you expected. Well, here's a tidbit for you—life doesn't revolve around you, and one of these days you're going to learn that the hard way. You're just pissy because Hunter didn't fall at your feet, and Tyler can't get over the fact I would rather clean a toilet than let him put his hands on me."

Jen visibly blanched, and her sharp inhale a sure sign she had no idea Tyler had put the moves on me, too. A fleeting moment of guilt bit into my stomach, but I squashed it. I wanted her to leave me alone.

With an aggravated breath, I hiked my bag higher onto my shoulder considering my words. "Hey, I'm sorry. The thing with Tyler was ages ago, but that's not the point. Just leave me alone, okay? It's over. Hunter and I are a done deal. Get used to it."

The girl said nothing, just blinking at me with a shocked expression. I uttered a disgusted sigh and headed to class. Jen would have to learn to deal.

Hunter and I left school the minute we got the chance, each blowing off our last two classes to make the most of our meeting with Libby. As usual, mid-day traffic was at a snail's pace on Main Street, forcing him to inch our way toward the traffic light and the right turn that would take us toward the Historical Society.

Horns blared at a car stopped in the intersection, and Hunter cut around the momentary chaos, his wheels screeching in the process.

We turned right up the hill and then right again onto Grove Street, parking down the block from the stately Victorian that housed the Historical Society.

The celebrated brick building, with its intricate wrought iron fencing and red shuttered windows, was at the heart of the historic district. Built in 1848 by Jacob O'Dell for his new bride, the structure was now home to preserved artifacts and an extensive library of archival materials.

"It's so quiet," I murmured as we got out of the car. The tree lined road was nothing like the sea of traffic a block and a half away.

The street was awash with color, the afternoon sun adding to the riot of autumn leaves shimmering in hues of gold and red. Halloween decorations graced the walkways and front porticos of the modest homes set back from the sidewalk, turning the quiet suburban street into a supernatural fantasy land.

Libby was expecting us promptly at twelve-thirty, and as she had gone out of her way to accommodate us on such short notice, neither Hunter nor I wanted to be late.

We stood on the front path and surveyed the high, narrow structure with its steep front stairs and tall, thin door.

"After the crypt, this should be a cake walk," Hunter teased, stepping through the open gate with me in tow.

At the top of the stairs, I reached for the door, but stopped with my fingers barely an inch from the brass knob.

"What's the matter?"

"There's a sign warning visitors not to push or pull on the vintage handle."

"They know we're coming, just ring the bell," Hunter pointed out, gesturing to the small round circle to the side of the antique door.

A harsh buzzer sounded on the opposite side of the glass, and after a moment a silhouetted figure stepped out.

The door opened inward to reveal an attractive older woman. "You must be Hunter and Rowen," she greeted with a warm smile.

I nodded. "Yes, ma'am. We have an appointment with Mrs. Scarborough."

Her eyes glittered with humor and she took a step back, waving us in. "That you do. Come in, but watch your step on the door saddle."

The woman was of average height and build, and was dressed in a chic executive cut suit, dark shoulder length hair swept back from her face. She didn't seem the type to pour over dusty records. In fact, she looked as though she belonged on the board of a Fortune 500 company.

"You're Mrs. Scarborough?"

The woman nodded, laughing lightly. "Not the stuffy historian you envisioned, huh."

Immediately embarrassed, I wagged my head back and forth. "Sorry, I didn't expect you to be the one answering the bell."

"Budget cuts affect everyone," she replied, closing the door behind us. "Though, the real reason is we're not officially open for business today. The Historical Society is only open to the public on Wednesday, Thursday and Saturday afternoons. Private access is a little...irregular."

The vestibule opened to the main floor of the house which was set up as a museum of sorts. From what I could see, the narrow front hall broke into various rooms, the closest an antique front parlor. We followed Libby until she stopped at the base of a staircase situated near the end of the hall.

"As you see, we're pretty cluttered around here, so we make do with the room we have. The museum takes up the entire first floor, while Historical Society offices are located upstairs." She gestured, lifting her arm in the general direction of the second floor. "Where would you like to start?" she asked, looking at us from one to the other.

In the dim light, Libby looked even more out of place with the dust. "We don't want to get in anyone's way, so wherever is the most convenient for you," I said, hoping to redeem myself from my initial gaffe.

She paused, considering the both of us. "You could come upstairs to the conference room and start sorting through the archival materials: genealogies, books, diaries, etc., or you can start in the basement with the artifacts and objects of interests that are not currently on display."

Before I could answer, my nose wrinkled and I sneezed. The house was musty, with an aged trace coming from years of dust and layers of time. Libby handed me a tissue from the box on the antique sideboard against the wall.

"You'll get used to that," she said. "Comes with the territory. Why

don't you come upstairs and I'll introduce you to Cameron and Tara. Cam is our intern, and he'll be here with you 'til about five p.m., so you'll need to wrap things up by then. Tara is our archivist, so if you have any questions and I'm not available, she's your go-to-gal. Unfortunately, neither of us will be around for much of the afternoon. Tara and I have a fundraiser to get to, but if you leave a list of questions and your email address with Cameron, I'll make sure to get back to you with the answers tomorrow."

"Thanks, Mrs. Scarborough. We really appreciate your help."

She smiled at me "Anytime. I was surprised to get a call from your grandmother about your research project. Kids come every year to look up different things, but this was the first time I've had a request for a singular appointment. Anne must have called in a few favors to arrange it."

I glanced from Libby to Hunter and back again, a confused frown pulling at my forehead. "My grandmother called you?"

Libby looked surprised. "Well, yes. You didn't know I was doing this today as a favor to her?"

I peeked at Hunter whose expression was just as thrown. "No. I thought Hunter set this up."

Libby patted my arm and moved past me, placing one foot on the bottom stair. "He did. However, it was the call I received over the weekend that stressed how important it was for you two to get in here posthaste. I know your grandmother, and she doesn't usually get involved unless something serious is brewing...pardon the pun. I can only guess what's behind this research of yours, but I know better than to question Anne Dederick Ekert."

That made two of us.

Libby settled us in a conference room that appeared to be part storage room, part office space with an old-fashioned dining table at the center serving double duty. Books and piles of paper were crowded into shelves and on top of surfaces all around the room, making it clear why the Historical Society needed college interns for slave labor.

How anyone found anything in this place was beyond me, but Libby seemed to have everything at her fingertips in this controlled chaos. She bustled in and out, finally coming back with an arm load of books and

documentation.

"Here are the genealogies for the prominent families living in Sleepy Hollow and the surrounding areas during the time of the revolution." The heavy stack dropped to the table with a dull thud.

"This one, in particular, should be of interest," she added, patting top of the pile, and with a wink, handed the thick black volume to Hunter.

The book was dust-stained and dog-eared, but one word written across the binding left no question as to why she handed it to him.

Van Tassell.

He took the book from her hand, and studied it for a moment as if memorizing every crease. Tiny cracks in the ornate gold lettering along the spine gave the volume a museum-like quality, similar to old paintings at the Metropolitan Museum of Art. Hunter slid his fingers over his mother's maiden name, and opened the cover to yellowed pages filled with looping script.

"I'm sure it's a safe bet I'm not listed in this one," he teased, glancing up at Libby with a wink of his own.

With a small laugh, she shook her head. "Nope, sorry. Though I did bookmark the pages in most of the records pertinent to the time frame you mentioned. Take a peek. While they might not help much with your research, I still think you'll find them interesting."

She patted the books again, and then turned to leave. "Let Cameron know when you're ready to go downstairs. Happy hunting, kids."

"If I look at one more family registry, I swear I'm going to go blind." An unflattering yawn slurred the end of my sentence, and my eyes watered. I reached over my head and stretched, arching my back. "This is as bad as wading through the genealogy of Adam in the Book of Genesis. Want to call it a day? We've been coming up empty for hours."

Hunter's answering sigh was surprisingly severe. "No. Even with a pinpointed search based on your grandmother's stories, we haven't found anything that remotely correlates to Irving's legend. This sucks." He shoved the wide volume in front of him forward.

His voice was harsher than I'd heard before, but then again, I hadn't experienced a frustrated Hunter, yet. The amount of paperwork, coupled with tiny, almost illegible writing would tax the patience of a saint.

Maybe what we needed was a change of scenery.

"Tell you what. Let's finish with these last books and then go down and play with the artifacts. If anything, it'll at least wake us up." I took his hand in mine and bounced his fingers up and down teasingly. "…and, we haven't even looked at *your* lineage, yet. Come on, let's play the name game with the Van Tassells and see if your family has a forename that was used to death. So far we've had twenty people named Jan, ten named Pieter, and four named Bram."

The grandfather clock on the first floor chimed the half hour, and he looked up from fidgeting with the torn edge of one of the books in front of him. "You've got a bizarre sense of fun, you know that?" he said, his expression soft. "It's three-thirty already, and I didn't expect we'd still be plodding through birth and death records. I thought we'd be reading accounts of Emmerick and his crimes. If they were so bad, you'd think someone would have written about them."

Hunter stopped fidgeting, and pulled his hand away from mine to close his book, placing it on the dead soldier pile. "Maybe the stories about him were just that—nothing more than stories. Every timeframe, every age has scarlet letter stories. Perhaps the families needed an out and Emmerick was the best candidate to lay blame. He was a Hessian, right?"

I nodded.

"So, at that time Hessians were the boogie men, feared and hated. Makes for a nice, tidy way to clean up a daughter who had an illicit affair, don'tcha think?"

I didn't know what to say. Hunter didn't know my grandmother like I did, and her stories were never just stories. Then again, there was always a first time.

"I don't know. Maybe you're right." The words were sour coming out my mouth. Gran was never wrong, and it tasted like treason for me to even entertain the idea, let alone voice the possibility. I switched gears, dismissing the wayward feeling, and picked up the book with his family's genealogy. "Come on. Let's see where you come from."

Scooting my chair around, I moved closer to his and plopped the book between us. "From the way the pages layout, it looks as though this one covers every branch of your family in generic order of births, deaths

and marriages. Back in the day, who was your direct ancestor? If we start from there it shouldn't be too hard to trace." I said, skimming a few more pages.

"I think it was Jan Cornelissen Van Tassell or Van Texel. The name got corrupted at some point."

"More Jans," I shot back with a snort. "They weren't exactly a creative bunch, huh?" I scanned chapters, running my finger down the list of names and dates until I found the right family line, and then scrolled down to find the correct 'Jan.' "Got it."

I shifted the book closer to Hunter so he could get a better look, and pointed to the last entry at the bottom of the page.

"That says 1667, Rowen. We need to add about a hundred and ten years' worth of ancestors to that."

I smirked and turned the book back to face me. "Haven't you been paying attention to how this all works? All we need is to follow the dates of the children and grandchildren that came afterward, and that should… lead…us… right… here!" I exclaimed, flipping a half a dozen pages to the one that read, *Van Tassell and Allied Lines: Fourth Generation.*

"Cornelius Van Tassell and Elizabeth Storm. Those were your direct ancestors from the time of the revolution." I announced triumphantly.

He shrugged. "So?"

I wrinkled my nose at him. "So? It says right here Cornelius was involved in the infamous patriot burnings." I tapped the page with my index finger. "There's even an accounting…see…"

With my finger on the footnoted section, I moved the book closer for him to see. "You said you wanted an accounting, well here you go. First hand, and from the exact time frame we've been looking for."

He took the book from me and scanned the page. When his eyes met mine, it was as if a light had gone off in his head. "I think this is something important, Rowen."

"For the project?"

"No…" He shook his head, unease and uncertainty warring in his eyes. "…I don't know, maybe. But I've got gooseflesh up and down my arms, and the hair on my neck is tingling."

"Read it," I said, scooting the book even closer to him. "Out loud."

Hunter began slowly, the language being unfamiliar and old

fashioned.

"The British scouting parties having met with many humiliating defeats at the hands of these [Americans], Governor Tryon determined to adopt harsh measures to exterminate them....

"On the night of Nov. 17, 1777, Peter and Cornelius Van Tassell were taken prisoner at their homes by Captain Emmerick's command from King's Bridge, a part of which also proceeded to the house of Major Abraham Storms, which they partially burned.

"The enemy having collected the Van Tassell's stock of cattle, made sure their prisoners should not escape as they tied their hands to their horses' tails, in which position they compelled them to drive their cattle to their camp [dragging the imprisoned men behind].

"While they were preparing to burn the dwelling, Lieutenant Van Tassell's [teenage] son, Cornelius, Jr., having secreted himself in the attic, was driven out by the smoke. Throwing a blanket over his head he came down stairs and sprang over the lower half of the hall door and ran rapidly to the Saw Mill River, pursued by the enemy, who gave up the chase when they found that he had broken his way through the ice in order to escape. [The boy] died later as the result of his exposure at the time of his father's capture. Captain John Romer, husband to Leah Van Tassell Romer, gave the following account in 1845..."

"*The night on which the houses were surprised and burnt was one of the coldest of the season. Cornelius Van Tassell on the first alarm sprang from the windows and tried to escape, being almost naked. He was taken, but never recovered from the exposure of that night. The Tory Captain, Joshua Barnes, acted as guide for [the devil] Emmerick that night and his voice was heard above the tumult: 'The houses are both owned by damned Rebels—burn them!' My wife, Leah Van Tassell, was the only daughter of Cornelius, and she was the infant taken out of the house in a blanket by a soldier, [compelled by kindness and humanity] and laid carefully in the snow, and the mother, distracted and distraught, was seeking her babe when he told her where the child was. The only son, Cornelius, Jr., fled for safety half naked to the roof of the house and held on by the chimney, from which when the fire began to reach him he jumped to the ground. He escaped that night, but caught cold from which he*

never recovered."

The report continued, but paraphrased by the historian. "It was about this time that Governor Tryon issued his infamous order to "Burn Tarrytown," which provoked swift reprisal, and so Lieutenant(s) Cornelius and Peter Van Tassell were cruelly and ignominiously carried away to New York as prisoners of war. While the [Van Tassell] dwelling was burning, one of the soldiers actuated with praiseworthy feelings of humanity obtained a feather bed and threw it over the mother and child, who were then secreted away to a dirt cellar, [the only habitation left upon the farm] to care for themselves."

I sat thunderstruck. "So Emmerick *was* the bastard Gran told me about."

Hunter made a face, and sorted through the spiral bound documents Libby had left along with the genealogies, tossing some papers aside, and examining others.

"Hunter…what are you doing?" I asked, watching him plow through the archival material like a man possessed.

"I want to find out if there's anything else on this guy."

He stopped, lifting one of the booklets from the pile. "This is it," he said showing me the cover.

"The King's Men," I murmured, scanning the title.

He opened the pamphlet, his eyes scouring the regiments listed on the inside pages. He exhaled, shaking his head in frustration. "Emmerick's Chasseurs," he muttered, his eyes flicking back and forth as he read. "The language is way formal, but it's not hard to read between the lines. The man was a Hessian, and based on that alone it's not a far stretch to assume also a mercenary—still, he was promoted to Lt. Colonel. According to record, his legion was, *'very ill-disciplined, particularly among the officers, which directly led to its disbanding in 1779.'"*

His eyes scanned the paper again. "Very ill-disciplined. There's no need for a formal interpretation of that." He made a face, and shifted his gaze to me, gesturing with the pages. "Your grandmother did a good job of filling in any blanks, plus the timeframe matches the account she told you. If Emmerick did what town legend says, then it follows suit Governor Tryon would have gotten wind of it, eventually tossing the man out on his sorry ass—and *not* because of what he did to the

townspeople, but because he cheated the British Governor."

I shook my head, research project forgotten. "That means the rest of what Gran told me is probably true, too."

He nodded slowly, a deliberate smirk gracing his mouth. "That he's got descendants running around town somewhere. Most of the families stayed local, right?"

I bobbed my head up and down. It was true for the most part.

Hunter got up and paced. "Irving published his *Legend* in 1820. He had to have known who was who, and like Mr. Conover said, Irving was privy to everything, both past and present..."

"And took walks through the cemetery taking names for his story," I interjected.

Hunter sat. "It's needle in a haystack time, babe. We need to find which family in town had Emmerick's bastard child."

Without waiting for me to say anything, he pushed his chair in and maneuvered around the end of the table, his fingers grazing my shoulder as he passed. We needed Tara, and if I knew Hunter, that's where he was headed.

Chapter 12

Tara brought us every diary she could find that had any connection to the families or the timeframe we were looking for. We worked feverishly, pouring over the records, until Tara came back with one last volume.

In addition to the slim book, she had two pairs of white cotton gloves in her hand. With one glance it was easy to see this particular diary was one of extreme age. Its cover was threadbare and frayed at the seams, and its pages had moved beyond simple yellowing to a crumbling brown.

Tara placed the book on the table, resting her fingertips on the cover. "I'm leaving now, as I'm already hours late and need to get to the fundraiser. Libby is already there; however I wanted to give this to you, first. I'm sure I don't have to explain how delicate and valuable this volume is. It's the diary of Maritie DeBoeck."

Hunter held out his hand for the gloves, gesturing for me to do the same. My hand shook at the thought of handling something so precious.

"It's written in Dutch, so you won't be able to read it."

My hand slumped along with my shoulders. Why show it to us, then?

"It's been translated, but unfortunately I don't have the complete transcription," she said, holding out a handful of typed sheets. "But I think I have what you're looking for."

Hunter took the book, holding the diary in awe before placing it flat on the table and carefully opening the cover. I took the typed copies from

Tara's outstretched hand.

"I have one email left to answer and then I'll be heading out. I can't leave any of the diaries with you without either Libby or me present, so you have about five minutes to finish up with them. Please be especially careful with that one," she said, eyeing the DeBoeck volume.

She turned, but Hunter interrupted before she could leave. "Tara, who was she?" he asked, gesturing to the book she just handed to us.

Tara paused as if considering her words. "She was the Dominee's wife, the first lady of the Old Dutch Church. From all accounts, a truly spiteful woman." she hesitated again. "Ironic, really."

"Why?" I asked.

She raised one shoulder and let it drop. "Because in her youth she was sentenced to stand pillory for lewd behavior. She was one of Captain Emmerick's infamous conquests."

Tara didn't elaborate further. With a nod, she left to answer her emails, leaving Hunter and me to wonder about the diary and its author. Everything suddenly seemed fishy. Did Gran tell Libby and Tara what books to hand us, or was this all just coincidence?

"Do you want to read this, or should I?" I held the typed sheets between us.

"You do it." He set the diary to the side and peeled off the white gloves.

I scanned the cumbersome pages, reading quietly to myself before glancing up at Hunter. "She was Emmerick's mistress all right. Brags about it in spades. It's just like Gran said. She was her father's pawn to save their farm, and when Emmerick was disgraced and his legion disbanded, her own father turned on her, accusing her of debauchery. She was to be lashed and tied to a pillory, but threw herself on the mercy of the Dominee."

He snorted. "What a tool. Her father trades her like cattle, and then turns his back when it comes time to ante up. Sounds to me like she went into survival mode and did what she had to in order to stay alive. I feel bad for her, even if she was narcissistic. I guarantee it was her father's betrayal that caused her to become bitter and puritanical."

"Look at you, psychoanalyzing a two hundred year old head case."

He frowned. "I'm not psychoanalyzing anyone, but people get

messed up because of things in their life they can't control."

Hunter was quiet after that, and I didn't comment. I didn't need Psychology 101 to know he was talking about his own dad.

"Listen, we'd better head downstairs before it gets much later. Is there anything else in that transcript that might help?" he redirected, changing the subject completely.

I shook my head, exhaling a low whistle as I flipped through more of the pages. "Nope, just that the name DeBoeck gets its origin from people who lived by a brook." I paused skimming the same page again. "There's one footnote that's interesting, though…"

"What?"

I shrugged. "Nothing really, just that it was family tradition for the name DeBoeck, or a variation of it, to be included as a second or third name for every baby born into the line. It says here it was a custom carried over from the Netherlands as a way to differentiate the families, since so many shared the same forenames and surnames." I folded the thin document and stuck it in my notebook. "Makes sense, I guess. After all, how many *Jans* did I say we counted?"

Hunter was quiet.

"What?"

He shook his head.

"No, come on…what?"

"We need to take that transcript and match up the DeBoeck lineage straight through the last census," he said, pointing to the printout poking out from the edge of my notebook.

I eyed him. "What's going on, Hunter. What just happened?"

He hesitated, before meeting my gaze head on. "I think I know who Emmerick's descendant is."

A quick covetous grin spread across my face. "Who?"

I watched his expression, and felt the excitement in my own fade.

"It's not you, is it?" I kept my voice low, immediately sorry for my initial gossipy tone.

He shook his head, glancing down at his fingers laced together on the table. "No, it's not me." And he answered the look on my face before I could voice the words. "…and no, it's not you, either."

"Who then?"

"Tyler."

My eyebrows flew into my hairline, and I was practically bouncing in my seat. "No way!" From the table, my hand came down in a thump, sending dust everywhere from the pile of old linens tucked onto the chair beside me.

He nodded. "Tyler's middle name is Boeck."

My enthusiasm waned into uncertainty. "Okay...but a guess based on a middle name is a bit of a stretch, don't you think?" I didn't exactly like Tyler, but this was too unbelievable, even for me.

"I can't argue with that. We have to prove the truth by finding the right records."

Still trying to play devil's advocate, I hedged, "Yeah, but those records wouldn't be here. Libby and Tara will most likely have archives up 'til the turn of the century at most and neither one of them is here to answer the question."

He pushed back from the table. "I know. We can hit town hall tomorrow, especially if we ask Cameron to email us the DeBoeck genealogy, we can take it from there."

There was so much to think through, so much more we needed to ask. Moreover, none of this proved anything or moved us closer to a correlation for our project.

"Come on, let's see what they have downstairs. There isn't anything else we can do until we get that list."

I tucked my notebook into my bag, my mind churning. "Even if all this is true, it's not like we can use any of it."

"Why not?"

"Because the assignment was for us to research town events that possibly correlate to the legend and Irving's character creation, that's why."

The clock chimed downstairs. We had one hour before we had to clear out, and we'd wasted enough time chasing shadows.

"Are you telling me you can't see the possibilities here?" Palms pressed into the table, Hunter leaned forward. "Have you even read the legend?"

I stood, annoyance biting into my brow. "That's a stupid thing to ask. Of course I have."

"Katrina was the belle of the town, right? She beguiled every guy she ever met, including the bad boys. It's not hard to imagine she was a bit of a tease."

"So?" I shoved the rest of my research notes into my bag.

"Then you have Brom Bones. A bad boy prankster with a disorderly crew, tearing up the town until all hours."

"Again, so?"

He stood, his body language screaming single-mindedness. "Think, Rowen. The schoolmaster and the bad boy. Don't you see the connection? According to record, Maritie DeBoeck married the Dominee of the town after her fall from grace."

"Hunter, I'm still not following you."

He exhaled, raising his hand and letting it drop. "Dominee is the Dutch term for schoolmaster or church master." Anticipation glinted in his eyes, and he cycled his hand encouraging me to follow his train of thought.

A long minute passed, and I opened my mouth, but shut it again.

"Oh come on, Rowen, you're not thinking outside the box. Ichabod Crane was Irving's fictional schoolmaster! Get it? Irving could have taken town gossip and reworked it, especially if Maritie turned out to be the hard-ass Tara mentioned. In real life she married the Dominee, but she *wanted* the bad boy that got away—Emmerick. In the story, Irving gives her what she wants, but at a cost."

"I...I don't know, Hunter. There's a lot of academic speculation already as to who inspired the character of Brom Bones. I don't think Emmerick is one of them."

His hand sliced the air horizontally. "Yeah, yeah, but the operative word is *speculation*. If that's the case, then why is my theory any less valid? We've studied this in class, Rowen. The language used in the Legend of Sleepy Hollow, especially when it came to Katrina Van Tassel, was battle-like, stating that women must be 'captured' and a man must 'maintain possession' and 'battle for his fortress.' Don't you think that makes more sense if Irving had a soldier in mind, rather than a country prankster?"

"Yeah, but..."

He was on a roll and cut me off. "Plus there's the whole self-serving

attitude of the townspeople in his story. Ichabod was a poor nobody, an outsider, and no one gave a rat's ass when he disappeared. The entire town was more than hot to believe a ghost spirited him to hell than admit one of their own took a prank too far and actually killed someone.

"Think about it. In your grandmother's account, the townspeople peddled their own daughters to Emmerick to protect their wealth. Irving's tale reeks of the same self-centeredness, especially in his description of the Ichabod the Schoolmaster—and that babe, is where we can draw our correlations."

His nod at the end felt more like an exclamation point, and I half expected him to sing out, "Tah dah!"

A slow grin itched at the corner of my mouth. Hunter was definitely excited, but in an eager, almost cocky manner. "Sounds like someone did his homework."

With a self-conscious smirk he dropped his chin, keeping his eyes on the table. "Yeah, well. After yesterday's mysterious crypt caper, I didn't want to show up here unprepared. I did some last minute reading before I went to bed."

"Some? You could write a thesis on the subject."

Cameron poked his head through the doorway, his tall lanky frame almost filling the space. The muffled tick-tick-tick of a bass beat rose from the iPod stuffed into his jacket, and one ear bud hung loosely around his neck while the other was still plugged into his left ear.

"Hey..." He gestured with a quick pop of his chin. "I unlocked the door to the basement in case you still want to head down to look at the artifacts. I've got some transcription to do," he said, motioning toward the back office with his loose ear bud. "Give me a heads up when you're done so I can lock up."

He angled off, already stuffing his other ear bud back into place.

Hunter snorted. "Transcription my ass. That was a GreenDay backbeat coming from his pocket."

"Let's go," I said, slipping my shoulder strap over my head.

The basement opened into a large rectangular space with small egress windows that gave a ground level view of the gravel parking lot to the side of the historic house. A narrow corridor led to a series of rooms, each housing different sets of antiques—from furniture and clothing to

artifacts from the infamous capture of Major Andre and the treasonous plot hatched by American turncoat, Benedict Arnold.

Libby had drawn a makeshift map, showing which artifacts were stored in what room. She had even set up a long folding table for us to use while examining each piece.

There were swords and dirks from the time of the revolution, as well as bits of pottery, candlesticks, choir books and even a collection plate from the Old Dutch Church. In one box there were dozens of grave rubbings, buttons, shoe buckles, and bits of lace from the 18th century.

We carried a few items to the table and laid them out. I took a turn examining the grave rubbings, while Hunter busied himself with the weaponry.

He held up one of the regimental dirks, holding it in the flat of his palm. The blade was ten inches long with an intricately carved handle inlaid with silver. "This is amazing," he said, wrapping his hand around the hilt. "It fits so perfectly into the palm of your hand."

I sorted through the tray with the buttons. The items were mostly brass and dull, tarnished silver, but one caught my eye. It was a single cufflink, most likely silver, but what piqued my interest was the crest embossed into the front circle.

"Hey, take a look at this," I said, tapping Hunter on his sleeve.

He looked up, craning his neck slightly. "That's the Van Tassell crest." He put the knife on the table and took the cufflink. "I remember seeing this in my grandfather's house," he said, turning the small rounded discus over in his hand.

After a moment, he glanced up. "It's a miracle this survived in such good condition. I know it's a long shot, but take a look and see if its match is in the box, as well."

I rummaged around, picking up and discarding item after item, but luck was with us and at the bottom I found its mate. "Whaddya know!"

Holding up the second one, it was my turn to examine the design, from the engraved banner flags and plumed helmet, to the baroque lion at the center.

Hunter put the cufflink down and picked up the knife again. "You don't suppose Libby would let me take the pair home, do you?"

I shrugged, watching as he examined the dagger again. "She might,

after all it's your family crest. Here, you'd better keep the two together," I offered, handing him the one I had.

Our fingers touched and a wave of vertigo hit me hard. I gasped, squeezing Hunter's fingers, the cufflink pressing painfully into both our hands.

Hunter's face changed, and his breathing became shallow and rapid. Beads of sweat formed on his forehead and his knuckles whitened around the hilt of the dagger in his opposite hand.

I let go, the cufflink dropping to the table with a dull plink, and rushed around to the opposite side of the table.

"I can't let go," he rasped. His eyes were saucers as his other hand came up of its own volition and wrapped around the hilt, forming a double fisted grip.

I didn't know what to do, my eyes glancing between him and the stairs. "I'm going to get Cameron." I took two steps away from the table, only to have Hunter whine in pain.

"Don't. Leave. Me," he struggled out.

I stood frozen in fear, realizing what Hunter must have felt being on the watching end of my visions. He was fighting some unseen force, and I didn't know what to do.

Pressing my lips together, I reached for my phone in my back pocket. "I'm calling my mother." I announced it as if I were calling in the marines, only to find I had no signal.

"Crap on toast!"

Hunter's eyes grew even wider, and we both watched as the blade turned in his hands, his forearms shaking with the effort to stop it as it pushed its tip downward, tilting straight for his heart.

"Oh, my God!" I rushed to the table and tried to pry his fingers loose from the hilt. His hands were a vice grip, and I looked at him, my heart sinking at the fear in his eyes.

I dragged in a breath and tried to think of everything my mother ever taught me about directing and redirecting energy. Why didn't I pay more attention?

Regardless of who raised the energy, the source needed a conduit in order to travel. It was the same in the physical world as in the magical. Power formed in a spiral either from the earth upward, or in reverse from

the universal crown, but either way it could always be directed back into the earth.

"Hunter, listen to me. We have to pool our energy and form a block, a wall of will, and send whatever this is into the ground."

His lips were dried and cracking. His tongue darted out to try and wet them. "Hurry, Rowen. I can't hold on much longer."

Ugh. This place was solid concrete. My eyes searched the floor and the base of the walls, finally moving up to the egress window. Alarm tape covered the corners as well as the connecting alarm wire, but I was sure Cameron had turned the system off with us down here.

The window was street level and butted against landscaping, which meant dirt. With a hiss of, "yes!" I grabbed Hunter's chair and pushed against it with all my might, turning him around to face the window. With no time to worry about the consequence, I grabbed one of the other blades from the table and dragged my chair to the base of the window. Hopping up, I sliced through the connection tape, severing the alarm wires and opened the window.

Fresh air drifted in, and the cool feel fortified me as I pushed the hair away from my sweaty forehead.

"Okay, let's do this. Like Gran said, I'm a conduit and you're a magnet, so let's send whatever this is back to hell."

Hunter moaned and I swallowed back on the panic squeezing my throat. I wrapped my hands around his, digging my fingers beneath his as far as they could go. My fingernails tore at his skin and he hissed at the pain, but I ignored the pang of guilt that washed passed, concentrating all my energy into breaking whatever it was that held him in thrall. His grip gave slightly, and I slid my fingers even further in, breaking the invisible hold at bit more.

Our eyes locked and I pressed my forehead to his. "Together," I murmured, and kissed the bridge of his nose.

I concentrated, gathering my thoughts and my desires, focusing on my longing for Hunter, my want of him, both physical and emotional. The air around us chilled to freezing, and I knew it wasn't from the open window. My breath sucked inward, the sharp intake almost knocking me backward. Hunter was trembling, and I squeezed his fingers, not caring if I broke them in the process.

Hollow's End

The air swirled around us, and vertigo took me, nausea biting into my throat and I tasted bile. Images danced on the periphery, and I pressed my forehead harder into Hunter's, willing the vision to take us both.

We weren't in the basement store rooms any longer. The wind howled, and the icy cold bit into our arms. Across a winter barren front garden, fire billowed from the cottage farmhouse I saw in an earlier vision. A woman was on the ground in her nightclothes, and I felt the snow turning her exposed flesh red and raw. Anguish and fear lashed through me, and suddenly I knew her child was inside the inferno.

Watching from a distance, I cried out, as her husband was beaten and dragged through the snow and muck, a dagger at his throat as his captors lashed him to the back of a cow.

"Hunter, can you see this?" I asked in a low hiss, but he shook his head. I pulled one of my hands free and lifted his chin so I could see his face, screaming when I saw his eyes had been hollowed.

Helpless tears stung my cheeks in the cold, and I turned back, watching as the woman begged on her knees in the snow for the life of her children, only to be backhanded and sent sprawling to the ground. Cruel laughter and drunken jeers followed as she landed with her night dress pushed around her naked thighs.

A single soldier took off his coat and offered it to her, but she shook her head, instead pointing to the house, a plea of desperation in her voice as she begged again. The man looked to his commanding officer, but he stood laughing with the others. Disregarding orders, the soldier plunged his coat into the well and tossed the soaked garment over his head, rushing headlong into the burning house.

Injured and coughing from the smoke, the man emerged holding the toddler in his arms. The soldier's eyes held such pity as he wrapped them together in a feather bed, but his empathy was short lived, as his commander seized a whip from the confiscated barn and beat him, a curse on his lips with each lash.

Vertigo whirled again and we were back in the basement, but the entity's hold on Hunter hadn't lessened. The air churned in the room, whipping up papers and sending artifacts flying.

In the depths of the din a voice called out as if struggling to be heard. "Revenge and justice only found if blood and truth meet." The voice was

ethereal, nothing more than a moan in the swirl of the air, yet its words were clear.

The howling stopped and the room settled, but just as I thought it was over, the concrete groaned and the thick basement walls breathed in an out, and the air was heavy and loathsome. I drew in a deep breath and focused everything, all my fears and hopes, and issued a final and definite demand. "Leave. Us. Alone!"

Glass exploded outward and Hunter's hands were released. With a sharp draw he sucked in breath as if starved for air, letting the dagger clatter to the floor. Without missing a beat, I stepped on the blade, flinging my arms toward the patch of grass outside the shattered window, my mother's words on my lips: "Return to earth all energies, and go to the greatest good. I banish and bind all that seek to harm."

It was over, and I slid down onto the floor beside Hunter's chair, exhausted. How much time had passed? Had Cameron heard anything, or was he so plugged into command central upstairs he was oblivious to the supernatural hell hole we just encountered?

I stood, taking the blade with me, and stalked to one of the dusty sideboards. I then threw the dagger in a drawer that had a key and turned the lock, tossing the key into the far corner of the room.

Hunter sat up, his face drawn. I ran to him and sank to my knees in front of him, gathering him into my arms. "Are you okay?"

He inhaled again, his breath still ragged but better than before. "Okay is relative," he mumbled into my shoulder.

He pulled back to look at me, and my heart squeezed with how pale he seemed.

"You heard the voice?" I asked, not wanting to push it but still needing to know it wasn't just me.

He nodded. "Whatever it was, it wasn't the same energy that kept me pinned. It broke through. It was meant for us to hear."

I didn't answer; I was too scared to think about the implications.

Hunter slid his hands to my face and cupped my chin. "It's a war, Rowen. Whatever is going on here is a battle. I don't know if it's between good and evil or between two spirits who have unfinished business, but for some reason it involves you and me and the vision you saw and I heard." He paused. "The voice…"

I nodded. "I know. It was the same message carved into the wall in the crypt."

"We have to figure this out, Rowen. It's getting worse and I think we need to tell your grandmother what happened."

I shook my head, my own reservations gripping me. "No. Not yet." I exhaled harshly, knowing Hunter thought I was just being petulant. "I know we should, but Gran will stop us from seeing each other at all. I wouldn't put it past her to spell us into forgetting we even know each other, let alone like each other."

I flopped down on the floor, and folded my arms in front of my chest. Maybe I was being peevish, but I refused to let some supernatural entity bully me from another realm.

I set my jaw, yet Hunter was as stubborn as me. A frustrated sigh escaped my lips and I got to my feet to help him up, then handed him what was left of my water bottle.

"What time do you think it is?"

He took a huge swig from my bottle, finishing the water with a gulp. "I'm not sure. He fished in his pocket for his phone. "Mine's dead. Check yours."

"I don't have service…" I reached for mine, only to see it was eleven p.m. and I had full bars. "What the?" I held up the phone so he could see.

"The entity knew enough to mess with our cellphones. This is bad, Rowen."

"How did Cameron lock us in and set the alarm even though the window was shattered?"

Hunter shook his head. "I don't know. Look, I want to get out of here. Call your mother and have her get in touch with Libby. After we call we won't have a choice but to tell them what happened."

I chewed on my lip. "Okay. But we need to downplay the whole knife thing, or we're both in a spelled bubble for our own protection, courtesy of our own mothers. Got it?"

Grim faced, he nodded in agreement. "Deal. Now let's get the hell out of here."

Chapter 13

The Silver Cauldron was busy all afternoon, and I stayed an extra hour after closing so Gran didn't have to come in. I felt bad; especially since Mom had gotten her out of bed for our supernatural recap late the night before.

With my mother's consent, I stayed home from school, too traumatized to deal with the day to day of classes and homework. Hunter didn't go in either, but his Wednesday schedule was a light as mine, so it was all good.

As agreed, we gave the Stygians a watered down version of what happened in the basement. Neither of us was fooling anyone, least of all Gran, and Hunter and I knew it. She stared at both of us as we recounted the details of the vision and what we thought sparked it, even going as far as to tell them about the walls breathing in and out, and the disembodied voice that was separate from the slick, oily feel of the all rest. We deliberately skirted the part about the dagger and the hold it had on Hunter, but from the way Gran's lips were pressed together in a thin bloodless line, she knew. She didn't say anything, but she knew.

Of course, we gave Libby a totally separate story, explaining how I panicked and broke the window when Hunter and I couldn't get out. My mother assured her she would cover the cost of any damages, but Libby was less than impressed to say the least.

I felt bad, considering the woman had gone out of her way for us, but

what else could we say? *"Sorry, Lib, but your basement is haunted, and Hunter and I inadvertently triggered a paranormal event that caused all the damage?"* I don't think so. The woman would either call the cops, or call for a straitjacket.

While Mom, Britt and Gran tried to piece things together, I felt worse when we heard Cameron had lost his internship as a result. None of this was his fault. All I can say is thank God the old building had a history of electrical system glitches, because faulty wiring was the only explanation Libby was buying as to why the alarm never sounded when the window shattered.

Surprisingly enough, none of the Stygians overreacted as I expected. In fact, they were calm. Too calm. Nevertheless, my mother's watchful gaze hovered at a distance all day, until it became unbearable. I was standing at the register when the bells on the front door jangled, and I glanced up thinking it was Hunter, but I didn't see anyone. "We're closed!" I yelled to whoever it was that came in.

"Hey, Rowen."

Money in hand, I looked up again to see Tyler and Benny standing across the front counter from me. "Tyler. What are you guys doing here?"

"Hunter texted he planned to meet up with you around five, something about the two of you heading out to the Van Cortlandt estate to blaze it up."

I rolled my eyes, stuffing the cash back in the register. "We're not blazing it up, Tyler." Disdain dripping from my voice at his childish Mary Jane joke. "Hunter was talking about *the Blaze*, as in jack-o-lanterns. These particular pumpkins don't get lit 'til Halloween. If you must know, we're volunteering to place the new ones being carved. Still interested, or was it just the idea of playing with fire that appealed to you?"

"Ha. Very funny, but I'm not the only one who likes to play with fire around here. You and Morrissey had your own little blaze going, getting locked in at the Historical Society and staying out all night," he said running his fingers across the top of the counter, his eyes glued to mine. "And here you had me fooled into thinking you preferred to go it alone. I guess the Fair Ms. Frigidaire is actually a tease, go figure."

"Piss off, Tyler and take your minion with you," I shot back, shoving his hand off the counter. I was suddenly very aware of just how alone I

was in the store with them, especially with Benny chuckling behind one the bookshelves. "I told you we're closed. Don't let the door hit you in the ass on your way out."

A full grin broke out across his face. Hunter was right; it was obvious Tyler enjoyed getting under my skin. "Relax, Rowen. We actually came in to look around. Hunter told me he invited you to our cemetery soirée, right? So what's better in a bone yard than a séance, complete with props and creepy music? Got anything good we could use? I want to scare the pants off Jenny."

I had to press my lips together to keep the snide comments to myself. From what I heard, he didn't need to bother. Jenny's reputation said she'd striptease for a snow cone.

I turned my back, not trusting my facial expressions, and busied myself behind the counter. "We're not a costume shop, Tyler. We don't sell props. There are books on séances toward the back of the store, next to the crystals and the case with the ritual tools," I answered over my shoulder, then paused. Why were Ty and Benny suddenly interested in spell craft? I shook my head dismissing the foolish worry. It's not like either would know what to do with the items, anyway. "Don't touch anything. If you want to see something, I'll get it for you. You've got until Hunter gets here, then I'm throwing you out."

Tyler headed back toward Benny. I reopened the register to finish counting out the drawer while I waited for Hunter. He was late, and I found myself watching the clock. Finally, the bells on the front door jingled again, and this time it was him.

"Hey," I said, locking the cash register for the night. Despite everything we'd been through, things between us were still so new I wasn't quite sure how I should greet him. Hunter took care of that, coming around the back of counter and pulling me into his arms for a quick kiss.

"Ready to go?" he asked, brushing my hair back from my cheek.

I rolled my eyes and shook my head. "Not exactly. Tyler and Benny are here," I said, motioning toward the back of the store with my head. "They're looking for stuff for the cemetery party. Tyler wants to scare Jenny."

Hunter made a face. "She's about as sharp as a doorknob. He'd do

better with just shouting *boo!* at her."

I laughed, smacking him on the shoulder.

"Hey, Rowen," Benny called from the back behind the bookcases. "This cool black knife with all the funny carvings on it. What's it for?"

I rolled my eyes, and Hunter chuckled, shaking his head. "It's a Wiccan ritual knife called an athame, used for casting. The carvings are not funny, they're rune symbols. That particular knife is inscribed to portent primal energy, spiritual journeys and to break constraints. It's not a toy and it's not for you."

I paused, unease pecking at me the minute the words left my mouth. Looking at Hunter I gestured toward the back of the shop. "Go check on them, will you? They've been back there awhile. I bet they're trying to read some of the package information and got stuck on the bigger words."

Hunter smirked, a comment on his lips when a huge crash echoed from the back of the store. Running toward the sound, we stopped short when we found ourselves staring at books and packs of tarot cards, candle paraphernalia and broken glass from the curio case all over the floor.

"What the hell? Didn't I tell you I'd get whatever you wanted to look at?" I said, staring at Tyler and Benny in disbelief.

"Sorry, Rowen. I reached for the statue with the horns on it and everything sort of happened," Benny said, embarrassed. "It was an accident, really."

I exhaled, looking around at the broken glass and crushed candles. Benny never said much, in fact that was the reason Tyler liked him around. He was the fall guy for Tyler's clown act, and I'd bet anything Tyler instigated this entire mess, letting Benny take the blame. One glance at Hunter told me he had the same thought. "It's all right Benny, but you guys better get going."

Tyler put his hand on my shoulder, and it took all my self-restraint not to jerk away. "You sure you don't want Benny to stay and help you clean up?" he asked, a little too close for comfort.

Hunter's eyes narrowed and he took a possessive step in my direction. "No. That won't be necessary. Neither of you need to stick around. I've got Rowen covered, but thanks for your offer to help, Tyler."

Sarcasm coated his every word, and the two Sleepy Hollow boys eyed each other for a moment.

It was plain Tyler got Hunter's meaning loud and clear because he stepped away from me. Benny might be a hanger-on, but not Hunter. No way. I smiled up at him, slipping my arm just as possessively around his waist. "Thanks, babe." I said giving his cheek a peck.

The set of Tyler's mouth gave me a tingle of self-satisfaction. He was ticked off, and I knew my public display of affection added to it, regardless of how he played it off. He all but snapped his fingers for Benny to follow him out, and I handed the keys to Hunter to lock the door behind them.

Hunter returned, and the two of us surveyed the mess. The best we could do was clean up the broken glass and put the damaged merchandise on a shelf in the back. The showcase was destroyed, so its contents would have to be moved as well. Everything would have to be inventoried at some point, but my mother could take care of that. Halloween was only three days away, and we were both too preoccupied to worry about it now.

We were still in the back when the bells on the door jangled again.

"It's only me," my mother called from the entry.

I peeked around one of display racks at my mother, already feeling her pique.

"What?" I said, watching her eyes narrow.

"Something happen this evening that I should know about? I'm getting an uneasy vibe, something unrelated to the visions."

"Jeez, Mom. It's like living with the psychic network plugged into my head. But to answer your question, yeah, something happened. There was an accident toward the back and somehow the curio was shattered, along with some of the books and candles on the back shelves."

"Rowen! How?" She put down her grocery bags and walked past us to the back of the store.

"I don't know exactly, but Hunter and I cleaned it up," I hedged.

"Was anyone hurt?" she asked, surveying the damage.

"No, but I wish I could say the same for some of the merchandise."

"Don't worry about that, just as long as no one got hurt. That's what insurance is for—are you sure that's it?" she asked, still watching me with

a question in her eyes.

I nodded. "Yeah, but we'll need to inventory everything. Do you want me and Hunter to do it now, or can it wait 'til Friday? We have tonight and tomorrow to finish Mr. Conover's stupid project."

She sighed. "Speaking of which, I called the Historical Society earlier to see how Libby made out with her insurance adjuster. All I can say is thank God you two had the presence of mind to clean up that basement and put everything back before we got there. If she saw the condition of those artifact trays and the mess you described..." my mother's voice drifted off.

"Anyway," she continued, "I was happy to hear she decided not to go through insurance after all, and let us settle things privately. She gets her window and her alarm fixed, and I get to write off the check as a donation. It's a win-win for both of us, at least that's how it seemed when I dropped off the check to cover costs, plus." She paused. "That reminds me..." Turning on her heel, she headed back toward the front counter.

Hunter and I followed, and next to the register she opened her purse and rummaged through papers and coupons. "Here it is." She handed me a thick packet stapled together in ten sheet bunches.

"What's this?" I asked, taking it from her.

"Libby gave me this for your research. She found Cameron's note taped to her computer after she let him go. Poor guy."

From across my shoulder, Hunter's eyes scanned the top sheet along with mine. It was the entire DeBoeck line, including the latest from the town clerk. Libby must have even called over to the town hall for us and had the records sent.

"I suppose she felt bad the two of you got locked in," my mother added with a shrug. "In her mind this makes up for Cameron not checking on you before he left."

"It wasn't his fault, Mom. There had to be an illusion, a deception or something. He knew we were there..." I paused, faltering for words. "I can't explain it."

At the look on my face my mother put her hand on my cheek. "You're right. The house *was* spelled. Cameron swears before he locked up he checked every room, including the basement, and you two were nowhere to be found. Unfortunately, his internship is collateral damage in this

war, and there's nothing we can do about it."

"War," I said with a snort and glanced across at Hunter before meeting my mother's gaze "That's exactly what Hunter said."

"He's right, sweetheart."

Hunter took the papers from me and set them on the front counter. His forehead creased, expression guarded. "Even though I couldn't see what you saw in the vision, I felt and heard and smelled everything. The voice that spoke? You said it was muffled, but I heard it loud and clear." He shrugged. His uncertainty evident in the way he shook his head. "Maybe I heard the message more clearly because I was blinded in the vision. Who knows? I do know this though, the energy behind that voice didn't feel cruel like the one blinding me or pinning my hands. The energy felt restless, yet purposeful. It wants us to make connections. The other one doesn't, and that's why it keeps trying to scare us off."

I didn't say a word, and the silence between the three of us hung in the air along with Hunter's words and their chilling conjecture.

My mother went to snap off the light, telling us to head upstairs. "I'm going to get dinner started so we can eat early and then head over to the Blaze. We can take two cars, but I want the two of you close to me on the estate. Understood?"

Hunter and I both nodded.

"Good. Gran is meeting us there at six p.m., so we've got back up. Britt is spending tonight going through Van Tassell family papers for further clues. The veil is thinning, and the battle lines are being drawn. I want us ready, so no one trips over them on accident."

I grabbed the genealogy and the town records Libby sent, re-clipping the top sheet as I walked toward Hunter waiting for me. "It won't take long to trace the family line to date. We can finish the comparison over dinner, that way we can get started writing first thing tomorrow."

I stopped short, letting my words clip. A weird feeling crept over my skin as if something watched and waited in the darkness behind me. The hair on my neck stood on end and I turned. At that moment a driving wind blew against the door, the gust sending in tiny pieces of rock from the sidewalk beneath the weather stripping. I spun around shielding myself from the fragments. Another gust rattled the display window, the force cracking its wood frame, and the air in the room chilled to the bone.

"Upstairs now!" My mother's voice resonated power as Hunter and I ran for the steps.

Halfway through the door, I glanced over my shoulder. Mom's arms were raised, and I knew she was in full caster mode. My heart dropped and I wheeled around to help her, but Hunter grabbed my arm.

"Let go of me!"

"No, Rowen. If you distract her, you'll both get hurt. She knows what she's doing."

I nodded, ignoring the wet sting at the corner of my eyes and swallowed the lump of fear lodged in my throat.

Hunter tucked me under his arm and together we hurried up the steps. I spent the next thirty minutes pacing, before my mother called an all clear and I ran down the stairs to make sure she was still in one piece.

The store was a mess. Groceries strewn across the front entrance, and the display window was ruined. I looked at my mother, afraid to say anything. She held out her arms, and I rushed into them, holding her close, all my fear welling to the surface as I sobbed into her shoulder.

"It's okay, Rowen. I'm fine. Whatever this entity is, he wants us to back off, but I don't think he expected the battle of will he got with me, or to get a dose of his own medicine thrown back at him."

Sniffing, I stepped back from her, wiping my nose and my eyes on my sleeve. "Him? This thing is male?"

She nodded. "Yep. And it's strong, but it won't underestimate us again. We have feminine energy in spades, and all it has is hate."

Hunter looked at my mom and me, and cleared his throat. "Only feminine energy?"

My mother chuckled, crossing her arms in front of her. "Well," she said with a teasing smirk on her face. "feminine energy, plus. How about that?"

She looked over at me and the expression of doubt I knew I had on my face.

"What?"

I shook my head. "You just fought a dark entity that wants to make creamed corn out of us, and your cracking jokes?"

She slid her arm around my shoulder and gave me a loving shake. "Yes. That's half the battle, sweetie. Not letting your fear paralyze you. If

you're afraid, the entity's power grows, but if you show confidence and strength in your abilities, you take power from it."

She pressed a kiss to my cheek, and then pulled her arm back, clapping once. "Come on, help me get this place cleaned up." She bent to pick up the torn box of spaghetti, glancing at the squashed vegetables and dried pasta littering the rug in front of the door. "And, I guess we are eating out, tonight. We'll hit the Colonial Diner near the Blaze. Rowen, you can help me do the display window in the morning before you leave for school."

She straightened, eyeing the two of us and the rest of the mess. "I'll call Britt before we leave and let her know what's going on. I want you both close. There's only two days left 'til Samhain, and hopefully all of this will just vanish behind the veil as it thickens."

Provided no supernatural entities insisted otherwise.

Everyone was quiet for the calm before the storm as we filed into class. The whole of yesterday passed in a blur, between writing the final research paper and standing in front of the mirror fighting back nerves and nausea as I practiced for the oral presentation. But now it was Friday morning, and ready or not, it was showtime.

Mr. Conover employed a bit of originality in choosing who got to give their oral synopsis first, by using a deck of cards. High-Low was the name of the game, with high card going first. Hunter and I each scored a low card, a three of diamonds and a two of spades, respectively. Sweet! Now we got to sit back and watch everyone else squirm before we hit the hot seat.

Our supernatural shadows notwithstanding, I was amazed anyone could even focus. Between the away game tonight, and the cemetery party set for tomorrow, the air in the hallways buzzed with excitement. I could deal with excitement. Temperatures dropping metaphysically to freezing like in the shop the other night, not so much.

Mom sent me out with an absent wave this morning, assuring me I would be fine. She and Gran had cooked up something else to put in my mojo bag, and this time I didn't question what, not caring if it was something gross or smelly. I slipped it over my head and immediately a feeling of quiet protection cascaded over my senses.

Damn they were good!

I was ready for my day, and Hunter's game tonight. The Horsemen were battling the Somers Tuskers on the opposing team's turf, as they had field lights while Sleepy Hollow had yet to upgrade their stadium.

Of course, Hunter had to go on the bus with his team, which meant I had to drive the half hour north to Somers High School. Chloe was coming with me, but Talia had plans again with Mike.

After our last conversation, I hoped to God Talia stuck to her guns and didn't let her fear of slipping back in to social Siberia make up her mind about Mike. It was her choice, obviously, but I wanted her choice to truly be *her* choice. If she wanted to be with Mike, then go for it, but only if it was what she wanted, too. As much as I wanted to either shake her or hug her, I couldn't worry about Talia. I had enough to deal with.

The clocked ticked, and the atmosphere in the classroom thickened from anxious to comatose in thirty-five minutes with people droning on with the same tired comparisons or stumbling over themselves. Even so, I glanced across to the third row and caught Hunter's eye. It was time to pay up or shut up.

From his perch atop of one of the empty desks, Mr. Conover watched and listened to each presentation from the cheap seats at the back of the class. With a gross wet sound, he cleared his throat, probably as much to wake himself as to be in good voice to stick it to me and Hunter. He tapped the side of his chair with his glasses. "And we've saved the best for last. Hunter? Rowen? You're up."

Hunter slid out of his chair, its metal feet scraping across the linoleum floor in a short, sharp screech. He walked to the front of the classroom and plugged a flash drive into the laptop situated on Mr. Conover's teaching desk. The Smart Board flickered on, and he moused over to the computer file that read, "DeBoeck and the Legend of Sleepy Hollow."

I moved to his side, and stood in awkward silence with everyone's eyes on us as they watched and waited. With a self-conscious pivot, I shifted around, giving my back to the peering eyes of my classmates, determined to find out what the hell Hunter was doing.

"When did you put together a PowerPoint presentation?" I whispered, leaning my head close to his as he bent over the laptop.

Intent on what he was doing, he answered without looking up. "Last

night when I got home from your house. I was too wired, so I made some slides."

"It would have been nice if you had told me. Are they just the talking points we discussed?"

He nodded, glancing across his shoulder at me , however his crooked half smile said otherwise.

"Just wonderful, Hunter." I murmured, moving to turn back around, but he tugged on the bottom of my sleeve.

"It will be great. Just wait and see."

We both turned at this point, and I caught Mr. Conover's disapproving look.

"Sometime this century, Ms. Corbett, please?"

Snickering chirped in pockets around the classroom and I gave Mr. Conover a nod, shooting Hunter a dirty look.

"Sorry for the delay, Mr. Conover, if I may, I'd like to begin." Hunter said, standing up straight and flashing me a confident grin.

"Rowen and I spent the better part of the last week researching not only the Legend of Sleepy Hollow, but the other lesser known legends the town is known for, including the Bronze Lady. Needless to say we came up empty."

At Mr. Conover's raised eyebrow, Hunter put up his hand.

"But we were determined, and decided instead of researching the known legends, we would try and see if we could find events that occurred in town around the time of the revolution, or during the timeframe in which Irving wrote his Legend, and correlate those.

Mr. Conover's eyebrow rose even further. "And?"

"And, we hit the jackpot."

Nausea took control of my stomach and my nerves churned. Hunter was going to do it, he was going to mention family names and cause a big brouhaha in town, and of course, I was going to be blamed for coercing the golden boy to join the dark side.

"The Legend of Sleepy Hollow is basically a love triangle," he continued. "We have Brom Bones, Ichabod Crane and Katrina Van Tassel...oh, and by the way, did anyone ever notice that Irving spelled the Van Tassell surname incorrectly? It's got two 'L's, not one....but anyway...it's a triangle.

"At that time, Sleepy Hollow wasn't the quiet little God-fearing, patriotic town everyone thinks. No. It was a hotbed of intrigue, treachery, and sex."

Snorts and laughter broke in nervous bursts throughout the class, and Mr. Conover had to bang on his chair to get everyone to quiet down.

"Please continue, and Ms. Corbett, I'd like to hear your voice, too," he added with a chastising tilt to his head.

I swallowed, nodding, again. *Christ, I must look like a bobble head, because lord knows that's what I feel like.*

Hesitating, I tried to pick up Hunter's thread, and as if sensing my nerves were in overdrive, he clicked on the next slide, an easy flowchart for me and everyone else to follow.

I winked, giving him a warm smile, and took my place at the center podium. "In 1777, the revolution was in full swing, and the fighting was getting fierce. As we all know, the Hudson Valley is steeped in history, because where we live is where much of the war happened. Neighbor turned against neighbor, and people were torn between the unhappiness of the life they knew, and the uncertainty of what life would bring after the war. Tories and patriots went head to head, and friends turned their backs on people they knew and loved.

"Resistance was high, and the cost paid to the British at the time was ever higher. At the time there was a Hessian captain in town by the name of Emmerick. He was the one who carried out Governor Tryon's orders to 'Burn the Tarrytowns,' to set fire to patriot homes and families in order to teach the rebels a lesson. Nevertheless, Emmerick was a ladies man, and soon local families realized they could save their fortunes if he took a fancy to one of their daughters."

My voice quavered at this point, because I knew I was glossing over the facts. Hunter squeezed my hand and took over from there.

"Emmerick's conquests were many, but no one caught his eye more than Maritie DeBoeck. Her family lived on the outskirts of the hollow, close to the Croton border, and her father was a wealthy merchant with a mill and lands. His properties were spared because of his daughter's liaison, but as war stories go, Emmerick was in it for the short haul. So when he shipped out, Maritie was left alone and pregnant."

Hunter continued the story, highlighting every parallel and

association he touched upon at the Historical Society—even citing that the name DeBoeck meant "brook dweller", and quoting the number of times Irving alluded to and actually used the word "brook' in the story.

Mr. Conover put his glasses on his head and leaned forward, resting his elbows on his knees and his chin in his hand. After a moment, he nodded, clapping his hands, slowly.

"Now that's what I was looking for. It's wonderful to see how you paired the historical with the metaphysical nature of the story, and allow the reader to take a peek at the particulars that may have inspired Irving in his writing. You gave the modern reader all kinds of interesting tidbits to chew on. Well done."

I went to sit down, but Hunter stopped me. Mr. Conover had his hand up. He wasn't finished.

"So, if Maritie DeBoeck stayed in town and married the church master as you say—yet the child she bore was illegitimate—did the Dominee adopt the child, or did her offspring solely bear the name DeBoeck?"

Hunter and I exchanged glances. "Well, that's hard to answer," I began. "The genealogies are so long…"

Hunter interrupted. "We know from record the child was adopted and raised as the Dominee's own, but kept the name DeBoeck. It was family tradition the name be kept in some form for all children born into that same line—then and since."

"Thank you both, good work."

The room was quiet, and no one seemed to make the connection between Tyler, his ancestors and the legend. If someone did and it got back to him, I prayed the infamous nature of the story would appeal to his bad boy ego, and that he'd laugh it off, rather than take it the wrong way. It could go either way, as Tyler's family was one of the town's *holier than thou* types.

The day wasn't over, but so far so good. I left school and went home to change, doing my time at the shop before picking up Chloe around six p.m. I pulled up to the front of her house in my mother's minivan, ignoring the eye roll she shot my way from the edge of her driveway.

"You know, you don't have to come with me," I said with a sniff as she climbed into the front passenger seat.

"What? And give up the chance to be seen climbing out of a mommy mobile? You must be mad." She snorted, shoving my shoulder sideways.

"What's in the bag?" I asked, gesturing to the drawstring pack between her feet.

"Everything we might need."

I glanced in the rearview mirror, checking the side one as well before pulling into the street. "We're going to a football game, not an all-night rave. What could we possibly need that we can't buy?"

"You've only been to one game, Ro. You'll see."

The game against Somers High School was a real nail-biter, the tight score keeping everyone on their feet. We had three injuries already, and the game was tied. The Horseman had been battling the Tuskers for over two hours, and the ref blew the whistle announcing overtime.

The wind whipped across the bleachers with a vengeance. Chloe and I huddled together under a fleece blanket, and through chattering teeth I thanked her for being such an über-fan. "I don't know what we would have done if you hadn't thought to bring this. I can barely feel my feet."

She laughed. "Didn't I say I had everything we might need? You freeze your butt off once, and you learn not to make the same mistake twice. When it comes to outside sports, I come prepared for any scenario—cold, wet, hot, whatever."

"Hey, did your research grade post yet? I checked before we left, and mine's not up. Conover must be having a hard time, considering."

Chloe snorted. "A hard time? After the thesis dissertation you and *sir snoops-a-lot*, did? Jeez, Ro, how many hours did you spend in that yawn of a building, mulling over moldy records?"

I made a face. "You don't want to know."

She countered with something halfway between a chuckle and a shiver, and then took a sip from her big gulp. "Well, you certainly nailed Tyler's family to a cross. Everyone's talking about it."

My hand froze with a piece of soft pretzel half way to my mouth. "Who's talking about what?" I asked, hoping she missed the hitch in my voice.

She rolled her eyes. "Oh, come on, Rowen. The whole thing about the DeBoeck name? Everyone knows Tyler's middle name is Boeck. Every member of his family has it in some form or another. Even his mother has

it attached to her maiden name."

I nibbled on the corner of my pretzel so I wouldn't chew on my lip. Chloe knew me well enough to know my trademark nervous tick. "Does Tyler know?"

She nodded, inhaling with a sharp hiss, immediately pressing her hand to her forehead. "*Ugh.* Brain freeze."

I took the big gulp from her and put it on the floor between us. "Damn it, Chloe, if you stopped drinking that chemical slush you're so fond of, your brain would stop protesting! I swear I will never stop at 7-Eleven for you again."

She squeezed the bridge of her nose and pressed her thumb to the roof of her mouth and breathed out.

"Well?"

"Well, what?" Her words were mangled as she tried to talk over her thumb.

I sat back in a huff, the crowd around me on its feet for something that happened out on the field, but I was no longer interested. I spared a glance to make sure Hunter wasn't being carried off on a stretcher or anything, but turned my attention back to Chloe the minute I saw he was safe and sound on the sidelines.

"Chloe! You nodded that Tyler knows. What did he say?"

She nodded again, licking blue Slurpee off the side of her hand. "Oh boy, does he know. And from what Benny told me, he was cool about it until one of the jerks in the locker room started in about his great-great-plus grandmother being a slut, and how funny it is that his mom is so buttoned up and butt-clenched."

I slumped in my seat. "Great…just, great."

She picked up her drink and took a careful sip. "I wouldn't sweat it if I were you. Benny said Ty's not mad at Hunter or you, for that matter, because neither of you said it was him, directly. People are just putting two and two together. He was eating it up at first, I mean you know his ego, but then the jerk from the wrestling team had to bring Tyler's mother into it. What a tool."

I had a million questions, but I wasn't going to push the issue. If Tyler wasn't blaming me or Hunter, then maybe it was all good.

At that point a breathless hush took over stands as Hunter took the

field with Tyler for a crucial play. Even I knew it was now or never. We needed this to win, and I turned my full attention back to my gorgeous boyfriend and his tight football pants. The ball was snapped and Tyler grabbed it, running for a seamless hand off. The ball sailed smoothly into Hunter's hands like a guided missile and he ran, dodging and weaving for a spectacular touchdown.

The crowd exploded, and I stood holding my breath, watching as Hunter and Tyler banged helmets, grabbing each other in a giant bear hug. I smiled to myself. Yup. It was all good.

Marianne Morea

Chapter 14

It was finally Halloween, and the day dawned wet and cloudy. I peered out my window, running a pick through my wet curls, the dreary weather putting a damper on my spirits.

Trudging downstairs in my slippers and sweats, I made myself a cup of raspberry coffee and took a croissant from the wax paper bakery bag on top of the toaster and sat down with a napkin to eat.

The phone rang, and I eyed it over my mug.

"Rowen! Can you get that? I'm in the laundry room," my mother called from the bottom of the stairs.

No one I knew called on the house phone, so Mom was going to have to talk to whoever it was, regardless.

I got up from the table and picked up the cordless receiver. "Hello?"

"Hi, Rowen, it's Britt Morrissey. Your mom around?"

"Oh, hey. Yeah she's doing laundry. Just a sec." I held the phone to my chest and yelled down the stairs. "Mom! It's Britt."

"Tell her I'll call her back in five minutes. I'm up to my elbows in tie-dye."

Tie-Dye?

"Britt she said she'll have to call you back, she's tie-dying or something."

She chuckled on the other end. "No problem. Tell her to make sure to do a shirt for me."

197

Britt hung up and I took my coffee and headed downstairs to see what my mother was up to.

I stuck my head into the laundry room to find two large tubs splattered with dye: one orange and one black. A stack of white tees rolled and wrapped in rubber bands sat to the left of them, while plastic Ziploc bags filled with wet, freshly dyed tees sat to the right.

"What on earth are you doing?"

She looked up, brushing the hair out of her eyes with her rubber gloved hand. "I'm making tee-shirts for tonight."

"I can see that. But why?"

"I thought it would be cool to have the Blaze staff wear black and orange tie-dyed shirts. It's Halloween so I wanted it to be a little different from the other show nights."

I inhaled, putting my mug on top of the washing machine. "Need any help?"

She smiled, rolling back onto her feet from where she knelt in front of the tubs before pushing herself to stand. "Yeah, sure. If you could start rinsing the ones that are done, that would be great. Cold water, and leave the rubber bands on. Don't forget to squeeze out the excess. We can wash them all in one big batch later."

I helped my mother organize all day, from arranging the shirts and the thank you gifts for the Blaze volunteers, to helping out in the shop on the busiest day of our year.

The downpour was relentless, and I finally curled up on the couch with a cup of cocoa to watch *Hocus Pocus* like I did every year, waiting for the first trick-or-treaters to ring the bell. The first group of mini-monsters wasn't set to descend for a couple of hours, and I was already impatient for the night to begin.

The TV flickered, and I listened to the rain patter against the window. This stunk. With an ugly exhale, I tossed the cable remote onto the coffee table, and the clatter had my mother poking her head in the doorway.

"Still got the rainy day blues?"

"Hmmm."

"Well, you've earned my help today, so let's see if I can salvage tonight's events," she proposed with a jaunty tilt to her head.

Brows knotted, I sat up swinging my legs around to face front. "What

are you talking about?"

"Tonight's a packed night for you and your friends, socially I mean, and I thought a little weather spell might help you feel less restless. There's nothing worse on Halloween night than a twitchy witch."

"Yeah, right," I shot back blowing stray hairs off my forehead. "We'd need a full coven to chase away this kind of rain."

She laughed out loud. "You sound like Gran. Come on grumpy gills, let's give it a whirl. I've got a few tricks up my sleeve for just such an occasion. I started perfecting it when you started dating. I wanted to be sure I had it down pat in case the weather on your wedding day needed a push in the right direction."

My mouth dropped. "My wedding day?"

Her gaze grew soft and a little far away. "I know it's not on the horizon, but a mother can dream can't she? Plus this is a perfect opportunity to test the waters, or better yet, the rain."

She held out her hand for me, and with a grudging sigh I put my hands on my thighs and stood. "Here goes nothing," I muttered, and followed my mother into the kitchen with her spell books and copper pots.

Amazingly enough, the rain petered out and the sun came out in time to dry the streets and the grass enough for trick-or-treat. Whether my mother's weather spell had anything to do with it, I couldn't say, but lately stranger things have happened.

I stayed on the couch standing vigil over the doorbell and the candy bowl. Every ten minutes or so there would be a knock on the door followed by the cutest chant of *"trick or treat, smell my feet."*

The kids liked coming to our house because they knew my mom gave out full-size candy bars, but they also learned if they didn't get to us early they would miss out when we left for the Blaze.

Of course, we always placed a large black cauldron on the front porch for whatever candy was left, and it only took one time for pranksters to crack eggs inside the black iron pot for my mother to spell the entire porch. Now only kids with honorable intentions were allowed up the stairs, while children with more nefarious aims were left feeling a little queasy the minute they stepped one foot on the steps.

It was ingenious, actually, because parents always blamed their

child's tummy ache on too much candy. Needless to say, we haven't had another egging episode since.

The doorbell rang again, and I got up to open the door, one hand on the handle and the other in the candy bowl.

"Trick or treat," Hunter said, holding out a single white rose, the tips tinged with orange.

I grinned, putting my hands on my hips. "What, no candy?"

Stepping through the door, he smiled his sexy half smile before kissing me hello. "Nope, but I brought this instead."

My heart fluttered as his lips touched mine, and I reached up, winding my arms around his neck. "Mmmmmm. Now that's what I call sweets for the sweet."

He broke our kiss, his voice a husky murmur against my ear and my heart went from flutter to full out skip a beat. I took a step back, and moved aside to let him in the rest of the way. "We've had kids nonstop for the last hour. What's it like at your house? The same?"

He walked past me into the foyer and peeled off his black jacket, draping it over the stairs "Pretty much. You know we have to leave soon if we're to make the last candlelight tour at the church." He fished in his inside pocket, brandishing two long white tapered candles. "I swiped these while the team was setting up."

I shook my head, closing the door behind me. "Stealing from the church. I don't know about that, Hunter. Bad karma, dude." I replied, mimicking my best surfer impersonation.

His smile met mine, and he laughed. "With the way things have been going lately, I figured it can't get any worse."

"Ha. Famous last words."

I rubbed my arms to fend off the chill from the front porch. "If we have time, I can make us hot cider. I have to carry the black cauldron from the kitchen to the porch, and put the rest of the candy in it with a note saying 'one per customer.'"

"The honor system? Really?"

I raised an eyebrow and cocked a hip at him. "You're forgetting who lives here, and I don't mean me. My mother is a pretty formidable witch, in case you didn't notice."

"I did take notice, but I think you're a pretty formidable witch

yourself, Ms. Corbett. You've got me under your spell."

My stomach flip-flopped, and heat coursed from my neck to my cheeks.

"Plus, it wasn't your mother that saved our butts the other night."

His confidence in me was palpable, and I saw pride reflected in his eyes, but just remembering the feeling of vulnerability and panic left me a little queasy. What if it was up to me to save us again?

I shook my head. "That was pure fear, and I don't ever want to face that again."

He moved past the stairs and wrapped his arms around my waist. "You won't. Besides, it was the two of us together that pulled us out of that pickle, remember?"

"Hmmm. Us against the supernatural world. I never thought of it that way." I grinned. "I like that."

"Me, too," he whispered, kissing the top of my nose.

I slid myself back from him, and hooked my arm in his. "Come on, let me bribe you with cider and homemade spice bread, then maybe you'll carry that monstrosity of a pot to the porch for me."

Candles burned in equal measure around the crumbling grave markers, bathing the Old Dutch Cemetery in an otherworldly glow as we listened to Jonathan Kruk narrate the *Legend of Sleepy Hollow*.

Residual clouds had cleared, and the full moon hung in the sky adding to the mysterious tale, its pale yellow hues courting the darkness with an eerie light. An iridescent ring around the moon was tinged with red, and I stared at the sign of trouble to come wondering what else the universe held in store for us.

In their eagerness, Hunter and the boys had already hidden flashlights and water guns at strategic places in the cemetery for a game of Assassin. The thought of hiding behind gravestones and in the shadows of the tall mausoleums left my skin tingling. This party was going to be scary good fun.

Gran warned Hunter and me again about our physical ban, cautioning the veil between the living and the dead was at its thinnest tonight. She actually used the words, *no hanky panky,* and I visibly cringed, causing my mother to turn so Gran wouldn't see her laugh.

Neither of us was cocky enough to completely ignore Gran's warning, but we weren't missing out on tonight for the world, supernatural or otherwise.

The tour was breaking up, and Hunter took my hand. We followed behind the crowd with Mr. Grayson leading the way in full revolutionary garb, his lantern held high while he signaled for everyone to follow him to the parking lot.

"Thanks, Mr. Grayson. It was great," I said as we filed passed, stopping to give the old man a kiss just above his whisker line.

"Not at all, lass," he replied, feigning a brogue. "I trust nothing is amiss with you and your young lad?" Leave it to the old caretaker not to miss a beat in his role play.

I giggled, earning a wide toothy grin from him.

"Aye, good sir. He is a fine lad at that." I answered back, adding a bob of my head and a courtesy for good measure.

"Oh, jeez…" Hunter rolled of his eyes despite the grin on his face.

Mr. Grayson guffawed, his wheezy laughter threatening another coughing spasm. Hunter banged him on the back, but the man raised his hand, sucking in a breath.

"I'm fine, thanks." He waved off Hunter with another breathy chuckle. "Go on with the two of you. I bet your mother's waiting at the Blaze."

I gave him another peck on his cheek, and we started down the dimly lit path toward Hunter's car.

"I'll leave the flashlights where you boys stowed them, but I'm trusting there'll be no food wrappers or beer cans left behind, right?" Mr. Grayson called after us.

I stopped in mid-step, the knowledge of how bad this might be paralyzing me where I stood.

The old man's question was obviously rhetorical, but Hunter laughed out loud, anyway. "You got it, Mr. Grayson. I promise," he answered, waving back in acknowledgement.

Stunned, I slid into the passenger side of Hunter's Mustang.

"That was some kind of passive aggressive warning, wasn't it? Mr. Grayson is going to call the cops on us."

Hunter slid his gaze to me. "Relax. He's not going to call the cops.

You had to have guessed he would know about our plans. Didn't he tell us this was *his* cemetery? We aren't doing anything different than any other senior class in the last fifty years. Why else do you think he said what he said? He's letting us know he's watching. That's all."

We drove in silence the few miles north to the Van Cortlandt Estate, but I couldn't help but wonder about the ring around the moon and what else Mr. Grayson knew.

The air was wet and raw, and it had started drizzling again, but clearly not enough to discourage the tourists. The Blaze parking lot was packed, and we followed the line of cars as volunteers in reflective orange vests directed us toward the overflow parking on the lower grass.

"Wow, this is has got to be the biggest success the Blaze has had to date. Halloween night is always popular, but this is nuts!" I said looking at the sea of cars.

Billowing banners, each with the image of a flaming headless horseman graced either side of the arched walkway. Harvest corn stalks and piles of fat ripe pumpkins and colorful knotty gourds were set in festive arrangements along the main path leading to the entrance.

Vendors lined the admission tent, selling Halloween trinkets, hot cider and donuts. At the far end was the starting point for the jack-o-lantern lined path winding around to the old Van Cortlandt mansion. From there the path trailed through the grounds, the walk taking visitors past various themes designed completely of lit jack-o-lanterns.

My mother was at the entrance collecting tickets and checking time stamps. The crowd was thick, and the line to get in extended around the parking lot.

"Hey, you two," my mom called, waving to Hunter and me as we hovered near the back of the tent.

We walked past the rows of people patiently waiting for their time stamped turn to go in, hoping no one thought we were trying to cut the line.

"Hi, Mom," I said, planting a kiss on her cheek.

"How was the candlelight tour? I bet Jonathan Kruk was in good voice tonight. No one tells the Legend like he does."

I shrugged. "It was good. Everyone seemed to like it."

She chuckled, waving in the next group of sightseers. "Don't excite

yourself, Rowen, jeez… What about you Hunter? You haven't heard Jonathan's performance before. What did you think?"

Hunter gave my mother the same classic noncommittal teenager shrug that I did. "I liked it. After deciphering the Legend in class and all the research Rowen and I did, it was nice to hear the story narrated for the simple pleasure of storytelling. Considering when and where it was written, Irving really did pen a masterpiece."

My mother laughed out loud, clapping her hands full of spent tickets. "Now that's what I call appreciation." She went up on her toes, giving Hunter a peck on his cheek.

Hunter was red to the tips of his ears, and I wanted to wince.

"Mom…"

"I know…" She smirked, but was clearly pleased with herself. "Listen, I've got staff badges for you if you want to go in and see what you helped put together, but you'd better do it now. The later time slots are more jammed than this," she said, gesturing to the throng of people waiting.

I took the lanyard badges from her and slipped mine over my head, handing Hunter his.

"Stop and say goodbye before you leave for your boneyard party." she said, with a wave.

Gape-mouthed, I swung my head around to stare at her over my shoulder.

"Have fun! But not too much fun!" She winked, making me want to cringe, again.

It didn't take long for us to wind our way through the themed paths and the requisite gift shop visit before realizing it was time to go. The rain had stayed at a steady drizzle the entire time. It was more annoying than wet, yet Hunter's phone buzzed every ten minutes with people canceling last minute on the cemetery party.

Everyone was supposed to meet at Gory Brook Road at ten p.m., and then head into the cemetery from there. Now we were down to our original ten. Most parties moved indoors, and I was about to suggest the same thing, when Tyler texted that we had better not bail, ranting about senior tradition, plus he said he had something planned to safeguard against the rain and the cops.

The dead end was perfect cover for us to sneak into the cemetery via the hiking path at the end of the road, but by the time Hunter and I worked our way out of the crowded parking lot, we were running late.

"They're not going to wait for us, are they?" I said, holding Hunter's hand as we hurried through the grass field toward where we parked.

The wind whipped, snapping the banners and creating the illusion of the headless horseman in full gallop. I dug in my pocket for a pair of gloves, slipping them over my frozen fingers and wishing I hadn't decided against a hat. *Vanity thy name is Rowen.* With a sigh, I pulled my hood up knowing it made me look like a gnome.

Hunter pulled up the collar on his jacket, and put on a pair of driving gloves. "Don't worry. I know where they're headed. Mike wants to start the game by Millionaire's Row. He's obsessed with the statue of the Bronze Lady."

"Gran told me that story. It's so sad to think about that poor woman and how she killed herself over a love that wasn't even reciprocated." I shivered, but not just from the cold. The idea of someone that miserable and distraught left me feeling a little hollow.

"You look like you're freezing. Do you want to stop at your house to change or grab a hat or something?"

I shook my head, clenching my jaw to stop my teeth from chattering. "Nah. This parking lot is completely open, so the wind is worse here. Once we get to the cemetery, I'll be fine."

He slid his arm around my shoulder. "Okay, just stick close to me then. We'll keep each other warm."

For a dead end on Halloween night, Gory Brook Road was deserted. In fact, we pulled up to the end and parked in the darkest corner off to the right.

I looked around but didn't see any other cars. "Where is everyone?" I asked, still peering through the gloom.

We got out of the car, and Hunter closed his door and came around to where I leaned against the back bumper. "This was supposed to be the meeting place. Maybe the cops came by and chased everyone out while they were waiting for us." He opened the trunk and took out a small black nylon backpack.

Lifting the end of his glove, he checked his watch. "It's twenty past ten. Maybe they parked closer to Peabody Park and snuck in through the new cemetery."

There were voices in the distance, and we turned toward the woods, listening. Hunter put his finger over his lips and gestured for me to stay close.

The trees looked black and forbidding, and faint rustling in the ground leaves made me jump. I took an instinctive step backwards.

"Come on, Rowen. We can't stand here much longer or someone *will* call the cops," he whispered. His hands were in his pockets and he held an elbow out for me.

I hurried to his side, and hooked my arm with his plastering myself hip-to-hip with him. All my previous bravado about him and me against the world, faded. I swallowed hard, praying my mother and my grandmother were on their game with whatever they stuck inside the little bag hanging around my neck.

We crossed the street and headed into the trees, stepping over deep puddles from all the rain. Thank God I was dressed for it, with black jeans and a pair of purple and black plaid rain boots. I had on a deep plum colored blouse topped with a cropped black silk sweater to highlight my waist. Too bad they were hidden under my rain jacket.

The grass was wet and squishy, yet we managed to move quickly until we stopped to navigate across the Pocantico River. Normally just a babbling brook, the picturesque stepping stones took on a treacherous feel with the rushing water from all the rain. Hunter grabbed my hand and we moved carefully from stone to stone until we made it across and headed for dryer ground. It wasn't until we hit the hills that I stopped feeling as though we were slogging through marshland.

"I think we'll go the long way round when it's time to leave, and take the Headless Horseman Bridge over the river."

Hunter nodded. "I'm with you on that," he said, shaking out one of his hiking shoes. "At least your boots are waterproof."

This was turning into more of a hike than I expected, and the deeper into the trees we went, the darker and more eerie the night seemed. Ground fog swirled in spots like apparitions taking shape. In other places the mist hovered as if guarding something it didn't want us to see. Even

Marianne Morea

with the full moon, the canopy of brown trees and the remaining autumn leaves obscured whatever light filtered through, leaving patches of the woods as dark as pitch.

Hunter pulled his pack forward and dug inside for a flashlight. With one click a single beam of warm yellow light illuminated a narrow swath for us to follow. Despite the heat from Hunter's body and the comforting light from his flashlight, I still jumped at every twig crack and rustle.

We angled our way south and hopped over a low stone wall.

"The cemetery is right through this last bunch of trees," he said, pointing toward the thick, black copse ahead. "I think…"

"You think?"

In the gloom, low hanging branches obscured any view of the cemetery road.

"Is there any way we can check?" I asked, cringing at the sound of my own voice in the stillness.

He pulled his pack around again, and from the slim side pocket he took out a trifold brochure and opened it to a map of the cemetery

"You have a map?"

He nodded. "Of course. Did you think I would take you traipsing through the woods at night and not come prepared?"

With the map between his teeth, he handed me the flashlight to hold while he pulled the drawstring open on his pack. Inside he had a folding knife, two water bottles, matches and a waterproof blanket.

"See?"

"A gentleman and a hero," I said, and handed him back the flashlight.

He pulled the strings on his bag closed and slid his arm behind my waist. "I'm glad you think so." With the flat of his palm, he gave me a playful shove. "Ladies first."

He held the back of my jacket so I wouldn't fall, but I still stumbled forward a step.

"Hunter!"

One of the branches pulled back with a low crack, and both of us wheeled around to peer into the darkened tree line. Benny and Chloe stepped from the shadows, each wearing a silly smirk.

"Chloe, you brat! You nearly gave me a heart attack!"

She giggled. "Sorry. But you were just too cute acting out your *boy*

scout rescues frightened damsel in distress gig.

"Yeah. I'm impressed, Rowen. I thought for sure you'd be on your ass after Hunter's little love tap."

"If you must know, Benny, I have perfect balance," I said with a sniff. "It comes from wearing heels all day in school."

At that all three of them burst out laughing. "No offense Ro, but I've known you since you stopped being homeschooled in fifth grade, and you are the clumsiest person I know," Benny replied with a snort.

Hunter put his arm around me and pulled me close, tucking my shoulder under his. "That's all right. As long as I'm around I won't let you fall."

Chloe put her hand up. "Enough, I'm getting a cavity. Let's find everybody else and get this party started." She took Benny by the hand and marched him into the darkened trees. "The road is straight through here. Follow us."

Hunter looked at me with one eyebrow arched. "Jeez, bossy much? Well, you heard the lady." He gave my shoulder a squeeze. "Let's go."

After about ten minutes, we caught up with the rest of our group, my breath puffing out in short, wet clouds. Cardio was not my thing, and if I had known training was a prerequisite I might have reconsidered the whole evening.

Mike and Talia were waiting for us at the general's tomb, along with Constance and her new boyfriend, Eric. He was on the football team, as well, but I had never met him. The only ones missing from our little party were Tyler and Jenny.

I heard far away muffled shouting and noises from other parts of the cemetery.

"Are there other parties around tonight," I asked. "I thought everyone else bailed because of the rain?"

Constance shrugged. "Maybe. But it's more likely people hanging out in Douglas Park."

A huge burp echoed from the side of the mausoleum and Tyler came around the edge pulling his zipper up. "Like my dad says, you don't drink beer; you only rent it." He glanced over at me and Hunter, a grin spreading across his lips. "Itchy Witch! Nice of you to join us!' he announced with a mock bow.

I exhaled low, stifling the urge to say something nasty. "I asked you not to call me that, Tyler. Remember?" My tone was sweet and sing-song and earned a snort of laughter from Eric.

"He actually calls you that?"

I rolled my eyes, nodding. "It's long story, but unfortunately, yes."

Squatting down, Tyler reached into a plastic grocery bag stowed under one of the bushes and pulled out two cans of beer, tossing one to Hunter. "That's right, and Rowen is our one and only," he replied with a wink.

Stunned, I stiffened a little at the unexpected compliment, not sure how to respond.

Hunter caught the beer. "You mean *my* one and only." With a wink of his own, he clicked the inside of his cheek and cracked the can open.

Jenny came around the opposite side of the tomb, almost as out of breath as I had been. "Tyler, why did you leave me alone back there? Didn't you hear me calling? I could have been killed for all you care!"

She was tucking in her shirt, and I wasn't sure if it was because she trekked up to where we were or because she and Tyler had a quickie behind one of the tombstones.

He belched a third time. "If complaining were an Olympic sport, you'd win a medal. Don't you have a mute button?" He held his hand up pretending to press a remote control.

Jenny made a face. "You're a jerk, and I'm going home."

Tyler grabbed her arm, pulling it harder than he should, and Jenny yelped. "Get off me!"

"Fine. I'll get off you. How about I permanently get off you? You wanna go? Then go."

Jenny stormed off the way she came, and I looked at Hunter. We only just arrived, and already this little get together was heading south.

"Don't go, Jen…" Hunter called after her. "Rowen and I will give you a ride home when we leave."

"What do you care, Hunter? You and your girlfriend can save your concern for someone who needs it. I'm fine." Her voice echoed behind the mausoleum, the telltale tap-tap of her boots along the path.

Constance exhaled, stamping her foot. "Tyler, do you always have to be such a jerk?" She took off into the gloom, and after a minute or so she

brought Jenny back, and the two sat on the front step of the tomb.

"Is this the fun part? Are we having fun yet?" Mike said, shoving Tyler's shoulder back. "Come on, man. Don't be a tool tonight. You said you had a surprise, so what gives?"

"Well, we still have enough people for a quick game of Assassin, so what do you want to do?" Eric asked, looking to Hunter and Tyler for their say.

The wind picked up blowing the drizzle into an annoying spray, its low howl followed by branches cracking in the darkness.

"Sounds like the cemetery is singing our song. We don't have enough people for even teams, so it's every man for himself. Last one standing wins. How about we make the Old Dutch home base?" Eric continued.

"Home base? What are we, ten?"

Eric flipped Mike the bird. "I meant the safe zone, dumbass, and you know it, so shut up. I don't hear you coming up with alternative suggestions."

"Quit it, you cretins. I've got a better idea." With a nod and a crafty smirk Tyler reached into his pocket and pulled out a skeleton key with what looked to be a luggage tag tied to the end. "Anyone up for a game of tomb-raider beer pong?"

Benny clapped once, rubbing his hands together. "Sounds like we've got a plan. Grab the beer and let's go!"

Tyler laughed. "Oh, we're not going anywhere, son...at least not yet. Anyone got a flashlight app?"

"Hold on." Hunter motioned to Benny, and the two of them disappeared into the shadows. A few minutes later, they came back carrying several flashlights.

"Here," Hunter said, handing us one each. "We hid them earlier in case we needed to bolt."

Tyler's trademark smirk grew into a grin. "Morrissey, you were always a goodie-goodie boy scout, at least now it's come in handy. Hold the light up for me, willya?"

I moved to stand next to Chloe and Talia, a feeling of dread crawling its way across my chest. Tyler put the key in the lock and I felt the color drain from my face. I rushed forward, almost tripping over the uneven concrete in front of the mausoleum.

Marianne Morea

"Wait a sec! You're not going to pick the lock on that tomb, are you?" I asked, aghast. "Tyler this is such bad karma it's not even funny."

My eyes sought Hunter's. I didn't want either of us involved in desecrating someone's resting place, especially not tonight, but he was intent with helping Tyler. "Doesn't anyone else think this is a dangerous idea?"

Except for Jenny telling Tyler to hurry up, no one said a word.

"Hunter?" I questioned, hoping the anxious tone in my voice would register with him.

Still holding the flashlight, he glanced across his shoulder at me. "It's fine, Rowen. Tyler has the key. No one is breaking into anything. We're only going inside to get out of the rain. And if it makes you feel better, we'll keep the beer outside. Right, guys?"

Everyone nodded in agreement, and my mouth dropped open. I pulled my hood farther over my forehead and closed my arms in front of my chest.

"What's the matter with you?" Chloe whispered, moving closer. "Is your *bad feeling* a Corbett specialty bad feeling, or just an 'I'm a wuss and don't want to get into trouble' bad feeling?"

"Really, Chlo?"

Talia snorted. "Come on, Rowen. This is what seniors do on Halloween night. Haven't you been listening to the stories around school? The rain is the only reason this isn't turning into a rave. I bet there's worse going on in basements and garages all over town."

Talia was right, of course, and I was being naïve. Nevertheless, I couldn't quell my gut feeling that a shadow hovered in the distance.

"Come on, you stupid lock! Give!" Tyler grumbled, striking the tarnished bronze with his palm.

"Don't force it, man. Try wiggling the key," Mike suggested.

A moment later there was an audible click.

"All right! Let's get this party started." Benny sauntered over, sliding his arm around Chloe.

It took three of them to push the heavy bronze door open.

"Gimme the flashlight," Tyler said, holding out his hand to Hunter, but the single beam of soft white light didn't do much to illuminate the dark interior.

"We're going to need more than one light, Ty," Mike commented behind Tyler's shoulder.

Tyler turned his head, giving Mike a sideways stare. "You think?"

"Don't be a tool," he shot back.

Talia grabbed a couple more flashlights from the concrete step and handed one to Mike and the other to Hunter. Everyone else stayed back. I did too, but then again I knew a little more about what lurked in the shadows than they did.

"Whoa... now that's creepy!" Mike said half-aloud. He shot Talia a thumbs-up, and she walked away from us to get a closer look.

Eyes wide, she glanced back at me and Chloe. "Come on," she said, waving us over.

With me last, the rest of us went in. I put my hand on the door, moving slowly, tentatively. The tomb was a perfect rectangle, but unlike the crypt beneath the church, this one didn't have bones scattered about. If it had, I would have been gone.

The general's coffin was recessed into a stonewall at the back. Two large iron candelabras flanked both sides, covered in cobwebs and dust. Half melted candles sat in each holder.

A bronze plaque hung above the niche, dust obscuring half the Latin verse embossed on its surface. A narrow table, much like a hall credenza was pushed against the side wall. It was bare, but ink stained, as if it once held a book of remembrance.

Everyone else may have been creeped out, but this was nowhere near as bad as what I experienced this past week alone. Hunter caught my eye and held his hand out for me. If he was game, I was too.

I slipped in beside him and he pressed a kiss to my temple. "At least it's dry, right?"

"Mom and I did a weather charm before you picked me up earlier. I guess it was an epic fail."

He chuckled. "Maybe...but then again maybe not. The last two Halloweens were brutal around here, or so I've heard. One year, monster snowstorms, and then last year Hurricane Sandy. Maybe your spell sent whatever was supposed to hit out to sea or something."

"I didn't even think of that. People were without power for weeks." I made a face at the thought. "And the Jersey Shore still isn't back to

normal."

"Benny, grab the beer and bring it in here."

Tyler's directive jerked my attention back, and my gaze flicked to Benny headed toward the doorway.

"Oh no, you don't. This is still someone's grave, and we are not turning this into frat party central." I said, scrambling to block the entrance.

"Come on, Rowen. Lighten up." Mike took a ping-pong ball from his pocket and lobbed it at me. "It's a party, not a funeral."

"Red solo cups are in the bag with the beer," Mike called after Benny as he scooted under my arm. I turned to Chloe for a little backup, but all she did was shrug.

Mike took another ping-pong ball from his pocket and bounced it on the concrete, catching it in his hand. "You're outvoted, Rowen," he said, shifting his gaze to mine. "Now it's up to you. You can either stay and hang with the big kids or go home like a little girl."

Hunter snatched the ball in the air on its next bounce. "Put a cork in it, Mike. We're all a little weirded out being here, and Rowen is only trying to be respectful."

Mike put his hands up neutral. "Just saying, man. This is supposed to be a party, and if she's going to be the pooper then maybe you should take her home."

Benny came back in and shook his hair like a wet dog, earning twin shrieks from Jenny and Constance. Talia took a beer from the bag and settled herself on the ground between Mike's legs, leaning against his chest. "Too bad we don't have music," she said, cracking open her can.

"Who says we don't?" Jenny wiped her hands on her pants before reaching for her small leather backpack on the floor between her and Constance. She opened the top flap and pulled out her iPod along with a small dock and built in speakers. "Voila!"

I cringed, and Eric laughed out loud at my obvious disapproval. "Oh man, Rowen. You are going to need serious therapy after tonight." He motioned for Jenny to give him the rig. "How about I set it up next to the door, that way it's nowhere near the dead dude? Would that make it better?"

"Hey, I don't want my iPod getting wet. Set it in the corner near you

and Constance. I'll sit with Ty."

Tyler grinned, slapping his lap. "Come to papa, baby!"

With a giggle she eased herself onto Tyler's lap, his arms immediately sliding around her waist, pulling her against him even more. Hunter and I sat by the door across from Constance and Eric, the cool air from outside clean against the scent of dust.

The music was low, and Benny paired with Chloe against Mike and Talia for beer pong. Tyler, of course, went into his diatribe about how if he was old enough to be given a gun and sent to Afghanistan, he was old enough to have a beer. Of course, that's not what the law said, but hey, who was I to judge?

I finally relaxed against Hunter's chest, his arm slung tightly around my shoulder. I wasn't drinking, and he was still nursing his one beer. With what we had both witnessed lately, neither of us wanted to tempt fate—though breaking and entering a mausoleum seemed to trump that idea.

"Hey Tyler, how did you come across the key to this place, anyway?" Benny asked, tossing him the ping-pong ball.

He tapped Jenny on the side of her thigh, motioning for her to move to the side as he lined up his shot. "I snagged it from old man Grayson's cottage. He sent me inside for more brochures when the team was setting up the candlelight tour. The key was right there on a peg board with the others, tagged and bagged and just waiting for me to take. It was too easy. Like it was fated or something."

"You suck, you know that. Old man Grayson probably has the cops on speed dial." Eric said, throwing a handful of tomb dust at Tyler.

"Relax and listen to the tunes, man. You're as uptight as Rowen. Mr. Grayson isn't calling the cops. The old guy is as blind as a bat. Trust me, he doesn't even know the key is missing, but if you're worried I promise I'll return it tomorrow before the 10 a.m. service at the Old Dutch. He's always outside helping direct cars in the parking lot."

At Tyler's bombshell, I sat up and exchanged glances with Hunter. From the expression on his face, I knew he was thinking the same thing as me. Tyler was an idiot, and his little heist was the reason Mr. Grayson let it slip to us earlier that he knew about the party. Now the question remained, why wasn't he stopping us?

Marianne Morea

I settled back against Hunter's chest, chewing on my lip.

"You're doing it again," Hunter whispered against my ear.

"What?"

"Nibble, nibble little mouse."

I exhaled. "I'm sorry, but doesn't it seem off to you? I mean, I don't care what Ty says. After the tour at the church, you know as well as I do that Grayson knows we're here."

He shrugged. "Maybe this isn't as strange as it seems. There's always a senior party of some kind at midnight on Halloween. Maybe he leaves the keys out in plain sight just because. Who knows? If it wasn't for the rain and the wind there might be other tombs being used for the same reasons."

I didn't reply, just sat, watching the others have fun.

"Come on, Rowen. You were just starting to relax." The song changed, and *Mirrors* by Justin Timberlake began playing. Wearing a sly smile, Hunter leaned over and sang the chorus, deep and sexy in my ear.

A sideways smile tickled the corner of my mouth just as the stubble on his chin tickled my tender skin. I leaned into him and he nuzzled my neck. "Dance with me," he whispered.

I shook my head.

"Yes," he said against my neck. "I'm not taking no for an answer."

He rose to his feet, and pulled me up to mine. "This song is perfect for us. Two people making two reflections into one. I couldn't say it any better if I had written the words myself."

Without waiting for me to say or do anything, he pulled me against him, sliding his hands around my waist, moving slowly to the beat. I knew everyone was watching, but I didn't care. Eric and Constance got up and joined us, and when he dipped her, planting a big fat kiss on her mouth, Mike and Tyler's cat calls made everyone laugh.

Hunter kissed me, pulling me back down onto the floor, but this time onto his lap. I caught Jenny's eye and she gave me a small smile.

"Ugh. I can't believe we don't have another day off until Thanksgiving," Jenny moaned, nuzzling Tyler's neck.

Mike laughed. "What are you talking about? We have a long weekend because of Veteren's day in two weeks."

Jenny reached for an empty plastic cup, falling forward off Tyler's lap

in the process. Tyler laughed, slapping her butt. "She's not the sharpest knife in the drawer, but she does have her good points, eh Mikey-boy?" Sliding his gaze toward Mike and Talia. "Jen's good for a lot of things." He shot Mike a knowing wink then held his beer can up in a mock salute.

Talia's jaw tightened. "And what's that supposed to mean?" she asked.

Tyler shook his head, pulling Jenny back onto his lap. "Don't get your panties in a twist, Talia."

She looked from Tyler to Mike who wore a huge smile on his face.

"You'd have to blast those babies with dynamite before anyone could get them in a twist! Or get them off for that matter!"

For Mike to say something like that, it was clear he'd crossed the line. His words weren't slurred, but his swagger had gone into overdrive.

"Um, Mike. Don't you think maybe it's time for us to take you and Talia home?" Chloe interjected.

"Why? The night's just getting started!" Laughing, he scrambled to his feet. "You game, Eric? Let's see if the legend about the Bronze Lady is true." He gestured with his head toward the door.

Without waiting for anyone, he darted out the tomb entrance slipping on the wet concrete. "Bring on the nightmares, baby!" he said, climbing onto the side of the statue. "Woo hoo! Tal, grab my beer for me!"

"Maybe you shouldn't be up there, Mike. It's really slippery," Talia hedged, clearly not wanting to provoke him.

"Just give me the damn beer, Talia. Jesus! First, you won't put out, and now you're nagging me? He burped an expletive and Talia threw her empty can at his head.

"Oh, would you look at that. The statue feels for you, Tal," he said, stroking the wet cheeks of the famed statue. "What's the matter metal lady, you think I treat my girlfriend like crap. I know what they say about you and your curse. Ha! Whaddaya you think about this?" He smacked the statue's face, the cold bronze ringing in the night.

"Mike, don't!"

He shot Talia a dirty look. "Nothing's going to happen, so just shut it." He turned back to the statue. "Did I hurt your feelings, too? Oh, come here, baby..." Mike slid onto the statue's lap and started kissing its cheek, then let his had travel down to the statue's chest. "Honk, honk, hey she

likes, it! Come on, bronze baby, give it to your daddy, let me love you long time."

Talia tried to pull him off the statue. "Let's go. This is boring." Her voice was almost desperate.

Mike jumped to the ground, taking his half-full beer from Talia's hand, finishing it in one gulp. "You got that right." He tipped the top of the can at her. "But, the only thing more boring than this, is sitting with you in the backseat of my car." He winked, making a clicking sound with his tongue and his cheek before tilting up the can to drain the last drops.

"Not tonight it won't," she said, lowering her voice to a husky purr. "Let's go, and I'll show you just how unboring it can be."

A lewd smirk tilted Mike's mouth into a drunken parody of a smile. He grabbed Talia around the waist and kissed her hard.

Talia looked at me and Chloe standing in the doorway, and for a split second she looked as scared and desperate and we both knew she was, but it was short-lived, and she stuck out her chin and chest, taking off with Mike into the darkness. The only sound, the tinkle of her giggles fading into the night.

Jenny came to the door and stood between us. "Another virgin bites the dust," she snickered, giving us the eye. "And when are you two going to join the club. College is just months away. Tick-tock, ladies. Tick-tock."

Tyler joined us, sliding his arms around all three of us from where he planted himself behind Jenny. "Nothing like watching two good friends heading into the darkness to get it on!"

I didn't comment, just scooted out from under his arm, back into the tomb. I took Hunter's arm, turning his wrist my way so I could see his watch. Midnight. A loud knock on the door startled me, and I turned with a gasp.

"It's Witching Hour, kiddies. Who's up for a séance?" Tyler said, holding Jenny's leather pack up by its straps. "I've got everything we need right here, plus we have Rowen."

My head jerked around. "Me? Oh no. Count me out. Between helping my mother and Mr. Conover's lame research quest, I've had enough of Halloween legends and things that go bump in the night." I shook my head, staring down his overconfident smirk.

Still watching me, Tyler's upbeat air faded as he slipped Jen's pack

over his shoulder. "Yeah…" He paused, his brow creasing in a measured frown. "I almost forgot you two had a field day in Conover's class with my family history." With a slow calculated nod, he walked farther into the tomb eying the mess. "Come on. We need to clean up this mess and lock it back up. It's time for a game of truth or dare."

"What's that supposed to mean?" I asked, not liking where Ty was taking this.

He smiled, but his grin was off, almost to the point of being creepy. Tyler didn't answer my question, instead shifting his attention to Jenny. "You up for a game of truth or dare, babe? Too bad Mike isn't here though, 'cause that would make telling the truth a whole lot more interesting, don'tcha think?"

Jenny visibly paled, glancing at Constance, and I groaned.

"Now's not the time, dude," Hunter interrupted clearly trying to defuse the tension from ratcheting to level ten.

Tyler slid his eyes to Hunter, and they narrowed. "Maybe, but then again maybe not. We need to take this party to the source for a real game of truth or dare."

"What are you talking about? What source?" Eric asked.

Tyler grinned that creepy grin again. "The Old Burial Ground. Let's play truth or dare with the dead and see what they have to say."

Chapter 15

Eric was still hell-bent on organizing a quick game of Assassin, so after we locked up the tomb, we planned to play our way to the unmarked grave at the Old Dutch Church and Tyler's séance.

Flashlights had already been retrieved, but Benny and Hunter headed back into the darkness to find the water guns.

"Rules are there are no rules." Eric said, waving the guys over as they emerged from behind the trees with the bag of mini super soakers. "You get tagged you're out, unless you make it to the church first, but there's a lot of ground between here and there." He marked the distance with his water gun like he was Dirty Harry.

"And no cheating, lover boy," Tyler interrupted, pointing at Hunter before shifting his gaze to Eric and Benny. "And that goes for you two, as well. The girls are on their own. I, of course, will be waiting at the church for you losers."

"You're not going to play?" Jenny asked, her disappointment a little surprising.

"Not my bag, sweet cheeks," he retorted slapping her on the butt, again.

Chloe burst out laughing and held her fist out for me to punch. "See you on the other side!"

The seven us of took off in different directions, with me cutting through the grass and shrubs in the general direction of the Old Dutch. I

stopped for a quick breath behind the Rockefeller mausoleum, moving ahead to crouch low between two shrubs. Mike was right. This was lame, plus it was wet and muddy and thoroughly gross.

I spotted Chloe kittie-corner from where I squatted, and watched her peer around the edge of the immense granite structure before sprinting across the grass to the path.

Following her, I worked my way through the graves, careful of the upraised roots and uneven ground, when I heard someone fall not far behind. Colorful expletives in a harsh exhale let me know it was Benny.

A large angel perched on top of an arched gravestone gave me just the cover I needed. Benny was rubbing his ankle, and for a second I considered letting him go, but decided he wouldn't do the same for me, so too bad.

Circling around, I tagged his shoulder from behind. "Gotcha!" I chuckled. "You're out, Benny."

"Crap!" He threw a handful of grass after me. "Hey! Rowen's over here and she's wide open!"

I sprinted past him, giving him the dirtiest look. "Sore loser!"

Somehow I made it to no man's land where the headstones were small and relatively no cover. I had no idea where Hunter or the others were, so I scanned the area for the largest tombstone and crawled to it. My pants were soaked and full of muck, but they were black so they wouldn't stain. I wished I could've said as much for my blouse. My cuffs were ruined despite my rain jacket. *Ugh. I should have bailed with Tyler.* I shook my head at the errant thought.

I slumped behind the gravestone and pulled in my knees. This area was known as Irving Ridge, which meant Lincoln Avenue was to my left and would lead me straight into the Old Dutch Churchyard. It was odd enough the graveyard named the roads within each section, but that I recognized them to mark my position in this silly game was even odder.

Shadows were long, and the gloom seemed thick where the moonlight was obscured. My skin prickled and I shivered, hoping it was because I was cold and wet and not because something spectral stirred. Either way, I wasn't waiting around to find out.

I rocked back onto the balls of my feet and scanned the graves ahead, listening. I glanced at the sky and waited for the moon to slide behind a

cloud, and then took off running, keeping to the grass to muffle the sound of my footfall.

Footsteps echoed behind me, and I knew there were at least three people on my heels. Sharp pain dug into my side, but I forced myself to run the last ten meters into the churchyard.

Sucking in breath, I kept one hand on my side-stitch while I leaned over thinking I would puke.

"Need some mouth-to-mouth, itchy witch?"

My head jerked up to see Tyler leaning against one of the historic gravestones, his arms crossed in front of his chest.

One glimpse and I knew his entire demeanor had changed. He was sullen and drunk. "No. I'm good." I shook my head, careful to keep my voice pleasant. "And you promised you weren't going to call me that."

He unfolded his arms and moved away from the stone. Warning bells went off in my head and a surge of adrenaline spiked, its rush hiking me to standing.

"I know you're good, Rowen. I can tell by watching the way you move. I've wanted to feel you move beneath me for ages now."

"Tyler…no!" I put a hand up turning to run, but he was faster.

He grabbed a handful of my hair, and jerked me back. Darts of pain fanned across the base of my head. He twisted me to face him, then slid his free hand over my arm and shoved my wrist behind me. My back arched, jutting my breasts upward. "You even smell good sweaty."

Tyler crushed his mouth to mine and I struggled, trying to get my knee into his stomach or his groin, but he was so much stronger, I couldn't move. With another jerk, he let go of my wrist and shoved me to my knees. This time he fisted my hair, forcing me to look up at him.

He looked off, with an expression unlike any I ever saw. "You look good on your knees, Rowen. It's where I've pictured you since our last date."

"Our only date you creep!" With both hands I fought him, shoving him back to try and make him let go.

With a punishing tug, he jerked my head back. I hissed in pain, but anger boiled, bubbling up white hot and I balled my hand into a fist and punched him in the groin.

His body pitched forward, and he let go of me, wrapping his arms

around his middle.

"What the hell?" Hunter flew past me, tossing his backpack to the ground and grabbed Tyler by the throat. With a single shove, he threw him backward onto the open grass. "Dude! What do you think you're doing? That's my girlfriend!"

Tyler landed in a heap at the center of the unmarked grave, as the others arrived at the church. His knees were in his chest and he gulped down air.

"Tyler!' Jenny cried, before whirling on Hunter. "Why did you hit him?"

Chloe saw me on the ground and rushed to my side, helping me to my feet. Hunter stood with his fists clenched, waiting for Tyler to try something.

"Somebody tell me what the hell is going on here!" Jenny yelled, her eyes traveling from me to Tyler to Hunter and then back again.

Tyler shifted himself around, leaning up on one arm. "Shut up, Jen. Your voice is worse than the pain in my balls."

From the side of the church, Constance moved toward Eric, both looking at the scene with disgust. "No offense, Tyler, but you're an ass. Why did you have to get drunk? Everything was cool until..." She exhaled, shaking her head. "This blows."

She took Eric's arm. "Let's see if anyone is still hanging out at Horseman's Hollow. This year it's supposed to be wicked scary."

Eric shrugged. "Sounds good to me. Sorry, dudes, lady's choice."

They left, hopping the stone wall leading to the street. Hunter glanced at me standing with Chloe in the shadows of the church.

"Party's over, man," Hunter said.

"Yeah, well, you're all a bunch of tools anyway. Who needs you? I have my own scare plans tonight," he said, slurring his words. "Wanna see?"

He reached into his back pocket and pulled out a knife. Staring at the silver blade and the black rune-carved handle, my eyes widened. He held it up, turning the blade so it glinted in the moonlight.

"That's right, Rowen! I took it from your shop." He stressed the syllables of my name in a taunt, waving the ritual knife back and forth in front of his chest. "Want it back?" he asked, laughing at me and the look

on my face.

My shock faded into anger again. "I should call the cops on you, jerk. But since you have no idea what that knife is for, I'll make sure you're never allowed back into the Silver Cauldron. I know my mother won't press charges, but if it were me I'd do something worse like make you go bald or have your private parts shrivel up."

He snorted. "You think I don't know?" He turned on his heel.

"Tyler, what are you doing?" Hunter asked, raising his hand. "Give me the blade before you fall and hurt yourself or someone else. You're drunk, dude. Don't be stupid."

"Yeah right, Mr. Holier than Thou! I know what you meant to do with that little speech of yours in Conover's class."

Hunter and I exchanged glances. This was it, I knew it was coming, and here it was.

"Want to see what I planned for tonight, Rowen? Originally I was just going to scare Jenny, but she's a pig who sleeps with my friends, so she's dead to me."

Jenny's sharp intake left me wincing, and when the poor girl dissolved into tears, Chloe patted my arm and went to comfort her.

"But you two gave me another idea." Tyler ranted, not missing a beat. "You let the whole school know that my mother's family was descended from a whore. Well, fools, I asked my mother, and she told me the girl was raped. So let's raise the dead and find out for ourselves, shall we?"

"Tyler, no! It doesn't matter what happened in the past," I said, trying to reason with him before he did something he'd regret.

"Oh, but it does. I did a little research myself last night. Emmerick was scum. He was dishonored and his detachment disbanded. He lost his commission because he was such a tool, yet here I am with his blood in my veins. I want to confront the bastard!"

Tyler raised the athame above his head and recited passages from a book he must've stole from the shop as well.

Holy crap! He'd memorized a resurrection chant! I took a step away from the back windows of the church.

At this point Chloe clutched at both me and Jen. "Holy bat poop! Is this what he meant by séance or has Tyler just flipped?"

Hunter shook his head. "I don't know if he's crazy or not, but that's

no séance. That's a spell to raise the dead."

"Tyler! Stop! You don't know what you're doing! Hunter! Do something before he raises a real demon or some poor soul that's been at peace for two hundred years!"

Hunter rushed Tyler. The two struggled with the knife between them before crashing against a headstone. Hunter's jaw clenched as they hit, taking the impact with his shoulder. "Drop the knife!" he said through gritted his teeth

"No! I will clear my name!"

Hunter freed the athame from Tyler's grip and tossed it into the grass. Ty snatched Hunter by the hair and smashed his head on top of a square headstone. Hunter slumped to the ground, blood streaming from his hairline.

"Hunter!" I lunged forward but Benny held my arms.

"Rowen, no! Tyler's got the knife again!"

Hunter's eyes fluttered open, and he touched his head, wincing.

I screamed his name and his head snapped up at the panic in my voice. With a groan he tried to stand but slumped again.

"Get up baby, please! Hunter!"

I struggled against Benny's hold on me. Hunter waved me off, reaching over his head to grab the headstone to pull himself up. Blood smeared the front of the old sandstone, and I gasped. The name on the stone read *Cornelius Van Tassell*. Hunter's ancestor.

Tyler wandered in a frenzied state, blade in hand, moving from and stone to stone. "Where are you, you bastard? Show yourself!" He sobbed. "Not true, it's not true!"

His emotions shifted between anger and inconsolable regret, though I had no clue as to why. Tyler's actions were beyond reasoning, *he* was beyond reasoning. His instability was more than just the beer talking. Prickles iced my arms, and a cold descended around me taking my breath and setting my teeth chattering.

Tyler wiped his nose on the back of his hand, and laughed, stumbling toward the center point of the unmarked grave. "If it's true, then I'll show you what I think of you!"

Unbuttoning the front of his pants, he cackled, pissing on the barren grass. "This Buds for you granddad! Wherever you are!"

"Tyler, don't! Emmerick isn't even buried here." Chloe said, trying to reach him. She and Jenny moved closer to us, and Benny put his hand on her shoulder, shaking his head.

"Come on, Chlo...Let's get out of here," he whispered, gesturing toward the street with his head.

She shook her head. "I'm not leaving Rowen."

Tyler stumbled forward a couple of steps, wagging the knife in Chloe's direction. "If he's not here, then let's ask someone who knows where he is!" He stalked to the center of the grass and sliced the blade across his hand, squeezing his blood into the grass, slurring the words, "blood calls to blood."

"Tyler! No!" My hands flew to my mouth. Blood in any spell, even a half-assed one was bad. Very bad.

Benny let go of me, and grabbed Chloe's arm dragging her toward the path. She stumbled, but he yanked her to her feet and the two ran toward the shadows, heading for the street.

Tyler turned to me, holding the knife in his other hand. "Maybe all I need is blood from our itchy witch to seal the deal," he slurred, lunging toward me, but I was too far away.

"No!" Hunter scrambled to his feet, grabbing Tyler by the back of his jacket. Ty wheeled around, swinging wildly, his fist connecting with Hunter's face.

Bones crunched, and Hunter's nose poured blood, but he didn't stop, just wiped the blood on his sleeve. He rushed Tyler again, and the two fell on the unmarked grave, their blood mingling as they wrestled in the wet grass and mud.

Tyler elbowed Hunter in the face, and got to his feet. He stood with the athame in his hand and his fist clenched. The ground was smeared red, but in the dark it looked black. Crazed, Tyler threw his head back and yelled, the sound so full of rage it seemed inhuman.

Ice crystals formed on the grass around Tyler's feet, and the ground fog swirled, obscuring the unmarked grave. Jenny sobbed, cowering in the corner of the church. When Tyler finally calmed, she called to him. He turned his head and looked at us, but his eyes were unseeing.

"Tyler!" Jenny tried again, but he ran into the woods, the athame still in his hand.

I hurried to Hunter, wiping the blood from his face with my jacket. "Should we follow him, or go to the police?"

Hunter shook his head, wincing with the effort. "Neither. He's just drunk and he'll sleep it off. If we go to the cops, then we'll all be in trouble for being here tonight."

I shook my head. "No. Something more happened here. Something evil, powerful."

Police sirens echoed in the distance, and lights flickered across the parking lot at the caretaker's cottage. Mr. Grayson stuck his head out the door, and we ducked, hiding behind two of the tombstones.

"We have to get out of here," Jenny hissed.

When the lights went out, I crawled to Hunter's pack, and rummaged for his keys.

"Jenny, stay here with Hunter. I'll get the car."

"Rowen, I'm fine." Hunter said.

"Yeah, 'cause you look like you can drive. Give me a break. I'll be right back."

"But you hate the dark."

"I know. But I hate seeing you like this more." I blew him a kiss and hopped over the stone wall and ran toward the woods and the dead end.

We got back to my house, and I helped Hunter up the stairs and through the door and finally onto the couch. My mother wasn't home, but it was Halloween, she had unofficial *official* town witch duties to attend to.

I got Hunter an icepack for his nose, and did the best I could to clean him up, giving him one of my plain oversized sleep jerseys to change into. With my mother and her medicinal skills unavailable, I made do with Bacitracin and Band-Aids, and gave Hunter two Tylenol to hold him until she got home.

I turned on the TV and we settled in to wait.

Next thing I knew, I woke to the whispered sound of my mother's voice in my ear.

"Mom?"

"Yes, sweetie. It's late. Go on up to bed."

"Hunter…"

"I got him covered, honey. Go on up."

"He was hurt fighting with Tyler. I think his nose is broken and he's got a gash on his head."

She nodded. "I saw the bloody shirt in the garbage. All I can say is thank God this was something easily handled. I'll take care of Hunter. Not to worry. Now scoot."

I didn't sleep well, tossing and turning all night, my mind racing with thoughts of what Tyler could have done, haunting me until I fell into a dreamless coma just before dawn.

I woke to bright sunshine a little before noon, and had just stripped out of my pajamas and turned on the shower when I heard the doorbell ring. My mother's footsteps echoed from the hall, and I cracked open my bedroom door to hear who was there.

The voices were too muffled to distinguish, but when the front door shut again, I heard my mother's footsteps on the stairs headed toward my room. A bad feeling closed over my heart, and I clutched at my suddenly sick stomach.

"Rowen?"

"Come in, Mom." I said grabbing my bathrobe.

She pushed open the door to my bedroom and her face was ashen.

"That was Libby. Someone broke into the Historical Society last night. They stole a dagger and a sword."

My mouth went dry. "It wasn't us, I swear."

"I know it wasn't you. It was Tyler Cavanaugh. Libby has him on the security cameras. She called me because the police found a ritual athame at the scene of the break in, the same one missing from the shop."

I nodded. "Tyler had it with him last night."

My mother inhaled a deep breath and then sunk onto the edge of my bed. "Turn off the shower water. You need to tell me exactly what happened at the cemetery last night."

I was halfway to the bathroom to do as she asked, when I turned to look at her "What about Hunter? How is he, is he still downstairs?"

My mother shook her head. "Britt picked him up a little while ago, but I have a sinking feeling they're going to have to turn around and come back. Go do what I said. We have a lot to talk about."

I exhaled slowly, closing my eyes at the nightmare my life had become in a few short weeks.

"Rowen?"

I opened my eyes as I took in my mother's worried expression, and my shoulders slumped. "I think you better call everyone. This is going to take longer than you think. In the meantime, I'm going to grab a shower while I can."

My mother, Britt and Gran sat at the kitchen table, each one eyeing me and Hunter.

Gran shifted her gaze to Hunter. "Did the voice in the basement actually say, 'Blood calls to blood'?"

He shook his head. "No. That's what Tyler muttered, along with 'it can't be true.' He was in some kind of a drunken rage, and then vacillated between sobbing and laughter. The voice in the basement said 'revenge and justice are only found when blood and truth meet.' It was the same saying someone scratched onto the wall of the Philipse crypt over two hundred years ago, or at least that's what Mr. Grayson said."

I caught the look my grandmother shot my mother. Was Mr. Grayson involved in this somehow?

"Hunter, did any of you bleed on the graves last night?"

"No, Gran. No one bled on the graves, but Tyler pissed on them, does that count?"

"Rowen."

My mother's tone was an admonishment, and guilt washed over me at the look on her face. I was being a brat, but I was working on no sleep and this was getting tedious. What happened last night was teenage drunken stupidity, and Hunter and I simply got caught in the crossfire. Case closed. Whatever Tyler did after the fact was his problem, not ours—except I didn't really believe that.

The ticking from the clock above the stove underscored the time we'd spent sitting and rehashing. At least the kitchen was warm and inviting, with the smell of Mom's spice cake cooling on the rack next to the toaster.

I fidgeted with the embroidered table cloth, tracing the delicate thread of its harvest fruit motif with my finger. The silence was unnerving, and I sighed. I really wasn't paying attention, because when I finally looked up from my doodling, Hunter's face was wan. He looked at his hands, and then rubbed his head below his now bandaged wound.

My eyes widened, and his gaze met mine. "Gran...there was blood...I forgot. Tyler cut his hand and squeezed it over the unmarked grave." What I didn't want to tell her was that both Hunter and Tyler smeared their blood all over the Old Dutch burial ground during their fight.

I looked at Gran, feeling the weight of her dirty look. "I'm sorry. It was a very stressful night and I forgot. Tyler cut himself with the stolen athame. He even tried reciting some of the incantation from the Book of the Dead, but his words were slurred and half-assed."

The three women looked at each other.

Gran shifted her gaze to Hunter, giving him a perfunctory smile. "You look like you took quite a beating last night, and that's quite a gash on your head. How are you feeling?"

I froze. Gran was not exactly the nurturing type. She had a reason for her sudden concern for Hunter's wellbeing.

Hunter looked at his mother and then at me before addressing Gran, directly. "I'm okay, Mrs. Ekert."

"I'm glad," she said, patting his hand. Of course the moment she touched him she looked right at me with narrowed eyes.

"Laura, give this girl of yours a tincture of peppermint, stinging nettle and skull cap. She's suffering from memory loss."

"Gran!"

Gran pointed to the phone, and then it rang. No one made a move to answer it, but she banged on the table and I jumped. "It's John Riverton, so somebody answer the damn phone."

Why the chief of the Sleepy Hollow Police Department was calling on a Sunday morning I could only imagine. Maybe the blood on the stones caused mass panic at the Sunday morning services. After all, wasn't that one of the town urban legends, too? That the tombstones bled on Halloween night?

My mother got up from the table and answered the phone. "Hello, John. How are you?"

Nobody who called here was ever stunned that most of the time we knew who it was before we picked up. It was just an uncanny talent we all possessed. I would have chalked that one up on my freak-o-meter too, but it was actually better than caller I.D. for screening prank calls.

Everyone's eyes watched my mother's face as she talked to the chief

of police, especially mine and Hunter's. We were the ones facing possible criminal mischief charges.

My mother's expression paled, and her hand went to her mouth. "Yes, John. I understand. I'll make sure to bring Rowen down as soon as possible." Her voice cracked, and she suddenly seemed to go weak, pulling a chair from the table so she could sit down.

"What? Are you sure? Yes…yes, they're here. Okay, just a minute."

Mom covered the phone with her hand. "Britt, Chief Riverton would like to speak with you, too. He wants to question the kids about last night, and says he'd rather do it here than having us take them down to the station."

Britt's face drained of color as she took the cordless phone from my mom's shaking hand.

"Hello?"

She listened for a moment, her fingers trembling at her lips. Finally, nodding, agreeing to have the chief come and speak to Hunter here, along with me.

Britt handed the phone to my mother, and Mom placed it back in the cradle. Both women were more ashen than before, and my mother sat in her chair as if in a daze.

I watched Gran, fear settling in and beginning to race through my veins.

"Mom, what did he say?"

She lifted her eyes to mine and they were wet with tears. "Talia's dead, honey. Mike, too."

My hand went to my mouth, my eyes filling. "No, that's not possible. How? When?"

"Their bodies were found at the Tarrytown station, under the overpass. According to John, Talia was attacked. Her body was covered in slash marks. She was raped in the backseat of the car and left to bleed to death. Mike was dragged from the car and…" she hesitated, as if knowing what her words would do to me.

Her eyes locked with mine. "He was gutted and partially scalped. Like what you saw in your vision." She took my hand, shaking her head. "It wasn't Hunter you saw, it was a manifestation of what was to come. Hunter is your magnet so it was his face you channeled."

Tears ran down my face and over my hands pressed to my mouth in horror. Restrained sobs shook my shoulders, and Hunter wrapped his arms around me.

"There's more, honey," Britt said, her heart breaking in her eyes as she looked from me to my mother.

My mom took my hands from my face and held them in hers. I looked at her, my head moving back and forth in denial. "Not Chloe, please tell me it's not Chloe."

My eyes pleaded with her, and she shook her head. "Chloe is fine. It's Jen. She was attacked as well, beaten terribly, but not cut. Somehow she managed to get away and got herself to the emergency room. They did a rape kit on her, but she fell unconscious before the police could question her. The hospital won't have DNA results for at least two weeks. I'm so sorry, sweetheart."

I took a cleansing breath, the air hitching in my throat, but I squared my shoulders and looked from Hunter to the three women who watched my face and every my emotion. "I don't need DNA results. It was Tyler. He went crazy last night. Yes, he was drunk and had a meltdown, but I think there's more to it. Maybe he's schizophrenic."

Gran was adamant. "This is not your fault, either of you. This is what happens when magic is used in a fickle and irresponsible way. I know Hunter's blood mixed with Tyler's," she said looking at me, but neither her voice nor her expression was accusatory. In fact, she seemed genuinely sad for me. Sad and pissed off.

I shook my head. "Gran, first of all Tyler doesn't have a magical bone in his body. Second, he mangled the incantation and didn't cast a circle. It's not that."

Gran got up from her seat at the table and moved to sit beside my mother. She laid her own hands on top of ours, in effect interlacing the three generations.

"Sweetheart," she began, "intentions are all you need for magic, and yes, it helps greatly if you come from magical blood. All the other rituals we do, our candles and our circles of salt are to ensure that whatever we bring forth stays contained. Without those rituals, you can still open a portal, especially on a night like Halloween when the veil is at its thinnest. Blood was sacrificed, and the incantation set, regardless of how

inept, it was enough. Tyler let the demon loose, and now it's up to us to put it back."

"The headless horseman?" I asked.

Mom and Gran just looked at me, and Gran shook her head.

"No. Emmerick."

Moonrise Sunday night. Mr. Grayson stood to the side, and with a single nod from my grandmother he marked the graves with salt to protect those at rest, but also to prevent any unwanted spirits from rising. When finished, he handed Gran the silver pitcher engraved with runes and Gaelic writing. Without a word, he went back to his cottage and closed the door behind him.

Gran looked to the darkening sky where the moon sat just above the horizon. She nodded, handing the pitcher of salt to my mother.

"It's time to prepare," Gran said with another nod, but this time to Britt.

My grandmother situated herself at the center of it all, while Britt and my mom walked to the eastern most corner of the burial ground. Britt took the pitcher from my mother's hand and moved clockwise, pouring a salt line around the entire perimeter. My mother followed behind, tracking the four directions and moving her birch stick wand in a counter clockwise motion for purification until they enclosed us in a large circle.

Gran held her own athame high; both arms flung to the heavens and called the watchtowers for each direction, invoking power and protection for all within the circle.

"Come, children." She gestured to Hunter and me, moving her athame in a circular motion to urge us toward the center of the circle. She had us face each other, and then bound our wrists using a threaded silver chain to hold the conduit and magnet together as one.

The air was still and the forest behind us eerily quiet. Even the water in the brook receded to a whisper of what it was the night before.

Earlier, Gran had me lay a twelve inch square piece of white linen on one of the flagstones, making sure I pinned down the edges. On the cloth she placed a flat silver dish with a mixture of crushed star anise, clove and dragon's blood. Once untied, Hunter and I were to strike a match and recite the banishing spell to send Emmerick's spirit back through the veil,

sealing him there forever.

Ideally, since Tyler's blood called Emmerick, we needed him to expel his ancestor. However, Hunter's blood was included in that unfortunate mix, so he was our ace in the hole and I was the means to the end. I just prayed it wasn't the kind of end you don't come back from.

"Are you okay?" Hunter asked, his eyes and the set of his mouth telling me he was as freaked out as I was.

I nodded, giving him a quick smile. "Piece of cake." I even lifted our bound hands to try and snap my fingers, but his answering smirk said he wasn't buying my bravado for a second.

"Maybe we can try this tie me up, tie me down thing next time we're alone." Both of his eyebrows lift suggestively, and I pressed my lips together so as not to laugh.

The mental image he painted gave my current butterflies a different reason to wing around my stomach.

Gran put her finger to her lips, shushing us.

Everything was ready, and Hunter linked his fingers with mine, whispering the word "together" before giving my hand a gentle squeeze. With a deep breath, my grandmother motioned for my mom and Britt to take their places, flanking her like sentinels.

Gran's arms were in the air, and my mouth went dry. This was it. My previous composure fled, and fear sent my heart pounding so hard, I heard my pulse in my ears.

"Guardians of the spirit realm hear me. Guide my words and those of all here. The hour rings true. I summon Emmerick, destroyer and debaucher. Come now."

There was no sound, no quaver, in the graveyard. Time ticked, each breath a counterpoint to the surrealism of what we were doing.

The moon rose higher, and Gran watched as if waiting for an appointed time. Then with loud exhale, she stabbed her athame upward as though piercing the sky. Pulling the knife down in a wide arc, she drew a pentacle intertwined with the four points of the cross in the air in front of her, and then thrust her blade upward again.

Three times she repeated this, each time invoking the spirit realm.

My mother and Britt joined hands, and each rested their free hand on Gran's shoulders, forming a circle within a circle, with me and Hunter at

the center. The three of them chanted in unison, and Gran pierced the sky once more, this time with both hands.

The graveyard rumbled, and everyone jumped to the edge of the circle, my mother and Britt pulling me and Hunter with them. My mom untied our hands though Gran yelled for her to stop.

The barren earth of the unmarked grave cracked across the center of our circle, ominous like the start of an avalanche. The ground shook, splitting further, and the cracked edges crumbled inward until there was nothing but a gaping hole.

A skeletal entity rose from the loose earth, his skull tucked beneath his arm. Long bony hands gripped the side of the gaping jaw and lifted the head, reattaching it to the top of its neck.

Gran pulled herself to her full height, all five foot nothing, and stood with her athame pointed at the specter. Nervous laughter bubbled up in my throat, with me half expecting her to utter one of the unforgiveable curses from *Harry Potter*.

The air vibrated, swirling in a mini vortex around the skeleton as layers of muscle and flesh reformed. The air stilled, and a man stood on the edge of the ruined grave in place of the skeletal remains.

"Who are you?" Gran asked, still brandishing her athame like a magic wand.

The man was handsome, dressed in revolutionary style and wearing the blue coat of the German infantry, his brown hair tied back with a ribbon to match. "My name is lost to time, and it is of no matter where I am now," he replied, his English accented and choppy.

"Then why have you come. Are you Emmerick?"

The man scowled, his handsome features taking on a look of disgust as if Gran had uttered profanity. "He is the reason I am summoned. Our fates are intertwined."

"I'm sorry your rest was disturbed. We mean you no harm. You are released from my summons if you wish to return to your slumber," Gran said, her voice soft.

"Rest? I have no rest. That man robbed me of my rest though I lie in hollowed earth."

"You're the Hessian soldier, the headless one the legend is based on, right?" I blurted the words, catching my hand over my mouth too late.

The soldier turned his sad eyes to me, and bowed. "Yes, good lady, I am. Though there is nothing of truth in the tale of my undoing save the loss of my head. It wasn't even a hero's loss. Before dawn one morning, I was made to ride out from the cannon line to check the range of our guns, when my commanding officer ordered a mortar to be fired.

"You took a direct hit?"

He shook his head. "No, child. I was wounded. The cannon did not take my head as history imparts, though the injuries I sustained were grave. I knew I was dying, and I wanted the solace of making my peace with God, but I was denied that final comfort."

He held out his hand and with a single nod signified we do the same. Our hand formed another circle and the air vibrated again, but this time there was nothing in it that felt like a calling. It shimmered in layers, and we watched time fall away. Our collective sight expanded until a vast field appeared in the heat of battle.

Smoke billowed upward into the starless sky from the ground where cannons had puckered and charred the soil. Bodies lay strewn across the field, as men marched in formation for yet another advance. Rows of cannons rutted the earth behind the lines, their barrels scorching hot despite the winter chill. A voice above the din yelled, "Fire!" and the air was once again broken by the roar of guns.

The commanding officer astride his black horse rode the line, his face grim. "You!" he said, pointing to his men.

The soldier raised his head.

I gasped at the answering face. It was the same soldier standing now with his hand outstretched in accord with ours in the safety of our circle.

The air shimmered again, and the vision changed to the outskirts of the field. My knees buckled with pain and the copper taste of blood in my mouth.

"Rowen!" Hunter moved to help me, but one look from my grandmother froze him.

"Let her be, Hunter. She's safe."

He eyed my grandmother, and then slowly shook his head. "No. If she's the conduit and I'm the magnet, then I'm drawing this to her. I won't have her suffer alone." With strength of courage I never expected, he defied my grandmother and took my elbow, helping me up.

Pain still sluiced through my body, the feeling crawling through my skin and burning my insides I bent forward, but Hunter grabbed the threaded silver chain from the ground between us and took my hand, rebinding our wrists.

The pain dulled immediately, and though I still sensed every injury, it was as if from a distance. I smiled. "Thanks," I whispered.

Tiny beads of sweat broke out on Hunter's forehead, and he squeezed my hand.

"Bad?" I asked.

He shook his head. "Manageable."

Together we lifted our joined hands to the circle once again, and the air shimmered as if waiting for us to continue.

Through the smoke, the sound of the horse's hooves like thunder echoed. Relief poured through my body, and I felt the soldier slump back against the ground, hope giving him a quick ease of breath.

Instead, the commanding officer on his black horse rode out of the haze, the beast's nostrils breathing wet clouds in the darkness. Uncertainty laced with fear added to the already metallic tang of blood in my mouth. He slid from his horse, and grew larger in my sight as he menaced forward, his sword drawn. A cry of "No!" was lost amid the sound of guns, and everything went black.

Panting, I dropped my hand, taking Hunter's with mine. Slowly everyone did the same, and the scene before us returned to the dark of the cemetery.

"It was he who took my head. It was payment for breaking rank and disregarding orders."

I shook my head, confused. "But you did what he said, I don't understand."

He smiled sadly. "My commander waited for the perfect time to repay me for the sin of showing kindness in the face of his utter cruelty. I refused to burn a child alive, although he ordered it so. I broke rank and saved the little girl's life, restoring her to her mother."

Hunter and I exchanged glances, and I took a step forward, my mother reaching her hand out to stop me. Hunter stepped forward with me, our fingers laced together regardless of our silver bond.

The Hessian looked at the two of us and recognition dawned on his

face. Stepping a foot back, he bowed low, crossing one arm across his chest in formal assent. He straightened, and regarded us with a soft expression. "Thank you," he said.

The soldier held up his hands and the scene around us changed again, this time without our combined energy. The grounds surrounding the cemetery hills were now tree covered and dotted with cottages. Twilight cast a dark purple hue across the sky, and soft snow covered the ground.

Smoke rose from the chimneys of the Philipse estate across the frozen dirt road, and from our vantage point outside the vision, we watched Cornelius and Elizabeth Van Tassell standing graveside with their young daughter, Leah, as the Deacon of the church offered prayers for the soul of the departed soldier laid to rest in the earth.

The soldier waved his hand and time fast forwarded to spring, showing Elizabeth holding the hand of a little girl as she placed flowers on an unmarked grave.

The little girl's face lifted to look at me, and she smiled and waved, just as she had done in one of my earlier visions. She was the child the Hessian soldier had saved and then died for.

I opened my mouth to ask another question, but the air around us changed again. This time it grew dense, and the feel of it on my skin was clammy and slick. Emmerick's image wavered on the perimeter of the circle like an oasis in the desert, all shimmery, until Tyler walked amid the headstones, disoriented.

He was covered with blood and dragging the sword from the Historical Society behind him. "Ty!" I yelled, taking a step toward him, but both Hunter and Gran held me back.

"That's not Tyler, sweetheart," Gran said, her grip on my arm tight enough to bruise. "He's in there somewhere, but he is being used like a puppet."

My head jerked around and the expression on my grandmother's face scared me. Her mouth was a grim line and her eyes were hard, though I knew she was grappling with herself over how to try and save Tyler.

"Gran, he's just a kid. Isn't there anything you can do? He's not responsible for what happened. It wasn't him."

She shook her head. "I'm afraid we've lost him, honey. This has moved way beyond possession. Look at his eyes. They're black."

I shifted my gaze to where Tyler stood, staring at nothing. His gorgeous candy blue eyes were just as Gran said.

The hole in the ground belched, and dirt showered everywhere, as another spirit swirled from the depths. The air vibrated again as it did for the Hessian, but this time what manifested was a corpse. It was Emmerick, and he clasped his skeletal clawed hand on Tyler's shoulder. The words *blood calls to blood*, a whisper on the air.

The Hessian soldier raised his arm, pointing his finger at Emmerick. "You are to blame for the atrocities committed against these good people. Your actions gave me the yoke I carried for centuries, blamed for the evil that tainted this hollow with fear and horror."

One by one spirits gathered, each pointing their fingers at Emmerick, accusing him, calling for justice. Men and women alike, Tory and Patriot, British and Hessian, every one of the men he forced to help carry out his crimes, every girl he abused, every soldier he wrongfully killed, every family he victimized.

The corpse opened its mouth and laughed. Their indictments weren't enough, and in that instant he seemed to grow stronger. Emmerick moved in closer, sliding his bony arm around Tyler's shoulder, its gaunt mouth pressing a parody of a kiss to his cheek.

"This isn't working." My voice was a harsh whisper in Hunter's ear.

Gran's concentration seemed to be weighing and discarding options, but I knew we were running out of time. Dawn approached and we needed to banish Emmerick before he took over Tyler body *and* soul. What we needed was a distraction that would give Emmerick pause and buy us a little more time.

I yanked Hunter to the side, the sudden movement startling everyone, including Gran. Using the momentary disruption, I grabbed the athame from her and sliced the palm of my bound hand, doing the same to Hunter.

"No!" Gran shouted.

Without sparing my grandmother a second glance, I forced the carved handle into Hunter's palm, ignoring his wince of pain before wrapping my own palm around the bloody grip. Together we plunged the blade into the ground, our mingled blood running in cooled rivulets down the knife-edge and into the punctured earth.

Hunter's eyes widened. "I hope you know what you're doing," he murmured as we straightened.

I didn't answer, but Gran's lips peeled back from her teeth, her smile as creepy as it was cunning. Realization glowed in her eyes, and a single nod was all I needed to continue.

I untied my wrist from Hunter's and moved fast, scraping our blood from the handle and both sides of silvered blade into my palm. Gran shouted rune symbols to me as I traced each onto the ground between us and where Emmerick stood with Tyler, the blood in my palm like cosmic finger-paint.

When I finished, Gran took my cut hand and placed it in Hunter's. "Keep your hands together and your blood fused. It will protect you. Whatever happens, don't let go of each other." Her voice was low and she eyed me circumspectly. "Invoke the summons."

Hunter squeezed my hand and I winced, the warm, sticky feel of fresh blood between our palms. Gran bent, taking the athame by the handle and handing it to me.

The quiet was unnerving, and time and space seemed suspended. I squeezed my eyes closed and whispered a silent prayer. Opening my lids, I thrust the athame's point toward the sky. "I summon Marite DeBoeck. Come now as I call. Come and witness the desecration of your line, the defilement of your blood."

Emmerick's hollowed eyes jerked toward me and he snarled. The sound was evil, making the blood against my palm writhe as if alive. I squeezed the handle tighter, willing myself not to freak out and drop the blade though it felt as if a thousand insects crawled around my hand.

The spirits in the graveyard moaned, swirling between us, chilling the air even more. Ice formed around my feet, spreading in a wide swath toward the open space midway between Emmerick and the nameless Hessian. The air at dead center became thick and murky, gaining a palpable texture. The thickness coalesced, taking shape and the figure of a woman appeared.

She stood quietly and blinked, as if awakened from a deep sleep. Awareness dawned, and she focused her gaze on the skeletal form directly in front of her. "Andreas," she called, holding one arm out.

Emmerick let go of Tyler and took a step forward.

"No," she said, her voice rising. Her features were hard and full of hate. "You took what I gave and discarded me and the babe I carried, yet you still seek to take more. You have no claim here. Begone!" Her outstretched arm waved wide, the motion sharp and definitive.

The wind picked up blowing leaves and debris into a whirlwind, forcing branches to bend an crack.

Emmerick laughed, his bones clacking with the mirthless motion. He stepped into the swirl of leaves and dirt and took shape, solid in flesh and muscle but varied in density as if he didn't possess the strength to complete the job.

Marite shrieked. Lifting one arm, she raised a tombstone and launched it at Emmerick's head. "I should have killed you when I had the chance!"

Emmerick let go of Tyler, shoving him to the ground and catching the ancient stone with both hands. "You want claim to your blood line? Then I give it to you in spades!" The spirit lifted the stone above his head and a brought it down, aiming for Tyler's skull.

"No!" I lurched forward, my blood-slick hand slipping from Hunter's grip. "Don't hurt him!" My arms and legs were heavy, and the athame in my hand cold enough to burn my skin, but I rushed ahead, lunging with the blade's sharp point aimed at Emmerick's heart.

The spirit sidestepped and I fell, pitching forward onto the grass. Hunter charged, knocking Tyler out of the way just as the stone crashed to the ground where he lay.

The nameless Hessian held his hand out to me, and when I slid my palm into his the blood on my skin sent current through my arm and into my chest. I cried out, and Hunter scrambled to reach me.

The blood in my veins raced, even as vertigo hit making me slump against Hunter's chest. The Hessian held on, the slick red between our hands growing hot. His grave cold fingers grew warm to the touch even as my own body chilled. Life's blood. He was drawing some of my life force, growing stronger and more sold even as I grew weak.

Power spread from the shared essence, and my soul infused the Hessian, his body becoming stronger, more flushed with life and vigor as the seconds passed.

"Do not be alarmed, sweet lady," he murmured. "No harm will come

to you." He eyed Hunter, gesturing to the blade in my other hand."

Hunter tightened his grip around my middle and slid his free hand across my outstretched arm toward the blade. He unwrapped my fingers from the hilt and handed the razor-sharp athame to the Hessian.

The ground shook beneath us as soon as the Hessian clasped the carved handle. Energy infused the air and the surrounding earth. The Hessian let go of my hand, releasing me, but my imbued strength stayed with him.

He raised both arms, calling Marite and all the spirits in the graveyard to action. They swirled, circling Emmerick, flaying the skin from his bones as he screamed in real pain. In the midst of the fray, the Hessian lunged, using his borrowed strength to slit Emmerick's throat down to the bone. Thick, unctuous blood, black and noxious oozed from the wound as Emmerick's hand rose to stem the flow.

One by one, each spirit flew into the gaping maw circling in and through and out until a great vortex formed around the corpse. Emmerick reached for Tyler, dragging him back. What was left of our friend stood mute, his eyes blank as Emmerick's bony fingers tried to hold on to this world, but the force of the vortex pushed him back, sending him stumbling toward the open wound in the earth.

I screamed for Tyler, my gaze flying toward my grandmother for help. Marite shrieked again, using what energy she had against the swirl, but the force was too strong. Fire spewed from the hole in the ground, engulfing the skeleton. Emmerick screamed, and the sound echoed into the darkness. At the Hessian's command, Gran matched fire with fire and lit the pyre with the banishing herbs for our spell.

Hunter and I got to our feet and ran to the edge of the circle, joining my mother and Britt as their chant formed a ring of protection ensuring the outside world heard nothing but the sounds of the night. Gran raised her arms and the rest of us followed. She began her own chant, layering power upon power, and with our hands and voices crying out for justice, she raised her face to the sky and intoned her spell, her voice rising above the rest, above the din of the swirling spirits.

The flames turned blue, then finally white as they consumed Emmerick. His fiery arm reached out, his fingers tightening on Tyler's arm, pulling him in until they were both sucked into the hole in the earth

from whence Emmerick came. The ground healed itself, and nothing was left but the sound of our chants.

In the silence that ensued, the Hessian soldier turned toward Gran, offering her a formal bow. "Dear lady, the truth has been brought to light and justice is served. My spirit can sleep." He then turned toward his own grave, but hesitated, turning once more to face Hunter and me. "You gave your blood freely this night—impetuous, yet filled with good intention. Be careful how you next choose to spill it."

Gran stifled a smirk, and let her arms down. She inclined her head, giving him a small courtesy. "I could not have admonished them any better. Thank you."

He vanished, and the wind was the only sound left in the cemetery, the graves as they always were, untouched and beautiful...their history and secrets as silent as the stones that marked each plot.

I clung to Hunter, and my mother and Britt circled us with their arms. All my strength returned as if it had never left and I sighed, letting my shoulders slump in exhaustion.

Gran joined our huddle, resting her hand on my cheek. "It's over, sweetheart. Let's go home."

Epilogue

Hunter and I stood hand in hand at Talia's grave site. The first snow of the season dusting the cemetery in a feeling of unsoiled peace. Talia had no memorial yet, no stone to mark her life and what she meant to all of us save the flowers dotting the blanket of white with color. It was the same at a grave across the cemetery for Mike.

Autopsies had been completed, and police files were put to rest along with our friends. As for Tyler, the police believed he was on the run. Jenny had come out of her coma and gave the police a detailed account of what happened, naming Ty in the attack.

I had no more tears to cry. Tyler was gone along with the others, yet his memory would be tarnished for the crimes he committed. But how much of him was cognizant at the time? Gran said his presence was there somewhere inside his body, but he was no more than a spectator to his own actions. Did that make him responsible? Could he have fought Emmerick? We'll never know. It was a giant circle, and his innocence paid the price along with the others.

I let go of Hunter's hand and knelt in the snow, clearing a path. I sprinkled rosemary, mullein seeds, and rue and placed black obsidian, smoky quartz and garnet into the not yet frozen earth, muttering my spell to protect and ward her grave against evil. I had done the same thing for Mike, and tried to give Jenny a pretty little mojo bag, but she refused it. My mother said she'd come around in time, but I had my doubts.

Hunter handed me the bouquet, and I placed it on top of the others,

and whispered a prayer. Layering the old religion with the new.

"That's quite a charm you've woven, missy." Mr. Grayson's voice called from behind.

Hunter helped me up and I turned, dusting the snow from my wet knees. "I don't know if it will help, but I don't want their rest disturbed," I replied, earning myself a curious look from the old caretaker. "Every one of my friends died or suffered needlessly, including Tyler. I just want them to have peace."

"You're worried about Tyler, aren't you?"

I looked at him, but this was too fresh, too painful for me to discuss with an outsider. I knew my eyes had narrowed, and I was sure from the look on his face that Mr. Grayson knew I thought he eavesdropped on what happened after he left.

"Look, Mr. Grayson. We performed a…a…" I hesitated, not sure what to call what we did, exactly. "…an exorcism of sorts. And I know that Gran had you protect the graves of those not involved by having you spread the salt. You're the caretaker, it was proper. But as to what happened after you left…."

He held up his hand. "Rowen, I didn't peek through the shutters if that's what you're worried about. Your gran visited me the other day because she was worried about the same thing. You're afraid that Tyler has taken the Hessian's place as the wronged spirit in the cemetery, and that history will repeat itself at some point."

He shook his head. "Honey, it's always been and always will be. This time it took two hundred years." He looked at the rolling hills and the graves, turning to gaze into the distance. "The writing on the wall in the crypt was a truth meant for all, it was both warning and call to action, but it wasn't the first."

He pointed to the bell in the steeple. "Do you know what's engraved on the bell, the same bell that has been there for three hundred years?"

Hunter nodded. "Romans, Chapter 8, Verse 31: '*Si Deus Pro Nobis, Quis Contra Nos?*—If God be for us, who can be against us'?"

Mr. Grayson flashed his wide, blocky tooth smile. "Very good. It was an invocation. Oh, it's Christian, and it's fitting for a church bell, but church fathers put it there for another reason. Like Irving said, this place is steeped in mysteries that go beyond the natural world. It lives in the

very earth.

"Those who carved their message into the rock behind the crypt were here when the worlds breached and malevolence showed its ugly head in human form. And just as the church fathers warned, we were ready for it this time. When the time comes again, there will always be those willing to carry the torch. Those with a fire for the truth."

I exchanged glances with Hunter and then faced Mr. Grayson. "I don't understand."

He patted my cheek with his fingers. "Truth and justice always come at a price, and the innocent sometimes pay with blood. It's a hard lesson…" he paused, "for anyone so young to learn. This world teeters on a precipice between light and dark, and there are lives meant to help maintain that balance. Those lives give light to this world."

He smiled bending down to pick up a single rose from Talia's grave and held it out to me. "Welcome to the fight, itchy witch."

Chills washed over me, and I sucked in a breath. The only person in the world to call me that was Tyler.

I looked at Mr. Grayson as if seeing him for the first time, and his eyes twinkled. Candy blue. "Thank you, Rowen," he said with a wink, and turned to walk away with a wave.

"Wait!" I called after him, but when Mr. Grayson turned his eyes were once again a watery blue.

"Happy Thanksgiving, Mr. Grayson."

He nodded. "You too, sweetheart."

I watched him head slowly down the slope to the road.

"Rowen?" Hunter put his fingers under my chin, shifting my gaze to meet his. "What's the matter?"

I shook my head, absently. "What color eyes does Mr. Grayson have?"

Hunter looked at me like I'd lost my mind. "Like a milky wet blue, why? I think he's got the beginning of cataracts."

I dragged in a breath and went up on my toes to press a kiss to his lips. "No reason."

He took my hand and walked ahead of me down the slope. "Do you think your spell will do any good?"

I smiled to myself. "I think it already has."

Note from the Author

This book is a work of fiction, though there are many elements of fact cited throughout the book. Like many authors, I was inspired by true historic events and the story grew from there. While some of the historic names have not been changed, and the quoted accounting of events from Captain John Romer, husband to Leah Van Tassell Romer, is true—the rest of the story is fictionalized.

Captain Andreas Emmerick was a true historic figure, and yes…he and his men did arrest Cornelius Van Tassell and tie him to the back of his cattle before leading him away as a prisoner of war. Emmerick did burn the Van Tassell house with the child Leah still inside, and the Hessian soldier that became the legendary Headless Horseman did rescue her, subsequently secreting the child and her mother to safety. The soldier was killed, decapitated at some point afterward, but the facts surrounding the event are sketchy. There is an unmarked grave at the Church where town legend holds the Hessian soldier was buried in a secret Christian ceremony courtesy of the Van Tassell family as a tribute to the man's kindness and mercy.

As for Captain Emmerick, records show that later in his career he was removed from his British command and his men disbanded for disgraceful behavior, but not much else is known except he returned first to England and later Germany. Unsettled, Emmerick attempted to write a book, but never finished. His restless nature continued and he became involved in a political rebellion against the French occupation of Westphalia, was captured and later sentenced to die in front of a firing squad.

The Bronze Lady is a real monument that can be viewed today, and the urban legend about the weeping statue is one that is still told.

Sleepy Hollow and the surrounding Hudson Valley are full of history and tales that speak to American enterprise, freedom and our never-say-die spirit. The Great Jack'Olantern Blaze is a yearly event held every autumn at the Van Cortland Estate, as are the Candlelight tours at the Old Dutch Church and Burial Ground and the Fright Night at Horseman's Hollow. For more information, follow the website information below.

Oh, and enjoy the pics!

Marianne

The Sleepy Hollow Historical Society on Grove Street
http://www.thehistoricalsociety.net/

Old Dutch Church and Burial Ground
http://www.odcfriends.org

A glimpse inside the Old Dutch Church

Another look inside the Old Dutch Church

Where the floor boards were replaced sealing off
the entrance to the Philipse crypt.

A view of the village and the Hudson River
from Sleepy Hollow High School

Cornelius and Elizabeth Van Tassell

Catrina and Petrus Van Tassell

The Bronze Lady
http://www.visitsleepyhollow.com

http://www.hudsonvalley.org/events

Acknowledgements

Hollow's End is my fourth book, but it is my first in the Young Adult genre and a story I am very proud of. So many people have helped and encouraged me during the creation of this historic fiction.

My unbelievably patient husband, Bill, for putting up with the insanity and verbal barrages that accompany being glued to my laptop for hours. Our three kids for knowing enough to leave mom alone when she's writing, despite laundry piling up and pasta for dinner, yet again.

I need to send my gratitude out to Sara Mascia, Archeologist and Executive Director of the Tarrytown and Sleepy Hollow Historical Society, and Tara Van Tassell, Historical Society Archivist and also direct descendant of Cornelius and Elizabeth Van Tassell. I can't thank them enough for their patient help during my research—for the historic books, pamphlets and genealogies they let me be privy to, and for answering my incessant questions.

I would be completely remiss if I didn't send my thanks out to Kyle McGovern, volunteer docent at the Old Dutch Church. This unbelievably patient young man spent hours with me at the Old Dutch Cemetery, answering my questions and canvasing his friends at the high school to help fill in the gaps regarding town folklore and urban legend. Kyle was the Senior Class President at Sleepy Hollow High School when I was first introduced to him, and as this book goes to print he is now halfway through college. He is truly a talented and kind young man.

To my father and mother and my wonderful mother-in-law for their guidance, and my siblings for their support.

To all my hometown friends, especially Karen Marsh, Ginger Hardman and Ginny Ryan.

To my wonderful Street Team beta readers, Gloria Lakritz, Penny Nichols, Susan Firtik, Teri Zuwalla, Patricia Statham,

Bonnie-Jean Aurigemma, Douglas Meeks, Kelleyann Langlois, Ebony Laprocina and Heather Gabriel.

My special thanks go out to author C.J. Ellisson, for her undying support and friendship, and for backing my decision to leap into cross-genre writing.

And to my teenage beta readers who told me point blank when the story didn't work, and helped me master 'teen-speak' (even though I opted to keep the book clean!) My thanks go out to Bridget Mollaghan, Olivia Ottinger, Kelsey Butera, Ali Robeson, Lily Messina, Lauren Martelli and Danielle Morea.

I thank you *all* for reading, critiquing and for being the best cheerleaders anyone could want.

And last but certainly not least, I want to thank God for all his blessings. The longer I live, the more I learn to appreciate what could very easily be taken for granted. God bless.

I hope you enjoy the book.

Research Bibliography

Amrev-Hessians –l Archives. *Lt. Col. Andreas Emmerich*, by John Helmut Merz
(Archiver.rootsweb.ancestry.com/th/read/AMREV-HESSIANS/1999-08/0934952078)

The Kings Men: Loyalist Military Unites in the American Revolution, by Todd Braisted. Online Institute for Advanced Loyalist Studies. (www.nyhistory.net/~drums/kingsmen_02.htm)

Ghost Stories: The Other Legend of Sleepy Hollow, by Robyn Leary. New York Times, Sunday, October 29, 2000

Genealogies, courtesy of the Tarrytown and Sleepy Hollow Historical Society.
(www.geni.com/people/Lea-Romer/60000000005921936766)

About the Author

Marianne Morea was born and raised in New York. Inspired by the dichotomies that define 'the city that never sleeps', she began her career after college as a budding journalist. Later, earning a MFA, from The School of Visual Arts in Manhattan, she moved on to the graphic arts. But it was her lifelong love affair with words, and the fantasies and 'what ifs' they stir, that finally brought her back to writing.

Visit her website: http://www.mariannemorea.com